Desert Storm

Crisis in the Desert Series, Book Three

By
Matt Jackson
&
James Rosone

Library of Congress Control Number: 2021921745

Table of Contents

Chapter 1
Addressing the Nation

1 March 1991
Oval Office, White House
Washington, D.C.

Since October 5, 1947, when Presidents needed to address to the nation via television, they did so from the Oval Office. President Harry Truman was the first, and every president thereafter had followed suit. The American public and the international community were familiar with the setting: the President seated behind the Resolute desk, the flags framing the right and left of the picture, the credenza behind the President in front of the windows. Often, the message to the nation was one of distress. This speech would be no different.

"In three, two, one," the producer said and pointed to the President.

"Good evening, my fellow Americans. I come to you with grave news that I believe needs to be told. Our nation is in a state of war with the nation of Iraq, and I feel you are owed an explanation for why that is and, more importantly, why this war needs to be fought to its rightful conclusion. Approximately six months ago, the armed forces of Iraq invaded the country of Kuwait. Iraq claims Kuwait is a rogue province of Iraq. They also claim that Kuwait had been stealing oil from their oil fields via slant well drilling. The Iraqi government, under the leadership of Saddam Hussein, has justified this wanton act of aggression based on the 1890 Ottoman Empire treaty with Great Britain, which referred to Kuwait as the Basra Province. At the conclusion of World War I, however, the boundaries were redrawn, establishing Kuwait as a free and independent country.

"The government of Iraq could have stopped their military adventurism in Kuwait, but they did not. Instead, Iraqi forces continued to advance across the Arabian Peninsula, invading the Kingdom of Saudi Arabia and the United Arab Emirates. These overt and blatant acts of aggression cannot stand. America cannot allow a rogue dictator to assume control of over fifty percent of the world's oil production."

The President paused for just a moment, letting his words sink in before continuing. "In the past six months, we have attempted to negotiate a withdrawal of Iraqi forces from these lands and restore the established international borders. Our overtures of peace were instead met with violent attacks on the forces we sent to stabilize the situation. Our forces have defended themselves, but make no mistake, our forces have fought gallantly and will continue to do so. Up to this point, our responses have been defensive in nature. We do not wish to harm the Iraqi people, who have no say in the decisions made by their unelected leaders.

"This continued aggression must stop. Iraqi forces must withdraw to the international border established and recognized between Iraq and the Kingdom of Saudi Arabia, and Kuwait. Therefore, in response to Iraq's continued aggression, the following steps are being taken. One, effective at 1200 Greenwich Mean Time tomorrow, March eighth, 1991, no ships—cargo, oil or container as well as military shipping of any kind—will be allowed to enter the Strait of Hormuz regardless of where it is bound. Two, all shipping in the Persian Gulf must depart by March fifteenth or remain in port, as any shipping in transit at that point will be considered hostile. Third, on March thirtieth, Iraqi ground forces must initiate a withdrawal from Kuwait and Saudi Arabia as well as the UAE. After the March thirtieth deadline, US forces and our allies in this conflict will take appropriate action to remove Iraqi forces from these countries.

"It is my sincere desire that the Iraqi government will recognize the futility of their aggressive actions and comply with these demands. The American people only wish for a lasting peace in the Middle East and the Arabian Peninsula. We take no pleasure in having our sons, our daughters, our husbands, and our wives committed to this conflict so far from home. But we are also determined to defend the oppressed and stop the aggression that has been thrust on Kuwait, Saudi Arabia, and the UAE. Tonight, I ask for your prayers that the Iraqi government will comply with our demands and avoid further bloodshed and violence. I ask for your prayers for our soldiers, sailors, Marines, and airmen as they prepare to remove the Iraqis from these nations.

"Good night, and God bless these United States of America," the President concluded. He held his stare at the camera until he heard the word "Cut" from the director as the programming cut to the major studios.

****

Halfway around the world and seven hours ahead of the Washington, D.C. time, Saddam sat watching the president's address on CNN. He had already received a written copy of what the president was reading on his teleprompters, so nothing was a surprise, but it still pissed him off. Others sitting with him did not move or say anything as they watched a slow burn of anger and frustration consume Saddam. Finally, Saddam turned to the assembled officers, surprisingly calm.

"Have all preparations been made?" he asked.

Sultan Hashim Ahmed al-Tai, the Minister of Defense, glanced over at Ibrahim Ahmed Abd al-Sattan al-Tikrit, the Armed Forces Chief of Staff, and received a reassuring nod indicating that all was prepared before he spoke.

"Sir, all preparations have been made. Our forces are well supplied and are in position to blunt and destroy any advance by the American Army. The Arabian Gulf is closed with our minefield, and only those that have transited it with our pilots know the way through the minefield. Our navy has trained extensively in ambush tactics, so if any ships exit the minefields, they will be prepared to deal with them. The air force has taken some losses but is capable of meeting the Americans—" al-Tikrit expounded before he was interrupted.

"How many fighter aircraft can we surge to meet the Americans?" Saddam asked, looking at Hamid Raja Shalah al-Tikriti, the Air Force Commander.

"Sir, we can surge around three hundred and fifty aircraft and sustain that for thirty days. We are prepared for them. This also does not include our close-air support aircraft or our helicopters. This, combined with our air-defense systems, should be sufficient to stop any American attacks," al-Tikriti said confidently.

"It better," was all Saddam said, looking across the audience. His eyes focused on one man who had not said much, nor had he been asked to speak.

"What is our status?" Saddam asked the individual identified on CNN as Chemical Ali, a name he did not appreciate.

"We have not moved anything from our stockpiles. Our Soviet advisors have told us the American satellites are watching them like a hawk. If we move anything too soon, it will tip them off as to our intentions. When ordered, we are prepared to move them and load the Scuds with them when the time comes," Ali Hassan al-Majid said. Saddam simply nodded.

"Admiral, is our newest gift from the Chinese functioning properly?" Saddam asked, turning to Admiral Ramd Gha'ib Hassan.

"It is, sir. Our crew training was completed several weeks ago thanks to the cooperation we received from Rear Admiral Morteza Safari of the Iranian Navy. In August, they did their first shakedown cruise in the Arabian Sea and watched the American PrePo ships from Diego Garcia make the transition. The instructor crew would not allow them to fire on those ships at that time, but they did run drills against them and evaded one American destroyer that moved into the area. They returned to the Arabian Gulf and have completed their training. As we speak, they are preparing to get underway from Bandar Abbas Naval Base, where they have been undergoing their training. If an American satellite happens to spot it, it would appear to be one of the new submarines Iran has purchased," Hassan indicated. Continuing, "It has been brought to our attention that the Soviets have been training the Iranians in one of their Kilo subs and will put to sea accompanying our submarine."

"Good. I think it is time for us to put our Chinese gift to sea and be prepared to engage the American Navy, particularly their aircraft carriers or amphibious ships, beginning on March fifteenth," Saddam said as he stood and turned to face the assembled officers.

"Gentlemen, the Americans are not going to be a pushover, as we have already seen with the XVIII Airborne Corps. The American attack helicopters and antitank weapons are formidable. We must inflict maximum damage on them and, if possible, we want these attacks on their forces to be spectacular. Remember, the American public is our target. The American public cannot accept a protracted war with heavy losses. We must show them the destruction and suffering we are inflicting on their sons and daughters and will continue to inflict until they leave our lands. If in the opening days of this war we can demonstrate how heavy the losses on the American forces will be, then the President will be forced to sue for peace, and it'll be on our terms. We will give him back the UAE and half of Saudi Arabia, but we will keep Kuwait and the northern half of Saudi Arabia. We will retain a port on the Red Sea and the ports in Kuwait. We will no longer be a desert beggar and a land-locked nation. Alright, you know what must be done. Now go do it."

Chapter 2
Plans Change

2 March 1991
Iraqi 3rd Squadron
50 Kilometers East of Abu Dhabi, United Arab Emirates

Major Vitaly Popkov banked his MiG-29 Fulcrum hard to the right as he dispersed another barrage of flares. Moments later, the AIM-9 Sidewinder missile passed under his fighter and slammed into one of the decoys.

Popkov breathed a sigh of relief just long enough to pull his aircraft hard again, only this time, he pulled the nose up and applied his air brakes, enabling his aircraft to bleed off nearly half his airspeed as he cut power to his engines. The maneuver was called the Cobra as it involved using the entire aircraft as an air brake by flaring the nose and body of the aircraft nearly vertical while cutting its thrust, thus allowing the pursuing aircraft to fly right past you. If the pilot acted quickly enough, he could acquire the pursuing enemy aircraft and take him out before he knew what had happened. In the case of Major Popkov, he'd mastered this maneuver and shot down five enemy aircraft with it so far.

As he executed the maneuver, the large American F-15C Eagle flew right past him. Popkov closed his air brakes and immediately applied maximum military power to his engines to give chase. The instant g-forces of going from near zero kilometers per hour to over eight hundred and climbing slammed him into his seat. The Eagle driver realized what had just happened but was powerless to stop what he knew was about to happen. He desperately tried to put some distance between them, lighting his two Pratt & Whitney F100 turbofan engines to maximum. By dumping fuel right onto his engine to light up his afterburners the pilot creating the perfect target for Popkov's missiles the perfect target to chase after.

Popkov activated his R-73 AA-11 Archer missile and waited for the infrared seeker head to indicate it had a solid lock on the Eagle's two engines. It took only seconds for the seeker to lock on, and once it had, Popkov fired. The missile dropped briefly away from his left wing before its rocket motor kicked in and accelerated to Mach 2.5.

The Eagle driver banked hard to his right, spitting out flares as he did. Popkov did his best to make sure he stayed on the pilot. For a brief moment, he thought his missile was going to go for one of the flares. He activated another R-73 missile and waited for the tonal sound indicating it had a solid lock. As soon as he heard it, he depressed the firing stud one more time. His second missile leapt after the F-15.

The American pilot pulled up hard and took his aircraft nearly vertical, lighting up his afterburners again. *He's trying to outrun the missiles*, Popkov thought.

The American fired off additional flares. To Popkov's frustration, one of the R-73 missiles went for the flare and blew up harmlessly. Then the second missile got within range of its proximity fuze and blew up. The shotgun blast of steel ball bearings ripped into the rear of the F-15. It took part of the left stabilizer off and caused the left engine to catch fire. The fighter started to level out as the pilot changed direction, looking to get closer to the Omani border.

When the aircraft leveled out, Popkov could see the flames spreading from the left engine up the spine of the aircraft. He was lining up to finish the American off with his guns when the pilot decided he was done. He ejected. Less than a minute later, the F-15 blew apart. The fire had reached the internal fuel stores and ignited.

One down, now to see who's left.

The warning tone in his headset alerted him to glance at his SPO-15 Beryoza radar display, confirming that he was being locked up. The Eagle driver he'd just shot down had a partner that was angling to get a shot on him. Popkov then did something crazy. He dove straight for the ground. As he was diving, he was picking up speed and bleeding altitude like crazy. Instead of pulling up or leveling off, he continued to aim down and pushed even steeper into the dive, then rolled inverted, essentially pulling off a somersault in the air with his aircraft.

His RWR stopped screaming in his ear as the American lost its lock on him. Pulling up hard and applying more power, Popkov saw he was just three hundred meters above the desert floor. He was whipping past Iraqi ground units spread out in their defensive positions on the ground. Aiming his aircraft back up into the sky, he caught sight of the American that had been chasing him. The Eagle driver was already angling in to attack one of his comrades.

Looking at his radar, he saw the American fighter was roughly twenty-six kilometers away. He was clearly giving chase to another one of Popkov's fighters. Applying more power to his engines, he looked to close the distance and checked his ordnance load. He still had two R-27 missiles left and two R-73s.

"Artem Leader, Lynx Actual. How copy?"

Popkov crinkled his eyebrows at the call. *Why is ground control calling me?*

"Lynx Actual, Artem Leader. I'm a little busy right now."

"Artem Leader, we are tracking a flight of twelve medium bombers approaching from sector three. They are flying at an altitude of one hundred meters, speed seven hundred kilometers. Can you intercept?"

Damn, those must be F-111s looking to slip past us to bomb the airport.

"Lynx Actual, understood. Breaking off current attack, will attempt to intercept. Out."

Sorry, my friend, you're on your own against the F-15, Popkov thought.

Changing course, he headed right for the bombers. They were unfortunately a little far off from him right now. Popkov wasn't sure he'd be able to intercept them before they overflew the airport if that was in fact their intended target.

****

495th Tactical Fighter Squadron

Major William "Gunslinger" Kidd's F-111 Aardvark was screaming across the desert barely one hundred meters above the ground. He was leading a strike of twelve bombers to make a run across the Abu Dhabi International Airport. Each aircraft was carrying a stick of twenty-four BLU-107 anti-runway cratering bombs on their four underwing hardpoints. The US variant of the French Durandal bombers were specially made for use on the F-111 for this very type of mission. The other four hardpoints were carrying another twenty-four five-hundred-pound Mk 82 dumb bombs, which they'd look to drop on their second pass over the airport's fuel farms and supporting maintenance hangars.

13

After this attack run, the Iraqis and their Soviet contract pilots won't be able to use this airfield again, Gunslinger thought, a mischievous grin spreading across his face.

Then his radio chirped, "Karma Leader, Oz Actual. We're showing a lot of SAM activity around the target. We count five SA-10 radar trucks, two SA-12 radars, six SA-4s, and twelve SA-6 trucks intermixed with at least fifteen other radar-guided gun trucks. You need to do your best to stay below one hundred feet," called out the E-3 Sentry from a few hundred kilometers behind them.

Good grief, how are we supposed to fly through all that? Gunslinger thought.

He depressed the talk button. "Oz Actual, Karma Leader. Good copy. Break. Wizard Six, you copy all of that?"

"Karma Leader, Wizard Six. We copy. Going hot with the magic. Halo element is moving to engage. Good luck and happy hunting. Wizard Six out."

"Hot damn, I hope those Spark Varks are able to jam all those radars," Kung Fu said, a bit of concern in his voice.

"Hey, we've flown through this kind of stuff in the past. We'll get through it like we always do," Gunslinger said, trying to reassure Kung Fu, his weapons officer, and himself at the same time. "Don't forget, we've also got the Fighting Hawks—you know, the 23rd Tactical Fighter Squadron. Those F-4s are outstanding Weasel platforms. They'll handle the SAMs, you just make sure our weapons are ready to drop when the time comes. I don't want to have to make any more passes over the target than necessary."

No one spoke for a few minutes. They continued to monitor their radar and what was going on all around them. Some twenty thousand feet above them, the F-15s flying escort duty for them were mixing it up with a group of MiG-29s. The damn MiG pilots were good. This wasn't the first time they'd flown against them.

"Hey, my scopes are going a little haywire," Kung Fu announced, a bit of concern in his voice.

"It's OK. It's the jamming from the Spark Varks. See?" Gunslinger pointed to the airport off in the distance. "We're almost to the target. I'm going to line us up to fly across runway 31L. Go ahead and get our stick of Durandals ready."

As Gunslinger lined their aircraft up for its attack, the other Aardvarks were doing the same. Each aircraft had a specific part of the runway they were going to crater. Some would hammer the runways, others would hammer the taxiways, and still others would nail the parking ramps. Once each aircraft had released their initial stick of bombs, they'd line up for a second pass, only this time they'd overfly the terminals, fuel farms, and anything else of value to plaster with their remaining five-hundred-pound dumb bombs. Then they'd hightail it out of there back to the Gulf of Oman, where they'd link up with the tankers to top off their fuel before flying on to their home in Egypt along the Red Sea.

Once he'd lined up for his attack run, Gunslinger pulled back on the throttle, slowing them down. He needed to make sure they didn't overshoot the runway. Keeping his eyes on his speed, altitude, and position, he told weapons officer it was his show now.

"Preparing for weapons release," Kung Fu called out.

As their aircraft closed in on the runway they were about to bomb, the sky all around them lit up with anti-aircraft fire. Red and green tracer fire flew right at them. Some of it was being spread wild, while some of it looked like it was going to rip them right out of the sky. Then Kung Fu started releasing their first stick of runway-cratering bombs. When the first stick had fallen away, the second stick released, then the third, then the fourth and final stick.

Gunslinger could feel the aircraft practically lift a hundred feet as the weight of those bombs fell away. Applying some additional power to the engines, he pulled the stick to the right a few degrees as he angled back out over the desert. He now wanted to realign the bomber for the final attack run on the airport. As they finished making their turn, he caught a great view of the Abu Dhabi airport. The runways looked thoroughly wrecked. Fire and smoke billowed from some of the commercial aircraft exploding and being torn apart.

Holy crap, we made it through that storm of AA fire.

Just as he was starting to breathe a sigh of relief, their RWR lit up, telling them an enemy radar was attempting to lock them up.

"Missile, six o'clock!" Kung Fu shouted urgently.

Gunslinger banked hard to the left and lit up their afterburners. He saw the body of a missile zip right through the space where they had just been. He dispensed flares and chaff in an attempt to throw off whatever radar was trying to lock them up.

Craning his head around, he tried to see who or what had shot at them. Then he saw a missile slam into Karma Three and blow it apart. The missile hit the aircraft in the center of the fuselage, and the entire aircraft erupted into flames.

Then a gray object flew right past them, shaking their aircraft as it did.

"What the hell was that?" Kung Fu shouted as he tried to catch a glimpse of whatever had flown by.

"I think that was a MiG!"

"Where the hell did he come from?"

"Who cares. Drop our ordnance. We're going to go supersonic and get the hell out of here," Gunslinger ordered. "All Karma elements, dump your ordnance and go supersonic. Head to the rally point now! We got a Fox in the henhouse," he called out to his bombers. If they had a MiG inside their formations, they needed to get out of here.

As soon as Kung Fu dumped their sticks of five-hundred-pound bombs, the aircraft again lifted a few hundred feet. Adjusting their wings to their fully swept back position, Gunslinger accelerated the aircraft up to Mach 2.3.

"Karma elements, sound off."

One by one, the Aardvarks sounded off. It became apparent they'd lost four aircraft. What they'd start to figure out as they sped away was who had been taken out by the lone MiG that seemed to have gotten within their ranks rather than by groundfire or SAMs. In any case, the Abu Dhabi airport was officially done as a forward airbase for the Iraqis. This was a key target that had to be taken out in preparation for the ground offensive that was slated to start on April 1, just twenty-eight days away.

****

CENTCOM Forward HQ
Military Technological College
Muscat, Oman

Major Stube had been called to General Schless's office. *What now?* Stube thought as he approached the open door to the general's office, pausing there. He was about to knock when General Schless, who was on the phone, motioned for him to come in and take a seat.

"Yes, sir. We will go over it and get back to you," Schless said, hanging the phone up.

"Sir, you wanted to see me," Stube said as he took a seat opposite him.

"Jack, we got a problem. It appears that the 35th National Guard Division will not be ready in time to get here. Instead they're sending the Tiger Brigade from the 2nd Armored Division, which was alerted three weeks ago and is already on their way. Typical snafu at the Pentagon. They forgot to tell us until just now. It seems that General Boomer now has reservations about the 1st Marine Division being able to attack the Iraqi 10th Armoured Division through those mountains. He's concerned that the 1st is going to get hung up in Fujairah and not be able to put any pressure on the 10th, and that would leave the 2nd Marines in dire straits coming ashore," Schless explained, hoping Jack might have some insight into what they should do.

"Sir, the 1st MarDiv has almost no one opposing him in Fujairah. He should be through there in hours and not days. And, yes, he is going to be pushing through some very rugged terrain that will impede his forward progress. It also impedes anyone attempting to attack him. As he breaks out of the rugged terrain, he has an avenue to the north that he can flank the 10th. Seven miles to Maleha puts him on the northern flank of the 10th. On the south it's the same—nine miles to Al Madam with open terrain," Stube pointed out.

"That was my thought as well. General Boomer is pretty adamant that he wants three divisions to go against the 10th Armoured," Schless said in resignation. "Look this over again and get back to me before the end of the day with a proposal."

"Sir, it's too late for us to put the Tiger Brigade in the task organization for this first phase. The only thing we can do is steal from Peter to pay Paul, and that's going to piss off some other commander," Stube explained, hoping his boss would see that.

"I know, but we have to come up with something. If people complain, then Schwarzkopf is going to have to decide. Not our fight there, we just recommend," Schless said. "You really think four MEBs are enough to take the 10th?"

"Sir, the Marines have their own air force. They can pound the 10th into the Stone Age before we launch the ground assault," Stube said in frustration.

"Well, Boomer doesn't see it that way, so come up with something and then the dogfight can begin between the heavy hitters. Just get me something before this evening's brief. We'll brief the changes there. Now go," Schless said, pointing to the door.

As Stube walked back to the office of the Jedi Knights, as they were referred to, he was mumbling to himself at the thought of having to change the plans and the orders at this point. When he got to the office, the others were waiting in anticipation of this event.

"Alright, listen up. General Boomer feels that he needs more forces to take out the 10th Armoured. He feels that 1st MarDiv will have a tough time getting through the mountains to take them head-on. So, we have to see where we can get more forces from and move them to support the Marines," Jack explained. The looks on the other majors' faces showed exhaustion and frustration with this latest request.

Jim Rumgay pointed out, "First, we need to see how another division could attack. Shit, there are only two roads through those mountains in his sector and the 1st would have them both. If we put another division in there, how could they even move through there? This is crazy."

"Let's look at another avenue of approach to the 10th and see what we got," Roy McClain said, pulling out a map of the AO. Everyone gathered around to examine the map.

"We've identified these two highways that come through the mountains from Fujairah, but that's all there is. No other way through those mountains," Major Bob Peters indicated.

"What about the Marines air-assaulting over the mountains?" Major Fred Thompson asked.

"The choppers will all be tied up with the amphibious operation for the 2nd and they won't be able to do double duty," Major Mike Monroe clarified.

"Well, is there another approach we aren't seeing?" Stube asked as everyone continued to study the map.

"Certainly nothing north of here. Hell, how do these people get around in this country? You'd have to be a mountain goat to live up in this northern area," Rumgay observed.

After a few minutes, Thompson said, "Hey, look at this." He dragged his finger across the map. "Highway 7 approaches Al Ain and Al Buraimi, but before it clears the last of the mountains, there's a road cutting north behind this low ridge, and then at Nuway it opens to flat ground. We could bring a division down Highway 7 to Humaydah and position them between Humaydah and Nuway the night before. On order, they attack west to Margham and Al Madam. That would put three divisions on the 10th with the 1stMar coming from the east, an amphibious landing coming from the west, and another division coming from the south. Why the hell didn't we see this before?" Thompson said with a bit of excitement in his voice.

"Looks damn good to me," McClain said. "Now the fun part. Who do we get to pull another division from?"

"There's only one corps that we can look to. That's VII Corps, and I can tell you General Franks will not be happy. Who do you think he would be willing to give up?" Stube asked.

"1st British Armoured," Monroe said. Everyone looked at him. "The Marines have worked with British units before in some of the maneuvers in Norway. I believe they were supposed to do it again this winter. Frank's forces in Germany have trained with the British but the Germans aren't exactly fond of having the British running loose in the countryside with US forces. Last time that team pretty well tore Germany up. Franks would want to keep his US Forces and would rather cut the Brits loose. I think the Brits and Marines would get along just fine given how many exercises they've done together."

Everyone exchanged looks, seeing if there was any counterargument. Stube spoke up then. "All in favor?" Everyone's hand went up. "That settles it. We recommend that 1st British Armour be transferred to MARCENT and that the battle plan be changed, having them stage out of... um, what should we call this staging area?" Stube asked.

"Tactical Assembly Area Biscuits," McClain said with a smirk on his face.

"Staging out of TAA Biscuits to attack northwest to Margham. Any questions?" Jack asked. There were none. "Why call it Biscuits?" Jack asked, looking at McClain.

"The Brits are always eating their biscuits with tea... it fits," McClain said.

That evening at the commanders' brief, the change was briefed, and surprisingly, no objections were raised. Approved!

Chapter 3
1st British Division Shift

4 March 1991
1st British Division HQ
Adam, Oman

"You have got to be bloody kidding me," the commander of 4th Brigade, Brigadier Christopher Hammerbeck, said with disgust.

"Brigadier, I assure you that I am not kidding," General de la Billière, the commander of British Forces, explained. "We are loading up our kit and heading north. Seems the Marines don't think they have the force to take on the 10th Armoured Division and we are going to come to rescue them. CENTCOM is sending all the transport we need for the equipment, and planes will be landing in Fahud to fly the troops north to Sohar, where our wheeled vehicles will be waiting. The HETs will deliver our tracked vehicles and we'll hop in them when it's time to go."

He paused for a second before adding, "I've been assured that the military police will have a traffic schedule and clear the roads for this move. For this to work and for us to maintain the element of surprise, this must all come off quickly and smoothly with the least amount of radio traffic. The order of movement will be 4th Brigade, followed by 7th Brigade. The deputy will develop the flow and provide you all with the timetable. Have your number two get with him for you transport requirements by 0600 tomorrow.

"I know this will appear confusing to the lads, but deception is part of any good plan, especially when it deceives those that are to carry it out," General de la Billière said with a smile.

"Sir, if I may, just when is this move to take place?" asked Brigadier General Patrick Cordingley, 7th Brigade commander, trying to figure out when his brigade would be on the road.

"In seventy-two hours, General," de la Billière declared. "As soon as it gets dark, we'll get on the move. It'll provide us good cover, don't you think?"

General de la Billière could tell by the stunned looks on everyone's face that the reality of going into combat was suddenly hitting them.

"Gentlemen, this needs to stay quiet and kept to yourselves. On April first, the air campaign that will kick off this entire offensive will start. General Schwarzkopf believes the air campaign will last at least two weeks and maybe three before he gives the official go order to launch the attack. That means we'll have some time to get ourselves ready, but not much. We need to be ready to move sooner if an opportunity presents itself. So do what you can to get your forces moved to Rabi. I would think it unprofessional on our part if General Schwarzkopf felt compelled to extend the air campaign because we could not be in position and ready to do our part. Anything that can be packed and ready for the move should be prepared now and over the next seventy-two hours." The general paused for a moment, then closed, "I think that about covers everything. Would anyone care for tea, or have I just stymied your appetites?"

****

"Sergeant Major!" Lieutenant Colonel Belew called out as he returned from a meeting with Brigadier Cordingley. Turning to his runner, he said, "Find the sergeant major and be quick about it." Belew was not in a good mood. He'd been commander of the 1st Battalion Royal Scots for less than a year. Like the families of everyone in the battalion, his family remained in Münster, West Germany, where the battalion was permanently stationed. A graduate of Sandhurst, he had always been a soldier and liked serving in the oldest regiment of the British Army, which had been formed in 1633.

Sergeant Major Smith had been born and raised in the regiment. He'd joined the army right out of high school and found the military lifestyle to be exactly what he needed and longed for. While he was a model soldier now, he'd had his time of hellraising as a junior enlisted. He was the epitome of what Hollywood pictured as a sergeant major. Solid build at six foot four with not an ounce of fat at 235 pounds. He loved to play rugby on the battalion team and took the hits as well as any man and gave them too, regardless of rank. His well-trimmed handlebar mustache was a thing of beauty, highlighting his square jaw.

As the sergeant major approached the colonel's quarters, Major Saunders, the battalion executive officer, arrived at the same time.

Saunders was the opposite of the sergeant major. A short man at five foot six, he had attended Sandhurst, graduating as a second lieutenant.

"Any idea what this is about, sir?" the sergeant major asked.

"No, but I understand he is in a fit," Major Saunders indicated. "He has been up at Brigade most of the evening and I have no idea what that was about. Sort of a spur-of-the-moment thing. I suspect we are about to find out."

As the sergeant major and the executive officer entered the tent, they saw a world map spread out on a table with Belew studying it.

"Sir, you wanted to see us?" Major Saunders inquired.

"Yes, we have orders to move," Belew muttered, still looking over the map.

"Move, sir? Yes, sir, how far?" the sergeant major asked.

"A couple of hundred miles north, and we have three days to get ready for it," Belew fumed. The sergeant major was unflappable, but Major Saunders had that three-thousand-meter stare going on at the idea of moving in less than three days.

"Did you say a couple hundred miles and only three days to be ready, sir?" the major asked.

"Are you ears full of sand, Major? That is what I said." Belew was normally a very polite and even-keeled leader, but not today.

"The bloody Yanks couldn't get their foocking act together and the United States Marine Corps sniveled—to General Schwarzkopf, mind you—that they needed help. And rather than take an American division, they are sending us to pull their bacon out of the fire."

"Where exactly are we going, sir?" the sergeant major asked.

"We are being flown to Sohar up here," he replied, pointing at the map, "where we will have transport to here at Rabi and join our track vehicles. HETs will arrive in forty-eight hours to load them up. MPs have our convoy clearances and schedules. I will be leaving in the morning with the company commanders and driving up to Rabi to check the area over and look at the Tactical Assembly Area that we will stage out of to launch our attack. Number Two, you and the sergeant major will have to get things organized back here and get it loaded and moved out. Any questions?"

"How much can we tell the lads, sir?" the sergeant major asked.

"You can tell them they are moving to a new location and that is all, although I suspect they will figure it out. We move under the cover of darkness, so any Iraqi aircraft won't spot us. The lads will know something is afoot. These kids are not dumb."

"Aye, sir. They will figure it out very quickly," the sergeant major agreed.

Standing up straight to stretch his back, Lieutenant Colonel Belew looked at the two gentlemen. "I think it is about that time. Anyone care for tea?"

Chapter 4
The Plan, Phase 1

7 March 1991
ARCENT HQ
Muscat, Oman

"Gentlemen, if you take a seat, we will get started," General Yeosock said as he entered the room. The gentlemen consisted of every division commander under ARCENT and MARCENT as well as regimental commanders and combat aviation brigade commanders.

"Whenever you're ready, General Taylor," Yeosock directed. General Taylor was the G-3 or operations officer for ARCENT. The ground tactical plan rested on his shoulders, and he had worked closely with the Jedi Knights in the development of the plan.

"Yes, sir. First slide, please," he requested. "Gentlemen, this is the task organization for this first phase of the operation. There is one change that I want to point out. The 35th Infantry Division will not be joining us as we anticipated. It seems they couldn't get ready fast enough, so the Tiger Brigade of the 2nd Armored Division will be joining us instead. Once they arrive, which will be at the end of phase one, we anticipate them being attached to MARCENT. For phase one, 1st British Armoured

Division will operate under MARCENT." Taylor paused long enough for everyone to read the slide. "Are there any questions?"

TASK ORGANIZATION
PHASE 1

MARCENT	VII Corps	XVIII ABN Corps
1st Marine Div	1st Infantry Div	28th Infantry
2nd Marine Div	24th Infantry Div	29th Infantry
1st British Armoured Div	1st Armored Div	82nd Airborne
	3rd Armored Div	101st Airborne (Assault)
	2nd Armored Cavalry Rgt	TF West
	6th Cbt Avn Bde	
	12th Cbt Avn Bde	

III Corps

	TF "Abu Bakr"	TF "Tariq"
1st Cavalry	2nd Saudi Bde	Saudi Marine Bn
50th Armored Div	Northern Oman Bde	TF Othman
3rd Egyptian Infantry Div	UAE Mechanized Bn	Bahrain Motorized Co
4th Egyptian Armoured Div		
Kuwaiti Al Fatah Bde		
Kuwaiti 2/5 Mechanized Bn		
18th Cbt Avn Bde		
3rd Armored Cav Rgt		

NOTE: Upon arrival of Tiger Brigade, 2nd Armored Division, it will be assigned to MARCENT

There were none, as everyone had known from the beginning who was going to be with who.

"Next slide." Again, Taylor paused as the slide came on the screen. He allowed the audience to read the slide.

MISSION
On order, ARCENT attacks to destroy Iraqi forces in sector and prepares to continue the attack through Saudi Arabia and into Kuwait. Be prepared to continue the attack.

PHASE 1

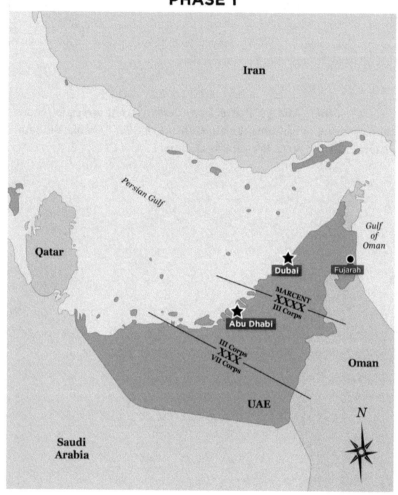

"In preparation for phase one, mine-clearing operations will commence on 10 March. On G-day, offensive operations will commence, with 1st Marine Division attacking to clear Fujairah and continuing the attack to clear the highway from Fujairah to Maghribiyah and Mleiha. Be prepared to conduct linkup with 2nd Marine Division on G plus one, vicinity of Dubai.

"The 1st British will attack northwest under the command of MARCENT to clear Al Hiyar, Al Faqa, Murqquab, and Al Madam. Conduct link up with 1st Marine Division.

"III Corps attacks in center of the western sector and to seize Abu Dhabi. This will also cut off any chance of the Iraqi force breaking out of Al Ain."

General Taylor paused just long enough for a question to be posed, but none came. "VII Corps will attack the southern portion of the sector here"—he pointed to a spot on the map— "and look to destroy the Iraqi forces in that sector. This will allow them to seize Alyhyali, Zayed City, and Al Ruwais along the coast, which will put VII Corps in position to continue attacking west."

Taylor then waited for a new map to be brought up, one that showed the western side of Saudi Arabia. "In the west, the XVIII Airborne Corps conducts offensive operations to seize Tabuk. Once they seize Tabuk, it will position our forces to attack eastward. As our forces push out of Tabuk and continue to advance east, the Iraqis will have to withdraw the 2nd Republican Guard Corps from Medina or face the likelihood of them being completely encircled and cut off from their supply lines and any avenue of retreat."

Many of the generals nodded in agreement. "On G plus 2, the 2nd Marine Division will conduct their amphibious landings between Dubai and Abu Dhabi. This will further cut Iraqi supply lines and prevent them from withdrawing north unless they act quickly. If they fail to see the avenues of retreat closing, then there's a good chance we may be able to encircle these divisions in the UAE and Saudi and destroy them. That concludes my brief—what questions do you have?" General Taylor asked before moving on.

Again, there were none.

General Taylor continued, "The main effort is VII Corps. The commander's intent is for a swift penetration by the VII Corps to destroy the 52nd Armoured Division and be prepared to repel a counterattack by 1st Republican Guard Corps should they launch one. The big unknown variable we have right now is how aggressive these corps and division commanders may be and if they'll be micromanaged from Baghdad. On paper, these corps and divisions look formidable. They even look like they may be on par with our own units. But it remains to be seen how they'll behave when pressed by a non-Arab adversary.

"Gentlemen, if there are no further questions, this concludes my portion of today's briefing. I will be followed by the G-4, who will provide the logistics plan," Taylor concluded.

He knew there would be no questions as he had individually briefed each corps commander and their staff ahead of time. Now it was a matter of execution and minimizing the Iraqis' vote. In war, just as in politics, the enemy always gets a vote.

Chapter 5
Underway

8 March 1991
USS *San Juan*
Gulf of Oman

Commander David Osborne could not be happier. His first command and one of the newest subs in the fleet to boot. The USS *San Juan* SSN-751 had been commissioned only a year ago. She was a *Los Angeles*–class fast-attack submarine equipped with the latest AN/BSY-1 sonar suite, Mk-48 ADCAP heavyweight torpedoes, and twelve vertical launch tubes for her highly capable Tomahawk cruise missiles. The boat's Mk 2 Combat Control System/All Digital Attack Center integrated sonar, targeting, and tracking into one system and allowed for accurate and quick responses in a tactical situation. While this was Commander Osborne's first command, he had been in the Silent Service his entire career, and his twelve officers and ninety-eight crewmen were old hands when it came to undersea warfare. For all the crew, this was at least the second boat they'd served on.

For the past week, the *San Juan* had been monitoring traffic traversing the Strait of Hormuz. As the President's deadline approached, fewer ships were attempting to enter the Strait and more ships were coming out. Several ships that had been waiting to receive a pilot to take them through the minefield had departed the area in search of a port outside of the Persian Gulf.

"Conn, Sonar, we have another contact coming out at this time. Appears she's a tanker. Designating Sierra 3."

"Roger, Sierra 3," Commander Osborne said, returning to watch the view being transmitted through the ship of what the periscope was seeing and looking at the geographic plot on the combat system. The display showed two ships at eight thousand yards for one, and ten thousand yards for the second, heading towards the Strait, and one ship at fifteen thousand yards heading out of the Strait. The ship coming out, designated Sierra 3, was getting out before the deadline, but Sierra 1 and Sierra 2 looked to be pressing their luck. The 1200 GMT deadline was passed by thirty minutes. Osborne's orders at this point were to observe and report. While he wasn't sitting near the entrance with his torpedo doors open, he did have them loaded and the tubes flooded and ready to fire should the need arise.

As they watched what was going on via their periscope, two SH-60 helicopters came into view and circled above Sierra 1, an oil tanker that appeared to be empty based on how high it was sitting in the water. In contrast, Sierra 2, a container ship, was fully loaded and sitting low in the water from the added weight.

"Conn, Sonar, Sierra 1 and Sierra 2 are reducing revolutions."

"Roger, Sonar," Commander Osborne said, still watching the screen. It was becoming obvious that both ships were slowing. Then, as expected, Sierra 1 commenced turning to port, followed by Sierra 2.

"I think the tanker may be going to Fujairah to take on a load and the container might be going to Khor Fakkan. That's a container terminal," Osborne said to his COB, Master Chief Mark Young.

Master Chief Young was coming up on his eighteenth year in the Navy. Like most who neared retirement, he'd started thinking about what he might do next. Raytheon had already sent someone by to talk to him about a position with their company if and when he decided to retire. Besides a very lucrative salary on top of his Navy retired pay, they also offered a stable home life, something his wife and teenage children would enjoy immensely after following him around from assignment to assignment. His son was at the age where a strong father figure was needed at home.

"Those ports are in Iraqi hands now, aren't they, Captain?" the master chief questioned.

"Yeah, but we have no orders about stopping commercial traffic entering ports outside of the Persian Gulf, at least not yet."

Master Chief Young looked over at Commander Osborne. "Sir, when was the last time you got some sleep? You look like shit, sir," he said with a grin. "With all due respect, sir, of course."

"You know, you're right. I'm going to lay down and get some sleep." Osborne turned to the executive officer. "XO, how about you take it for the next four hours? Let's go deep to monitor Sierra 3 as she leaves the Gulf and listen for any other contacts."

"Aye, sir, XO has the Conn," the XO stated as Commander Osborne made his way forward to his cabin.

Commander Osborne's quarters were nothing as extravagant as the captain's quarters on the Love Boat, but for a submarine, they were comfortable. The quarters consisted of a bunk, a washbasin, and a writing desk—about as fancy as it gets on a submarine and a private room to boot. A single chair accompanied the writing desk. Under the bunk were drawers for his clothes and a small closet to hang uniforms. Underway, everyone wore a blue jumpsuit that was wash-and-wear and sent to the boat's laundry for cleaning. Usually the supply officer was the laundry officer, supervising a couple of crew members.

On his writing desk, Osborne maintained a clean desktop with only a picture of his wife and daughter always kept out. When submerged, you didn't experience the same wave action as you did on the surface, so things were fairly stable unless an emergency surface or dive was executed. When he knew he'd be executing those maneuvers, he'd make sure to put the pictures away in his drawer so they wouldn't get flung off his desk.

Kicking off his rubber-soled canvas loafers, he climbed into his bunk and pulled a blanket over himself. Although the boat was kept at a stable and comfortable temperature, Commander Osborne had to have some weight on him, such as a blanket, in order to sleep. Once his eyes closed, he quickly dropped into REM sleep and became dead to the world around him.

****

"Cap'n, Cap'n. Wake up, sir," Master Chief Young said, gently tapping Commander Osborne's foot.

"Yeah, COB, I'm awake," a drowsy Osborne said. "Is that coffee I smell?"

"Yes, sir, I figured if I was to wake you, I should at least make it pleasant... like your wife would," Young said with a smile.

"You don't know my wife, COB. She would have poured it on me. What's up? How long was I asleep?" Osborne asked as he accepted the cup of coffee and swung his legs out of the bunk, feeling for his shoes with his feet.

"You've been asleep for six hours. The XO said to let you sleep. He's training that new officer right now in the Conn and didn't want you to witness the kid's mistakes," COB said, chuckling.

"That bad?"

"Sir, nothing you didn't do when you went aboard your first boat. You learned and he'll learn too. Life teaches us lessons until we learn. Actually, sir, the reason I woke you is we have something in Sonar that might interest you. At first they thought it was nothing, but the longer they listened, the more they were convinced it was something. We've been tracking it for a couple of hours now," the COB explained. That immediately got Osborne's interest.

"It's not another gray whale whistling Dixie, I hope," Osborne commented, slipping on his shoes and standing. "Let's go see what we have."

They departed his cabin and walked down the passageway to the sonar room. The two sonarmen were seated, watching the waterfall on their digital screens. Grabowski was the senior sonarman and a petty officer first class. He was "training" Davis, who had served on a previous boat but had changed his rating to sonarman, so he was still learning according to Grabowski.

"Grabowski, what you got?" Osborne asked when he came up behind the two.

"Sir, we were tracking Sierra 3 as she came out of the Strait. She was only making about ten knots, which I thought was a bit strange for a tanker. She also didn't sound quite right. I was thinking she may have been having propulsion problems to be moving that slow. When she passed near us, the XO took us up for a peek and she was identified as a Chinese-registered ship."

"Nothing unusual about a Chinese tanker coming out," Osborne countered.

"Well, sir, as we continued to listen to her, the sound changed and we began to track two vessels instead of one," Grabowski said. "Sierra 3 moved off to the southeast, but this second vessel continued to the southwest, and the further it separated, the more distinct the sound was. Sir, it's a Chinese submarine, Type 033 Romeo class."

Osborne lifted an eyebrow at that. "Are you sure?"

"Positive, Captain. Tracked them on my last boat out of Sasebo. We've designated him Sierra 4."

Osborne quickly left sonar and entered the Conn. The XO saw him and announced, "Captain on the Conn."

"Sir," the XO started, "we're tracking a—"

"Sonar filled me in."

"Sir, Sierra 4 is two thousand yards ahead and we're right behind him. He's doing ten knots and noisy as hell. Not the usual silent types we're used to tracking. His heading is one hundred and ninety degrees, and he's been on that track for the past hour. Sierra 3 turned to a one-hundred-and-forty-degree heading and that's when we picked up Sierra 4. He was right under Sierra 3," the XO indicated. Osborne glanced at the depth indication—three hundred feet.

"XO, let's get a message to NAVCENT and notify them of what we have here. Tell them my intentions are to track this guy and await instructions."

"Aye, sir." The XO departed to get the report ready to send.

The COB reached over and took the empty coffee cup from Osborne's hand. Osborne hadn't realized that he had finished the cup but was still carrying it. His mind was somewhere else, like trying to figure out why a Chinese submarine was operating in an area that was about to turn into a war zone.

Chapter 6
Tracking

8 March 1991
USS *San Juan*
Gulf of Oman

It had been a couple of hours since the *San Jose* had sent a message to NAVCENT indicating that they were trailing a Chinese Type 033 Romeo-class submarine. Osborne was in the wardroom, which wasn't much bigger than the table that the twelve officers could sit around. He knew he was eating a very satisfying dinner but wasn't sure if it was breakfast time or supper time unless he looked at the ship's clock, which indicated 1900 hours. Two of the junior officers that were off watch were with him at the moment when the XO stuck his head in the doorway.

"Cap'n, we got a response back from NAVCENT," he said.

"What did they have to say?" Osborne asked, taking a drink of milk to wash his food down.

"Sir, they said that sometime yesterday morning, a Romeo-class left Bandar Abbas Naval Base and hasn't been seen since. It went out with a Kilo-class sub as well. However, intel says there were no Chinese personnel at the base in the past year. They want us to maintain contact with the Romeo and report its movement. We're not authorized to engage unless they engage us first, or present a threat to friendly vessels," the XO said, handing Commander Osborne the message to read. He scanned it quickly and thought about what it meant.

"XO, let's maintain a track and plot every time there's a course change to see where he might be heading. Also, let's get a fix on where our fleet is operating, to include the Brits. I don't want to be following this guy and have to wait for him to put a fish into someone. Let's see if we can determine hostile intent before it happens."

Finishing his dinner, Osborne was trying to figure out what this new contact was all about. They knew they had detected a Russian sub a few months back, but now a Chinese one. Something wasn't adding up. *Could the Soviets and the Chinese have sold some of their older-model subs to the Iraqis and the Iranians? Could the Iraqis and Iranians*

possibly be working together? The big brains at naval intelligence need to sort this out so we know what we're facing out here.
****

Captain Adil Kazemi was forty-eight years old and had served in the Iraqi Navy since he was eighteen. He was quickly noted for his intelligence and sent to further schooling at Britannia Royal Naval College in Dartmouth, England. He was one of several foreign students attending the thirty-week course and graduated in the top ten percent of the class. Returning to Iraq, he had become proficient in ship handling and developed an interest in submarine warfare. He'd written several papers on the need for Iraq to possess submarines in order to ensure freedom to the sea through the Strait of Hormuz.

Soon he was off to Moscow for three years to learn more about the submarine service from the Soviets. Returning to Iraq, he had become vocal about the need for submarines. Finally, he had been noticed by Saddam, who had sent him to China to tour the Chinese submarine force. When he'd returned home, he'd brought with him an offer from the Chinese government to sell Iraq one of their older submarines as long as it wasn't advertised to the world. However, since Iraq had no port for a submarine to operate out of, a deal was worked out between China and Iran for the sub to base out of Bandar Abbas. To the Iranians, this was like poking a sharp stick in the eye of the Americans and more than worth putting their ire for Iraq aside. The enemy of my enemy is my friend sort of agreement.

Captain Adil Kazemi was excited about his first command of Iraq's first submarine. He had received extensive training in submarine warfare from both the Soviet Union and China. He'd then undergone sea trials supervised by a Chinese submarine officer. In their training, the graduation exercise was a dry run on an American Navy cargo ship with a down-the-throat attack. It impressed the hell out of the Iranian skipper. With his crew trained, he now had his sailing orders: proceed into the Gulf of Oman and Arabian Sea and sink the American carriers.

Kazemi found it convenient that a Chinese oil tanker was in port in Iran and the captain, with some guidance from the Chinese embassy, had agreed to sail out of the Persian Gulf at a speed of no more than ten knots for forty-eight hours on a heading of 131 degrees.

The merchant captain knew better than to ask questions as to the low speed—he likely had his suspicions but played along. When the forty-eight hours were up, he increased his speed to fifteen knots and continued westward across the Indian Ocean. He was off the southern coast of Oman and had seen several military vessels, the most impressive being an aircraft carrier off the horizon roughly twelve miles to the east. The captain thought it might be a bit further as he could only see the bridge and the aircraft landing.

Below the waves, Kazemi also took note of the heavy screws—an aircraft carrier or maybe one of the American battleships. At surface level, the horizon was only three miles away, so viewing through the QZHA-10 attack periscope would be a worthless and possibly dangerous exercise. He would have to rely on the H/AQ2-262A sonar system to guide him to the American fleet. He was content to continue a plot towards the heavy sounds and exercise some patients.

"Sonar, distance to target," Kazemi asked.

"Estimated range is twenty kilometers."

"Roger," he acknowledged. "Helm, maintain course and depth."

"Understood, maintain course and depth."

****

Several days later, Commander Osborne had been making the rounds throughout the boat. He enjoyed these walks. It was a chance for him to see the crew as it was working and get to know the sailors and let them get to know him. It also gave him a good perspective of the crew's morale. Like so many leaders, he had learned that if the crew was getting mail from home, if their pay was straight and if the chow was good, then they were generally happy. If any one of those three got messed up, then he knew he would have a crew member with a less-than-perfect attitude, himself included.

"Captain to the Conn," he heard over the ship's speaker system as he entered the engineering section of the boat.

Hmmm, that might not be good. Commander Osborne turned and proceeded to the Conn. The officer of the deck was a lieutenant and solid officer. When Osborne entered the Conn, the OOD and the XO were there along with the navigation officer and weapons officer.

"What's up?" Osborne asked, looking around the confined area.

"Sir, Sierra 4 has changed course and is heading on a track to the fleet," the OOD indicated as the others remained silent.

"Any indication that he's opened his outer doors?" Osborne asked.

"No indication, Cap'n," the OOD stated.

"Range to target?"

"Five thousand yards."

"Roger, plot a target solution. If he opens his outer doors, we'll engage as I consider that hostile intent. I want him sunk if he does that. Understood?"

Everyone acknowledged, knowing this might be the first time a US submarine had fired its weapons in anger since World War II.

****

Captain Adil Kazemi was feeling confident as he gave the order to raise the periscope. His sonar station gave him no indication that they had been detected. As the periscope broke the waves, Kazemi could see that his target, the American aircraft carrier, was in the perfect position for his torpedo attack. Without looking away as he concentrated on his target, Kazemi ordered, "Open outer doors and prepare to fire."

It was the last order he ever gave.

****

B-808 Yaroslavl IRIS *Taregh*
Indian Ocean

The IRIS *Taregh* had slipped out of Bandar Abbas the same time and way as their Iraqi counterpart—underneath the belly of a giant freighter. Captain First Rank Aleksandr Nemits was glad as hell he wasn't on one of those Chinese rust buckets. They were loud and noisy and attracted all sorts of unwanted attention. He knew even his Kilo-class wasn't quite as good as the American boats, but they weren't far off.

Standing on the bridge, Captain Nemits asked, "What is the status of the Iraqi boat?"

One of the Iranian officers replied, "She's eight thousand yards to our front, but she's picked up a tail."

Captain Sayyet looked surprised by the announcement. He turned to look at Nemits. "How did you know there would be an American submarine waiting for them like that?"

"It's what I would if I was an American."

"Now what do we do?" Sayyet pressed.

"We slide in behind the American and we stay in their baffles and we wait."

Sayyet smiled a devilish smile. While the Iraqis didn't know it, they were being used as bait. While the Americans were busy playing cat and mouse with the Shchuka and now following the Iraqi sub, the Iranian sub would slip in behind the American sub and put her on the bottom when the time came. Then they'd fire a spread of torpedoes at the American aircraft carrier not far away.

For several hours, they waited. The American sub continued to follow the Iraqis as they got closer and closer to the American fleet. They had practically slipped through the outer perimeter of the carrier's escorts. The American submarine was the last and final line of defense for the carrier.

"Are submarine operations always this boring?" Sayyet asked.

Nemits lifted an eyebrow in surprise at the question. "Boring? Are you kidding me? This is the most excitement I've had in years. As submariners, we spend most of our careers playing cat and mouse with the Americans. When we leave our home ports, they usually have a submarine waiting for us. The Yankees…they like to follow you around, see what you are doing. We know they are there, so from time to time we'll try and mess around with them. We'll conduct some crazy maneuver we know will make them angry, but it'll usually get them to back off as well."

"Crazy maneuver like what?"

Smiling, Nemits regaled him and the rest of the Conn with some of the stuff they'd do, from the Crazy Ivan turn to the occasional torpedo launch to blow up some underwater rocks or a sunken ship on the bottom of the ocean. Things the Americans would complain about feverishly if they could. From time to time, a news story of an encounter with a Soviet submarine playing war games off the coast of New York would warrant a splashy headline. Most of the time, people were generally oblivious to what was going on under the waves off their coasts. The Russians liked to remind the Americans they weren't as safe as they liked to think they were.

As they waited to see what the Americans would do next, Sayyet lowered his voice so only the two of them could hear. "What should we do with this American sub we're following?"

This was one of those moments where years of experience in the silent service made all the difference. It was the reason he was still on board this sub, providing them with his expertise. Sayyet just wasn't ready to be thoroughly on his own in combat.

Taking a deep breath in, he quietly responded, "I'm thinking when those Americans fire, we fire. With our torpedo being fired into their baffles, they'll never hear it coming until it's too late. Once they are down, there will be some confusion amongst the surface ships. They'll all go to flank speed, which means it'll be too noisy for them to listen to us. I propose we close the gap with the American carrier just a bit and then we fire a full spread of torpedoes at them. Then we go deep and we slip away, back to Bandar Abbas, or at least away from here, and reassess. If we're lucky, we might sink the carrier. If not, we'll have put her out of the war with the damage we'll cause," Nemits explained. The opportunity to torpedo an American carrier was every Russian submariner's dream.

Sayyet nodded in agreement at the plan. They briefed the others on what they were going to do so that when the time came, they'd execute.

Another hour went by with little in the way of action. The trio of subs continued to move closer and closer towards the American fleet at a steady pace of ten knots. Then out of nowhere, the action began.

"Conn, Sonar. I'm detecting the sound of torpedo doors being opened. I can't make out if it's the Iraqis or the Americans, but whoever it is, they are likely preparing to fire."

Nemits asked, "How far away is the American carrier relative to the Iraqi sub and then us?"

One of the crewmen replied, "Um, they are six thousand meters from the Iraqi sub and nine thousand yards from us."

"Conn, Sonar. Torpedo in the water. The American has fired on the Iraqi sub."

Nemits nodded to Sayyet—it was time for him to give their own order.

Captain Sayyet grabbed for the handset. "Weps, Conn. Fire torpedoes one and three at Sierra 1. Reload tubes one and three."

It felt like an eternity as they listened to their torpedoes race after the American sub. In a way, they felt bad about their brothers-in-arms on the noisier Chinese sub. There was nothing they could do. They were doomed, and they either knew it or were about to find out. The only consolation was that their deaths wouldn't be in vain. They'd nail the American submarine, and if all went according to plan, they'd land a few blows against that American aircraft carrier.

Then they heard it. An explosion, followed by a second, likely the second torpedo. These explosions were followed by the breakup of the Iraqi sub as its internal compartments imploded from the water pressure.

While the Iraqi sub was beginning to sink, the screws on the American submarine had jumped to full speed. The American sub had turned hard port as it released some countermeasures, but it was too late. On the advice of Nemits, Sayyet hadn't cut the wires to their fish until they were practically on top of the Americans. By the time they had, the torpedoes had already fully acquired them. They zoomed right past the noisemakers and zeroed in on the American.

Boom. Boom.

The first torpedo had nailed the rear of the submarine, crippling its engines and propulsion system. The second torpedo had hit the sub amidship, nearly ripping it in half. In fractions of a second, the sub had flooded nearly every compartment and room on the boat. It began to break apart and join the Iraqi sub on an eternal patrol.

"Conn, Sonar. The surface ships are increasing speed. I'm showing two frigates heading in our direction. The closest one is thirteen thousand yards, traveling at twenty-five knots. They look to be Knox-class ASW frigates."

"Weps, Conn. How far away are we from that carrier?"

"Conn, Weps. We're now six thousand yards from the carrier."

Nemits asked the sonar room which American carrier it was. That would tell him roughly how fast it could travel away from them.

"Sonar, Conn. The carrier is the *Midway*. She's now accelerated to thirty-three knots. She's also turned onto a new heading that is going to take her on a track that will lead her towards us if we turn to a heading of two-two-three degrees. This will allow us to be in weapons range before they are able to flee the area."

Sayyet looked at his helmsman. "Turn us to two-two-three degrees. Make your depth two hundred and twenty meters."

Nemits nodded in approval at the orders. It was exactly what he'd do if this was his command.

They stayed on this course and heading for another ten minutes as the distance between them, and the *Midway* continued to close. When they were within four thousand six hundred yards of the carrier, Sayyet gave the order every Russian submariner could only dream of giving.

Once all six of their 533mm heavyweight torpedoes had been fired, they began the process of reloading their tubes and turning away to make their great escape. It was now a race to put as much distance as possible between themselves and the fast-approaching frigates now hunting for them.

As the time ticked by, they eventually heard the sound of four impacts. It sounded like two of the torpedoes had missed. They heard a couple of additional explosions, but it didn't sound like the carrier was sinking. In any case, they'd successfully hit an American carrier with four torpedoes, and that was a huge win.

Chapter 7
Shift Forces

9 March 1991
Basement Level, Pentagon
Arlington, Virginia

"What the hell is this?" Bob Daley mumbled as he examined the morning satellite pictures. As he stared at the photos on his computer screen, he noticed the 10th Iraqi Armoured Division moving south. He also noticed that the 49th Iraqi Infantry Division was moving north.

"Hey, Cliff... you want to take a look at this? I think they're shifting forces around in the UAE. I'm surprised, the way the air strikes have been hitting them, that they would be doing that," Daley said.

"Let me take a look," Cliff, his supervisor, directed, walking over. He pulled his glasses down from the top of his head, leaning over Bob's shoulder. "Hmmm... hmmm. It sure appears that way. Now why would he be doing that? Pull a tank division down from the north and replace it with an infantry division."

"I might have an idea," a voice behind Bob and Cliff said. They both turned. There stood Paige Harrison. She had recently come to work in the office, having completed her military service as an intelligence analyst at CENTCOM in Tampa, Florida. She was a graduate of the US Naval Academy and had liked her time in the Navy but wanted a more stable home life in order to start a family—after she found the right man, of course.

"What's your idea, Paige?" Cliff asked.

"Well, up north, what have we got for terrain? Mountains and a major city on the southern coast. Horrible tank country. I think he's moving that infantry division north to occupy Fujairah and Khor Fakkan. Moving his tank division south puts three tank divisions all in close proximity, with two up and one back where he thinks the main attack from us will come. And I'll bet he isn't far off the mark. Our tanks aren't going to attack through those mountains, and he knows it. Somebody smart is starting to look at his battle plans and he's making adjustments."

"Paige, how long do you think it'll take him to complete the shift?" Daley asked.

"Well, he's doing it at night, and it looks like he's covering a hundred miles or more. So I figure his track vehicles travel somewhere around thirty-five miles per hour, so that would be what… a three, four-hour road trip. Moving two full divisions, it'll probably take him a week to complete the move and another week to get positions prepared for the tank division. The infantry division has the same hundred miles to cover, plus another thirty miles over to the coast. But he won't have to worry about preparing positions. That will likely have been done by the unit he's replacing. Most likely he'll just move into the city and the beach obstacles that were already installed when the 1st Republican Guard divisions were operating in that area. So probably two weeks for him to be ready. I'd say probably by 1 April, both would have been in position and completed their respective moves," Paige surmised.

Cliff and Bob considered what she'd just said. They knew she was probably right. Finally, Cliff broke the silence. "Okay, you two write up what we're seeing and our analysis that it appears the Iraqis are placing their forces in more advantageous defensive positions. I want you both to brief the Assistant SecDef this afternoon. I'll get it on his calendar."

Chapter 8
Commence MCM Operations

13 March 1991
USS *Tripoli*
Off Masirah Island

The ten minesweepers rode gently on the afternoon tide. It was so calm that the water looked like a mirror. All had dropped anchors in the forty-foot water earlier in the day. The skippers were directed to join the admiral on the USS *Tripoli* for a meeting of the minds. The two commands had been exercising for the past months in the vicinity of Masirah Island, working out interoperability issues. It had been no secret where they were going to clear mines. Right now, they were just waiting on the order to proceed.

The assembled skippers were in the wardroom of the *Tripoli* when the admiral walked in. The table was set for dinner, so they all assumed they'd be around for a meal on the helicopter assault carrier.

"Attention," the first officer seeing the admiral announced.

"At ease, gentlemen. As you can tell, you all are joining me for dinner tonight. I figured we can make this a working meal while we go over some things before this next operation kicks off." The admiral moved to the head of the table and motioned for everyone to take a seat. Once they were seated, he bowed his head and said grace. When he finished, the mess stewards entered and began serving. The conversations varied, but the three "taboo" subjects in the officers' mess were not discussed: sex, politics, or religion. Navy tradition considered these three subjects off-limits as they would offend someone and a lack of harmony aboard ship was not invited. As coffee was served and dishes cleared, the conversation died down and then ceased.

"Gentlemen, now that I've fed you the good food, it's time to serve you the bad news. As you all have heard, the *Midway* took four torpedoes. She's no longer in danger of sinking, but she's out of the war. They managed to limp her back to Salalah Port, where she'll be tied up until they can make the necessary repairs to get her seaworthy again. It was by the grace of God she didn't sink. One of her aviation fuel bladders erupted and nearly tore the guts of the ship apart. As it is, they suffered three hundred and ninety killed in action and another nine hundred plus injured. About a third of their aircraft were also damaged in the hangars from the fires. What's left of her airwing is now stuck, unable to rejoin the war as they can't take off from the ship when she's tied to the pier."

The officers at the table all grumbled a bit. Some cursed softly to themselves. Most of them knew a friend or two on the *Midway*—she had a crew of more than four thousand. Losing the carrier meant they were going to be down a major capital ship until another one could get on station to take her place.

The admiral continued, "Beyond the news about the *Midway*. We've determined there are mines present in the Strait on the north and south sides of the channel. This means the Iraqis have created a narrower channel for us to operate in than before the hostilities. In addition, it's estimated that between one and two thousand mines have been laid by the Iraqi Navy, stretching from Kuwait to Saudi Arabia and along the north shore of the UAE.[1] Our reconnaissance has assessed the mined area limits as well as the type and number of mines. That isn't to say we've accounted for all the mines, however. We're looking at a combination of both magnetic and acoustic influence mines. The magnetic moored mines are MYaM, Soviet M-08 and Iraqi LUGM-145 mines. The acoustic influence mines are Italian Manta, Soviet KMD, Soviet UDM and Iraqi Sigeel mines.

"Our mission is to clear fire support areas for the battleships, then clear the sea echelon area, and lastly, clear the channel itself. Initially, we need to take the intelligence we have on the existing minefield that the Iraqi Navy has put in along the south side of the channel and clear it to expand the channel so that more than one ship can safely negotiate the Strait. At this point we want to stay, if possible, out of waters considered by Iran to be theirs, although they consider the entire Strait their waters. If we stay to the south side, it's felt they won't challenge us, but if they do—well, we have a right to self-protection and I intend on us making short work of them.

---

[1] After the war, it was determined that Iraq had placed 1,270 mines along the Kuwaiti coastline. https://www.vernonlink.uk>the-gulf-wars

"The existing route through the Strait is Q-Route 1. This is the Q-route that we want to expand on the south side. The minefield is a defensive minefield with mostly moored mines at varying depths. There are some floaters in the area as well.

"The deadline for all ships to remain in port inside the Persian Gulf is in two days, and then we'll move into the Strait and begin clearing the minefields on the south side of the channel. You've all been provided the operational plan for what's going to happen and how. Do any of you have further questions about how we'll clear the south side of the channel?" the admiral asked.

Not seeing any, he continued, "The *Princeton* will be providing air-defense coverage for us, and if the Iraqis or Iranians try to get froggy, they'll handle them as well. Air cover will be on call if the need arises, but considering our air campaign will be underway, I don't think we'll have a problem unless it comes from Iran. You are free to engage any threatening moves towards your ships. However, let's try to get the frigates and naval air support to do any heavy lifting. They've got better firepower than our minesweepers do. Our tactics in clearing the southern side will be as we discussed. MH-53E helicopters from the *Tripoli* will proceed and sweep.

"Also, just so you're aware of what ships will run the gauntlet first, the *Avenger*-class minesweepers are going to lead the way in. They've got the AN/SQQ-32 MCM sonar, which is specially built for this kind of mission. They also have the remote-piloted AN/SLQ-48 mine vehicles that will look to neutralize the mines directly. Once we've sufficiently neutralized the mines, the fleet will proceed through the Strait to include the amphibious forces. Escorting the vulnerable troop ships will be the *Iowa* and *Missouri* battleships. Once the fleet is through, we'll proceed north to begin clearing fields that have been identified further north.

"We will not deploy any EOD divers initially. The water depth and currents are too great. If we get in close to the area where the amphibs will be landing and find mines and obstacles, then we'll put divers in the water. But not unless we absolutely need to," the admiral explained.

A hand then went up. "Excuse me, sir, but the departure time was TBA," said Lieutenant Commander Ford, skipper of the USS *Impervious*.

"We'll weigh anchor at 2300 tonight and proceed to the Strait in accordance with the order. Gentlemen, if there are no other questions, my launch is standing by to take you back to your ships. Oh, one last thing. Good hunting," the admiral said as he stood, indicating the meeting was over.

Chapter 9
Reliefs in Place

20 March 1991
XVIII Airborne Corps Sector
Medina Ridge

"Sergeant Murphy, I hear track vehicles," Private Mendoza said as he came running up to Murphy's foxhole. Mendoza was a new kid, having come in as a replacement for guys lost in the Battle for Medina Ridge. He was a tough little guy who was enduring the hardships of an infantry soldier like a champ, without complaining. Murphy was beginning to like the kid, as he was dependable and really seemed to like this infantry stuff. Mendoza had been back at the slit trench, depositing whatever it was he'd eaten the night before, which had been tearing up his insides all night. It was not advisable to leave your foxhole after dark, even to relieve one's gastrointestinal ailments. It was a good way to get shot by one of your own people.

"Calm down. It's behind us, which means it's probably that Saudi mechanized unit that's coming to replace us. They're taking over our positions while we get to go back to Jeddah for a rest. We've been out here for what now… six months? I could use a hot shower, a change of clothes and some good, fresh hot chow. Only thing missing would be a cold beer—better yet, a twelve-pack of ice-cold beer," Sergeant Murphy said wistfully.

"Besides, the pounding those Iraqis have been getting from the artillery and the air force has reduced their capability to do much against us. Near as I can tell, we're pretty much at a stalemate along this front. I heard that the 3rd Brigade got pulled out last night and is back in Jeddah already. They damn well better save some hot water for us," Murphy said, digging in his shirt pocket for a cigarette, a nasty habit he'd recently picked up.

"You know, Sarge, you shouldn't smoke. It's bad for your health," Mendoza commented as Murphy lit another cigarette up.

"Bad for my health! Mendoza, being out here for the past six months has been bad for my health. Eating this stuff someone calls *food* is bad for my health," Murphy countered, almost laughing. "How's your stomach this morning? I heard you last night."

"I think I'm doing much better now. I was able to pay the slit trench a long visit. I think I may have cleared myself out. We'll see," Mendoza replied as he pulled out a plug of chewing tobacco and bit off a wad.
****

"Lieutenant Ainsworth," Captain Bodine called out, approaching Ainsworth with another officer. "This is Captain Mohammed from the 1st Company, 1st Battalion, 45th Brigade. His company is taking over our positions. The official changeover is at 1300 hours today. At that time, you will withdraw your platoon to the company rally point. We will load trucks and pull back to Jeddah. Captain Mohammed is going to take you to one of his platoons, which you will then guide up to your positions. I want you to brief their platoon leader then as well. You have any questions?" Captain Bodine asked. The man looked exhausted, like he hadn't slept in a month.

"No, sir," Lieutenant Ainsworth said as he extended his hand to Captain Mohammed. Captain Mohammed hesitated; he wasn't used to this familiarity in the Saudi Army. Finally he grabbed the outstretched hand and shook it.

"Come, we go," Mohammed said as he walked towards a Toyota Land Cruiser.

Ainsworth fell in behind him with a glance over his shoulder to Captain Bodine. The look on his face said it all. "What the hell!" *Are these guys seriously riding around the front lines in a luxury Toyota Land Cruiser?*

Bodine just shrugged his shoulders and shook his head.

Arriving at an assembly area for the Saudi unit, Ainsworth saw that they were using M60A1 tanks and M113 armored personnel carriers. Armored was a misnomer as a 12.7mm round would pass right through the side and rattle around the interior of the M113, injuring or killing everyone in it. It would, however, offer some protection from small arms to those inside the vehicle. Judging by the looks of them, they'd equipped the tracks with an M2 Browning .50-caliber machine gun.

When the Toyota came to a stop, another Saudi officer ran up to open the door for Captain Mohammed. As Captain Mohammed got out, he motioned for Ainsworth to follow him. Captain Mohammed said something Ainsworth couldn't understand to the officer and then walked off, leaving the young Saudi officer standing there with him.

"Glad to meet you too, Captain," Ainsworth said under his breath.

"He does not speak English," the Saudi officer said. "I am Lieutenant Mohammed, platoon leader."

With a look of surprise, Ainsworth asked, "Is he your father or something?"

The lieutenant chuckled. "No, Mohammed is like Smith in your country. Very popular name in the Middle East."

"Well, I'm Ainsworth. Your English is pretty good, by the way."

"Thank you. I went to university in Virginia. Maybe you heard of it—VMI," Mohammed said with a bit of pride.

"Oh yeah, I've heard of it. I'm a Citadel graduate. Ever heard of it?" Ainsworth asked.

"Yes, we used to kick your ass in football," Mohammed said with a grin.

"You wish," Ainsworth retorted, and they both started to chuckle. After a moment, Ainsworth dug out his map and placed it on the hood of the Toyota. "Let me show you my sector that you'll be taking over."

Ainsworth proceeded to run his hands over the map to flatten it out better. Mohammed did the same with his own map. They discussed the mission, the enemy he'd be facing, the terrain, and time, with Ainsworth trying to give his Saudi counterpart as much detailed information as he could. He paused a few times to let his new friend ask a question or to pose one to him to make sure he was following along. It was a lot of information he was providing. He covered obstacles they'd emplaced as well as obstacles and defensive positions the Iraqi forces had built up.

Because Ainsworth was light infantry and Mohammed was mechanized, the terrain would be viewed differently when positioning the Saudi forces. Mohammed wanted his track vehicles where they could support the dismounted infantry. That made sense, but it was going to be very restrictive terrain. Ainsworth had taken advantage of that, but what worked as an advantage to his light infantry was actually a hindrance to Mohammed and their unit. It was clear the Saudis would have to choose his positions different from Ainsworth.

"We're running out of time, so why don't I just ride back with you and your platoon and I can walk the ground with you and get my people moving?" Ainsworth suggested.

"Sounds good," Mohammed said, raising his right arm and rotating it. Immediately, a group of five M113s started their engines and soldiers that had been outside started loading. "Come, that is my track," Mohammed said, pointing at an M113 with no one behind the .50-cal. Upon entering, Ainsworth found that the track had been modified slightly with a bench so two people could stand in the open hatch behind the .50-cal weapon. Putting on the TC helmet, Mohammed said something, and the vehicle lurched forward, almost tossing Ainsworth back into the cargo area.

Arriving to the rear of Ainsworth's platoon's position, the M113 tracks came to a halt behind a low rise so they weren't visible to the Iraqi OP/LPs. Initially, Ainsworth and Mohammed moved forward in a crouch walk to each position and Ainsworth allowed the soldiers to brief Mohammed on their fighting position. Each was dug down with a grenade sump and frontal cover. They were well camouflaged and had some form of overhead cover. The soldiers took great pleasure in explaining their sectors of fire and how they interlocked with the positions on the right and left. Range markers were pointed out for the fan of their coverage area, dead space in front of their positions, and final protective fire stakes. After Ainsworth and Mohammed visited each position, Ainsworth took Mohammed back to his foxhole and went over the wire comms and target reference points.

"You might want to take these predetermined artillery plots back to your commander and have them given to the artillery. Save you time trying to plot a target when things get hot and heavy," Ainsworth offered.

"Ah, yes, I'll do that. No point in reinventing the wheel, as you Americans like to say," Mohammed replied with a grin. "If you would, I would like one man from each of your positions to escort one of my men to their position and brief them on the position. I think that would be good?"

"Uh, yes, we can do that, but Mohammed, none of my men speak Arabic," Ainsworth explained.

"Okay, several of my men have a working knowledge of English, so they will go to the positions. American TV is popular here in Saudi

Arabia, at least some of it. Do you ever watch *Rawhide*? Very good cowboy show. Or *Bonanza*?" Mohammed asked. He already knew that these shows were no longer on American TV, but he couldn't resist jerking Ainsworth's chain.

Smiling, Ainsworth replied, "All the time." The two then laughed at the joke.
****

"Dean, your brigade is going to be relieved in the morning," General Peters said as he met Colonel Dean Anderson in front of his TOC. "The 28th Infantry Division is coming up and will arrive sometime tonight. They're a National Guard Division but have been in Jeddah for a month now, training pretty hard in desert operations. I must say, I'm pleased with what I've seen and the reports I'm getting."

"That's good to know. What's our next mission going to be?" Dean inquired.

He had been commander of the 2nd Brigade, 101st Airborne Division, for the past year. He wasn't one of those hard-chargin', full-of-himself type of colonels. Rather, he was one of those quiet, thinking types. Sometimes his staff wished he would demonstrate some bravado or at least bite the subordinate commanders in the ass now and then. He used his XO as the bulldog with the battalion commanders.

"I've been thinking about that. We're going to put you in an assembly area for now. Let you rest up a bit, get some good chow, some sleep and downtime. I want you guys to pull some maintenance and rearm. Then we're going to have you go out and do what you do best, air assault. We're going to put in a FARRP somewhere about eighty miles out towards Tabuk so the Apaches can get into the fight with the Iraqis as they try to withdraw to Tabuk. The 28th will be nipping at their heels and the Apaches will be biting them in the ass," General Peters explained.

Dean nodded at the information, then asked, "What have you heard about the air campaign? We see them flying every day, and from the looks of the contrails, exploding aircraft and parachutes, I'd say it's a wild dogfight up there. We've recovered four of our pilots and about a dozen Iraqi pilots."

"Yeah, it's been a real furball up there. From the reports I've seen, the air campaign is eating the Iraqis for lunch. The priority is to obtain air superiority first, bomb the crap out of the forces in the UAE and then go after the 1st Republican Guard Corps. To obtain the first objective, we have to take out as much of his air-defense assets as we can. That's the kind of hunting the Apaches and Cav have been doing and doing well. If we can thin out to the ADA systems, that gives more freedom for the fast movers to take out the armor and ground forces. If we can reduce the enemy's will to fight and end this war sooner, then I'm all for that. We've lost enough soldiers already. I don't even want to think about what it's going to be like once we look to push these guys back to their own borders."

****

"Colonel, you wanted to see me?" Lieutenant Colonel Gooderjohn asked as he entered Colonel Warren's office.

The 29th Division had been sitting on the outskirts of Yanbu, Saudi Arabia, for the past month, training in desert operations. They were tired of training and wanted to get on with the mission. Waiting was always the hardest part of war, especially as the time for the fighting drew nearer.

"Yeah, Gooderjohn," Warren said as he stood and walked over to the map hanging on the wall of his office. "Tomorrow, you're to move your battalion and head to the town of Al Ais. The 101st is operating a FARRP out of there, so the road is well marked. HETs will pick up your track vehicles at 0600 in the morning. I'm designating you to be the lead element for the brigade. Our brigade is also going to be the lead for the division. Somewhere around Murabba, you'll dismount your tracks and will be joined by the rest of the brigade. From there we're relieving the 1st Brigade of the 101st Airborne. We have a 'be prepared to attack north' order to seize an objective in the vicinity of Umm Shuyquq." Colonel Warren paused for a moment to point to a few areas on the map before continuing. "It's going to be a narrow avenue of advance. 101st attack helicopters will be out front, clearing a path for you as much as they can. Once we get out of this rough terrain, we get onto some open ground with the 28th on our right flank, and it's on to Tabuk."

Gooderjohn asked, "What kind of resistance are we looking at?"

"Good question. Intelligence says we're likely to be facing a division. The 2nd Iraqi Army Division, to be precise. Near as we can tell, they haven't been touched yet in the war, so we can expect a fight going into there. Any other questions?" Colonel Warren asked.

"Just one. When can I expect an operations order for this, sir?"

"The S-3 will publish an order tomorrow and we'll have an orders brief once we all close on Murabba. The 3rd Battalion, 327th Infantry, is securing that area now. They had a pretty good fight up there a couple of months ago, but it's been quiet for the past week," Warren stated. "If you have no other questions, I'll see you in Murabba," he concluded, a serious look on his face.

Chapter 10
Air Raid

1 April 1991
Prince Sultan Airfield
Riyadh, Saudi Arabia

Lying in bed, Major Ali Hassad had fallen into one of those dream states that felt as real as life itself. He was back home in Baghdad with his wife. They had only been married a year when the invasion had taken place, so this separation so early in their marriage was particularly tough on him. His wife was the most beautiful woman he had ever seen. As a young man, he had prided himself on his sexual conquests. But then he had met her, and she was something else. Her long dark hair and deep brown eyes could hold his stare. Only when she broke eye contact could his eyes drift down and draw in her firm breasts above her tight stomach. Naked, she had full control over him and he liked that. Her lips…

Ring, ring, ring…

The phone broke into his dream, much to his displeasure.

Groggily, he reached for the hand receiver. "Hassad here," he mumbled.

"Major, this is Sergeant Abu. You need to come to the center, please. It's urgent."

"Why, what is the matter? What time is it?" he asked as he swung his legs out of bed and ran his hand through his hair. Looking out the window, he could see it was still dark, so it was obviously early.

"Sir, it is 0300. But, sir, we have multiple American aircraft on our screen. I have never seen this many aircraft at one time. You must come," Sergeant Abu insisted. Major Hassad's eyes were fully open now. He stood, reaching over and turning the faucet on in the sink. He needed to splash some water on his face to wake himself up.

"Alright, I'm on my way in. Have you notified the air-defense batteries and the fighter command?" Hassad asked.

"We have, sir," Abu indicated.

"Alright, I will be right over," Hassad said and then placed the receiver in the cradle. *What the hell could this be?* he thought as he dressed quickly.

Since seizing the central air-defense center at Prince Sultan Airfield outside of Riyadh, the Iraqis had learned to operate the Saudi systems as well as their own. The two systems were not compatible for integration as the Saudi system was a Western system and the Iraqi system was Soviet. In addition, the Iraqi Air Force had destroyed most of the Saudi radar equipment during the initial seizure. They had managed to jury-rig the HAWK anti-aircraft missiles that they had captured well enough to fire them, but not very effectively. The Iraqi SA-6s with the corps were a dangerous weapon, and the SA-9s at the regiment level were also troublesome. The Soviets had also provided some new SA-300 anti-aircraft, known as the SA-10 Grumble by NATO forces. This was the most sophisticated anti-aircraft weapon in the AOR and was causing the Americans more than a little angst.

Arriving in Saudi, Hassad had been busy running the air-defense center at Prince Sultan. Thankfully the pace was nothing that would stress one out, but it was certainly busy. The general pattern of activity was that a flight of Iraqi aircraft would enter the AO and, as anticipated, American fighters would come up to meet them. Occasionally a flight of American aircraft would enter the AO on a bombing run; typically they'd be F-111s flying out of Egypt or B-52s out of Diego Garcia. What he enjoyed about this particular job was how much visibility he had when it came to pending attacks. The flights of B-52s were easy to spot, while the F-111s could be trickier depending on whether they tried to approach via nap of the earth or high-altitude like the big lumbering bombers. Knowing what was headed towards him also gave him a chance of organizing some sort of defense prior to their arrival. The job of manning this air-defense center had also become boring. Sure, when a raid by American aircraft was inbound, there were moments of excitement, scrambling MiG-25s. Soon, he'd be scrambling the vaunted MiG-31s if the Soviets actually let them.

In light of the massive aerial battles taking place across the desert skies, Major Hassad had heard several of his Soviet advisors talking about how a squadron of MiG-31 Foxhounds might join the MiG-25s already-flying intercept missions. Hassad knew the Soviets weren't helping his nation out of the goodness of their hearts. They were using this war as a means of testing their equipment against the American and European militaries.

58

****

Entering the command center, Major Hassad scanned the radar screens and could not comprehend what he was seeing. All five screens were almost a solid bright green for all the aircraft reflected on the screen. Each screen covered a different sector of the AO. One covered western Saudi Arabia, one southern Saudi Arabia and Oman as well as the UAE, one eastern Saudi and Qatar, one the Persian Gulf, and one Kuwait. Coverage of Iraq proper was located in Baghdad and partially Kuwait.

"Sir, we have alerted all the batteries," Sergeant Abu, the senior sergeant manning the night shift, reported. "Some have reported that their radars were destroyed as soon as they turned them on. Some are afraid to turn their radars on as the Americans are taking them out within minutes. Every command is reporting they are under attack. Right now it appears the enemy is concentrating their air raids against our forces in the UAE and in the west against the 2nd Republican Guard Corps and II Iraqi Corps." Sergeant Abu paused for a moment. "The Americans also appear to be going after our airfields at Tabuk, King Khalid Military City, King Fahd International Airport, and Al Jubail," Sergeant Abu explained, pointing at some of the screens depicting the attacks underway.

"Have there been any attacks against the 1st Republican Guard Corps?" Hassad asked.

"No, not yet. It appears they are concentrating their attacks on our airfields," Abu said, casting his eyes away from Hassad.

"What are you not saying?" Hassad asked, almost in a panic. "Have they hit our fields in Baghdad?"

"Yes, sir, they are hitting our airfields in Baghdad, Al Salman and Al Taqaddum," Abu responded, "as well as Balad and Tallil Air Base and the facility just north of there."

Hassad's face indicated he was almost in shock at how many airfields were under attack at the same time. *How many damn aircraft do the Americans have?* As he studied the screen, a picture began to develop—one that he didn't like at all.

"Abu, sound the air raid alarm. They are coming at us!" Hassad yelled. The sergeant sounded the base air raid warnings, alerting the defenders they had enemy aircraft inbound.

Watching the status board, Hassad noticed the radar vehicle for the battery of S-300s was up and running. They were launching their first volley of missiles at the inbound wave of bombers heading towards them. The four launchers were placed at different locations around the air base to minimize the likelihood of them being destroyed at the same time. Likewise, they had multiple radar vehicles scattered around the base and integrated the targeting trucks with multiple systems so that as one unit went down, it would still be able to provide targeting data to the missiles from another radar truck.

Thank Allah the missiles are getting off at the targets. Hopefully we'll at least down some of these bombers, he thought pensively. Deep down, he knew this kind of attack was going to hurt.

"Major, we can confirm a hit on two aircraft at this time. Six missiles are still tracking," a missile controller confirmed. Then his screen went blank.

"What has happened?" Hassad screamed.

"Sir, I think a Wild Weasel just took out the radar," the controller responded.

"That is passive electronic scanning array radar. They can't have locked on to that system," Hassad countered. "Can they…?" he asked with some concern.

Abu looked at the major. "Sir, it might have been one of the American Maverick missiles that took out the radar. They are TV-guided bombs—" He didn't finish his comment as a loud explosion overwhelmed the center, throwing everyone to the floor with a concussion wave that rained dust on everything. Several screens flickered as sparks cascaded out of one of the consoles.

Regaining his footing, Hassad called out, "Quick, get a fire extinguisher on that console. Is everyone alright?" No one had time to answer before the next explosion went off.

Luckily it wasn't as close as the first. Then several explosions rocked the base. Hassad was thankful that the center he was in was part of a hardened building. It was partially underground and covered with three feet of dirt on top and along the sides.

As the sound of the bombs died down, Hassad tried to regain control of the situation. "Sergeant Abu, do we have a status report from the fighter squadrons? How many got off before they were hit?"

"Sir, those reports have not come in as yet. As soon as I receive them, I will get them to you," the sergeant said, not really wanting to be the one to compile those reports and hand them to the major. The messengers of bad news tended to bear the brunt of their superior's anger.

Chapter 11
Air Surge

1 April 1991
Flying over Iraq
415th Tactical Fighter Squadron

Lieutenant Colonel David "Goldie" Goldfein checked his instruments one more time. Approaching Baghdad was both exciting and terrifying at the same time. So far, no one knew he was coming and he hoped it stayed that way. The city wasn't lighting up with anti-aircraft fire; neither was it exercising blackout procedures. He was detecting the occasional search radars, but it didn't appear they had turned on their ground radars to actively look for any possible air threats as of yet. Which meant they had no clue he was here, and that...was a damn good thing as far as he was concerned.

As the squadron commander for the 415th, he'd taken the most risky and dangerous mission his unit had been assigned. It wasn't that he didn't trust his other pilots—they were all extremely talented and very good. You had to be if you wanted to be a part of the stealth program. He just didn't want to ask his fliers to do a mission that he himself wouldn't do. Like his father before him, he learned from his dad that a good leader led from the front, and not from the rear. His father had served from 1949 until 1982, having retired an O-6 colonel. He'd flown combat missions in Korea and Vietnam.

Tonight's target was a tough one. His squadron would be carrying out attacks all across Baghdad. They were going after the command-and-control nodes, looking to eliminate the leadership's ability to communicate with their subordinate commands. His mission was to drop a two-thousand-pound laser-guided GBU-27 Paveway III right through the roof of a command-and-control bunker the Defense Intelligence Agency had identified. This particular building was supposed to be responsible for coordinating the air-defense response for the capital district. His second Paveway was earmarked for Al-Zaqura Palace, also in downtown Baghdad. This building housed the Council of Ministers. Attacking this building was meant to send a message to Saddam and his ministers that they, too, could be personally targeted and taken out.

As Goldie neared the target, he began to run through his checklist of procedures just like he had a million times before in training missions and the few combat sorties he'd flown over Panama. With the aircraft once again placed on autopilot, the computer flew the plane while he fought it by playing bombardier.

Activating the thermal-imaging infrared system, he typed in the exact coordinates of the building he was supposed to hit. Looking at the image, he visually confirmed the building. Next, he prepared to release his first bomb. He armed it and then opened the bomb door along the belly of the aircraft. He then turned on the laser designator and fixed it to the targeted building. Once he released the Paveway, the bomb would essentially ride the beam all the way until it impacted.

With the target acquired and locked, Goldie released the first Paveway. The aircraft lifted noticeably at the release of the two-thousand-pound bomb. At thirty-two thousand feet, the bomb had a few minutes of drop time before it'd hit. Right now, his only responsibility was to make sure the laser designator stayed pointed at the right building.

As the bomb neared the target, the entire environment around Baghdad suddenly changed. Where just a few seconds ago it had been a scene of tranquil peace and calm, now it was an eruption of anti-aircraft gunfire and the more dangerous high-hitting anti-aircraft artillery fire. The display of explosions from 130mm KS-30s all the way down to the Type 59 57mm cannons at altitudes all around his F-117 Nighthawk, caused his blood pressure to spike and his body to flood itself with adrenaline.

This is what it must have felt for the guys flying bombing missions over Germany, he thought pensively. It was downright terrifying what was happening below and all around his stealth fighter.

The building he had been watching on his little monitor suddenly exploded as the Paveway flew right down the center of it. With the first target neutralized, he typed in the coordinates for his second target. This one was also located in downtown Baghdad—the famous Al Zaqura Palace, whose exterior was reminiscent of an ancient ziggurat, the birthplace of Abraham. The Iraqis used this building as their cabinet building, so it housed the most influential and important people in the Baath Party. Sending a two-thousand-pound bomb through the center of this building was meant to send a message to the regime: that they could be next.

With the laser designator locked on the top of the building, Goldie released his second and final Paveway laser-guided bomb. The aircraft again felt noticeably lighter with the final bomb released. Now he had to hang tight and wait for the bomb to fall some thirty-one thousand feet before he could turn away and fly back over the western desert of Iraq, eventually linking up with a KC-135 Stratotanker to take on some fuel before heading back to the undisclosed Egyptian air base the F-117 Nighthawks were flying out of.

When his bomb finally hit, it dove through the first level or two of the building before exploding deep within the guts of the building, blowing out multiple stories' worth of windows. While all he could see was a black-and-white image, he was sure it made for a spectacular show down on the ground. Who knew—maybe he'd see it aired on CNN if he was lucky.

That's it. I'm out of here. Time to scoot while the scootin's good, he thought. Now he had a five-hour flight home. Plenty of time to think over what he was going to write in his after-action review. He hoped the rest of his guys fared just as well as he had. Seeing the amount of enemy ground fire being thrown at them, it wasn't out of the realm of possibility that one of his aircraft could somehow catch that golden BB—the one bullet that happens to hit something important and knocks your plane out of the sky. It happened from time to time.

I have a feeling we're going to be making trips like this a nightly thing, Goldie thought as he turned his aircraft westward, away from Baghdad.

****

511th Tactical Fighter Squadron
Near Kalba, United Arab Emirates

Around 0100 hours, a wave of twenty Tomahawk cruise missiles swept in from the sea, smashing multiple surface-to-air missile sites and critical air-defense positions. Immediately following the cruise missile barrage, Navy A-6 Intruders flying Wild Weasel missions looked to silence any remaining air-defense vehicles around the city of Fujairah.

Flying high above the flights of Wild Weasels, pairs of F-14 Tomcats prowled the skies, looking for MiGs to mix it up with.

This was the part of the mission Major Shawn Dunn was most nervous about. While the Navy made a show of going all out in their attack on the Iraqi 10th Armour Division, the A-10 Thunderbolts of the 511th Tactical Fighter Squadron would slip across the Omani-UAE border until they came across Route Blue, which connected the coastal city of Fujairah and ran all the way to Abu Dhabi. Their job was to travel along the road looking for targets of opportunity to attack.

Fortunately for Major Dunn, there wasn't a single cloud in sight, and the full moon tonight provided more than enough light for him to see columns of vehicles moving along the highway. Why columns of tanks and other armored vehicles were pulling back from the coastal city of Fujairah to Abu Dhabi was unknown to him. But right now, it created the opportunity of a lifetime for the flight of four A-10s.

Having approached the highway from an altitude of fourteen thousand feet, they hadn't been spotted yet by the enemy vehicles or any mobile air-defense vehicles traveling with them. It was highly likely the mobile AA vehicles were traveling with their radars off to avoid attracting attention from the nearby Wild Weasel prowling over Fujairah.

Major Dunn let his flight mates know he was going to swoop in first, instructing each of them to follow each other down the highway, one after the other, the four of them would tear this column apart. He'd start the attack by engaging the enemy armor with his four Maverick missiles. Once he'd expended those, he'd swoop down and deploy his cluster munitions across the column along the highway before breaking away to circle back around and reenter the stack of aircraft, then wait for his turn to make a gun run.

If things went according to plan, Dunn's flight of four A-10s might be able to reduce the enemy column of vehicles to nothing but burning wreckage by the time the sun came up.

Sighting in on the first T-72 tank, Dunn placed the Mavericks' targeting reticle on the rear of the tank, right between the chassis and the turret. He depressed the firing stud and sent the first missile on its way. He activated the next missile and repeated the process three more times, sending four of the Republican Guard tanks to a fiery end. He then dove like a Stuka dive bomber, dropping below eight thousand feet, then five thousand feet, then two thousand feet before he leveled his aircraft out at barely a thousand feet above the enemy column. At this point, ground fire was streaking up at him. Several gunners started firing their turret-mounted 12.7mm, DShK machine guns, intermixed with soldiers firing their AK-47s and AK-74s at him.

Major Dunn heard and felt a couple of metallic clinks, letting him know his aircraft was taking ground fire. He depressed the firing stud, releasing the first pair of CBU cluster munitions across the enemy vehicles. He then switched over to the second set of CBUs and released them as well. Pulling up, he saw a string of green tracer fire flash right past his canopy. Multiple strings of ground fire reached out for him, but fortunately they missed.

As he angled his aircraft away, he saw fires raging across at least half a mile of vehicles. Tiny explosions were initially followed by larger secondary explosions as fuel and ammunition vehicles exploded. He signaled to the next aircraft in the stack that it was time for them to commence their attack run and join the fray.

Major Dunn climbed back up to fourteen thousand feet, just high enough to stay out of range of the ground fire. He maneuvered his plane to get in line at the top of the stack while his three captains dove on the enemy and took them out. At this point, the other three aircraft were firing their Mavericks almost at will. The enemy vehicles were doing their best to get off the main roads where they could, but ultimately, they were trapped. Aside from a few spurs and spots along the side of the road, there was nowhere to hide. They were sitting ducks as they crossed the mountains, trapped on a single highway, a highway that was quickly turning into a graveyard, a highway of death.

When the other A-10s of Major Dunn's flight had fired their Mavericks and raked the column with their cluster munitions, Dunn ordered the flight to regroup behind the column. They now lined up to make a gun run utilizing the 30mm antitank gun the aircraft was famous for. One by one, they'd swoop down from the sky, spray a handful of rounds across half a dozen vehicles and then pull up and turn around to rinse and repeat. For the better part of thirty minutes, the four A-10s completely obliterated two entire battalions of Republican Guard tanks and armored vehicles. By the time their attack runs were complete, an eleven-kilometer stretch of the highway was nothing more than a cauldron of twisted, burning metal and blackened bodies.

For thirty minutes, Major Dunn and his flight of four A-10s had become death, the destroyer of men. Seeing their work was complete, they turned for home in Oman to refuel, rearm, and head back across the border for seconds.
****

Iraqi 3rd Squadron
Al-Kharj, Saudi Arabia

Major Vitaly Popkov had barely gotten airborne when the first barrage of cruise missiles cratered the runways of the Prince Sultan Air Base in Al-Kharj. He'd been a little late getting into his aircraft and it had almost cost him. His focus had been on getting his other pilots airborne and making sure they all got off before he did. His squadron had a couple of new replacement pilots from home, and they weren't as used to these kinds of combat operations—operations where you sometimes only got a few minutes' notice to get airborne and into a dogfight with the Americans.

As soon as Popkov got airborne, the ground station radar units started piping what they were seeing into his aircraft. They were guiding his flight of four MiG-29s towards what appeared to be a group of French Mirage 2000 aircraft. They looked to be flying fighter cover for a group of Omani Jaguars, likely flying a Wild Weasel mission to take out the S-300 batteries protecting the airfield.

Popkov saw the S-300 had already fired a dozen missiles at the Mirage and Jaguars. The fighters were breaking formation as they looked to evade the incoming threats. It was during this evasion that Popkov saw their opportunity to wreak havoc on their formations. He ordered two of his fighters to go after the Jaguars while he and his wingman focused on the Mirages.

Fortunately it was nighttime. The glow of the Mirages' afterburners lit their positions up nicely. Popkov angled his fighter towards the one he saw. He activated his R-73 Archer missile and waited until he had a tonal lock on it. Once the warble let him know the seeker head had firmly acquired the aircraft, he momentarily closed his eyes to avoid the bright ignition of the missile as he depressed the firing stud. The missile leapt from his aircraft and sped away. In seconds it was on the Mirage's tail. The French fighter barely had time to make a couple of maneuvers before the missile slammed into the rear of the aircraft, exploding. The pilot never made it out.

While Popkov had been battling his own Mirage, his wingman had lined up to go after a second Mirage. They saw two bright explosions not too far from their position. The S-300 had connected with two of the Mirages attempting to fly an escort mission for the Jaguars. One of the Wild Weasel Jaguars exploded from another missile, then two more went down from Popkov's pilots.

Another Mirage exploded when Popkov's wingman's R-73 connected with its prey. At this point, the remaining two Mirages and three Jaguars broke contact and headed back towards Jeddah, where they had come from. The French had lost four Mirages and five Jaguars in the attack against the Prince Sultan Air Base. As the Soviet mercenary pilots were celebrating their aerial victories, the ground station's radar they'd been leveraging went offline. Then the air base's primary search radar went offline.

Turning his aircraft slightly, Popkov got a good view of the air base. What he saw caused his heart to skip a beat, then sink in despair. Bright flashes of explosions and towering flames, some reaching hundreds of meters into the sky, greeted them. The airport was being pummeled by something even they couldn't stop. Cruise missiles. They'd fought valiantly and turned back an enemy air attack only to be outdone by wave after wave of cruise missiles.

The audio warning in his headset caused him to check his fuel gauge. He saw he had close to half a tank. A quick chat with the other aircraft revealed the same fuel status on their tanks. Under normal circumstances, they'd stay aloft over the area and look for more aircraft to engage, but seeing that their home had been thoroughly destroyed, they now had to start thinking about where to land. Turning to head north, Popkov told his pilots they would head for King Khalid Military City Airport and look to land there. Then they'd see what their next mission would be.

****

802nd Bombardment Squadron
Al Hofuf, Saudi Arabia

To say Captain Ian Maser was nervous about this mission would be an understatement. In his six years with the Air Force, the entirety of which he'd spent in SAC, or Strategic Air Command, he'd trained on the B-52G bomber to penetrate Soviet airspace and deliver nuclear weapons through one of the toughest-defended airspaces in the world. None of that compared to the pucker factor he was feeling right now as their squadron prepared to deliver the largest display of aerial might since the Arc Light bombing missions of the Vietnam War.

Just outside the Saudi city of Al Hofuf, the famed 1st Republican Guard Corps of the Iraqi Army had dug in. The same corps that had led the rampaging charge across Kuwait and then Saudi Arabia. During the last number of months, the Corps had built a massive integrated defensive line designed to prevent the coalition forces from dislodging them and forcing them out of Saudi Arabia. It had also created the perfect opportunity for the US Air Force to leverage its awesome bombing power to demonstrate why such defensive positions were utterly useless in an age when airpower alone could pulverize such a position.

Flying ahead of their bombers were a force of Wild Weasels, electronic warfare aircraft, and F-15 Eagles and a wave of Tomahawk cruise missiles. Still, despite that awesome display of aerial might flying ahead of them, the biggest threat they had to deal with came in the form of the venerable S-300 SAMs, and the two squadrons of MiG-25 Foxbats the Iraqis and their Soviet advisors had been flying. The MiGs had already shot down several B-52s in the prior months, along with a couple of E-3 Sentry AWACS planes. It was the job of their F-15C escorts to keep the Foxbats off their backs should they show up.

"Geez, would you look at that?" commented their electronic warfare officer.

"Whatcha seeing down there?" asked Lieutenant Haines, the copilot.

"The Iraqis have a ton of search radars going looking for targets, but as soon as they come on, they're getting nailed by the Wild Weasel flights."

"Hey, I count that as a good thing. Those S-300s are no joke," Captain Maser exclaimed. The more of those radars and batteries that went down, the better. In Vietnam, a lot of the B-52s that had been shot down were from SA-2 batteries over North Vietnam.

They flew on for another half hour in relative peace. The battles raging below them were largely keeping them safe. The few S-300 batteries that hadn't been destroyed by the initial cruise missile barrage were being wiped out by the relentless Wild Weasel missions. The initial onslaught of cruise missiles targeting the Iraqi air bases had succeeded in blunting their ability to get fighters airborne—none of the Foxbat squadrons were airborne before they were destroyed on the ground. The few MiG-29 squadrons that had gotten airborne were mostly over central Saudi Arabia, not close enough to intervene along the coastal areas where the B-52s were about to strike.

As the 802nd Bombardment Squadron arrived over the 1st Republican Guard Corps, the sixteen B-52s opened their bomb bays, releasing their payload of seventy thousand pounds of dumb bombs in a carpet-bombing mission reminiscent of World War II and Vietnam. Beneath them, more than twenty-four hundred five-hundred-pound bombs decimated the Iraqi positions in one of the most awesome shows of airpower in history.
****

Sitting in the open turret of his T-62 tank, Sergeant Aziz sat staring up at the night sky. The clear desert night was a curtain of a million tiny lights as the Milky Way was clearly visible. It was nights like this when Aziz thought of home and wished he was back there with his wife and young son. *The universe is so large, with so many planets that we cannot see. Truly Allah would have put intelligent creatures on those other planets as well. We cannot be the only ones out here in the universe*, he thought. As he stared up, he noticed that an occasional star he was watching would blank out for just a second or so. *Strange*, he thought.

Then he heard the sound of a screaming siren. The first bomb impacted about four hundred yards from him and blew him off the top of the tank. The second bomb landed at about 350 feet—the sound was deafening. Another explosion erupted closer, knocking him back to the ground just as he had tried to get up. Then he heard another noise, only this one sounded like it was being aimed right for him. He looked up. He couldn't see anything directly, but he knew in that instant that a bomb was going to land very close to him. He said a silent prayer for his family and closed his eyes. He heard an explosion and felt a wave of heat wash over his body, and then he felt nothing—nothing at all.

Chapter 12
LRRP Team Go In

1 April 1991
Long-Range Recon Patrol
Tabuk, Saudi Arabia

"Six minutes!" the jumpmaster yelled.

Lieutenant Skroggans was serving as jumpmaster for the night drop fifteen klicks from Tabuk. His ten-man team was part of the Long-Range Reconnaissance Platoon for the 101st Airborne Division. Their mission was to drop and then move to observe the airfield and barracks area at Tabuk. Specifically, ARCENT wanted to know the status of the airport after the intense air strikes that had paid it a visit over the last few days. They also wanted to know what the 2nd Iraqi Division was up to. They'd occupied the area for the past few months and had likely dug in, planning on defending it from an American attack.

The pitch on the engines of the C-130 Hercules changed ever so slightly as the pilot slowed the aircraft down. This was necessary when dropping paratroopers.

"Stand up," Skroggans yelled out to his men.

The ten soldiers, their faces painted in dark camouflage, struggled briefly to get to their feet. The pilots flying the aircraft were making a few last-minute turns and adjustments as they approached the drop zone. The soldier knew that just before the green light came on, indicating it was time to jump, the aircraft would make a final gut-wrenching climb to six hundred feet for the drop. With the unknown air-defense situation, the pilots didn't want to go any higher for fear of getting locked up by an enemy SAM.

Skroggans shouted, "Hook up," and used the hand signals he'd been taught. Each man connected his static line to the static line cable. Next, they inserted the safety pin. The last thing a jumper would want was for the static line not to be connected to the aircraft, especially jumping this low. A jumper wouldn't have time to realize that had happened before his body hit the ground. Jumping this low to the ground, a reserve chute was pointless and seldom worn.

"Check equipment," was the next command.

Each jumper checked the equipment on the back of the jumper ahead of him. He was looking to see that the static line was connected properly and that the static line wasn't wrapped around another piece of equipment, such as a canteen. If this was the case, then they would have a hung jumper and there would be very little they could do for the individual as he couldn't be dragged back into the plane. The jumpmaster would have to cut the static line and hope the jumper pulled his reserve, if he was jumping with one, which they weren't.

"Sound off with equipment check."

"One okay," the last jumper in the stick yelled and smacked the right rear thigh of the jumper in front of him.

"Two okay."

The count continued to the first jumper in the stick, who yelled, "All okay."

With that announcement, Lieutenant Skroggans stepped up to the open door of the C-130 and checked to see that there was no sharp exposed metal that could cut the static line. He also observed the pitch-black hole they were jumping into as cloud cover had moved in off the Red Sea and blanketed the full moon that eastern Saudi and Iraq were enjoying.

The loadmaster tapped Skroggans on the shoulder. "One minute," he said, which meant "hang on because we're about to make the power climb." Suddenly, the nose of the aircraft pitched upward. It took all the strength the jumpers could muster in their legs to keep from being forced to the floor of the plane. Once the aircraft reached six hundred feet, the pilot leveled them out and turned on the green light. He wanted them out ASAP so he could dip back below the enemy radars' effective limits.

"Go, go, go," Lieutenant Skroggans shouted as he motioned for them to jump.

The first jumper disappeared, and in less than ten seconds, all the jumpers were out of the plane. The pilots immediately dove for the ground and made a steep turn to the west and the safety of the Red Sea.

With the noise of the plane gone, the descent was rather pleasant until you hit the ground. The paratroopers were well trained in night drops, and everyone bounced up and began gathering their parachutes and equipment. They all knew to converge on the center of the stick, and with their night vision goggles, they could see the IR chemlite that Lieutenant Skroggans had activated.

"Sergeant Mallory, get a head count and let's get these chutes buried," Lieutenant Skroggans ordered. Sergeant First Class Mallory was an E-7 with many years in the Ranger battalions. He'd volunteered to join the 101st because its home base of Fort Campbell was close to Nashville, where his son could get medical treatment for a condition he'd had since birth. Since he'd joined the LRRPs, the level of proficiency had increased significantly across the board. All the members of the team were Ranger-qualified.

"Roger, sir," Mallory responded in a whisper and proceeded to get a head count and direct a place to bury the parachutes. While he took care of that, Skroggans verified their location with his GPS and studied the map for the route they'd previously chosen to move towards Tabuk. Skroggans determined that, to travel the fifteen kilometers with the one-hundred-twenty-pound packs and the desert terrain, it would be best to stop and hunker down for the day and make the distance over two nights.

"Alright, everyone, listen up," Skroggans directed as they finished burying the parachutes. In almost a whisper, he continued, "As we discussed, we'll move out on a heading of zero-three-zero degrees for five and a half kilometers. That'll put us in some rough terrain, but we need to avoid a couple of farm compounds in the area. We'll hunker down for the day there. Any questions?" There were none, and the squad moved out in a wedge formation. The night was relatively cool at seventy-five degrees, so the movement went slow and steady.

Reaching the higher, more rugged terrain, Sergeant Mallory had the squad members take up one-man positions in a circle around his and Skroggans' position. Daylight wouldn't be for another couple of hours, so members had time to dig down as best they could and camouflage their positions. A guard mount was rotated with one member always awake as others slept throughout the day. Fortunately, the squad was not discovered.

"What time is it, sir?" Mallory asked as he started to move from sleep.

"Time to push out to some hide positions for tomorrow," Skroggans said, handing Mallory a cup of coffee. Heat tabs allowed for water and food to be heated up without smoke to give away one's position. Of course, if a heat tab wasn't available, a piece of C-4 set on fire worked well too, but you didn't want to stomp that fire out. That was a good way to blow your foot off. "Who's first team tonight?"

"Sir, that's Sergeant Mays and Specialist Smith. I'll get them moving and over for their brief," Mallory said, standing and moving off to round up the two soldiers. Moments later, Mallory returned with both soldiers in tow. As they took a knee in front of Skroggans, he began to give them their orders.

"Okay, here's what you got. I want you to move six klicks to this stand of brush outside the military compound. Find a good hide position that'll allow you to observe the activities inside the compound. Plan on not coming back here for two days, so pack accordingly. You shouldn't be taking a lot of stuff. Travel light. Check in when you get there and give me your exact location. Only call when you have something significant and when you start back here. Any questions?" Skroggans asked.

"No, sir. We're good," Sergeant Mays said, looking at Specialist Smith, who just nodded.

"In that case, see me before you move out," Skroggans said, turning to Sergeant Mallory. "You want to take the next location and I'll relieve you in two days?"

"Sounds good. I'll get Sergeant Peppers and collect our gear," Mallory said, getting up.

A half hour later, he was back with Peppers and their equipment. They were traveling the longest distance, twelve klicks, and were lightly equipped with their load-bearing equipment, extra water, their weapons and ghillie suits. They had made the ghillie suits themselves and adapted them for the desert environment. The base was a jacket made out of what appeared to be a fishnet and matching pants. To this they tied on bits of burlap cloth with a mixture of tan, brown and green colors. They also had canvas "boonie bonnets" with a desert pattern and with similar camouflage. A soldier wearing the complete ensemble could be lying within a few feet of someone and not be detected.

"Sergeant Mays headed out on a heading of zero-one-zero before he shifted to a heading of zero-eight-zero," Skroggans said as Sergeant Mallory took a knee next to him and pulled out his map.

"Okay, I'm going to take a heading of zero-four-five and then swing north," Mallory said, tracing his finger along his map. "There's this drainage ditch here that goes right up to the perimeter of the airport and has brush in the bottom. We'll take a position there. I'll let you know when we get there and when we see something of interest." He stood up and put his map back in the cargo pocket on his pants.

"Be safe," Skroggans said. "No unnecessary chances." Skroggans had a lot of respect and admiration for the old sergeant, all of thirty-two years old. Sergeant First Class Mallory had joined the Army when he was seventeen, fresh out of high school. In five more years, he would be eligible for retirement. Skroggans doubted that he would ever retire, though. He loved this kind of stuff too much to leave it.
****

It had been a fairly easy trek across the desert that evening. The ground was compacted sand and limestone, so the walking was easy, especially with the cooler night air and the light loads that everyone carried. Everyone managed to avoid the civilian homes and compounds, so no dogs were barking at them. Sergeant Mallory and Sergeant Peppers slipped into the drainage ditch, which was dry and covered in brush, and made their way north, stopping at the fence that encircled the airport. In their ghillie suits, they appeared to be just another bush. They were positioned halfway down the east-west runway, having a clear view of the runway as well as the parking ramp and hangars across the runway. Mallory was sure that when the sun came up, he could write down the tail numbers on the aircraft as they took off. They could also clearly see any aircraft taking off or landing on the north-south runway.

"Peppers, let's get comfortable and get a couple of hours sleep in before the sun comes up. Then we can start watching. I'll take the first watch and wake you in two hours," Mallory instructed.

"Sounds good, good night," Peppers said, and within five minutes he was gently snoring.

She was standing on the beach, alone, with a towel wrapped around her. In the breeze, her red hair was gently blowing across her face. She was smiling a mischievous smile. Slowly, she brushed her hair away from her face with her left hand while her right hand held the towel together in the front. As the towel was also caught in the gentle breeze, she began to release the hold and as she did, so the towel began to reveal…

A hand over Peppers's mouth brought him fully alert and awake. Mallory was looking at him with one finger to his lips. Peppers understood immediately. Some uninvited guests were approaching.

Fifty yards to the east, on the outside of the fence, two Iraqi soldiers were strolling along with lit cigarettes. They were supposed to be on guard and checking the fence line for any indication that someone had entered the airfield. Given their level of discipline, it looked more like a stroll in the park, especially at five thirty in the morning.

Mallory just wanted them to keep walking their patrol. He and Peppers were here to observe, not kill the enemy. Both Americans remained perfectly still, with only their eyes moving as the two Iraqi soldiers approached. One was carrying a flashlight but was interested in the fence and not the drainage ditch outside the fence. As the two Iraqis walked nearby, Mallory and Peppers reduced their breathing so as not to make any noise. Mallory even managed to slow his heart rate. Then the two Iraqi soldiers began shouting. *If this is any indication of the level of discipline in these guys...* Mallory didn't speak Arabic, but from the body language, he could tell that one of them had said something the other didn't like. The argument became more heated when the shoving started.

The Iraqis were only about ten yards from the drainage ditch when the first blow was thrown. *Amateurs*, Peppers thought as he watched the two combatants smacking at each other. Mallory slowly reached his ankle and withdrew his Ka-Bar knife. Peppers imitated his movement as well. Without speaking, they were both thinking the same thing. If either Iraqi fell in the ditch, they might have to take them out. It would be a snap decision. As the two scuffled, they came closer to the ditch. One was now on top of the other and smacking the crap out of the guy, but with an open hand, Mallory noticed. *So he's not really trying to hurt the guy...* When the two started laughing and got up, Mallory was sure they were undisciplined fools. A sigh of relief went out when the two Iraqi soldiers walked off with their arms around each other's waist.

"Lovers' quarrel?" Peppers asked in a whisper.

"Could be. Glad we didn't have to intervene in that spat," Mallory replied.

77

"Well, they ruined a perfect dream I was having. I was even getting a hard-on," Peppers lamented.

"You'll get it back another night. My turn to catch an hour of sleep. Hell, maybe I'll pick up where your dream left off," Mallory said with a smile. "Night, wake me in an hour."

****

Sergeant Mays and Specialist Smith had an easy movement to their area. As they approached a hill mass that was covered in palm trees and brush, they heard a vehicle approaching but didn't see anything. Their maps hadn't indicated anything except some areas of vegetation that they were going to pass through on the way to their hide position. When the vehicle noise grew louder, they crouched lower until they were flat on the ground. Mays knew that unless the lights of the vehicle were directly on them, they would not be noticed. Looking up, he saw the glow of lights but not the actual headlights themselves. Something was blocking the headlights, and that something was between him and the vehicle. Then the lights went out.

"Let's move up and see what we have here," Mays whispered to Smith, who nodded and rose up. Together they moved forward in a low crouch and soon realized that a berm had been built—in recent days, from the looks for the soil. Reaching the bottom of the berm, Mays motioned for Smith to stay back as he crawled up the berm, which was about ten feet high. As he approached the top, he noticed a tent stake with a line attached and stretched to the other side of the berm. Reaching the top, he first found the edge of a camouflage net that was across the top of the berm. *What do we have here?*

Flipping his night vision goggles down, he soon found out as he wasn't fifty yards from an SA-6 launcher, all under a camouflage net. From the air, this must have looked like just another grove of trees. He eased back down to Smith.

"We have a target and will bypass this for now. Let's go," he said as he resumed his original course but bypassed the location of the SA-6.

Another two klicks and they reached their destination. The hill gave them a clear view of the military complex as well as providing ideal concealment. Smith quickly set up the radio with a directional antenna towards Lieutenant Skroggans's position.

"Dog Breath One, Dog Breath Three, over," May transmitted.

"Dog Breath Three, go," came the response.

"Dog Breath One, sitrep."

"Dog Breath Three, copy."

"Roger, Sierra Alpha Six, at Whiskey Bravo 82456137. How copy?"

"Dog Breath Three, I copy Sierra Alpha Six at Whiskey Bravo 82456137, over."

"Dog Breath One, you have good copy. Nothing further. Out."

Mays and Smith had no doubt that things would be lively in the morning. Then they settled in for a bit of sleep.

Chapter 13
Follow the Dust

3 April 1991
IX Corps HQ
Abu Dhabi, United Arab Emirates

Lieutenant General Juwad Assad Rasol Shitnah, Commander of the IX Corps, wasn't sleeping well with the constant American bombing. Nothing was impacting in the cities of Dubai and Abu Dhabi or Al Ain, but his troops and units were under constant attack outside of the towns and the continuous roar and thundering explosions pummeling the city was relentless. Somehow the Americans were finding his forces despite their best efforts at staying camouflaged. He had ordered that no equipment or vehicles be exposed, and all would be under desert-camouflaged covers. Yet somehow the Americans were still finding them and hitting them hard. To address the problem, he called in the division commander's staff, to include the air-defense commander as well as special staff.

"Gentlemen, why are we taking such losses from the American aircraft? Is all our equipment not under camouflage nets? General Nassar al-Hiti, when you took a helicopter up and examined the 10th Division, was not all your equipment under camouflage?"

"Sir, it was. We have completed the move south, replacing the 45th Division, and I could not spot one piece of equipment. It appeared that my division had left the theater of operations. I flew over every unit and saw nothing. I even landed in a few places to make sure they were still there. And they were. How we are being found, I do not know," General al-Hiti answered. The other commanding generals nodded as well.

"Colonel Abbu, have we not restricted all communications to landlines? Could the Americans be plotting our positions with radio intercepts?" General Shitnah asked of the signals intelligence officer for the Corps.

"Sir, we are wired into every location. We have laid out over two thousand miles of telephone wire. The airwaves are silent. There is no way they could be plotting our positions by signal intercepts," Colonel Abbu answered.

"Well, gentlemen, we have two problems and we best come up with some solutions quickly. First, our air-defense systems are not keeping the Americans off our backs, and second, we are not concealing our positions well enough to keep them from bombing us," General Shitnah said, stating the obvious. Looking over at the air liaison officer, he asked, "Colonel Saud Bahaa al-Deen, why do we not have sufficient air cover to clear the Americans from the sky?"

Al-Deen had known the question was coming, but still he let out a deep sigh. "The problem, General, is that the Americans have five aircraft carriers, with eighty-five aircraft on each ship, along with heavy bombers based in Diego Garcia and England and air force fighter/bombers operating out of Oman and Egypt—all this is overwhelming our capability. They are launching about two thousand sorties each day. We have just not been able to compete with those numbers. We started this engagement with about three hundred and fifty fighter aircraft, and we have taken losses. We have inflicted losses as well, but not in a sufficient number. We are getting the priority of coverage, but we are not able to reach the aircraft carriers, nor are we allowed to engage airfields in Oman or Egypt," al-Deen said.

"But I thought you placed an air strike in Muscat not long ago," General Shitnah stated.

"We did, but only against the port area. We have been ordered not to strike airfields, and even then, we lost several aircraft to the American air-defense systems. It is believed that there are too many air-defense systems around the airfields that the Americans are using. They maintain a constant air cap over their airfields, twenty-four hours a day," al-Deen said.

"What about our air-defense systems? Why are they not more effective against their aircraft?" General Shitnah asked, addressing Colonel Ismael Saeed Fares, the corps air-defense officer.

"Sir, anytime we turn on the radars to track a target, there is a high probability that a Wild Weasel missile will take out the radar. The radar site we had in the Gulf was destroyed by a Navy commando team, and that has created a huge gap in our coverage. They have been very effective in locating our air-defense systems and destroying them first. When we do launch a missile, their countermeasures have been somewhat effective in defeating the missile track. When a flight of naval aircraft strike, they include at least one aircraft dedicated to electronic countermeasures to jam our systems. When they have air superiority in an area, their Warthog aircraft loiter at altitude like a hawk and then swoop down and drop their bombs on a perfectly camouflaged position."

"Well, obviously, the positions are not perfectly camouflaged. They are destroying our forces faster than we can replace them. At this rate, they can stroll through our positions. We have got to stop this," General Shitnah said with an elevated voice. He reached over and picked up a glass of water that had been poured for him earlier. He sat for a moment, taking deep breaths. He knew what would be waiting for him if he were called back to Baghdad having failed to fix the situation.

****

"They are like the Arabian paper wasp, always present and always willing to sting," Captain Ghazali mumbled as he sat in the open hatch on his T-72 tank. He was under a camouflage cover, waiting for night to fall so he, along with the rest of the 37th Division, could move back towards Tabuk. It had become too dangerous to move in daylight with the American planes controlling the skies. More fearsome yet were the American attack helicopters. The first indication would be a vehicle exploding, and you would never see the helicopter—or if you did, it was beyond the range of your weapons. The air-defense weapons had pushed out further than they normally would, which meant that they no longer had overlapping coverage.

"Did you say something, Captain?" Sergeant Hafeez asked, sitting on the forward slope of the tank. It was too hot to sit inside the tank, so the crew lay around on the ground, napping or heating water for tea. The rest of Captain Ghazali's company was doing the same and was positioned around his vehicle. His was not a company with the newest T-72s, they were still operating the older T-62 models. They had been in a tank park, unable to move because of a lack of fuel, when the American B-52s had arrived and destroyed them. Fifty brand-new tanks all destroyed in a single strike. Who had been so stupid as to park them all together thinking the Americans would not find them? But he kept those thoughts to himself.

"Captain," Sergeant Hafeez called out, "there are two of those American Warthogs above us. They are just circling." He and the rest of the crew stood up, ready to run away from the tank if the planes made a hostile move.

"Everyone, just relax. They are maybe three or four thousand meters high and cannot see us. We are well camouflaged. They may be like the wasps, but they do not have eagle eyes," Captain Ghazali said in a calming voice. Everyone resumed what they had been doing, but with an occasional look skyward at the circling jets. Ghazali pulled out a small notebook and a pen. He had been maintaining a journal of sorts about his experiences since they'd crossed the border many months ago. The 37th Division had been full of excitement and confidence then, but now things were different. The 7th Division had been chewed up attempting to attack the Americans, and the 51st Division, rumor had it, was down to only one brigade as they had been hit so hard in their attempt to move through the mountains. Rumor also had it that the 14th had been destroyed in the mountain passes and had limped back to Tabuk. Only the 2nd, which had stayed in Tabuk, was unscathed. As he was writing, he heard a vehicle approaching and looked up. It was a Toyota pickup truck the battalion operations officer had liberated from a Saudi farmer. The dust trail following the vehicle indicated there had not been much rain in the past days, only the dew at night.

"Captain Ghazali, we have been attempting to get you on the radio. Why are you not monitoring the radio?" Major Jameel asked in a perturbed manner.

"Sir, if I keep the radios on, I am going to run the batteries down. Then I must start the vehicle and waste fuel while I charge the batteries. I thought fuel was critical and should not be wasted, or that is what we were told at the last meeting. You told us at the meeting this morning what time to be prepared to move out, and I will start my vehicle fifteen minutes before then. Unless, of course, you want me to run my engine now and then I can call and ask for a fuel truck before we roll out tonight," Captain Ghazali said, looking down on the major from the top of his tank. He really did not care for Major Jameel, who did not strike him as being very competent; many suspected Jameel had attained his rank because he was active in the Baath Party in his hometown of Mosul.

"Is there something you wanted to tell me, sir, since you came out here?" Captain Ghazali asked.

"No, we just wanted to know why we had no communications with any of you company commanders," Major Jameel said as he turned and walked back to his liberated Toyota pickup truck. *So none of the other commanders are on the radios either. Jameel should know better,* Ghazali thought as the major drove off in the direction of another company commander.

****

Seven thousand feet above the desert floor and Captain Ghazali, two A-10 Warthogs from the 511th Tactical Fighter Squadron lazily circled. They were originally out of RAF Alconbury, England, and had been one of the first A-10 squadrons sent to defend Saudi Arabia and the XVIII Airborne Corps. Flying out of Egypt, they had a relatively easy flight across the Red Sea to the area of operations.

"Buzzard Three-Four, Buzzard Three-Six," Captain Jim Cloore called his wingman, Captain Bob Dowling.

"Go ahead, Three-Six," Dowling responded.

"Three-Four, do you see that dust cloud down there at three o'clock? Over."

After a short pause, Dowling said, "Three-Six, I see it. Can't make out what's causing it, but someone is driving somewhere in a hurry. Let's just watch to see where he goes and stops."

"Sounds good. May just be a goat herder out for a Sunday drive, but who knows?" Cloore said as he continued his lazy orbit. As he watched, the vehicle stopped and the dust cloud began to dissipate.

"Three-Four, I'm going to drop down for a better look-see," Cloore said as he throttled back a bit and dropped his nose.

"Roger, I'll keep a watch for you," Dowling said, meaning he would be watching for an indication of a missile launch. He knew that he would be dropping to five thousand feet, which would give him a margin of safety from any SA-9 missiles that were down there and be out of range for the ZSU-23-4. They weren't too concerned with SA-300s firing on them as those missiles had been saved for the B-52s that were pounding the sand out of large groups of armored vehicles when they could be found massing. Dowling continued to watch as Cloore leveled off and continued his slow, lazy orbit. As he did so, he noticed the dust cloud commence again.

"Buzzard Three-Four, I have a white pickup truck starting back up and moving. I've plotted where he was and am going to wait to see where he goes now," Cloore transmitted. Dowling continued to observe.

"Buzzard Three-Four, the pickup has stopped again. I can see a guy walking… oh shit, he just disappeared," Cloore said with some surprise.

"Buzzard Three-Six, what do you mean he disappeared? Over," Dowling asked.

"Three-Six, he was walking and just disappeared into the desert. Come on down and take a look."

"Three-Four, I'm on my way." Dowling executed a wingover and dropped two thousand feet in an instant, coming up alongside Cloore's aircraft. He could see the white pickup but no one around it at first.

"Three-Six, there he is again. He just appeared and is getting into the truck."

"Three-Four, I'll bet money wherever he stops there are vehicles under desert-camouflage covers. Let's take a closer look. I'll lead on this pass and you lead on the previous location."

"Roger, Three-Six, I'm right behind you."

And with that, Dowling entered a steep turning dive with Cloore right behind him.

****

Thanks to Allah that Major Jameel is gone, Captain Ghazali thought as he continued to write in his notebook. *The quicker the colonel gets rid of him, the safer we all will be.*

"Captain, would you like a cup of tea? We just made it, so it is fresh," Sergeant Hafeez said, holding the cup up to the captain.

"Thank you, that would be—" Captain Ghazali's train of thought was interrupted by a loud ripping noise not far away. He turned towards the sound, which was now overshadowed by the explosions from his sister company's location. As he looked up, his eyes widened as he saw a gray aircraft with a shark's mouth turning left and right in an erratic fashion as if it was out of control. Then he realized it wasn't out of control but had turned directly towards his location. He never heard the ripping sound this time before he was floating in the air from the explosion of his tank.

Chapter 14
Concrete Bombs

3 April 1991
1st Republican Guard Corps
Al Hofuf, Saudi Arabia

It didn't take long before General al-Dulaymi realized that the Americans were exercising great restraint and not bombing any civilian populations. He knew that the Americans wanted to be perceived as liberators, and bombing the civilian population would not foster that image.

After some discussion with the division commanders, al-Dulaymi said, "Gentlemen, we are in reserve at this time with the IX Corps being the front line of defense. They are taking a beating by the American air campaign, and we are beginning to see it here as well. The Americans do not want civilian casualties or collateral damage, so they are reluctant to bomb in the cities. Therefore, we need to take advantage of this and move our tanks and vehicles into the cities. Once the ground campaign starts, we will have time to assemble our forces for a counterattack on the Americans."

"Sir, placing our vehicles in the cities will make them vulnerable to saboteurs where out in the desert they are relatively protected under their camouflage netting," General Jawad Rumi Dairi, commander of the 6th Nebuchadnezzar Division, said.

"General, if you feel that leaving your forces in the desert is better, then continue to do so. If you wish to move some into the safety of the cities, I am telling you to do that. As for saboteurs, the crews on those vehicles had best protect them."
****

Moving his BTR-60 into Al Hofuf was a pleasant exercise to Lieutenant al-Bakir's way of thinking as his platoon of six vehicles followed him. He had been told to take his platoon and park them at King Faisal University between the buildings. A company of tanks would also be there, so he was not to park next to them but close by. He was instructed not to just park in one of the large parking lots but between the buildings, where they would be difficult to see and impossible to bomb without considerable collateral damage. He was also told to take advantage of the dormitories for bathing and sleeping as the school had been closed since last August.

Once he entered the university grounds, he began positioning his individual vehicles, making sure they were between buildings and using the back alleys as best he could. He noticed that some of the tankers had also exercised the same technique. *Great minds think alike*, he thought as he motioned for his platoon to move into one of the dormitory buildings. They were all looking forward to sleeping in beds and taking hot showers.

That evening, after showers and a meal, the platoon had gathered in a dayroom with a television. Some soldiers were seated in the comfortable cushioned chairs. Others were reading magazines that had been left when the school had closed, and others were watching a television show called *Mr. Ed*.

"Lieutenant al-Bakir, did you know this horse can speak Arabic?" one of his enlightened soldiers told him.

"Yes, Private, they have some very intelligent horse in America," al-Bakir answered, shaking his head. *The stupidity of some of these goat herders. Next they will tell me that Mickey Mouse can speak Arabic too*, al-Bakir thought when a loud crashing sound shook the building.

"What is the name of Allah was that?" someone shouted as everyone moved to the windows. Dust swirled up from the street, obscuring their view at first, and al-Bakir remembered that a tank had been parked next to the dormitory building, although he couldn't see it.

"Everyone stay here. I will go see what happened. Some fool probably had an accident and drove his tank into the building," al-Bakir said as he headed to the door.

Leaving the building by the front door, he had to walk around the corner to the alley between the buildings. A crowd had gathered, and at first he couldn't see what had happened, still thinking a tank had rammed the building. What he saw shocked and amazed him.

The tank sat where it had been, but the turret was shoved down into what was left of the hull. The engine was shoved out the back and the road wheels were lying in the alley, detached from the hull, which was sitting on the ground, no longer on suspended tracks. A small fire was burning from fuel and the electrical system. On top of the turret appeared to be the fins of an American bomb. *Could this have been a bomb that did not explode?* he wondered. *But what is all this concrete on top of the tank?* He looked up at the side of the building and saw that it was undamaged. Slowly he came to the realization that this bomb was not supposed to explode as it was all concrete. It was supposed to smash its target without collateral damage. As he stood gaping at the carnage in front of him, another loud crashing noise could be heard. *The Americans are bombing us with laser guided concrete bombs...unbelievable,* he thought at people began to scatter as they all started to realize what this new American weapon was.

Chapter 15
Decision Time

15 April 1991
CENTCOM Forward HQ
Muscat, Oman

The air campaign had been progressing for the past two weeks. Air superiority was being seen over most of the forces, with only occasional hit-and-run attacks by Iraqi aircraft, and most were quickly disposed of by American or British fighters. General Schwarzkopf had some decisions to make based on the information he was about to receive. In the conference room sat the primary CENTCOM staff along with the ARCENT, AFCENT, NAVCENT, and MARCENT commanders and all the division and corps commanders. Everyone knew that this was a decision brief and would date-stamp the future. When Schwarzkopf walked in, everyone immediately stood.

"Keep your seats, gentlemen," Schwarzkopf said as he walked to his chair. "Let's get started, General Schless."

"Good morning, sir. This is a decision brief and at the conclusion we will ask for a start date for the ground operations," Schless said. Schwarzkopf already knew this, but it was said mainly for the benefit of anyone present who might not have understood the purpose of this meeting.

"Sir, this brief will be presented with the G-2 giving an intelligence update, followed by myself with a status of forces. General Horner will discuss the status of Air Force assets; Admiral Munz will discuss naval forces; General Yeosock will cover ground forces; and General Boomer the status of Marine forces. And lastly, the G-4 will discuss the status of logistics for the upcoming operation. The G-2, sir," Schless concluded.

Brigadier General O'Donnell took the stage and called for his first slide. It listed all the Iraqi divisions and their known locations. "Sir, as you are aware, the 10th Armoured Division and the 49th Infantry Division exchanged positions, with the 49th moving one brigade minus into Fujairah and one battalion from that brigade up to Khor Fakkan port. The other two brigades remain in positions between Al Madam and Maleha. A flight of A-10s did manage to catch part of this troop movement and summarily massacred close to an entire battalion's worth of troops and vehicles transiting through the mountains."

He paused for a second before continuing, "Moving south, the 1st Infantry Division continues to reinforce his positions in Al Ain. The 17th Armoured Division is in positions with Al Ain on the north flank and Al Wagan on the right flank. That's a thirty-five-kilometer front over fair terrain. The 10th Armoured Division has moved in with Al Wagan on its left flank and stretches south for thirty kilometers. The terrain here is sand dunes running east to west, offering some concealment for an attacker and difficult for a defender to laterally shift forces. The 45th Division is south of the 10th Armoured and is occupying positions on the northern fringe of the Empty Quarter. IX Corps reserve is the 52nd Armoured Division, located in the vicinity of Zayed City, and it appears he feels that our main effort will come this way. Any questions, sir?" General O'Donnell asked.

"What are we looking at in the west?" Schwarzkopf asked.

"Sir, in the west, the 2nd Republican Guard Corps has not moved from previous positions east of Medina Ridge. The bombing campaign and their bouts with the 82nd Airborne as well as Saudi partisan actions in Medina have cut the 2nd Republican Guard Corps down to thirty-five percent strength. ELANT sources indicate that he's desperate for supplies. The II Iraqi Corps is moving back towards Tabuk with the 7th Division down to forty percent strength, the 51st Division down to thirty percent strength and the 37th Division at sixty percent strength. The 14th Division is still attempting to recover south of Tabuk and is at fifty percent strength. The 2nd Division never left Tabuk and is estimated to be at eighty percent strength. As with the 2nd Republican Guard Corps, the II Iraqi Corps is hurting for resupply. Questions, sir?" O'Donnell asked.

"What are the other corps doing at this time?" Schwarzkopf asked.

"Sir, the IV Iraq Corps has not moved from the last positions he assumed around Riyadh, and indications are he's sucking off more of the supplies bound for the 2nd Republican Guard Corps than he's letting through. The VII Iraqi Corps, with its eight divisions, is scattered across the northern part of Saudi from the east coast, with a division in Dammam, a division in Al Jubail, another around the King Fahd International Airport, and one in the vicinity of Khafji. It appears these divisions are poised to repel an amphibious landing. The other four divisions he keeps to the west behind the IV Corps and rotates them with the divisions in the east on a three-month basis. His III Corps he retains in Kuwait and mostly in Iraq, watching his border with Turkey and Iran," O'Donnell stated. General Schwarzkopf nodded in approval.

"Sir, we haven't seen any movement from his chemical weapon stockpiles except for the one attack on the 82nd on Medina Ridge. We think there may have been an overeager commander on the scene that launched that attack as we've received reports that he was taken back to Baghdad shortly after that and executed. He continues to move his Scuds around, and we have teams looking for them and hitting them with air strikes whenever we find them. Three were located in the past week in the western desert, which surprised us as we didn't expect to find any there. They were destroyed in air strikes."

That got Schwarzkopf's attention. He turned to his aide. "After this meeting, get Colin on the phone, and I don't care if we wake him up." Turning back to O'Donnell, he said, "Please continue."

"Iraqi air strikes against our ground forces have dropped significantly, with only two air strikes reported in the XVIII Airborne Corps sector, and resulted in two Iraqi aircraft destroyed and minor damage to our elements.

"On the naval front, Iraqi surface vessels have remained in the Persian Gulf and have moved to guard the entrance of the Strait. We believe that once mine-clearing operations commence, they will attempt to disrupt that operation. They've ceased running supply ships to the UAE in support of IX Corps as we've sunk several that attempted to make the run. Those subs they ran out of Bandar Abbas really caught us by surprise. The USS *San Jose* managed to put one of them on the bottom, but it appears they were lost during the engagement. One of those enemy subs, we think it was the Kilo-class, managed to put four torpedoes into the *Midway*. As you know, we sustained nearly a thousand KIAs in that naval engagement and more than a thousand WIAs. The *Midway* is currently tied up at Salalah Port in southern Oman," O'Donnell explained.

Schwarzkopf turned to Admiral Munz. "That was a raw deal with the *Midway*, but at least she didn't go down. Do we have a way to find that Kilo-class and get a replacement for the *San Jose* and *Midway*?"

"Sir we believe we sank the Kilo by a surface attack. A replacement sub is enroute to replace the *San Jose.*

"Yes, sir, the *Carl Vinson* is taking the *Midway*'s place. Their strike group has a sub traveling with them, so their sub will take the *San Jose*'s place," the admiral replied. Schwarzkopf nodded in agreement.

"Sir, that concludes my portion of the briefing. If there are no questions, I will be followed by—" O'Donnell didn't finish.

"Let's move this along," Schwarzkopf interrupted. "Joe," he said, turning to General Yeosock, "are your boys ready to go?"

"Say the word and give me two days to move everyone into their attack positions and we'll be ready," Yeosock responded.

"Boomer, you ready?" Schwarzkopf asked, turning in his seat.

"1st Marine is in position, and we're ready to move the 2nd through the Strait and into position. Give me five days and we'll be offshore, ready to go in," General Boomer said.

"Gentlemen, then it's decided. G-Day is April twentieth. Plan accordingly."

Chapter 16
Keep Israel Out

15 April 1991
Pentagon
Washington, D.C.

"General Powell, General Schwarzkopf is on the phone for you," the aide said, turning on the nightlight.

"What time is it?" a half-awake Colin Powell asked.

"Sir, it's two fifteen a.m."

"Christ, what does he want now?" Powell mumbled as he reached for the phone. "Norman, what's up?" he asked, clearing his throat.

"Colin, have you seen these reports of Scud missile launchers being spotted in the western Iraqi desert?" Schwarzkopf asked.

"Ah... yeah, I got a brief on that yesterday. Why are you asking?"

"Don't you find it curious that they're in the western desert and not in southern Iraq, Kuwait or Saudi? The max range is eight hundred kilometers, and all have been located within five hundred kilometers of Tel Aviv. Colin, if he starts hitting Israel and they retaliate, this whole thing could fall apart. We have got to keep the Israelis on the sidelines. We cannot allow them to retaliate or the Omanis, Egyptians and the rest of the Arab world are going to turn on us," Schwarzkopf said.

"Well, we were sort of speculating on that fact, but we don't think Saddam would do that," Powell said, sitting up in his bed.

"And just who is we?" Schwarzkopf asked in a testy voice.
****

Paige Harrison was at her computer, observing the nightly downloads. They were boring as it was just the open western desert of Iraqi. The satellite had passed over Sinjar and a couple of airfields that she was interested in looking at. The airfields showed the damage that had been inflicted in recent bombing raids. Craters marred the runways. Some of the hardened aircraft hangars were caved in. It was determined that it was much easier to knock an enemy plane out of the sky, but cratering the runway that it had to use to take off or land worked as well. What she was seeing showed her that someone was attempting to repair the runways. *Hmm, time to call up another raid on this place*, she thought when something unexpected drifted into her screen. *What the...?* She sat up straight and leaned into her screen, freezing the picture.

"Bob, come over and look at this," she commanded.

Bob Daley needed to stretch his legs, and this was a good opportunity to do so. Standing, he picked up his coffee and wandered over to her desk. He was always eager to talk to an attractive woman, and Paige was certainly that.

"Whatcha got?" he asked as he leaned over to look at her screen, passing his eyes across her partially open blouse.

"What does this look like to you?" she asked, pointing at an object on her screen. It took a minute for Bob's mind to reorient to the satellite picture.

"Holy crap, that looks like a Scud launcher. What's it doing clear out here? It's well out of range to strike our forces. Even the XVIII Airborne Corps is out of range. Do you think he's trying to hide them?" Bob asked.

"I don't know, but let me think about this and give you my thoughts after lunch," she said.

****

That afternoon, Cliff came over to Paige's desk. "You got something to show me, young lady?"

"Oh, do I ever. This morning I found a Scud launcher in the western desert of Iraq. I had Bob look at it and he confirmed it. The rest of the day, I've been scrubbing through old pictures and comparing them to the new stuff that's coming in. I've found three more launchers out in the western desert that weren't there two weeks ago. We have four Scud launchers not in range of any of our forces, but well within range of Tel Aviv. I think he's going to hit Tel Aviv in hopes of dragging Israel into the fight and turning the Arabs against us," Paige explained, leaning back in her chair.

Cliff stood there for a minute, staring at her. "Write it up and brief the entire team in an hour. If everyone buys into it, let's get it upstairs to the boss."

****

"Come in and have a seat," the President said as Dick Cheney, General Powell, Jim Baker and John Sununu walked in. At 1800 hours, the workday was officially over, but not the unofficial workday. As they did so, the side door opened and the mess steward came in with a tray containing five highball glasses, a bucket of ice with tongs and a bottle of Pappy Van Winkle bourbon. The seal was broken but it appeared full. At $1,800 for a fifteen-year aged bottle (if you could find one), it was considered a bargain.

"Help yourselves, guys," the President directed as he took his chair.

"May I, Mister President?" Cheney said, gesturing that he wanted to pour for the President.

"Is a pig's ass pork? By all means and thank you." On that note, the others all picked up a glass and prepared their drinks before taking a seat on the two couches. Once settled, Cheney started the conversation.

"Mr. President, our satellite coverage has found several Scud launchers in western Iraq. The launchers weren't there last week. They're positioned outside the range of our forces, so they're not being positioned to strike our forces, but they are within range of Tel Aviv. The intel weenies think that Saddam may be getting ready to launch an attack—chemical, possibly—against Israel in hopes that they would retaliate and thus turn the Arab nations against us," Cheney said.

"Jim, what does State think about this?" the President asked before taking a sip of his fine bourbon.

"Bill Brown, our ambassador, has spoken with Prime Minister Shamir about this. Their position is that, if attacked, they will retaliate. Can't say I blame them, but we need to keep them out of the fight," Baker said.

The President thought for a minute, then looked at Baker. "Have you spoken with Ambassador Shoval?"

"I have, and he expresses the same opinion that Brown related to me."

"Okay, what do they want to stay out of this fight? They always want something, so what is it? Dealing with these guys is always something," the President asked with some frustration.

"If I may, Mr. President," Colin interrupted, "I've spoken to the Defense Minister, Moshe Arens. I think I know what would keep them out of the fight—Patriots. They want Patriot missile batteries positioned in Israel to protect them. If the batteries can intercept the Scuds, then they feel that they won't be under pressure from the populace to enter into the fight."

Silence followed as the others contemplated this latest announcement. Finally, Cheney broke the silence. "It would be a small cost to us and save us in so many ways if we could make it happen. How many batteries are we talking about?" he asked, looking over at Powell.

"I'm thinking four batteries, but I'll bet they ask for eight. One battery around each of their major cities and ports," Powell answered.

"Hell, eight would cover their two cities and their one port and the rest could cover the damn goat herds. That's too many," Sununu chimed in.

"Well, they start with eight and we negotiate down to four. Truth be told, they're holding all the cards at this point," Cheney interjected.

"Tell you what… let's offer to send four batteries over with US personnel manning the batteries. When the war is over, we can offer to sell them the four batteries. Jim, see if they'll buy into that for now. Explain that what batteries we have in production need to go into covering our forces at this point," the President directed.

"Yes, Mr. President," Baker said.

"Good. What's next for discussion?"

Chapter 17
Last-Minute Changes

15 April 1991
82nd Airborne HQ
Jeddah, Saudi Arabia

General Ford came through the door like a bear looking for a lost cub. Everyone knew to stay out of his way when he got like this. He was known to shoot the messenger at times like this, and he was heading to the Operations section.

"Where's Colonel Dobbins?" Ford yelled out as he entered the Operations area.

"Sir, he's in the latrine," a specialist clerk answered, fearful for his life. Without responding, Ford headed for the latrine.

Opening the door, Ford said, "Jesus Christ, who died in here? Dobbins, did that stench exit your ass? What the hell have you been eating?" He held the latrine door open and fanned the air.

"Sir, you wanted to see me?" came from behind a toilet door.

"Not in here I don't. Finish up and come to my office... and get this place aired out before someone dies in here. This is a damn biohazard area now," Ford said, slamming the door shut.

I don't notice any odor. Must be his mood he was smelling, Dobbins thought as he finished his dump and cleaned up.

Exiting the latrine, he went by Operations. "Anyone know what the old man is steamed about?" Dobbins asked as he picked up a pad of paper. He got no response, so he headed over to Ford's office.

"Okay, sir, what's the problem?" Dobbins asked, walking into Ford's office and bracing himself to hear about whatever he'd done wrong.

"Sit down," Ford said, pointing at a chair. "You've done nothing wrong except to stink up the latrine, so get that sheepish look off your face." As Dobbins took the chair, Ford continued.

"Our Trojan horse is now a Trojan pony. Seems the Navy couldn't find a big enough ship to move a brigade, so they got us one that can only hold a battalion. Instead of two brigades forward, we'll have only a reinforced brigade on Objective Wet," Ford fumed.

"So we transport the two brigades up to Wet by trucks and buses. Not a problem, sir," Dobbins commented, jotting down a note.

"No, we don't. I was told by Luck to keep one brigade here in Jeddah for security. A brigade minus will truck up to Wet. The other brigade will remain here as palace guards. Son of a bitch, palace guards on this damn airfield," Ford said, slamming his hand on his desk.

Oh shit, he's pissed, Dobbins thought.

"Sir, which battalion do you want to send up on the ship? We were going to send 2nd Brigade up—it should be one of their battalions. 1st Brigade is scheduled to make the drop," Dobbins offered.

"Yeah. Alright, send one battalion from 2nd Brigade on the ship, Have the rest of 2nd Brigade truck up the coast and we'll hold 3rd Brigade back here. Jim Irons is really going to be pissed about being the palace guard. Charlie!" Ford yelled out to get his aide's attention.

Charlie stuck his head in the doorway, attempting to avoid a flying coffee cup or a possible pistol shot. "Yes, sir."

"Charlie, call over to 3rd Brigade and ask Colonel Irons to come over and see me, now...and don't tell him I'm in a foul mood. Otherwise he'll take his own sweet time getting here," Ford growled.

"Yes, sir," Charlie responded. Charlie was a prior service captain who had attended OCS after two years in the enlisted ranks as an infantry soldier. Ford had noticed him in Panama and awarded him a Silver Star for his actions. Upon returning to Fort Bragg, Ford needed to replace his aide, who was leaving to another assignment, and decided to pull Charlie up to be his new aide. Another factor was the fact that Charlie wasn't married, which meant that Ford could work him all hours and not feel guilty about it. Ten minutes later, the knock on the door told Ford that Jim Irons hadn't taken his sweet time.

"You wanted to see me, sir?" Colonel Irons said, coming through the door. He noticed Dobbins's facial expression and suddenly realized he should have taken his sweet time.

"Yeah, Jim, sit down," Ford commanded as he also took a seat behind his desk. Dobbins's facial expression didn't change, Colonel Irons noticed.

"Jim, I'll get right to the point. We've been directed to leave a brigade here in Jeddah. You're it. You will assume duties to guard the

98

airfield and the port. I don't like it and I know you don't either, but that's it. Any questions?" Ford asked.

"Not much I can say about this, is there, sir? I guess I'll be rewarded someday for this noble task. Is there anything else, sir?" Irons asked.

"No, that's about it. We'll get you involved in this move. Just be patient," Ford commented as Irons saluted and departed the office.

"Charlie, get Colonel Allen up here," Ford called out. A few minutes later, Allen walked into Ford's office.

"Colonel, change in the plan. Only one battalion will be boarding the ship and sailing north," Ford said, getting straight to the point.

"Excuse me, sir. I thought the whole brigade was going by ship," Allen said, looking at Dobbins. Dobbins shook his head slightly in the negative.

"Well, Colonel, Luck and ARCENT see it differently. They couldn't get a big enough ship to haul you up there, so only one battalion is going and will be attached to 1st Brigade when they get there," Ford said.

"Sir, what's the rest of my brigade going to do, then?" Allen asked, not liking this situation already.

"Your brigade minus trucks up the coast to join the 1st Brigade and your battalion," Ford said, not looking Allen in the eye. Allen began to protest.

"Colonel, I talked to Luck until I was blue in the face. He even let me argue it with Yeosock, but I got nowhere. One battalion goes by ship and the rest truck assault—unless of course you want to stay here and replace the 3rd Brigade as palace guard. Now, which battalion are you sending?" Ford asked. Allen knew at this point he was not going to win.

"Sir, it'll be 3rd of the 325th. Is there anything else, sir?" Allen asked, hoping the other shoe wouldn't fall.

"No, that's it, and I am sorry, Colonel. It would have been an interesting exercise," Ford responded.

"Yes, sir, it would have been. If you have nothing else for me, sir, I need to go tell the boys the wonderful news. I'm sure they'll take it well," Allen said, standing, his comment dripping with sarcasm.

"Alright, Colonel, you have a better day," Ford offered as Allen saluted and walked out.

Chapter 18
First Naval Surface Engagement

17 April 1991
USS *Avenger*
Strait of Hormuz

The sun had set two hours before and there was no moon. As the minesweepers approached the south side of the Strait of Hormuz, everyone was on a high alert for not only mines but also Iranian gunboats and Iraqi vessels as well. The USS *Princeton* was behind the first of the minesweepers, with the flagship USS *Tarawa* to the south. The plan called for entering the Strait at first light and commencing operations to clear mines along the south side of the identified channel through the minefields. *Princeton* would provide support in the event of an attack by Iraqi naval forces. The Navy had provided a fighter cap over the Strait as well. Unbeknownst to US MCM Group, the USS *Florida* was still operating in the Gulf as well.

"Mr. Johnson," Captain Keys said, getting the officer of the watch's attention.

"Sir."

"I'm going to get some sleep before we get into the Strait. Wake me by 0430," Captain Keys instructed. Keys knew once they reached the Strait, sleep would be a luxury for him. Skippers didn't sleep moving through a minefield.

"Aye-aye, sir."
****

The ringing klaxon was so loud and sudden that it might wake the dead. Ramd Gha'ib Hassan had been asleep aboard the ship after a night of food and drink in Dubai, where he had transferred his flag to one of the Grisha-class corvettes. The past six months had been relatively quiet for the Iraqi Navy, who had been escorting supply ships to the UAE and watching the Strait. He'd suspected that an American submarine had been operating in the Gulf, but they hadn't detected it. As he started to roll out of his sea berth, there was a knock on the door.

"Come in," he said.

"Admiral, the American Navy is moving into the Strait," Colonel Muzahim Mustafa said with an anxious look.

"How many and what type?" the admiral asked, grabbing his pants.

"They were picked up on radar and it appears to be nine or ten vessels," Colonel Mustafa reported. "More could be following."

"What is their speed?" the admiral asked, continuing to get dressed.

"They appear to be moving very slowly along the southern minefield."

"They are minesweepers. They are attempting to clear the strait. A much larger force will follow soon. We must hit them in as they attempt to clear the minefield. What have the Iranians done? Do we have any word from them as to their intentions?"

"Sir, we have not had any contact with them. Their ships are all in Bandar Abbas. On radar, we watched some start moving into the port as the Americans approached."

"The Iranians are like dogs. They are tucking their tails and will not challenge the American fleet. I knew this would happen. What is the disposition of our other vessels right now?" Admiral Hassan asked.

"Currently, two Osa-class patrol boats are patrolling off the coast of Bahrain. The other two Grisha corvettes are tied up alongside us. One *Lupo*-class frigate is returning to the naval yard in Al Jubail. Two *Lupo*-class frigates are off Ras Tanura. One *Lupo* is en route from Al Jubail to here. The Lürssen FPB-57 and the four Lürssen TNC-45s are around the western approach to the Strait. The two Badr corvettes, 611 and 612, are in port at Abu Dhabi. The three Al Sadiq patrol boats are at Ras Al-Khaimah up north."

"Notify the Al Sadiq patrol boats to get to sea immediately and screen this American force. I want to know type and number. They are not to engage. Our attack must be coordinated and violent, but we must strike before they can clear the minefield. Notify the Osa patrol boats off Bahrain to get back here and take a position behind Sirri Island and wait for orders. Notify Colonel al-Hiti, commander of the Lürssen ships, to wait until we join up with him off Sirri Island. Notify the 611 and 612 to get underway and join us as we head for Sirri Island. We will consolidate the fleet there and attack the Americans in the minefield once we are joined. Now go and get that message out. All vessels to converge on Sirri Island."

****

The USS *Princeton* was following the shipping channel through the minefield that had been plotted by the USS *Florida* months earlier and updated several times since. On the port side were nine minesweepers along the south side of the Strait, beginning to sweep for and detonate mines. As the sun rose, explosions could be heard as the mines were destroyed or influenced to detonate. Two MH-53E helicopters from the USS *Tarawa* were also forward of the *Princeton*, towing a mine sled to cut floating mines and detonate influence mines. On the starboard side and a couple of miles away was the HMCS *Athabaskan*, a Canadian destroyer shadowing the *Princeton*. The minesweepers had been at general quarters since midnight.

"Captain, CIC."

Captain Hontz, commander of the *Princeton*, was sitting in his chair on the bridge when the call came over the loudspeaker. "CIC, go ahead."

"Captain, we're beginning to track surveillance radar on the Slick-32, range forty miles. Search radar has three small vessels moving at thirty knots coming out of Ras Al-Khaimah," the CIC announced.

"Roger, I'll be right there," Captain Hontz replied. He patted the officer of the deck as he left. From the bridge to the CIC was a matter of steps, and entering the CIC, he was always amazed at the number of blue and green computer displays, with the whole room bathed in the light they emitted. Personnel sat at chairs in front of each screen, generally with a keyboard. Stepping over to the SLQ-32(V)3 receiver, commonly referred to as Slick-32, he could see the images that indicated three vessels were departing Ras Al-Khaimah and spreading out.

"Notify the minesweepers that they may have company. I'll bet that's a screening or reconnaissance force coming to see what we're doing and how big we are," Captain Hontz said, addressing his executive officer, Lieutenant Commander Ed Harkins. Harkins was a very capable officer and was on the promotion list for full commander. He had commanded a destroyer in his previous assignment and hated to give up that command, as any officer worth his salt hated doing.

"Aye-aye, Skipper," Harkins replied but paused. "You know, sir, if that is a screening force, I wouldn't be surprised if we see some corvettes or frigates coming from behind Abu Musa or Sirri. Both have airfields on them as well."

"Let's make sure we have fighter coverage very close by as well," Hontz said as he returned to watching the computer screen.

****

Thirty thousand feet above the Strait, two Marine F-18 Hornets flew in lazy circles over Oman. Both aircraft had the distinctive tail markings of "VW," indicating they were from VMFA-314. The unit had arrived in Muscat in August and had maintained some aircraft in the air twenty-four hours a day. The mission for these two aircraft was to provide cover for the minesweeper force operating in the Strait.

They both had been painted by Iranian ground radars, but no warnings had been sounded and no countermeasures had been activated. If it was possible, the pilots were almost bored. They had drawn the short straws for this mission. Everyone else in the squadron was over the UAE, hitting Iraqi ground forces and forces inside Saudi Arabia. Both aircraft were similarly armed with two AIM-9 Sidewinder air-to-air missiles on the wingtips, four AGM-84 Harpoon antiship missiles under the wings, and three AGM-65 Maverick missiles under the fuselage. Both had the M61A1 Vulcan nose-mounted 20mm cannon capable of firing six thousand rounds a minute. It had been days since any Iraqi fighters had been seen in the area or even over the UAE. With air superiority achieved, this patrol was feeling more like a waste of two attack aircraft that could be pounding Iraqi positions rather than doing lazy eights in an empty sky.

"Slapshot, Dogbreath."

"Yeah, what d'you want?" The conversations between the two pilots were casual as they were the only ones on the frequency.

"I could go for a cup of coffee about now. How 'bout you?"

"No, otherwise I would be constantly peeing."

"When are we getting relieved?"

"We have another hour and then Birdbrain and Batman will be coming up." Their conversation was interrupted.

"Black Night Three-Five, November Delta India Hotel."

"Dogbreath, wait one. *Princeton* is calling me," Slapshot said and switched frequencies. "November Delta India Hotel, Black Night Three-Five."

"Black Night Three-Five, we're picking up traffic forty-five miles on an azimuth of two hundred degrees. It appears to be three patrol boats moving at thirty knots," the CIC aboard the *Princeton* indicated.

"Roger, November Delta India Hotel. We'll drop down for a look and get back to you." Slapshot changed his frequency back to air-to-air communications. "Hey, Dogbreath, did you monitor?"

"Yeah, let's go take a look."

Slapshot entered into a wingover maneuver with Dogbreath right behind him.

****

Admiral Ramd Gha'ib Hassan noticed the pink and blue colors of the eastern sky. The sun had not crested and would not for another hour. His flotilla of three ships was converging on Sirri Island. The other vessels from Abu Dhabi and Bahrain were further north and would not arrive for hours. The two captured Saudi Badr-class corvettes, 611 and 612, were already on station behind Sirri Island. *No problem*, he thought. The American minesweepers were made of wood and fiberglass with no real offensive weapons. They were slow vessels as well, especially if they were in the minefield, attempting to clear it.

"Excuse me, Admiral," Colonel Mustafa, his operations officer, interrupted his thoughts.

"What is it, Colonel?"

"Sir, I have a report from the As Sadiq patrol boats. They confirmed that there are nine minesweepers and one helicopter clearing the minefield on the south side. They also indicated that there appears to be an American cruiser escorting them along with a destroyer. They were not sure what flag the destroyer was flying. They also reported that two jets flew low over them," Colonel Mustafa indicated.

"The As Sadiq patrol boats have done well. Have them continue to screen the Americans. I want a position report every thirty minutes."

****

"Hey, Dogbreath, Slapshot."

"Yeah?"

"Did you notice those two Badr-class corvettes sitting behind Sirri Island? Also, the three Grisha corvettes coming from Dubai at max speed based on the bow spray?" Slapshot asked.

"Yeah, I saw them. With that bow spray, no doubt they were at max speed, but I couldn't make out what type they were. You think they know the mine-clearing operation has commenced?"

"Hell, I'll bet a month's flight pay they know we're there. Let me call *Princeton* and inform them," Slapshot said and switched frequency. "November Delta India Hotel, Black Night Three-Five."

"Black Night Three-Five, November Delta India Hotel, over."

"November Delta India Hotel, there are two Badr-class corvettes sitting behind Sirri Island and three Grisha corvettes coming out of Dubai in a big hurry towards Sirri, over."

"Roger, Black Night Three-Five, we're tracking the Grisha corvettes but weren't aware of the two Badr corvettes. Are you remaining on station? Over."

"That's affirmative. We have another hour and then will hand off to replacements, over."
****

As the two F-18 aircraft continued their descent, Admiral Ramd Gha'ib Hassan continued to monitor his Strut Curve air/surface radar. He could clearly see the small flotilla of minesweepers creeping along the southern edge of the channel. He also could see the two larger returns, indicating that there was an escort for the flotilla. Although he could see the flotilla, he had no weapons that could reach the ships, but the two Badr corvettes did with their American-made Harpoon missiles.

"Colonel Mustafa, contact the Badr corvettes. Have them begin their attack with their Harpoon missiles. Their targets are the two American escort ships. Once they are destroyed, we will move in and start taking out the minesweepers," the admiral directed.
****

"Slapshot, Dogbreath. Do you see the two ships behind Sirri getting underway?"

"Yeah, we best notify *Princeton*. Wait one and I will." Dogbreath switched frequencies. "November Delta India Hotel, Black Night Three-Five, over."

"Black Night Three-Five, November Delta India Hotel, go ahead."

"November Delta India Hotel, the two Badr corvettes behind Sirri are getting underway. Over."

"Black Night Three-Five, the Badr corvettes carry Harpoon missiles. They're a threat to us. Take them out. Over."

"Roger, understood. Commencing our run. Black Night Three-Five out. Slapshot, did you monitor?"

"I did, and I'm right behind you. Let's do this."

Both aircraft adjusted their attack profile, knowing that the Badr corvettes lacked any sophisticated air-defense missile system but did have a Phalanx Vulcan Gatling gun system. They wanted to be sure to stay out of the range on that system.

"Slapshot, let's use the Harpoons."

"Roger."

As they dropped to almost a surface altitude, both aircraft launched simultaneously. Moments later, both ships opened fire with the Phalanx Vulcan guns but were too late in the engagement as they hadn't anticipated an air attack and therefore had been lax in monitoring the system. They also weren't well trained on operating the system since this was a Saudi ship that they had captured.

****

As the Grisha corvettes raced towards Sirri Island to join the Badr corvettes, two bright flashes lit up the morning horizon. At first, the admiral thought it was the sun peeking over the eastern horizon, but he quickly realized it was not. The columns of black smoke told him what he feared most.

"Admiral," Colonel Mustafa interrupted his thoughts, "we have just received a request for assistance from Badr 611. He has been hit and is sinking. He requests we come quickly to pick up his crew. He is abandoning ship."

"And what about Badr 612?" the admiral asked, but he suspected he knew the answer.

106

"Sir, we have not had word from him. Badr 611 reported that 612 was hit as well, but that is all he said," Colonel Mustafa replied. There was a long pause as the admiral paced the bridge and stared off in the direction of the sinking ships. His thoughts were interrupted again. "Sir, what do you wish to do? Should we continue to Sirri and pick up the crews or…?" He did not finish before he had his answer.

"No, we move in and engage with our torpedoes against the two American escort ships. Bring us to general quarters. Make sure the SA-N-4 fire control system is functioning properly and engage those American aircraft if they come into range. They will drop countermeasures if we engage with the missiles, so be sure the MUFF-103 are up, but do not turn the radar on until the N-4 engages. Understood? The 57mm will back up the Gecko missiles. Have the four TCN-45 boats attack with their Exocet missiles. There targets are the two escort vessels. Once we have destroyed them, we will attack the minesweepers," Admiral Hassan ordered.

"Aye, sir."

"It will be a couple of hours before we are within torpedo range. I'm going to lie down. Wake me if necessary." And the admiral left the bridge for the last time.

****

"Captain, CIC," the squawk box on the bridge called.

"What you got?" Captain Hontz asked.

"Skipper, we have three targets closing at twenty-five knots at thirty miles on a due west heading. We believe they're Grisha corvettes from their radar signatures," the watch officer announced.

"Roger, I'll be right there," Hontz said, getting out of his chair on the bridge and making the short walk to the CIC, where he approached the watch officer. "Let's take a look." Hontz studied the screen and noted the three targets.

"The Grishas don't carry antiship missiles, as they're primarily an antisubmarine ship. They do carry torpedoes, however—the 533mm class, which is equivalent to our Mk-48," the weapons officer interjected.

"What's the range on them?" Hontz asked.

"Twenty-five kilometers, sir," the weapons officer said.

"XO, bring the ship to battle stations and let's engage these guys. I don't want to give them a chance to get a fish off after us."

"Aye-aye, Captain. Sound general quarters."

The watch officer hit the button, and an automatic voice sounded throughout the ship: "General quarters, general quarters. Man your battle stations. This is not a drill."

Sailors that had been asleep were suddenly jumping out of their bunks in their respective sleeping berths and moving quickly to their assigned battle stations. Most of the sleeping crew members, those not on watch, had been sleeping in their uniforms, so little time was needed before all compartments reported manned and ready. Hontz smiled to himself, knowing now that the drills had paid off.

There was a shudder throughout the ship as it fired the first Harpoon. The first was followed quickly by two more missiles. Skimming just above the water at over five hundred miles per hour, the missile was very hard to detect. The missile's homing radars were looking for the targets and found them, quickly locking on.
****

Admiral Ramd Gha'ib Hassan was lost in REM sleep when a pounding noise invaded his thoughts. The pounding was constant and rhythmic. The more it lasted, the louder it became. Hassan began to wake. As he opened his eyes, he recognized the sound. It was his ship's twin 57mm AK-725 anti-aircraft guns engaging a target. His last thought before all went black was *Why are they shooting?*

Chapter 19
Move Up

19 April 1991
Across the Board
Oman

Slowly, over the course of two weeks, the 1st Marine Division had been preparing for the time to come to start kicking the Iraqi forces out of the UAE. Task Force Shepherd, under the command of Lieutenant Colonel Myers, was given the mission to be the first to cross the line and initiate the attack. Task Force Shepherd was a composite light armored infantry battalion and consisted of a headquarters and service company, 1st Light Armored Infantry Battalion, which had four light armored infantry companies, an antitank platoon, an engineer detachment and an air-defense detachment. He was meeting with his company commanders one last time before they were to initiate the attack at 0400 the next morning.

"Any questions? Everyone understands what has to be done?" Myers asked, looking at the faces of some very young-looking captains. He had trained with them for the past year and was confident in each of their ability to complete the mission. *Breach Iraqi obstacles, to include the tank ditch, secure said breach, conduct passage of lines with main attack.* Once the main force passed, he would follow and be prepared for the next mission. "If there are no questions, get your men ready and I'll see you on the other side," Colonel Myers said as he stood. His company commanders followed suit and began to leave the tactical operations center. As they did, Colonel Myers shook each man's hand and wished him well.
****

The 7th Armoured Brigade's Royal Scots Dragoon Guards Battalion was the first unit lined up to cross the UAE border. During the night, they had moved from TAA Biscuit to the line of departure at Nuway. From there, it was a twenty-two-kilometer movement to contact across Oman before they crossed into the UAE. They had not crossed these twenty-two kilometers as it was open ground and they didn't want to alert any potential Iraqi reconnaissance units as to their approach. Unopposed, it would be a one-hour trek across the open desert. Their own reconnaissance unit had moved under the cover of darkness to Safwan and noted a few Iraqi vehicles across the border in Al Hiyar, but nothing significant.

"Sir, I think we're going to have a boring night of it and probably most of the day as well," Lieutenant Colonel Sharples said, standing in the dark and looking towards the UAE border.

"Well, I'd be very happy if we never fired a shot and just drove straight to Kuwait and home," said Brigadier Patrick Cordingley, commander of the 7th Armoured Brigade. "I'm looking forward to some nice cool weather and rain. Never thought I would say that. The weather in Sherborne will be quite comfortable in a few weeks."

"Are you from Sherborne, sir?" Sharples asked.

"I attended Sherborne School and did find the area quite pleasant," Cordingley answered. "Now remember, I want us to minimize civilian casualties and property damage. To be quite honest, this should never have got this far. Civilians are always the ones that suffer the most in these sorts of things. Let's not make it too difficult on them."

"Very good, sir, I'll have another talk with the lads about it just before we go over," Sharples said as someone approached.

"Excuse me, sir. I thought you might like a cup of tea. You are wanted in the command vehicle," the young sergeant said. Cordingley accepted the cup of tea but wasn't sure who the young corporal was, not recognizing him in the dark.

"Thank you, young man," Cordingley said as he turned back to Sharples and extended his hand. "See you on the other side. Do be careful." He then turned and disappeared into the darkness.
****

Lieutenant Colonel Dan Cory had not been in combat in twenty years—not since Vietnam, when he'd been a chopper pilot. He hadn't been married then and had no children. Now he had six hundred and fifty children that were assigned to his battalion and another hundred and fifty stepchildren, soldiers from other units that were attached to his unit for this operation. He considered every man and woman in his air assault infantry battalion to be his child, to include the stepchildren[2] The aircraft had been pre-positioned earlier in the evening and shut down. Each chopper load was already around the aircraft with the flight crew. Some were sleeping; some were in small groups, enjoying a cigarette and talking in whispers. Each UH-60 Black Hawk helicopter was carrying fifteen soldiers plus the crew of four. The seats had been removed and the fifteen passengers would sit on their respective rucksack for the thirty-minute flight to their objective. This was about to become the largest air-assault operation since Vietnam, and the 1st Brigade was making it.

Cory looked out over the twenty choppers that would carry the first lift of three hundred soldiers. It would take two lifts of twenty UH-60s to get the bulk of his battalion airlifted into the objective. Those not going in aboard the Blackhawks would come in on the CH-47s or the convoy. The other three battalions had twenty helicopters each to lift their units as well and an equal number of CH-47s. All toll, eighty Black Hawk helicopters and forty CH-47 heavy-lift helicopters making two lifts would get the entire brigade on the ground. Cory's as well as the other battalions vehicles, would be following the 29th Division lead elements. Cory could only see the first three aircraft as they were well spread out. Elements of the 29th Infantry Division had come past earlier in the evening, moving into their attack position. It was hoped that by the end of G+2, a linkup would take place eighty-three miles to the north at Prince Abdul Majeed bin Abdulaziz domestic airport, referred to by the command as Objective Cobra. The brigade's mission was to seize and

---

[2] Although women did not serve in combat arms at the time, women were attached to infantry units. In Colonel Cory's battalion, he had a female ambulance driver and a female ground surveillance radar operator. Both were on the front line and both served with distinction. Today a Ranger-tabbed woman commands an infantry company in the 101st Airborne Division "and I have been told she is tougher then a woodpeckers lips."

hold the airport so Apache helicopters could use it as a filling station to launch attacks against Iraqi formations. Cory was confident his kids could do their part and do it well—he just worried about someone getting hurt.

****

The 82nd had done a combat jump the previous year in Panama. A brigade had seized the airport in Panama City. On that drop, two thousand one hundred and fifty soldiers jumped. Almost that many would be placing their knees in the breeze on this night to seize the port. Thirty-five C-130 aircraft had arrived at Jeddah during the early evening to take the paratroopers to the objective. Their flight path would take them out over the Red Sea, away from potential enemy fire. Only with six minutes left to the drop zone would the aircraft turn over land.

"Delany, did you make the jump in Panama?" Private Slocum asked. This would be his first jump since graduating from airborne school and his first night jump.

"Yeah. What of it?" Delany asked. He had been in the 82nd for the past two years. His sergeant stripes were removed from his uniform at this time as he was working his way back up, having been busted for insubordination to a senior noncommissioned officer.

"I was wondering what it's like—I mean, to jump in and not know where the enemy is, and all the confusion on the drop zone and moving to rally points and—" Slocum lamented.

"Hey, slow down. You're going to talk yourself into a heart attack. First, when you land, breathe and look around. Get out of your chute and watch which way everyone is flowing. If there's shooting, move towards the sounds of the guns—our guns. More than likely, you'll land right with the rest of us and be fine. Relax, this will be just like at jump school when you jumped with your eyes closed," Delany said.

"Well, I'd rather jump than be one of those guys in the 1st of the 325th," Slocum said, pulling out a stick of gum.

"Why? What did you hear?"

"I was in a poker game two nights ago with a guy that works in the S-1 shop, and he heard from a guy that worked in brigade operations that the 1st of the 325th wouldn't be jumping or riding up to Objective Wet but be taking a cargo ship. The whole brigade was supposed to go by ship, but they couldn't find one big enough, so only that battalion is going. They're supposed to get there the same time as we jump."

"Oh, bullshit... we jump, Marines do things from ships. Get your gear ready."

Sergeant Schwartz sat in the turret of his Bradley fighting vehicle. Like most, he was wondering how he was going to do in combat. He'd joined the National Guard to get some money for college. It had never crossed his mind he would be going into combat. As he sat in the gunner's position, his platoon leader climbed up on the vehicle.

"Hey, Lieutenant, are we really going to be crossing the LD tonight?" Schwartz said, referring to the line of demarcation. "I saw those 101st guys back there and they said we were going to link up with them. Wished us luck. I think they're the ones that are going to need the luck." Schwartz was from Baltimore and wanted to join the family business—fur coat retailing—when he graduated from college.

"Schwartz, let's not worry about those guys but worry about ourselves. They're hitting the soft targets like cooks, bakers and candlestick makers. We're hitting the frontline tanks and BTRs. We're the ones with the real fight," Lieutenant Pile said.

Oh great! Why the hell could I not convince my father to pay for my college instead of this? Bet he'll want me to join the Israeli Army when my time in the Guard is over, Schwartz thought as the vehicle's engine came to life.

"Schwartz, get your helmet on. It's time to move toward the sound of the guns," Lieutenant Pile said, putting on his own helmet.

Chapter 20
G-Day, 0530

20 April 1991
IX Corps AO
Um Al Zumoul, United Arab Emirates

The eastern horizon was starting to show signs of day as the clouds over the Strait of Hormuz displayed some pink and orange color. On the ground, it was still dark and would remain so for another hour before the sand dunes would begin to heat up. Critters would be scurrying to their holes to seek out the cool sand and avoid the midday heat. Camel spiders and scorpions sometimes shared holes to avoid their common enemy, the heat, which could cook them in the midday sun. However, in the cooler morning air, they were still out and about.

Lieutenant Abd al-Rashid was enjoying his morning tea in what was the beginning of a planned solar power station. Little had been done so far; just one building had been constructed and it appeared to be the beginning of an office. At least they had plenty of water and some shade and electricity. As he sat outside, he noticed the eastern horizon beginning to show signs of the coming morning sun. He also noticed some flashes to the north and occasionally the sound of thunder. His favorite time of day was now, before the sun came up and the heat soared. Even back in his home of Mosul, it didn't get as hot in the day as it did here.

"Good morning, Lieutenant," Sergeant Baghdadi said as he came outside with his tea. They were the platoon leader and platoon sergeant for one of the brigade reconnaissance companies. Other platoons were scattered to the north along the same latitude as them, almost. Standing, Sergeant Baghdadi thought he heard something—the sound of a vehicle coming down the road from Al Ain, 235 kilometers to the north along the border highway. As he sipped his tea, he cocked his head, almost sure he was hearing a vehicle.

"Sir, do you hear a vehicle approaching?" Baghdadi asked. Lieutenant al-Rashid listened for a moment, then stood up.

"Yes, I do hear a vehicle, maybe two." Both strained their eyes to see into the night down the road but couldn't see anything until the muzzle flash of the 105mm main gun tank appeared and a round ripped through their sleeping quarters. The blast put both of the men on the ground.

"What in the name of Allah are those stupid camel jockeys doing?" al-Rashid said, jumping to his feet. "I will have them before a firing squad!" That was when Baghdadi grabbed his arm, spun him around and shoved him towards their own BTR.

"It's the Americans! Let's get out of here," Baghdadi screamed as he shoved al-Rashid towards their vehicle. The driver and crew were already there and had the vehicle ready to move out as soon as the lieutenant and Baghdadi arrived. Al-Rashid was the first to the vehicle, but it didn't matter as the vehicle exploded with the delivery of another round. Two minutes later, the lead elements of the 3rd Armored Cavalry Regiment rolled past the burning vehicles. They did not stop to collect souvenirs.

****

45th Division HQ
Alyhyali, United Arab Emirates

If one must endure the hardships of being in the infantry, then one should take advantage of all possibilities of comfort—that was Major General Omar Zeyad's attitude. He had graciously removed the family from the small palace he had commandeered for his headquarters and living area in Alyhyali. Here in the Liwa oasis, it was common to find lush gardens and green grass alongside the Moreeb Dune, one of the largest sand dunes in the world at over nine hundred feet. The pounding on the door brought General Zeyad out of a very pleasant sleep.

"General, wake up, sir," his aide was yelling through the door.

"Alright, alright, I'm awake. What the hell is so damn important? Get in here," the general yelled back as he sat up in bed. The aide didn't like to just enter the general's bedroom for fear of what or who he might see in the man's bed besides the general himself.

The aide approached the bed. "Sir, we're getting reports from our frontline units that the Americans are coming. We have lost contact with the platoon that was at Um Al Zumoul and the units that were north of there. Sir, that's only sixty kilometers from here!" Panic crept into his voice.

"Calm down. Have the staff assemble in the conference center and let's get the latest. Have the tank battalion in Asab put on alert and ready to move. Have they notified General Rasol Shitnah at Corps headquarters? If not, then let's get word to him that we believe the Americans have crossed and are attacking in our sector. Get General Nassar al-Hiti over at 10th Armoured Division on the phone. Now go," Zeyad ordered. As he stood to dress, he thought, *So now it begins. I hope I see my home again.*

"What can you tell me, General?" Zeyad asked of General al-Hiti, who was on his left or northern flank. He had known al-Hiti for many years, although they were in different branches of the army. They had served together on the General Staff in the Iraqi capital several years ago and had been in the same division in the war with Iran.

"Their first elements hit us at 0400 and they quickly breached out tank ditches," al-Hiti said with some anxiety in his voice. "It was still dark and we could see nothing, but their fire was very accurate and long-range. The coordination between their maneuver force and artillery is accurate and overwhelming," al-Hiti said.

"How did they get over your tank ditches so quickly? From what I saw, it should have taken them hours for that alone and another couple of hours to get through your minefields," Zeyad asked.

"They breached the tank ditches with metal culverts. Their infantry threw scaling ladders across the ditches and secured the far side, setting up positions in the ditch spoil, and then their engineers came up with prepared metal culverts and rolled them into the ditches until the ditch was full and they just drove across. The first vehicles across were bulldozers to push the spoil down, and then the tanks and infantry vehicles just drove across. It was all done in thirty minutes. Now they're pouring through and engaging my two forward brigades. I have to go. May Allah be with you this day, Omar," al-Hiti said before the line went dead.

Zeyad hung the phone up and turned to the faces in the operations section that were looking at him. They were hoping for a flanking maneuver from the 10th to strike the Americans in the side. The look on Zeyad's face told them it was not going to happen.

To no one, Zeyad said, "Get me General Shitnah on the phone." As he said so, he glanced at the clock. It was approaching 0600. This was a phone call that he did not wish to make.
****

1st Infantry Division AO
Al Ain, United Arab Emirates

MG Fadhil Jalil al-Barwari sat down for his breakfast. The morning was proving to be pleasant, and so he was taking it outside on the patio of the villa that he had so politely been given by the mayor of Al Ain. *This morning is unusually quiet*, he thought as he cracked the soft-boiled egg that was typical of his morning breakfast along with coffee, only one cup a day. A newspaper, the *Wall Street Journal*, lay beside his plate. He studied the American stock market closely as he did not intend to remain in the Army much longer and did not intend to retire on his military retirement pay. He anticipated retiring a wealthy man and living in the United States, maybe New York City. His concentration on the editorial page was broken by the sound of thunder to the south. He looked up. *Strange, there are no clouds in the sky this morning. The 17th Armoured Division may be exercising, although General al-Furayi said nothing about it when I spoke to him last night.*

"Sir," his aide said, bringing his attention back to the present. Before al-Barwari could answer, he went on, "The 17th just reported that they are under attack by two Egyptian divisions and a Saudi task force. One of the Egyptian divisions is attempting to flank him on his southern border between him and the 10th."

Standing quickly and heading for the door, al-Barwari asked, "What are our brigade commanders reporting?"

"Nothing in our sector, sir," the aide announced as he followed al-Barwari into the room and motioned for a soldier standing there to get the general's car.

"Nothing! Are they awake? We must have some news. Get Colonel Muhammed on the phone." Muhammed was the division operations officer.

"Muhammed, what is the status in our sector?" al-Barwari asked a few moments later, grabbing his hat but tied to his landline telephone.

"Sir, I have spoken with each of the brigade commanders and all report quiet in their sectors. We do not seem to have any activity at this time. I have a scout helicopter up and he reports negative contacts to our front or flanks but says there appears to be a major engagement to the south in the 17th's sector," Colonel Muhammed reported. He continued, "I did get a request from the 17th that we have our two tank battalions conduct an attack into the side of a Saudi task force that is hitting him on the northern flank."

"Absolutely not. If we release those two and then we get hit, we will lack a mobile reserve. I am not sacrificing my command to pull his feet out of the fire. No, unless Corps orders it, we retain all our forces. Be sure they all understand to remain in place and defend their positions. I will be there in a few minutes," al-Barwari concluded.

****

IX Corps HQ
Abu Dhabi, United Arab Emirates

The fog of war becomes thicker the higher the echelon of command. The fog is caused by many factors. Higher headquarters too far from the front lines, poor communications, untimely reports, and electronic warfare countermeasures all contribute. LTG Juwad Assad Rasol Shitnah was in the fog at this very moment at 0800 hours. Reports had been coming into the IX Corps operations center, and the staff was attempting to paint a clear picture of what was happening but was having difficulty.

"At this time, General, we know that the Americans, the Egyptians and the Saudis have launched an attack south of Al Ain. It appears to be just one corps and we believe it to be the American 7th Corps. The 1st Division in Al Ain reports no activity in his sector. The 17th reports some pressure but nothing serious and he is holding. The 10th Armoured says the Americans quickly breached his antitank ditches and are engaging his frontline forces. The 45th Division says they have had some minor contact with their reconnaissance platoons, but nothing serious. He has placed his one tank battalion on alert," Brigadier General Ejaz Husseim said, pointing out each unit's position on the wall map as he spoke.

"And what about the 49th Division? What have we heard from them?"

"They reported some light contact on the southern outskirts of Fujairah, but aside from that, all is quiet there."

"Are the Americans committing their attack helicopters?"

"No, sir. These are their heavy forces. We believe their attack helicopters are all in the Jeddah area. We have not experienced any problems with them in our area of operations."

"Their close-air support?"

"Likewise, we are seeing very little close-air support from their air force. There are reports of heavy bombing on the 1st Republican Guard Corps units at this time but relatively quiet in our area," General Husseim reported.

"Good, maybe the American Air Force is now limited in the number of planes they can commit to a battle. This is good. I want max effort of our attack helicopters committed at this time and coordinated with the 10th Armoured Division. I think this will be the main effort for the Americans. The 17th can hold the Saudis and the Egyptians. I saw the Egyptians in action in the '73 Arab-Israeli war. They got their dinner handed to them by the Israelis they were such poor fighters. The 17th will hold them, I am sure. Tell the 1st to maintain his positions but be prepared to attack south with one brigade on order. He is our insurance policy if somehow the 17th should fail. The 1st can hit the Saudis in the flank," Shitnah directed, then paused for a moment in thought. "Also, put the 52nd Armour on alert for a counterattack in accordance with counterattack plan Alpha."

"Yes, sir. Anything else, sir?"

"No, just keep me informed of any changes. I really think the Americans are probably just testing our mettle at this point as we have not seen any air activity. This probe will be over shortly."

Chapter 21
Attack

20 April 1991
1st Marine Division
Fujairah, United Arab Emirates
0430 Crossing the LD

"All Task Force Shepherd units, this is Shepherd Six, move out." Colonel Myers's vehicle lurched forward, crossing the Omani-UAE border five minutes later. As the unit cautiously moved down the road, the turret on each vehicle was searching for targets. The 25mm guns could take out almost any Iraqi vehicle save for a tank. The eight LAV-M vehicles displaced with the mortars to an overwatch position ready to fire quickly in support of the four scout LAV-25s that were fanning out across the terrain—very narrow terrain with the sea on the right flank and low hills and mountains on the left.

"Shepherd Six, Devil Dog Six, over."

"Go ahead, Devil Dog."

"Shepherd Six, we have a building approximately three hundred yards. I see two Bravo Tango Romeos and six paxs at this time."

"Roger, engage and bypass," Myers instructed. Before he could finish his sentence, he heard the roar of the 25mm Bushmaster chain gun open up. Checking his map, he knew this would be the UAE customs border post. He hoped his LAV-MEWSS electronic warfare vehicles were able to jam any transmissions from the Iraqi forces there. He'd wanted to get closer to Fujairah before running into the enemy's main elements. Combat in an urban environment was bad enough when you had the element of surprise. He suspected that the element of surprise had just gone out the window.

As Myers rolled past the burning wreckage of what had been a military truck, he could see his first company fanning out across the desert and moving into a high-speed maneuver. The eight wheels and powerful engine enabled the LAVs to reach speeds of up to fifty miles an hour, and at this point that was what they wanted. His mission was to get out front and find the Iraqi forces so the follow-on tanks and infantry could eliminate them. He knew on his left flank and on the other side of

120

a small hill, his second company was approaching the south side of Fujairah to the west of his first company. He just prayed he could reach the outskirts before any serious engagements took place.
****

Fujairah, Kalba District, 0500

"What was that noise?" Lieutenant Imam Jabal asked, sitting up on a rooftop and attempting to regain the dream he'd had earlier.

"That noise came from the south towards the customs checkpoint, Lieutenant. It sounded like a concrete drill. Maybe they're tearing up the road to prevent the Americans from coming up that road," the crusty platoon sergeant said, maintaining his supine position and hoping the lieutenant would resume the same so they could get some sleep. But no such luck.

"Sergeant, I'm going to take the vehicle and go south to see what the noise is. You stay here with the men, and I'll call you if I find anything," the young officer directed.

"Yes, sir, you do that and I'll come running," the sergeant answered, but he was thinking, *And if you believe that, I have a magic carpet I will sell you.*

Lieutenant Jabal went downstairs and rousted his driver. He would not take the entire squad, just the driver and gunner. Neither were happy about having to go out, but an order was an order, even in the Iraqi Army. Mounting up in the vehicle, they slowly started moving through the streets, which were fairly deserted at 0500 in the morning. Life would be moving by 0600, however. As they approached the Abu Dujanah mosque, Lieutenant Jabal thought he saw a red tracer round. His suspicions were confirmed shortly when a large flaming basketball appeared and passed through the side of his vehicle, then departed out the other side.

"Get us out of here!" Jabal screamed to his driver, who really didn't need any encouragement to do just that. The gunner had been facing in the wrong direction and couldn't bring his weapon to bear on the shooting vehicle. The 14.5 KPVT machine gun on the BTR-60 was comparable to the 25mm Bushmaster chain gun on the Marine Corps LAV. As Jabal's vehicle ducked behind a building, two more rounds

121

ripped through the empty troop compartment. Grabbing the hand mic, he transmitted his report to his company commander.

****

Fujairah, Kalba Lake, 0530

"Shepherd Six, Devil Dog Six, over."

"Go ahead, Devil Dog Six," Colonel Myers responded. There wasn't much traffic on TF Shepherd's command net at all, but Devil Dog had been attached to the other task forces. Myers was left with one company working forward of TF Taro.

"Shepherd Six, I got a problem. We engaged one Bravo Tango Romeo and he withdrew down a side street. Over."

"So, what's the problem, Devil Dog?"

"Shepherd Six, as soon as he left the area, fifty-seven, I say again fifty-seven Iraqi soldiers walked out of the houses and have approached my vehicles with white flags. They've surrendered. What do I do with them, over?" Shepherd had to consider this as they hadn't anticipated taking prisoners so early in the operation. They'd expected to take one or two prisoners, but not fifty-seven all at once during the first engagement. As Shepherd sat monitoring the radio, attempting to decide what to tell the young company commander, more reports were being made of similar actions on other parts of the 1st Marine Division area.

****

Fujairah, Kalba Bird of Prey Center, 0630

Colonel Fulks, commanding Task Force Grizzly on the left flank of the 1st Marine Division, was frustrated with the terrain they had to move through to reach the outskirts of Fujairah. The 2nd and 3rd Battalions, 7th Marine Regiment, had slow going through mountainous terrain before they moved out onto more favorable ground for mobility. As they began to fan out, ten Iraqi tanks moved out from the concealment offered by the town's buildings.

"Grizzly Six, Hammer Six, over," commander of the 2nd of the 7th called.

"Hammer Six, Grizzly Six, over."

"Grizzly Six, we have ten Iraqi tanks approaching our positions, over."

"Roger, engage. Over."

"Grizzly Six, I would rather not. Over."

"Well, why the hell not? Over." Grizzly Six was getting upset, as everyone hearing this conversation could tell.

"Grizzly Six, I would rather not engage because they all have white flags tied to their antennas and their turrets are facing to the rear over the engine decks. They're surrendering, over."

****

Al Aqdah, West of Fujairah, 0800

The sun had crested over the eastern horizon, but in the draws and valleys of the UAE north of Fujairah, the shadows of dawn were still evident. Sea Dog Two-Five and Sea Dog Two-Seven, two AH-1W Cobra helicopters, had been screening the left flank of TF Grizzly.

"Two-Seven, you see what I'm seeing? Over."

"Yeah, looks like the Long Island Expressway in morning traffic. You best report this to Grizzly, over."

"I will. QSY at this time." Two-Five switched from his VHF air-to-air radio to his FM air-to-ground radio. "Grizzly Six, Sea Dog Two-Five, over," he transmitted.

"Sea Dog Two-Five, Grizzly Three, over," the operations officer for TF Grizzly responded, as Grizzly Six was relieving his bladder at the time.

"Grizzly Three, Sea Dog Two-Five, we are vicinity Al Aqdah. The vehicle traffic is bumper-to-bumper and all heading southwest, over."

"What kind of traffic? Over," Grizzly Three asked, looking at Colonel Fulks, whose head had snapped around quickly hearing that report.

"All kinds: cars, buses, trucks, both civilian and military, even some Bravo Tango Romeos. Looks like rush hour on the LIE. Over." Grizzly Three was from Long Island and knew that LIE was the Long Island Expressway. In the mornings, it was worse than the 405 in Los Angeles.

"Roger, wait one," Grizzly Three instructed. "Hey, sir, what do you want me to tell them? If he starts hitting the military vehicles, it's going to clog that road, and that's one of only two roads we have to get to the coast. As narrow as those passes are, we'd never get to the coast for a week if we start strafing that highway. Besides, there are probably a lot of civilians on that road, too."

"I agree, but I hate to let the military vehicles slip through our fingers. On the other hand, if we let them know we're coming and let them pass, maybe they'll cause a panic in the 49th. Have him observe but not engage unless necessary," Fulks said and reached for the radio to Division.

"Sea Dog Two-Five, Grizzly Three, over."

"Grizzly Three, Sea Dog Two-Five, over."

"Sea Dog, do not, I repeat, do not engage. Let the vehicles continue to move south and west. Report any traffic jams. Let them observe you, but do not get decisively engaged. How copy? Over," Grizzly Three ordered.

"Grizzly Three, roger, have good copy. Sea Dog Two-Five, out."

The Sea Dog gunships continued to watch the mass exodus from Fujairah.

****

1st Marine Division TOC
Fujairah, 1200 Hours

"Sir, let me give you an update, because this is moving a lot faster than we anticipated," Colonel Lohman, the 1st Marine Division operations officer, requested.

Major General Hopkins had just come into the operations section after having to deal with a logistics issue. He had been gone for close to three hours and the staff was a bit worried that he might have gone forward with one of the task forces.

"Yeah, what have we got?" Hopkins asked.

"For one thing, we have too many prisoners. At last count, we had close to four hundred. TF Shepherd is just pointing them down the highway and telling them to walk with their hands up and with a white flag. TF Grizzly is reporting the southern road to the coast is a traffic jam of vehicles and has blocked E84 from the airport to the coast. TF Taro is at the Phase Line E84 and is preparing to move north to Sakamkam. TF Troy is clearing bypassed pockets south of the airport and TF Ripper is on the airport. We had TF Troy conduct his air assault to seize the port up at Khor Fakkan and he took less than an hour to secure it. Reported no contact. He captured the entire infantry company that was there without a shot being fired. Said when they landed, the company was in formation, standing next to the LZ. Damnedest thing. He said they had a formal surrender ceremony. Iraqi company commander even gave him his sidearm. He wants to know if he can fly the prisoners out. That was the request of the Iraqi commander at the surrender. What do I tell him, sir?"

"Tell him to sit on them until a linkup with TF Taro. We got better things to do with the choppers than fly the Iraqis around. On second thought, that might actually free up our ground transports. Tell him I'm considering his request. Where is the POW compound anyway?" Hopkins asked.

"Sir, to tell the truth, I'm not sure. Didn't think we would need it that fast," Lohman said.

"What are our casualties looking like?" Hopkins asked with deep concern.

"Sir, we have had one, fatal. One of our new privates was getting out of a vehicle and the pin on one of his grenades came out. He must have realized it when the grenade hit the ground because he threw himself on the grenade and covered it. Saved his squad with his life," Lohman explained.

"Damn. Get the word out to the commanders about safety. Don't need accidents like that, not now. Talk to the adjutant about an award for the young man. He did have the temerity to save his squad."

Chapter 22
Air Assault

20 April 1991
Tactical Assembly Area Campbell
Silsilah Anezah

The night before, twenty Black Hawk helicopters had landed in a pickup zone for the upcoming offensive. Across what had been the 101st sector before they were relieved by the 28th and 29th Infantry Divisions, Black Hawk helicopters had gone into pickup zones for the 1st Brigade. The 1st Brigade would make the first combat air assault to seize the airfield at Mogayra, sixty-seven miles to the northwest.[3] From there, additional units would land and continue to the attack north and use the airfield for a refuel point in support of future operations. The 1st Brigade would also conduct a linkup with the ground forces moving north. Airfield seizures were the 101st's cup of tea.

Lieutenant Colonel Dan Cory hadn't slept well the night before. Last-minute details had drifted through his head. The what-ifs of combat were always present and had to be considered. What if an aircraft broke down—could they move those soldiers to other aircraft quickly? What if an aircraft was shot down en route to the objective? What if there were enemy tanks on the objective? What if...? It went on constantly for a commander. And each contingency must be thought out and a plan made to meet it. Cory had been a pilot in Vietnam, and as he looked at a black sky full of lights from the Milky Way, he knew it would be a good night for flying. Flying over mountainous terrain in daylight generally meant a bumpy ride, but at night, this should be a smooth ride to the objective.

The mission called for two turns of twenty UH-60 Black Hawks and five CH-47 aircraft on each turn to support Cory's battalion, the 3rd of the 327th Infantry. Troops would be airlifted in the UH-60 aircraft, fifteen soldiers per aircraft, and sixteen of the antitank Humvees would be sling-loaded under the CH-47s, along with the S-3's vehicle and its

---

[3] This airport was nothing more than a dirt strip in the early 1990s and was not considered an airport until October of 2011.

radios and the TACP vehicle with its radios for close-air support. Cory knew it was time to load up when the Black Hawk pilots started the engines.

As the rotor blades began to turn, Cory took his position behind and between the two pilots. He hadn't had a chance to talk to them last night after they'd landed, and this was the first close look he had of them. It was then that he noticed the baby faces on both pilots. *Damn, these two are so young I doubt if they even shave yet. I guess that's what old grunt battalion commanders in Vietnam must have thought when they saw me on the flight controls.* Then Cory noticed both pilots were females. *Well, if they are shaving, it's not their faces.*

The aircraft commander turned, smiled and in a loud voice asked, "Are you ready, sir?"

Cory gave her a thumbs-up and pointed towards the front. The message was clear: "We're up and let's go." The pilot turned and nodded to the copilot, who pulled in the collective, and the aircraft broke ground with nineteen other aircraft right behind it. Both pilots were wearing NODs or night observation devices and could clearly see the ground and the other aircraft. To Cory and the soldiers on board, unless they had theirs on as well, it was just plain dark outside. The cockpit was bathed in a soft green light from the instruments. The aircraft remained low-level in their flight mode, which allowed them to clear the highest obstacles, in this case ridgelines and mountaintops, at a constant airspeed. Unlike scout helicopters, UH-60 helicopters operating in troop lift formations didn't operate in NOE or nap-of-the-earth mode. The flight time to the objective was approximately thirty minutes. There would be no artillery prep because of the range and no airstrikes for fear of damaging the runways and structures. Surprise was the key ingredient in this operation.

"One minute!" the door gunner yelled. He was a soldier from Cory's battalion who, along with ten others, had volunteered to fly as a door gunner from the very start of Desert Shield. Crew chiefs were assigned to aviation units, but door gunners were volunteers from the infantry units. Cory looked around at the fourteen others in his aircraft. His two radio operators were with him, as well as twelve soldiers that made up a squad from Bravo Company, the same squad that had been intoxicated a few months before and gotten in a ton of trouble over it.

They all had determined looks, but Cory didn't see fear in any of the faces. They were looking to atone for their past mistake.

Cory could feel the aircraft beginning its flare to land, and the side cargo doors were immediately thrown open. After the wheels touched down on the asphalt road, the soldiers were off the aircraft in less than three seconds. Cory was the last out, and the aircraft was already lifting off. As the aircraft departed, silence returned to the night. His soldiers and the other soldiers of the brigade began to move to their specific objectives. The battalion objective was a cluster of buildings at the northwest end of the airfield, and the chopper pilots put him down within two hundred feet of the edge of the buildings. As they stood to move out, lights flicked on in some of the buildings. Most of the soldiers reached the edge of the buildings before the first shot was heard, followed by a hand grenade going off. Then a hornet's nest of shooting began.

"Battleforce Six, Gator Six, we have contact. Appears to be platoon-size element with BTR-60s." Before Cory could answer Gator Six, he heard, "Battleforce Six, Bulldog Six, contact."

"All Battleforce elements, Battleforce Six. I can hear that we have contact. Get on with your business and inform me when you have a problem or have resolved the situation."

A few minutes later, he heard, "Battleforce Six, Dawg Six, I'm on the ground with eight vehicles and ready."

"Roger, Dawg Six, move to the northwest perimeter and close it off from reinforcing or escaping forces, over," Cory instructed the Delta Company commander with his eight antitank vehicles equipped with the TOW launchers.

"Roger, Battleforce Six, moving now." For the next thirty minutes, the fighting in front of Bulldog and Gator was intense with an exchange of red and green tracers and explosions from hand grenades. The mortars hadn't been employed due to the concern for the structures and the fact that the enemy appeared to be inside concrete buildings.

"Battleforce Six, Charlie Rock Six."

"Go ahead, Charlie Rock."

"Battleforce Six, our sector is secured. I say again, no enemy contact in sector." Cory quickly looked at his map. Charlie Rock had the southeastern portion of this complex.

"Charlie Rock, I want you to leave one platoon there to continue to secure your sector. Take the other two platoons and move northwest—start clearing the buildings with Gator and Bulldog providing suppressive fire. Break, break, Bulldog and Gator, did you copy? Over."

"Gator copied."

"Bulldog copied. Charlie Rock, be sure your people have a chem stick in their helmet bands. Don't want a green-on-green shoot."

"Roger, all Charlie Rock elements have a green chem stick in the right side of the helmet."

Over the next hour, the small-arms firing continued but slowly diminished as the companies swept the area clean of the enemy. Occasionally, the distinctive sound of a TOW being launched could be heard, which concerned Cory, but as Nick, the company commander, didn't report any trouble, Cory didn't worry too much about it. Across the airfield, Cory could hear the other battalions establishing their dominance on the airfield. As the eastern sky started to show light, the second lift of aircraft landed and that greatly improved the situation on the airfield. Now it was a matter of sit and wait for the linkup to take place.

Almost immediately, Apache helicopters began to land to take on fuel that was at the airport. CH-47 helicopters arrived with fuel blivets and pallets for ammunition for both the Apache helicopters and the infantry. Another flight of CH-47s arrived with 105mm howitzers under the aircraft, along with ammo. Three firing batteries were quickly established around the airfield and began engaging targets designated by the Apaches and the scout helicopters. Within three hours, the airfield was squarely in the hands of the 1st Brigade.

The 2nd Brigade would be flowing in by the end of the day and would conduct the next mission after the linkup with the 29th was executed.

Chapter 23
The Fall of the 49th

21 April 1991
Queen's Royal Irish Hussars
Murqquab, United Arab Emirates

The previous morning, the 1st British Armoured Division had crossed the LD right on time with both brigades abreast. They'd met some light resistance with no injuries when they'd rolled through and around Al Hiyar on the UAE side of the border. The open flat terrain allowed for rapid and unrestricted movement up to Murqquab, where the 7th Armoured Brigade now rested and refueled. Al Hiyar lay sixteen miles behind the 7th Armoured, which had stopped for the night. The other brigade was located five miles behind the lead in Al Faqa.

"Alright, Sergeant Major, let's get the lads up and ready to move," Lieutenant Colonel Benjamin Moore said, handing the sergeant major a cup of hot tea. "It's 0400 and I expect we'll get a call shortly from Division to move out. They're coordinating our attack with the 1st Marine Division, who will be coming from the east through the mountains. I guess from what was briefed last night, the 1st Marines had a pretty easy time of it. Lost only one man. Trying to figure out what to do with all the prisoners they're taking. Seems the Arabs didn't have much will to put up a fight," Moore said between sips of hot coffee.

"That wouldn't hurt my feelings one bit. Never did think the Arabs had much of a stomach for fights. I remember me dad, who fought in Egypt in the fifty-six Suez Crisis, saying that he wasn't impressed with the quality of the Arab soldier or their commanders," the sergeant major said. "He thought the Frenchies were pretty good as they had combat-experienced people that were at Dien Bien Phu in Vietnam. And the Israelis too were pretty good."

"Well, this should go quick as the 2nd Marine Division is coming ashore this morning as well if they haven't started already."
****

0600 Hours
Dubai

Colonel Dalil Ghazali had been notified of the attack on Fujairah the day prior, but the division had decided it would be more prudent to hold the Mi-24 Hind attack helicopters until the attacking armor forces moved into the open terrain. The 49th Division was tracking the movement of both the 1st Marine Division and the 1st British Armoured Division. Colonel Ghazali was up early and had made sure all his pilots were up and ready when the order came to commit the attack helicopters. Located just southwest of the Dubai International Airport, his aircraft were easy to maintain, although it would have been nice if they could have kept them right at the airport, he had argued.

As he stood enjoying the cool morning sea breeze, the distant sound of thunder caught his attention. He turned to look out towards the ocean when he heard what sounded like a freight train rapidly approaching. Then the earth erupted before his eyes, and most of his aircraft were gone in a cloud of sand. When he woke, he was lying on the ground and didn't know how long he had been there. He could see soldiers running, but in different directions. There was no order, just chaos. He couldn't hear anything either. Even his own voice had no sound to it now. The world was silent. He put his hands to his ears to clear the sand out of them, only to find that his hands were covered in blood. As he started to stand, a soldier walked past him and seemed to be in a trance. At first, Ghazali didn't notice, but then he did. The man's eyeballs were partway out of their sockets. Colonel Ghazali didn't hear the next rounds from the battleship USS *Iowa* fifteen miles offshore from Dubai.

****

0800 Hours
TF Grizzly
Al Manama

Alpha Company from TF Shepherd was supporting TF Grizzly, which had peeled off from the seizure of Fujairah and had traveled most of the night to Al Manama. To the south, in the town of Maghribiyah, was TF Ripper.

"Hey, Peters, you awake?" Lance Corporal Husky asked as he lay on the ground outside the LAV that served on.

"Yeah, I was able to get some sleep during the night when I was inside. Why?" Peters questioned.

"Well, I was driving all night and thought you might swap with me so I can sleep today while you drive," Husky said.

"What makes you think today is going to be a cakewalk that you can sleep?"

"We drove all day yesterday, and how many times did we give or take serious fire? Once—once in the entire day. Do you think it'll get any more interesting today? I doubt it." Husky's sarcasm dripped from each word.

"I heard from a guy in Supply that today would be the real fighting. That yesterday we were only taking out a company of Iraqis, so no serious fight was expected."

"A guy in Supply told you that. Have you got shit for brains? What the hell would a guy in Supply know about combat operations?" Husky retorted as the platoon sergeant walked up.

"Morning, Gunny," Peters said, sitting up.

"Peters, Husky, are you two ready to move out?" Gunny asked.

"Will be in a minute," Peters responded. "Just need to—" He didn't finish before the first incoming artillery round exploded.

"Incoming!" Husky yelled and dove for the ground as five more rounds impacted in close proximity. There was a pause.

"Mount up... let's roll!" Gunny commanded as the sound of a mortar round leaving a tube could be heard in the distance. He began to count seconds until the first round hit. By this time, the vehicle was loaded and they, along with three other vehicles from the platoon, were moving towards the sounds of the guns.

"Peters, head due west towards Al Bataeh. Those tubes are in that direction and not far. Husky, you stay on that gun and be watching," Gunny directed.

Over the radio, they heard, "All Grizzly elements, Grizzly Six, move out."

"Do you guys hear that? Grizzly Six just gave the order. This operation has just gotten serious."
****

0815 Hours

Maghribiyah

"All Ripper elements, move out," came over the D Company command radio. D Company, TF Shepherd, had been covering the engineers as they worked through the early-morning hours, clearing a lane through a minefield that was forward of the Iraqi 49th Division positions. As the sun came up, the white-tape lanes through the minefield were very clear, to both sides.

"Alright, Dunkin, let's move it," Lieutenant Triplett said, and the LAV lurched forward. Being the first through the minefield didn't excite anyone in the vehicle. Actually, an M60A1 tank with a mine roller on the front would be the first vehicle, but still, that didn't give everyone a warm and fuzzy feeling. As they moved in behind the tank, mortar rounds began impacting to the side and rear of the armored column. As soon as they were through the minefield, Lieutenant Triplett would peel off with his platoon to scout out Iraqi positions for the follow-on infantry battalions to take out.

"Lieutenant, we have an Iraqi BTR, three hundred meters to our starboard bow," the gunner shouted.

"Engage!"

The 25mm Bushmaster opened fire, sending a noticeable stream of red tracers into the BTR. Smoke was almost immediately seen, along with a white flag off to the side.

"Sir, it's a kill, and we have guys waving a white flag," the gunner reported.

Lieutenant Triplett had been studying his map during this brief engagement and moved to see outside the vehicle. *What the...?* he thought as Iraqi soldiers began standing up with their hands above their heads. At first it was a trickle, then a flow, then a flood. They'd expected to meet heavy resistance in this area, not a flood of enemy soldiers looking to surrender. This was not all how they figured this operation would unfold.
****

1500 Hours
Suwaydan

The two officers approached each other after climbing out of their respective vehicles. One British, one American. They wore different uniforms but sort of spoke the same language. In proper military fashion, both came to the position of attention and exchanged salutes. Then they broke out in smiles and exchanged handshakes.

"Colonel, it is good to see you," Colonel Hodory said as he approached Brigadier Harvey Wallbanger, commander of the 7th Armoured Brigade, 1st British Armoured Division.

"And how did Task Force Papa Bear fare this fine day?" Brigadier Wallbanger asked. The two of them had served together in Germany and how, here in the desert of the Middle East their two famed units had finally linked up.

"Sir, we had a few minor casualties, nothing that won't be cured by a week or so in a hospital bed. And how did the Desert Rats do today?" Colonel Hodory asked, a grin on his face.

"Very well, thank you for asking. Right now, Hodory, us Desert Rats are facing a serious problem. We're being inundated with prisoners. We just don't know what to do with them all. CENTCOM was supposed to be policing these people up, but so far we're guarding them and it's making it difficult for my force to stay on the move," Wallbanger explained, frustration clearly evident in his voice.

"Well, sir, I suppose that is a good problem to have versus a drawn-out fight. I don't mean to cut this short, but I do have to get back. There is still a war going. It was good seeing you again, maybe we can have a drink when this is over," Hodory said as he saluted and returned to the business of war and chasing the Iraqi's back to their own border.

Chapter 24
2nd Marine Ashore

21 April 1991
0545 Hours
Sahel Al Emarat Coastline, United Arab Emirates

Garcia Santos sat enjoying the quiet morning, watching over the sheep that were owned by someone else. He didn't know the owner. He'd been hired by a go-between to come from the Philippines to take care of the sheep. Garcia couldn't find work back home, and this paid enough that he could send money home to his family each month. Thankfully, his needs were small so he could send most of his money back to the Philippines.

Sitting on the ground, he had a plastic tarp to cover himself if and when it rained, a cup to eat and drink from, and a blanket for the cool evenings when they came. Aside from that, he needed nothing and had nothing. As he sat there in the early morning hours, he heard something. At first, he wasn't sure what it was. He thought it might have been a plane, if it was, it sounded like a slow moving propeller job.
****

0557 Hours
USS *Wisconsin*

"Turret One manned and ready" was heard, immediately followed by "Turret Two manned and ready" and "Turret Three manned and ready." Almost immediately, through the sound phones aboard ship, "Control, all turrets manned and ready" could be heard. Seventy-nine men in each of the ship's three sixteen-inch gun turrets waited in anticipation of the next command.

"Control, Command. Load!"

The order was quickly relayed to each turret. When each turret had completed its loading procedure of one shell and six powder bags, the control officer informed the ship's captain.

"Command, Control. Batteries ready."

"Control, Command. Fire!"

The nine sixteen-inch guns sounded together, launching nine two-thousand-pound shells twenty miles to the coast of the UAE—the first time they had fired a barrage like this since the Vietnam War.
****

Lance Corporal Harris didn't care for being inside the AAV or amphibious assault vehicle when it was swimming at eight miles per hour towards an unfriendly beach. The M242 Bushmaster 25mm gun along with the Mk 19 40mm grenade launcher and M2HB .50-caliber machine gun were a comfort, but they didn't overcome his discomfort when swimming. This discomfort had only begun when he'd found out the vehicle was manufactured by the FMC corporation—and not Ford Motor Company, but the Food Machinery and Chemical Corporation. He discussed the fact with the other twenty-five guys in his platoon that were riding with him, but it didn't seem to bother him.

"One minute," Gunny Cottle called out. Harris knew he would be on solid ground in one minute. *As long as no one else pukes, I'll be okay*, he was telling himself when he felt the vehicle lurch as it rolled ashore. The tracks pushed the vehicle for another minute before it came to a stop and dropped the back ramp. Everyone dashed off the vehicle and took up prone fighting positions, ready to meet the Iraqi Army. As Harris hit the ground and sighted his weapon, he realized they were surrounded by sheep and laying in sheep shit. He didn't see a lone individual not twenty feet in front of him.

"*Magandang umaga*," Santos said. Harris looked back at him and didn't know what to say.

"*Magandang umaga*," Sergeant Cottle replied to Santos. Cottle had taken a position right next to Harris. "He just wished us a good morning in Tagalog, the language of the Philippines. I learned some when I was stationed in Subic Bay on one of my many tours."

He turned back to Santos. "*Mayroon bang mga sundalong Iraqi dito?*"

"*Mayroon silang ilan sa pamamagitan ng Dubai at ng aliparan ngunit sa palagay ko hindi sila mga mandirigma.*" As Santos and Gunny Cottle were in conversation, the platoon leader, Lieutenant Duran, came over.

"Lieutenant, I just asked this gentleman if there were any Iraqi soldiers around here. He said there are some over in Dubai and at the airport, but he didn't think they were combat troops," Gunny Cottle explained.

"Give him a pack of cigarettes and let's mount up. Captain says we're headed for the airport," Lieutenant Duran ordered.

"You heard the lieutenant, load up," Cottle yelled. As he did so, he reached into his cargo pants pocket and produced a pack of cigarettes, which he handed to Santos.

"*Salamat*." Santos accepted the gift and nodded as Cottle headed for his vehicle.

Across the water, he could see the thirty-six ships that were delivering part of the 2nd Marine Division and support ships, to include the *Wisconsin* and the *Missouri*. Both were firing their big sixteen-inch guns at targets further inland that the AAI RQ-2 Pioneer UAV was spotting for the ship. It had spotted the Mi-24 Hinds that were on the receiving end of the naval gunfire.

Harris's battalion, 1st Battalion, 6th Marines, had been handed the mission to seize the north end of the Dubai International Airport. 6th Marines were going to secure the entire airport while 8th Marines and 10th Marines were attacking the 49th in the rear areas. They would then link up with the 1st Marine Division and the 1st British Armoured Division. Once they linked up with the 1st Marine Division, those 2nd Division assets that didn't participate in the amphibious landing would be able to rejoin the division. Getting their tanks back made everyone breathe a bit easier, although the attack helicopters were covering their movement.

"Hey, Gunny, we have an Iraqi Army convoy of trucks approaching us, and it looks like they're heading to Abu Dhabi," Lieutenant Cottle said as they approached the E11 highway from Dubai to Abu Dhabi.

"Sir, let's stop them and see what they have," Gunny offered.

"Driver, pull over. Everyone fan out," Cottle ordered, and everyone immediately complied. As they did so, Gunny walked out into the middle of Highway E11 and raised his hand like a traffic cop. A traffic cop with a Cobra Gunship right above him. The Iraqi convoy came to a stop. Slowly, an officer emerged from the first vehicle. His rank, as best as anyone could tell, was major. He slowly approached Lieutenant Cottle.

"I Major Mohammed. I am a staff officer with the 49th Transportation Battalion. We go Abu Dhabi for supplies. You let me pass. Yes?" Major Mohammed asked in his broken English.

"Afraid not, Major. You no go supply now. You prisoner now," Lieutenant Cottle said, taking the major's sidearm and motioning him to raise his arms. What surprised Cottle was the ever-growing smile on the major's face. He almost looked relieved to have been taken prisoner, that his part in this great war appeared to have been over and he had somehow survived it.

****

Lieutenant Colonel Brian Young's battalion, the 2nd Battalion, 6th Marines, was ashore in the first wave and, like everyone else in that first wave, his unit was surprised at the reception it received when they came ashore. Replaying in his mind the John Wayne movie *Sands of Iwo Jima*, he was expecting a major fight. Instead, he was met by some Pakistani guy selling fruit on the side of Highway E11. The fruit salesman couldn't care less about an invading force as long as the Marines would buy his bananas and papaya. Getting his battalion loaded back in their vehicles and moving to the airport took longer than he liked.

"Colonel, Cobra gunship reported taking fire from the main terminal building. He called for naval gunfire but was denied due to the damage it could cause," said Major Mike, the operations officer, who was riding in the command track with Colonel Young.

"Alright, get the word to the companies that they can expect small-arms fire but will not be able to use artillery or mortars without my clearance. Be sure the ANGLICO team knows that" Young directed. "Oh, and tell the companies no use of AT weapons except on Iraqi vehicles. I don't want them using AT-4s on buildings and blowing holes in the walls," Young added.

"Aye, sir," Major Mike said, picking up a hand mike to transmit the colonel's instructions.

Occasionally, the sound of a small-arms round could be heard pinging off the side of the amphibious assault vehicle or AAV. The gunner manning the .50-cal would return fire when he saw something worth shooting at. The Mk 19 grenade launcher attached to the turret was reserved for the more challenging targets. As the AAV bounced along,

Colonel Young reviewed his mission at the airport in his mind. Seize and secure the main terminal building, which was located on the southwest side of the airport, surrounded by smaller buildings. It was those smaller buildings that concerned him the most. Iraqi forces in those buildings could delay and impede his ability to quickly secure the main terminal. He had studied aerial photos of the airport as well as conducted a map recon. Rather than sticking to paved roads, his battalion was cutting cross-country and would come from the west into the airport complex. His battalion would pass between what appeared to be a housing development site and the outer buildings of the airport. This would position his battalion on the main road into the airport, giving them a straight shot to the terminal building. A Company would clear buildings on the left of the main road, B Company the buildings on the right side, and C Company would drive up the middle for the main terminal.

The Dubai airport was a major transportation hub, he recalled, starting as a hard-packed sand runway in 1957 before becoming what it was today, with the second paved runway just completed in 1983. Even the terminal building had been completed in 1983 with a second level. As they approached, it was obvious that someone had plans to build extensively around this airport. It was also obvious from the debris, craters and smoke that the big guns of one of the battleships had nailed a flight of Mi-24 Hind-D helicopters.

Young's thoughts were interrupted by Major Mike. "Sir, Alpha Company is about to crash the perimeter fence."

"Roger. What about Bravo?"

"Bravo is rolling up on his crossing point now."

"Good. Let's not bug them, but let them do their jobs. I'm sure they'll report if they get into something they can't handle."

For Colonel Young, this was the hard part—waiting for the first contact to be made—and he didn't have to wait long.

"Cavalier Six, Ambrose Six, over," a voice announced over the radio in an excited tone.

"Ambrose Six, Cavalier Six, go."

"Cavalier Six, we're in contact. Platoon-size element in the first two buildings on the left. All small-arms fire. No vehicles as yet. Over."

"Ambrose Six, roger, understood. Cavalier Six out." Tapping the AAV commander's leg to get his attention, Young indicated he wanted to move up for a better look. Major Mike knew what was coming next. *Son of a bitch, he's going to dismount and wants to get right into the middle of the firefight.* Major Mike was also keeping his ear tuned to the 6th Marine command net and listening to the reports from the other battalions that were moving into their assigned sectors around the airfield. No one else had reported any contact as yet.

"Hey, sir, don't you think we should wait to hear from Bravo Company before we get to Alpha and dismount?" Major Mike pointed out.

"The voice of reason... yeah, you're right," Young said, resigned to the fact that he was no longer a young lieutenant leading a group of hard-charging Devil Dogs. He knew his place was in the front, but with radios and communications and not running through the buildings like a private. The privilege of command was sometimes not as much fun as just being a Marine.

"Cavalier Six, Benevolent Six, over," came across the radio.

"Sir, Bravo Company is calling," Major Mike said, handing the handset to Young.

"Benevolent Six, Cavalier Six over."

"Cavalier Six, we've reached the outer parking lot at the main terminal. Our sector is clear. Do you want me to proceed to the main terminal? Over."

Major Mike and Young looked at each other in total surprise. *It can't be this easy*, Major Mike thought.

"Benevolent Six, roger, take it. Break. Campaign Six, Cavalier Six, over."

"Cavalier Six, Campaign Six, over."

"Campaign Six, bypass Ambrose Six's location and proceed to the main terminal building coming on Benevolent Six's left flank."

"Roger wilco," the Charlie Company commander acknowledged. The fight for the airport had begun.

Chapter 25
Love Fest

21 April 1991
III Corps Sector
Al Ain, United Arab Emirates

During the early-morning hours the day prior, elements of TF Sa'al had maneuvered to the north side of Al Ain while TF Abu Bakr had maneuvered to the south side. TF Tariq had made a show of force once the sun came up, keeping the attention of the Iraqi 1st Infantry Division in Al Ain. Loudspeakers accompanied TF Tariq and blared throughout the day that the Iraqi forces should surrender and prevent the destruction of the city. There was no intention of destroying Al Ain, but the Iraqi commander didn't know that, nor did the populace, which was in a panic. Leaflets were dropped from the air telling Iraqi soldiers to lay down their weapons and walk out. They would be treated well as prisoners for war. The city was nearly surrounded by the evening of April 20.

"General, we have a problem," Brigadier General Khalil Abdallah, commander of the Northern Omani Brigade, stated to Major General Muhannah Abbas, the commander of TF Sa'al.

"*We* have a problem, General? Or *you* have a problem and want to make it *my* problem?" Abbas asked with sarcasm dripping from each word. They did not get along as Abbas was a Saudi national and Abdallah was an Omani national. There had been a bit of a power struggle to see who the overall commander of the host nations would be, and Abdallah had lost.

"Well, it is my problem, but it is about to become your problem by close of business tomorrow," Abdallah said.

"And what is this problem I am about to have?" Abbas asked as he poured himself another cup of tea, not offering one to Abdallah.

"We are receiving prisoners from Al Ain. They are melting out of the city like goat's milk through cheesecloth. Tomorrow, either I won't be able to conduct combat operations as I will be guarding these people, or I can just tell them to walk back to Kuwait—or I can turn them over to you in a POW compound. What is your choice?" Abdallah asked.

"Don't be foolish. We cannot just turn them loose. They will simply rejoin other units," Abbas said, sipping his tea.

"So that gives you two choices. Which one will it be? Should I stop conducting combat operations or let you take them off my hands?" Abdallah said, starting to enjoy sticking it to Abdallah.

"Well, you cannot stop conducting combat operations. The III Corps commander expects us to lead the forces into Abu Dhabi. I cannot allow you to pull out to guard prisoners." Abbas had a worried look on his face.

"So that settles it. Where is the POW compound?" Abdallah asked. Abbas had not even thought about setting up a POW compound.

"I am sure that III Corps has designated a location and assigned some military police to establish such a place. I do not recall where it is. Go speak with Colonel Jabal, my operations officer, and he can tell you where it is located," Abbas said in a dismissive manner. "I have other important matters to attend to right now."

"In that case, General, I will leave you to your important matters. Have a good day," Abdallah said as he departed. He already knew exactly where the POW compound was and had been delivering prisoners there for the past four hours. He just wanted to jerk Abbas's chain a bit.
****

Sergeant Rami Habib was catching some sleep when someone kicked him gently in the foot. "Hey, Rami, wake up. Are you awake?" a familiar voice said.

"I am now, Lieutenant," Rami responded and was thinking, *I wonder if the American lieutenants are as dumb as this one.* "Why is it necessary to wake me? I was having a beautiful dream. She was just—"

"Listen, do you smell that?" Lieutenant Iqbal said.

Rami sat up and sniffed the air for a moment. "I don't hear anything, Lieutenant, but I do smell fresh-baked bread."

"I think it is coming from that house over there on the edge of town. It has a light on and I have seen a couple of guys go in. Maybe we should go over and get some fresh bread for the platoon," Iqbal suggested. With that, Rami stood up and they cautiously walked the two hundred meters to the house. Rami entered first and immediately noticed six Iraqi soldiers waiting to buy bread. Suddenly, he was grabbed from behind in a headlock. He struggled as the Iraqi soldier began rubbing his knuckles on Rami's head, just like his older brother had done when he was little. A swift elbow into the Iraqi's stomach released the headlock, and Rami turned and swung his fist into the Iraqi soldier's jaw. He was winding up for another punch when the Iraqi started laughing.

"You still punch like a girl," the Iraqi said. Rami then realized it was his brother!

"Jamal, what are you doing here and in that uniform?" Rami said, rubbing his fist.

"Rami, when the Iraqis overran Kuwait City, they rounded up all the young men. We had a choice—join the Iraqi Army or be shipped to Iraq to work in their factories. I chose this. We all chose this," he said, pointing at the others in Iraqi uniforms. "We are all from Kuwait City." The others were all smiling now.

"Rami, you must take us prisoner and get us out of here. There is almost no food in the city and morale is very low. They are just waiting for you to invade the city. Everyone is afraid of the planes and bombs. Please take us prisoner," Jamal pleaded. Rami looked at Lieutenant Iqbal, who was as surprised as anyone.

"Rami, is he truly your brother?" Iqbal asked.

"Yes, he is," Rami said as he threw his arm over his brother's shoulder.

"Then you may take them all prisoner and march them back to our positions. They must leave their weapons, and don't forget to get the bread, but we must hurry. You will probably be promoted for capturing so many of the enemy, but don't tell anyone he is your brother—otherwise you can forget the promotion. And stop hugging each other. It is embarrassing."

Chapter 26
Counterattack

21 April 1991
VII Corps Section
Asab, United Arab Emirates

VII Corps lead elements had broken through the frontline units of the 45th Iraqi Division and had pushed as far as Asab and Alyhyali. What hadn't been destroyed of the 45th consisted of either prisoners or those fleeing toward Zayed City or Ghayathi. General Shitnah had made it clear that the road to Zayed City was not to be used but left open for the 52nd Armoured Division to use in a counterattack. That plan was now falling by the wayside as units of the 45th were in true panic mode. Instead, the 52nd Armoured Division was heading across the desert to Asab.

"Rolling Thunder Three, Sabre Six," the commander of the 3rd Armored Cav Regiment said, calling the G-3 for the 24th Mechanized Infantry Division.

The 3rd Armored Cav, commonly referred to as the 3rd Herd, had worked with the 24th in many training exercises at the National Training Center at Fort Irwin, California. The Cav's mission was to screen ahead of the VII Corps and determine where the enemy's main thrust would come from. They would also screen the flanks of the Corps to ensure no surprise attack approached from the sides.

"Sabre Six, Rolling Thunder Three, go ahead."

"Rolling Thunder Three, have identified lead elements of enemy formation. Appears to be two brigades' abreast vicinity Hotel Juliet Tree Four Seven Four Eight Niner. Break. Artillery positions, two batteries, vicinity Hotel Juliet Tree Four Seven Four Eight Niner. How copy?"

This was the information Rolling Thunder Three wanted and could respond to. Sabre Six's information was passed to all the units of the Corps, and the Corps operations officer was able to respond to this new threat.

An hour later, the 24th Mech's G-3 called, "Sabre Six, Rolling Thunder Three, over."

"Rolling Thunder Three, Sabre Six, over."

"Sabre Six, contact Vulture Six, over."

"Roger, QSY at this time." Sabre Six changed frequencies. "Vulture Six, Sabre Six, over."

"Sabre Six, Vulture Six, I understand you have targets, over."

"Roger, two brigades." Sabre Six provided the locations and then ordered, "Commence attack in one-five mikes. How copy? Over."

"Vulture Six copies and is moving into position."

Vulture Six was the commander of the 12th Combat Aviation Brigade. He had forty AH-1 Apache helicopters, each armed with eight AGM-114 Hellfire antitank missiles with a range of eleven kilometers. Their attack was being timed to take place at the same time as the ground forces being attacked. As the armor and mechanized forces launched their attack, the Apaches would engage the deep targets deeper in the enemy formations and targets on the flanks of the attacking force. This combined ground and helicopter attack was designed to overwhelming the enemy force leaving them little to no chance of escape.

****

Captain Matt Poggi maneuvered his company of M1 tanks on the right flank of his battalion, 3-69 Armor. The engagements at Medina Ridge had taught him some valuable lessons about tank engagements. This was not his first rodeo; however, for the other company commanders in the battalion, it was their first combat engagement.

"All Black Panther elements, Black Panther Six. Hold short of this next ridge until we see what's on the other side," came over the radio. Matt recognized the voice of the battalion commander. The ridge was another three hundred meters to their front, and so Renshaw, the tank's driver, began to slow the vehicle and was just barely moving forward as they approached the top of the ridge. Poggi couldn't believe his eyes as the turret crested the ridge. An entire Iraqi tank battalion was spread out before him at about two thousand meters. He didn't need to request permission to engage. That decision had already been made for him on the command radio.

"All Black Panther elements, engage!"

Poggi relayed the order to his company, and they did as they had trained to do, hitting vehicles on the flanks first and working into the middle. The Iraqi T-72 tanks continued to press the attack and were

145

dying in doing so. The rate of fire of the T-72, although equipped with an autoloading system, it couldn't keep up with a well-trained crew of an Abram's rate of fire. In addition, the accuracy of the T-72s at that range couldn't be matched by the M1s while on the move; their gun systems didn't have the same type of stabilizer system the M1s had. And lastly, the T-72's accuracy diminished significantly at ranges of over nine hundred meters while the M1 tank's accuracy was excellent out to twenty-five hundred meters.

Poggi was concentrating on the overall battle while his master gunner, SSG Hernandez, concentrated on fighting his tank. As Poggi watched in his buttoned-up turret, a flash in the distance and on the flanks caught his attention. Then there were more flashes when he realized that a flight of AH-1 Apache helicopters was on the flanks and engaging enemy vehicles as they saw them. Those Apaches were hitting the follow-on brigade of the 52nd Division or the artillery positions and tearing them apart. That likely meant they wouldn't be dealing with wave after wave of enemy tanks and armored vehicles.

Twenty minutes later, all was quiet. In front of Poggi's position, beginning at one thousand meters, there were forty-two destroyed and burning Iraqi tanks, and that was just in front of his position. Across the battalion front, columns of black smoke from burning vehicles appeared as an orchard of waving black trees. Thankfully not one of the battalion's tanks had taken a hit and no one was wounded. Poggi, like all the soldiers, stared at the sight of what lay before them with mixed emotions. No one cheered; some wept as they were emotionally drained. The counterattack by the 52nd Iraqi Armoured Division had failed.

Chapter 27
Decisions

22 April 1991
1st Republican Guard HQ
Al Hofuf, Saudi Arabia

All night long, reports had been coming in from both Baghdad and frontline units about the battle raging in the UAE. Baghdad was reporting success, but that wasn't the word coming up from the frontline troops. General al-Dulaymi had gotten tired of the conflicting information, and on the previous evening, he'd sent two Mi-8 Hip helicopters to the UAE to report back on what they were seeing. Their report was disturbing.

"Get me Tahia al-Rawi on the phone," he instructed his aide. Tahai al-Rawi was the overall commander of the Republican Guard forces and worked directly under Saddam's son. Minutes later, the call went through to a palace in Kuwait City, where al-Rawi was enjoying life.

"Sir, what have you heard about the actions in the UAE?" al-Dulaymi asked.

"We have heard some glowing reports from Baghdad about the success of the IX Corps. Why, what have you heard?" Al-Rawi had learned in the Iraq-Iran War that not everything coming out of Baghdad could be trusted.

"My frontline units are reporting that they have been getting stragglers and elements passing through their lines all night. Reports of complete units being taken prisoner. Whole brigades of tanks being destroyed. I—" He didn't get to finish.

"Al-Dulaymi, I am sure that there have been some setbacks with some units, but let's not panic over a few minor losses," al-Rawi said.

"Sir, I sent two helicopters on a scout mission down there to see for ourselves. They had no problem finding the 52nd Armoured Division at night as their burning tanks have lit up the sky. The scouts couldn't make contact with the IX Corps headquarters either. They did see numerous American vehicles, all moving towards Abu Dhabi and along the coast road. What do you want me to do?" al-Dulaymi asked. There was a long pause before al-Rawi spoke.

"Hold your positions. If the situation is that bad, a counterattack would be foolish. Prepare to defend your current positions and I will get back to you. I must speak with al-Tikrit and al-Tai."
****

The phone call from Kuwait City to Baghdad was easier to make than the one from the front lines. Baghdad had seen some strategic bombing attacks, but nothing like what was taking place across the UAE and parts of Saudi Arabia and Kuwait. When Al-Rawi was able to connect with the people he needed to reach in the capital, he arranged for a conference call with Ibraham Ahmed Ard al-Tikrit, the Armed Forces Chief of Staff, and Sultan Hashim Ahmed al-Tai, the Defense Minister once everyone could be found and brought in on the call.

"What have you heard from the IX Corps?" al-Rawi asked, trying to sound respectful.

"We received a report late yesterday afternoon that the Americans had launched their offense and that Shitnah was committing the 52nd Armoured Division. After that, we have not had communications with them as the Americans are now jamming all of our radio frequencies," al-Tikrit explained.

"Well, I can tell you what al-Dulaymi is telling me. He has IX Corps personnel and scattered units passing through his lines in a panic. He sent scout helicopters to report, and they found the 52nd Division in flames and the Americans on the coast road. From what they could observe, the UAE is no longer in our control. They could raise no one from IX Corps command," al-Rawi said.

"If the Americans have overrun the IX Corps, then you should have al-Dulaymi counterattack immediately," al-Tai, the defense minister, stated with some trepidation in his voice. Before becoming Defense Minister, al-Tai had been one of the most respected and experienced combat commanders in Iraqi.

"And where do you suggest they counterattack? They cannot just plunge off into the desert looking for the Americans. The American Air Force would love that. It would be easy pickings seeing our tanks rolling out in the open. Without air superiority, we cannot go on the offensive," al-Rawi replied.

"Al-Tikrit, have you not heard anything from Shitnah? IX Corps is your responsibility—they report to you. What are you doing to regain contact with them?" al-Tai asked with a slightly elevated voice. There was no love lost between al-Tikrit and al-Rawi. Al-Tikrit was feeling the heat at this point.

"I will have to get back to you. The situation in the UAE is very confusing right now due to the jammed frequencies and the lack of communications with IX Corps. I am sure the situation is not as bad as al-Dulaymi is saying," al-Tikrit responded, trying to sound more optimistic than the news they were receiving was.

"Do you think he would make up a story like this? Do you think he wants to charge off into the desert with his divisions when we do not have air superiority? He would be insane to do so," al-Rawi almost yelled.

"Alright, enough!" al-Tai demanded. He knew the dislike between the commanders of the Republican Guard forces and the regular Army forces. "We cannot be having a fight amongst ourselves at this point. Here is what I want done. Find out what the situation is with the IX Corps and find out fast. Have the 1st Republican Guard Corps immediately put on alert to move so if we can execute a counterattack, they will be ready. We cannot let the Americans break out of the UAE, if it is in fact true that they have overrun the IX Corps. Let us have another call at noon," al-Tai said. Others agreed and understood their marching orders.
****

The high-level meeting at the Ministry of Defense featured all the military leaders responsible for the war and the defense of the country. With everyone present, the meeting got underway now that they had a better picture of what was going on in the UAE.

The meeting was being chaired by Tariq Aziz, the Deputy Prime Minister. He had called the meeting as he wanted to understand the situation and develop an approach on what to tell Saddam. Heads might roll over the outcome of this meeting.

"So, General al-Duri, would you be kind enough to explain what has happened in the UAE and with IX Corps?" Aziz began, wanting to get this meeting started.

"Mr. Deputy Prime Minister, on the morning of April twentieth, the Americans launched an attack from several points in Oman, striking the IX Corps positions. In the north, an attack was made by the US Marines and a British armoured division. In the center, the city of Al Ain was surrounded by a combination of Saudi and Kuwaiti forces. To the south, the two Egyptian divisions and two American divisions hit the 17th and 10th Armoured Divisions. The penetration was made in the south by the American VII Corps with four divisions. On the morning of April twenty-first, the Americans launched an over-the-beach landing between Abu Dhabi and Dubai, resulting in the capture of Dubai. That afternoon, IX Corps launched a counterattack with the 52nd Armoured Division. When the 52nd Armoured Division executed its counterattack, American attack helicopters joined the ground forces and engaged them. Our losses were significant. The Americans, according to CNN, have taken many prisoners in the process," General al-Duri explained.

"And to what do you attribute the Americans' success thus far?" Aziz asked as a follow-up question.

"I believe two factors contributed to the Americans' success. First, they had a superior-size ground force with a well-established logistic base. I said all along we should have been bombing their supply bases and sinking their ships, but—" General al-Duri was cut off midsentence when Aziz raised his hand.

"And the second reason, please," Aziz called in a calm voice. He realized that this could get out of hand quickly with finger-pointing.

"The Americans have air superiority. Our air force has not been seen in days. As long as the Americans control the sky, we are not capable of mounting an offensive operation," General al-Duri said.

Hamid Raja Shalah al-Tikriti took offense and jumped into the discussion. "So you're blaming this failure by the IX Corps on the air force, who have been the only thing holding the Americans at bay thus far. How dare you?"

"Gentlemen, let's keep this civil," Aziz said, restoring calm. "We are not here to place any blame but to determine what we must do for the future. The question really is, do we counterattack with the 1st Republican Guard Corps, do we hold in place and defend, or do we begin withdrawing? What are your recommendations?"

There was silence in the room as no one wanted to lead off this discussion. Finally, Ibrahim Ahmed Abd al-Sattan al-Tikrit spoke up. "As we do not know the location of the American divisions and cannot reach their logistic bases, or attack them from the flank across the empty quarter, I think it would be foolish for us to commit the 1st Republican Guard Corps to a counterattack, especially without air support, limited as it may be," al-Tikrit said.

"Do we all agree with this position? Is anyone opposed to this?" Aziz asked. With glum looks, they all nodded in agreement.

"So what is our best course of action given the current situation, then?" Aziz asked, looking at those seated at the conference table.

Sayf al-Din Fulayyih Hassan al-Rawi spoke up. "The Republican Guard are our most powerful and best trained soldiers and unit. We cannot waste them needlessly. The 2nd Republican Guard Corps has already held the Americans at Medina and needs to be withdrawn and refitted. I think we should withdraw both the 1st and 2nd Republican Guard Corps and bring them back to Kuwait, where they will have time to put in a proper defense to repel any attempt by the Americans to force their way into Kuwait. If you had left the 1st Republican Guard Corps in the UAE, this disaster would not have happened. Let the IV Iraqi Corps assume the entire defense of Saudi Arabia and pull the Guard Corps back."

Initially no one responded. They were all thinking the same thing. Al-Rawi spoke directly to Qusay—no one wanted to get on his bad side. They'd all heard the rumors about his zoo near the airport and how he liked to feed his pet animals…with dissenters and people who had gotten on his bad side. For him, it was entertainment.

Finally, Aziz asked, "How vulnerable will we be by making this move, and can the IV Corps stop the Americans?"

"The IV Corps has eight divisions and should be able to slide east to meet the Americans. Behind them would be the VII Corps, which has been in position since the beginning and can reinforce the IV. I think this would hold the Americans for some time for the 2nd and 1st Republican Guard Corps to be prepared," the Armed Forces Chief of Staff said.

Aziz thought about this suggestion for a moment and looked at the faces staring at him. It would be his decision. "Al-Tai, what do you think?" Aziz asked.

"I think this would be our best course of action, but what about the American XVIII Airborne Corps over in the west? What can we expect of them?" al-Tai asked the room in general.

"I am not worried about them. They are along the Red Sea, and just like II Corps, if they attempt to come west, their logistic tail will be so long, they will run out of supplies long before they reach Kuwait. The forces coming out of the UAE are our threat right now," al-Rawi answered.

"Then, gentlemen, I will recommend this course of action to Saddam. Prepare your forces for the moves, which should commence immediately unless you hear otherwise from me."

Chapter 28
Offensive Pause

23 April 1991
VII Corps HQ
Al Ruwais, United Arab Emirates

The VII Corps had sliced through the 52nd Armoured division and left nothing but burning Iraqi tanks and infantry fighting vehicles in its wake. The lead elements had reached the coastal highway in the early-morning hours, which was clogged with more Iraqi vehicles attempting to flee from Abu Dhabi and Dubai. Both VII and III Corps had a large population of prisoners, much more than was expected or anticipated, especially this early in the offensive. In addition, by a Joint Forces agreement, the Army was also responsible for taking in any prisoners captured by the Marines or Air Force. Brigadier General Joseph Conlon III was the commander of the 800th Military Police Brigade and responsible for the construction and maintenance of the POW camps. He was a reservist and had served in the reserves for twenty-seven years. In the civilian world, he was a full-time detective with the Suffolk County Police Department in New York.

"Bring him in," General Franks said to his adjutant.

A moment later, General Conlon appeared through the door of the office that VII Corps had taken over for its headquarters. Conlon noticed Franks straining to stand to meet him. "Please, sir, no need for you to stand. Very glad to meet you," Conlon said, knowing that Franks had lost a leg in Vietnam and it was probably bothering him about now.

"Well, thank you, sir. Please take a seat. How is my POW situation?" Franks asked.

"Sir, that question is a double-edged sword. It's good that you're capturing a large number of POWs, but it's bad that we're taking in more than we currently have the capacity to hold. We had constructed three POW camps at this point. One a small one in the MARCENT sector, one in the III Corps sector, and one in your sector. The plan was and still is that once we've secured the UAE, one large camp will be built and all the prisoners moved there, and the UAE will take responsibility for their feeding, sanitation, and medical needs. Those three camps are currently filled to capacity with eight thousand prisoners in each camp, but the UAE hasn't designated an adequate facility to handle twenty-four thousand prisoners. If this trend continues, we could be looking at over a hundred thousand prisoners. The Saudis have indicated that they'll take Iraqi prisoners off our hands once we move into Saudi Arabia, but not before, which sort of makes sense. They're planning on putting all the prisoners at Umm Athelah, as it's in the middle of nowhere but does have adequate freshwater wells and springs. They figure that once they get them there on the one road in the area, they just have to provide shade with haji tents. No need to put up wire or guard towers… there's no place for the prisoners to go, and if they did leave, they would be dead in three days from a lack of water."

"Why don't we do that?" Franks asked, half-joking.

"Wish we could, but we're a signatory to the Geneva Convention. Saudi is not, although they do honor it. We have to go a step further, and I think the Saudis will as well as we've offered to put a medical unit with their camp."

"Okay, so what can I do for you?" Franks asked.

"Sir, I've discussed this with the other Corps commanders, and they said if you would agree, they would as well. Your force is positioned the best to continue pressing the Iraqis right now. But if you could hold off for forty-eight hours from launching any further attacks, then we can turn the prisoners we've taken thus far over to the UAE and move three of the camps we've established into your sector for the next phase of operations?" Conlon explained.

"General, you're asking the wrong guy. Yeosock is going to have to sign off on this. I wouldn't mind a forty-eight-hour pause to rearm, refuel and pull some maintenance. Go talk to Yeosock, and if he approves or asks, I'll back you up," Franks said.

"Oh God, thank you so much, sir," Conlon said as he stood and saluted. He wasn't sure how General Franks was going to respond to his request. Knowing he was going to back his play made him feel a lot better.

Franks returned the salute from his chair and with a smile said, "Now get out of here. My leg is killing me and I want it off. Damn sand gets into it and rubs the hell out of my leg."

****

"General Yeosock, General Franks is on the line for you, sir," a voice said over the intercom, and Yeosock immediately picked up the phone.

"Fred, how are you doing?" Yeosock asked jovially. With the success of the campaigns, he was feeling pretty good these days.

"Good. I just had a visit from your chief MP, General Conlon. He asked if we could pause the attack for forty-eight hours because of all the POWs we're bringing in. Their pens are at capacity until we get more built or transfer the POWs to local control. What do you think?"

"Yeah, I heard he was making the rounds with you guys, begging for mercy. He has a point. We certainly didn't expect the Iraqis to be throwing in the towel this quickly once the ground war got going. I figured we'd eventually take a hundred thousand or so prisoners, but not in the first few weeks. This is kind of crazy. Would delaying forty-eight hours to give Conlon and his crew some extra time be a problem for you?"

"No. It would give us a short rest for the troops—a chance to refuel, rearm and pull some maintenance. It would give the supply guys a chance to move stores forward for the next push. I don't think it could hurt. In fact, it would give the Air Force a chance to pound on the 1st Republican Guard Corps before we get there," Franks explained.

"You haven't heard? The 1st Republican Guard Corps may not be there when you arrive. Intel got some message traffic between General al-Rawi, the commander of 1st Republican Guard Corps, and Hassan al-Rawi, the overall Republican Guard commander. Seems they're pulling the 1st Corps back to Kuwait and sliding the 4th Army Corps over to take their place. They're doing the same with the 2nd Republican Guard Corps over in Medina, pulling them back as well. They think since XVIII Airborne is going north that they may make a hook around and come at Kuwait from the west, so they want the II Iraqi Corps to be positioned to repel that. I guess they figure that the 2nd Republican Guard Corps will stand a better chance out of the mountains and in the open desert," Yeosock explained.

"Damn, now would be the ideal time to hit them, then," Franks said, surprise in his voice.

"Or the worst. It could be a trap to get us to attack with really just your corps and have you taking on the 1st Republican Guard when the 4th hits you in the flank. We're really not in a position to bring the III Corps or the Marines up on the line with you. If we were, then I would agree with you, but since we're not...," Yeosock said, not finishing his sentence.

"So we take a forty-eight-hour standdown is what I'm hearing," Franks announced.

"Yeah, I'll run it by Norm. I think he'll understand. Push out your cav regiment, but avoid decisive engagements. And your attack helicopters can go hunting too. How's the leg?" Yeosock inquired, referring to the leg Franks had lost in Vietnam.

"Hurts like hell."

****

The day had been long, hot and dusty for the members of D/3-69 Armor. They were down to less than fifty percent ammunition on the main gun and equally low on the .50-cal ammo. Water was another low point. When the order came to hold in place, it was a welcome call. As the evening approached, everyone dismounted and began pulling the operator's maintenance as well as resupplying the tanks with ammo and water. Fuel trucks would be around later in the night to top each tank off.

"Hey, Lieutenant Bagel, how long before we move out?" called out Staff Sergeant Scovel, a tank commander on one of the tanks in Bagel's platoon. His tank was thirty meters from Bagel's.

"Not sure. Captain Poggi didn't say. Said for us to just get ready to move as quick as we could, but he didn't know how long it would be before we did move out. Dismount, but keep someone on guard in the vehicles. Get some chow, some water and some sleep. Tank commanders, come over and let's review today and look at what might be tomorrow when you have a chance," Bagel ordered.

Ten minutes later, the three noncommissioned officers that were tank commanders converged on Lieutenant Bagel. Staff Sergeant Scovel was accompanied by Staff Sergeant Weik and Staff Sergeant Hanner. They each took a five-gallon water can for a seat. At night, it wasn't a good idea to sit on the sand, especially if one was a tanker and had other choices. Infantry soldiers could get in the dirt, but not tankers. You

156

wanted to try and keep as much of that fine sand and dirt out of the tank as possible, not unintentionally track or bring it in with you.

"Okay, let's look at what we did good today and what we did not so good," Bagel started off.

"Sir, I thought our fire discipline was pretty good. We were paced and accurate and we maximized the capabilities of the vehicles," Staff Sergeant Weik said.

"I agree, but we sort of fell short of designating targets. I noticed several times that some targets were getting two hits at almost the same time. We were shooting out of our lane on those occasions. In essence, we wasted some ammo," Staff Sergeant Scovel pointed out.

"We also lost track of target priorities at one point, I noticed," Staff Sergeant Hanner added.

"What do you mean?" Lieutenant Bagel asked for clarification. This was the first he was hearing about this.

"Well, sir, I noticed that at one point this morning when we were cresting the ridge, some of us, and I won't say who, were engaging the BMPs of the 52 and a few BTRs instead of tanks. The priority is tanks for us and air-defense vehicles next. Let the grunts take out the BMPs and BTRs," Staff Sergeant Hanner said.

"Let's work on all these points tomorrow. I still don't know what the plan is for the future, but—"

"*Alsalam alaykum warahmat allah wabarakatuh,*" came a voice out of the dark of night. All four Americans grabbed their weapons and immediately dove for the ground. They could see nothing in the darkness, and their night vision goggles were on the tank.

Bagel racked his brain to remember the Arabic phrase he wanted. Someone had said hello and peace be upon you, but what was the one he needed right now? Then it came. "*Aqtarab mae rafe yadayka.*"

"What did you just tell them, Lieutenant? I didn't know you spoke Arabic," Weik commented.

"I don't, but I learned a few phrases when you were reading comic books," Bagel replied. Slowly images began to appear before them, which grew into men doing just what the lieutenant had told them to do. The four Americans stood slowly with their weapons raised.

"Do you speak English?" Bagel called out as the Iraqi soldiers approached.

"I can a little," a voice replied. "Can we have some water, American?"

"Stop right there and sit down in the sand. Keep your hands above your heads," Bagel ordered. Slowly the turret of Bagel's tank rotated towards the Iraqi soldiers. SSG Adams, Bagel's master gunner, had heard the conversation and wanted to be sure he had the Iraqis covered.

Cautiously the four approached the group of Iraqi soldiers. Bagel began counting the compliant group. There were thirty soldiers sitting there. More of Bagel's soldiers heard the situation and came over to assist in the processing of the POWs. Some were sent to get water after each Iraqi was searched for weapons or explosives. Three cases of MREs, Meals Ready-to-Eat, were given to the Iraqi soldiers along with a demonstration on how to eat them. Some of them looked half-starved.

"Sergeant Weik, take charge here. I've got to report this to the CO. He's not going to believe me," Bagel said.

The CO believed him as the same scene repeated throughout the night across the entire front line of VII Corps. The Iraqi Army units were trying to surrender before the American tankers were able to get going again and started their murderous blitzkrieg across the desert again or the Air Force swooped out of the sky to plaster them with more bombs.

Chapter 29
Night Drop

20 April 1991
1st Brigade, 82nd Airborne
Jeddah, Saudi Arabia

Thirty-one C-130 Hercules aircraft were lined up on the tarmac at Jeddah airport. It was just after midnight and the soldiers knew that in a matter of hours they would be jumping into the start of Operation Desert Storm. As Colonel Kinser stood amongst the troops, he witnessed confidence and professionalism in the soldiers, noncommissioned officers and officers of *his* brigade.

The flight to the objective would be four hours long, so it was decided for everyone to chute up in the hangar and conduct the jumpmaster inspections there. The first order of business for each soldier was to drain their bladders as, once chuted up, you did not have the capability to take another piss, unless it was in your pants. Officers and NCOs were wandering through the soldiers, making sure that everything attached to rucksacks and the soldiers' LBE was properly fastened. Soldiers were assisting each other with their chutes and attaching their equipment, such as their M-4 rifles, Dragon rounds, radios, and AT-4 antitank rounds. Completely prepared for a combat jump, each soldier had about one hundred and sixty pounds of equipment on his body.

Finally, the word came over a series of loudspeakers: "Jumpers, man your planes."

With the aid of others, paratroopers struggled to get to their feet, helping the man behind them in the stick. Once everyone was standing, the soldiers proceeded towards the aircraft in four lines, each representing a stick. Each C-130 held sixty jumpers with fifteen soldiers in each stick, two rows down the middle of the aircraft, and a row on each side of the aircraft. Once the individuals were loaded, a pallet was loaded on each ramp that would be dropped after the soldiers, containing rations, ammo, batteries for radios, and other miscellaneous items. Finally, all the doors were closed and the engines moved each aircraft towards the runway.

Once airborne, the flight of aircraft moved out over the Red Sea, safely away from enemy air-defense weapons. Fighter aircraft watched over the flight of paratroopers, protecting them from any enemy fighters that might venture into the area. Inside each aircraft, most paratroopers went to sleep with their arms folded on top of their reserve parachutes and their heads resting on their arms. If they were tired enough, paratroopers could sleep anywhere in any conditions. The inside lights were turned off as well to aid them in sleeping, and the air conditioner was on to help prevent airsickness.

Suddenly, the interior lights came on. Soldiers began waking up and looking around. The two jumpmasters were standing by the back doors and talking to the aircraft loadmaster and crew chief. Both turned and faced the soldiers, holding their hands up with their fingers spread apart.

In unison, they shouted, "Ten minutes!" The soldiers knew the next ten minutes would pass quickly, especially once the six-minute warning was given. These four minutes were built in so they could wake up, tighten chin straps, and put away any paperback books or letters they might be reading or writing.

Again in unison, the jumpmasters shouted, "Six minutes!" holding up six fingers and immediately followed by the command....

"Outboard personnel, stand up!" Both jumpmasters raised their arms up from their sides with palms up. Struggling under the weight of parachutes and combat equipment, the paratroopers seated along the sides of the plane stood and formed one line.

Once the outboard soldiers were standing, the next command was given. "Inboard personnel, stand up." Those still seated stood and formed their own line.

"Hook up!" The command was given with the jumpmasters' index fingers raised above their heads in a hook position.

A moment later, when they were sure everyone had connected their static line to the anchor cable and inserted the safety pin, they gave the next command. "Sound off with equipment check."

The man in the last position inspected the equipment of the man in front of him, starting at the static line and tracing it to the parachute, ensuring that the static line wasn't wrapped around something that would prevent the parachute from opening. Once he did that, he turned, as did the soldier in front of him, and that soldier would check the last man's equipment. Satisfied, he slapped the rear thigh on the left side and sounded off with his stick number: "Fifteen okay." That continued until the first man in the stick pointed at the jumpmaster and announced, "All okay."

Moments later, the side doors on the C-130 opened and the jumpmasters commenced their checks to make sure there were no sharp edges along the door that could cut the static line after the jumper left the plane. They also hung out the door to see the drop zone to be sure that they weren't over water in this case. Satisfied, the jumpmasters stepped back and commanded the first jumper to stand in the door. As the jumper did so, he noticed the red light next to the door and stared intensely at it until it turned green. Before the jumpmaster could scream "Go!" the first jumper was gone and the stick was rapidly passing through the door. In less than fifteen seconds, the plane was empty of all sixty jumpers. The time was 0430 on G-Day.

****

Staff Sergeant Lopez enjoyed night jumps. The air was cooler and the wind was almost nonexistent, which made for softer landings. He stepped out of the C-130 in his tucked position and knew he had a good exit when he noticed that he was immediately looking up at the tail of the plane and then just as quickly he had swung one hundred and eighty degrees and was looking at the ground. With two more milder rotations, the chute settled down and he was able to concentrate on the business at hand. *Check canopy. Yeah, it looks good. Anyone around me or under me? Nope, good there. Where's those damn power lines the lieutenant told us about? Over there, good. And the ocean, way over there, good. Wow, the port's lit up like a Christmas tree. Looks like I'll be landing in the sand. Should be softer than on that road. Okay, release my rucksack. Feet and knees together, toes pointed down, don't reach for the ground.... just wait for it...*

"*Umpf!*" was the only sound he made as first his feet hit, then his calves and thighs and lastly his hips. Once on the ground, he made short work of getting out of his parachute harness. As he did, another jumper landed next to him. Before the other jumper could get out of his harness, Lopez heard the first shots being fired.

161

"Who are you and what unit?" Lopez asked the other jumper, helping him out of his harness.

"Sergeant Lopez, it's me, Jergenson."

"You okay?" Lopez asked.

"I'm good," Jergenson replied, grabbing his rucksack.

"Alright, let's round up the rest of the squad and get going," Lopez directed. The squad, platoon and company had prearranged rally points that were easily identified as they descended. This allowed the company to quickly assembly off the drop zone and move on to their assigned objective. Lopez's company had been assigned a sector on the south side of the port. Within the sector was a compound consisting of seven large buildings and several smaller buildings. Intel told the company that it was a living area for dockyard workers, but they didn't know much more than that.

Moving to the rally point, Lopez found his platoon leader, Lieutenant Bertone.

"Lopez, grab your squad and take point. We're going to clear this first building on the southeast corner. It's a two-story building, supposedly a barracks-type building." He pointed to it on his map. "I'll follow with the rest of the platoon when it's assembled. Questions?" Bertone asked.

"No questions, sir," Lopez said, standing up and motioning his squad to follow him.

As they moved off, he directed, "Jergenson, take point," and Jergenson moved out at a brisk walk to put a distance of twenty meters between him and the squad. Through his night vision goggles or NODs, Sergeant Lopez could follow Jergenson's movements and hand signals. The ground was level and consisted of hard-packed sand, so movement was fairly easy but devoid of any concealment. If anyone was watching, they were sitting ducks. The one piece of concealment was several trees and bushes along the base of the building, which would restrict some visibility of their movement. As they moved forward, Lopez noticed a single commercial ship sitting at the dock in front of a warehouse. Small-arms tracer rounds could be seen in both red and green colors coming from the direction of the warehouses. *Someone is in a firefight*, Lopez thought.

At two hundred yards from the building, Jergenson suddenly took a knee and threw up the hand signal to stop: a closed fist. Everyone immediately imitated his move. All except for Lopez, who, in a crouched run, came forward to Jergenson.

"Sarge, I heard voices. Someone's awake and moving outside the building," Jergenson said in a low whisper. Immediately, Lopez motioned for fire team A to move off to the right and set up an overwatch position. Then he motioned for fire team B to join him.

"There's someone moving around outside the building. A team is in overwatch. B, you're going to fan out, and we're going to approach. If we take fire, you know what to do," Lopez said.

"Roger, Sarge," the team leader answered.

"Alright, let's move out," Lopez instructed, and Bravo team began to fan out, creating a separation of fifteen to twenty feet between team members. They moved at a brisk walk, not wanting to spend too much time exposed if someone was aiming at them. They reached the outside walls of the building without incident. Lopez waited until Alpha team joined them before he issued instructions.

"Alpha, you take the front door. Bravo, take the back. Watch the window to make sure no one jumps out of a window to go warn others, so leave two people outside until the building is cleared. Bravo, give Alpha one minute before you come in. Just like we did in training at Fort Bragg. Let's go."

As they moved into position, suddenly all the lights came on in the building. *Shit, we've lost the element of surprise. No need to be crafty and silent now. Let's get 'er done*, Lopez thought as the first member of Alpha team hit the front door and the second member charged through the broken door and frame. The rest of the team was right behind him, weapons raised, fingers just millimeters from the triggers of their automatic weapons. In front of them were thirty Arab men with wide grins, holding little American flags. A "WELCOME AMERICANS" sign hung over their heads. They began cheering and approaching the soldiers, who had not lowered their weapons. Suddenly the grins disappeared from the Arabs' faces. One stepped forward.

"You American, yes?" He was hesitant in his speech.

"Yes, we American paratroopers. Who are you?" Lopez asked.

The grin returned as the Arab turned and said something to the group. Facing Lopez again, he said, "We work port. We like Americans. We afraid Saddam's soldiers come back. Welcome ... want cold beer?"

Suddenly, the weapons were lowered, and new friendships developed.

Chapter 30
Linkup

24 April 1991
FOB Copperhead
Prince Abdul Majeed bin Abdulaziz Airfield

The 1st Brigade had designated the airfield outside of Mogayra as FOB Copperhead. The 2nd Brigade had begun arriving the day before but remained on the airfield, preparing to go forward and seize the next objective that would support the 28th Infantry Division's move forward. The 28th Infantry was moving across fairly open terrain and had pretty much chewed up the 51st Iraqi Division, leaving only one regiment intact. That regiment was conducting a delay action, sniping at the 28th but not doing any serious damage to the forward progress of the division. 2nd Brigade would fly out once the linkup with the 29th was completed with the 1st Brigade. Their objective lay eighty-three miles to the northeast in Mudaysis.

It was early morning when 1st Brigade got indications that the 29th was not far away, and those indications were Iraqi units from the 37th Iraqi Division attempting to move past FOB Copperhead.

"Battleforce Six, Gator Six."

"Go ahead, Gator Six."

"Battleforce Six, we have six BTR-60s moving towards our positions at high speed. They have no flank security out that we can see and appear to be only interested in getting north. Over."

"Roger, Gator Six. You're cleared to light them up."

Cory turned to his operations officer, the S-3, and told him to contact Brigade and inform them. Before the S-3 could make the call, Bastogne Six made a net call.

"All Bastogne elements, this is Bastogne Six. Sabre Six is reporting a large Iraqi formation moving this way from the south with the Two-Nine right on their ass. Identify your targets and engage. Let's close the back door on these guys. Bastogne Six out."

Cory looked at his map and the locations of all his units down to platoon levels. As he studied it, he recognized the need to move some of the Delta antitank vehicles as they were all oriented for the most part to the north.

"Delta Dawg Six, Battleforce Six, over."

"Go ahead, Battleforce Six."

"Delta Dawg, Sabre reports Iraqi forces moving from the south. Leave a small element covering the north but move to engage. Let me know when they're in position."

"Roger, Battleforce Six. We're moving now."

****

"Williams, let's move it," Sergeant Dodge said as he smacked the top of the TOW Humvee.

Immediately, Private Williams started the vehicle and dropped it into gear. He knew exactly where they were going and how to get there as they had rehearsed this before, expecting the Iraqi forces to be coming from the south. They had prepared a new position and had it well camouflaged, offering concealment. *Now if it just had overhead cover, it would be an ideal position*, Williams thought. It took all of five minutes to reach the new position, located in an orchard south of the airfield. The brigade had developed a plan that positioned all sixty TOW weapons around the southern end of the airfield to engage in a kill zone. The kill zone was twelve hundred meters to the southeast of the runway.

As Sergeant Dodge's vehicle rolled into his position, the fire team quickly got to work preparing last-minute details. When all was ready, they played the waiting game as everyone else was doing. They could see dust clouds mixed with black smoke from burning vehicles in the distance but beyond the range of the TOW system. Occasionally they would see an attack helicopter.

"Hey, Sarge, do you think the attack helicopters will kill them all before they get to us?" Williams asked.

"Who knows? They'll damage a lot of them, I'm sure. We may wind up with a bunch of dismounted infantry coming this way if they lost enough vehicles." The team continued to watch the dust come closer, and soon the sounds of an engagement could be heard. Dodge had confidence in his team. They had all been together since the start of this war. They had all grown up together in this war as well, Dodge thought. They were no longer teenage dudes back on the block and wouldn't return home to that lifestyle, not after having gone through this war together. They would go home as men—men that had seen the worst of humanity and yet, at times, the best of it.

"Sarge, we have company approaching. I count six T-72 tanks and six BTR-60s in a wide formation. Can't see what's behind them because of the dust," Corporal Brown said, looking through the TOW sight.

"Put on the AN/TAS-4 night sight. That infrared capability will allow you to see through some of the dust. What's the range to the first elements?" Dodge asked as he handed the night sight up to Brown.

"I'd estimate they're five thousand meters. Brigade will start hitting them with artillery pretty soon," Dodge said. "First, they'll lay in FASCAM in the kill zone, then they'll hit them with VT fuze to make them button up. That's when we engage and not before. Got it?"

"I got it," Brown said as he finished mounting the night sight and started to look through it at the approaching enemy. What he was seeing was fuzzy red images of vehicles giving off a high heat resolution. "Sarge, I don't think we have enough rounds," Brown slowly said. "I'm looking at maybe thirty vehicles heading this way."

"This way or towards the Brigade kill zone?" Dodge asked with some concern in his voice.

"Towards the kill zone, but there are a couple heading towards us," Brown said.

"Okay, when the first vehicle gets to our marker, hit him. We should get off three shots before we need to move. Williams, start the vehicle," Dodge ordered and the vehicle came to life. Brown continued to watch the enemy vehicles that were approaching his hide position. Previously, they had paced off three thousand meters and placed a distinctive marker made out of a pile of rocks. Once those vehicles reached that point, Brown would fire. Time of flight for the missile was ten seconds. At three thousand meters, they were outside the effective range of the T-72 tank's main gun. Dodge had calculated that at the speed of the T-72, he could fire three rounds before the tank would be in range of the TOW positions.

"Brown, engage the T-72s first," Dodge directed as he stood by with an additional round to load as soon as the first hit its target.

"They're about there—" His words were cut off by the sound of impacting artillery on the Iraqi task force. The variable-time fuze artillery created airbursts that stripped away antennas, punctured external fuel tanks, and killed anyone that was outside the vehicle.

"On the way," Brown yelled as the TOW missile left the launcher with two guidance wires trailing behind the missile. Brown continued to hold steady on the target, a T-72. His aim point was the point where the turret met the hull of the tank as there would be no protective armor at that point if she was wearing any. When the missile impacted, there was a flash explosion and the turret popped off the top of the tank.

"Reload," Dodge shouted as he slammed another round into the launcher.

"Target T-72, twenty-five hundred meters," Brown yelled in a steady voice.

"Engage," Dodge ordered, and another round left the launcher for its eight-second flight to the new target. This time the turret didn't pop off, but a blinding flash in the side of the vehicle was noticed as it turned broadside just before the missile reached it. The next thing they saw was a column of flame roaring out of the turret's top hatch.

"Reload," Dodge ordered again.

"Target, BTR-60, command vehicle."

"Engage." And for a third time in less than one minute, another missile left the launcher. The TOW missile destroyed tanks and obliterated thin-skinned vehicles like the BTR-60. Killing this vehicle wasn't so important, but killing a commander was.

"Williams, get us out of here now!" Dodge yelled as small-arms rounds buzzed through the trees like angry bees.
****

Lieutenant Colonel Frank Hancock commanded the 1st Battalion, 327th Infantry Regiment, of the 1st Brigade. Like Battleforce, his battalion had participated in the airfield takedown and then pushed out to take up a position southwest of the airfield. He was uncomfortable not having his Delta Company as they had been attached to 2nd of the 327th to help defend the airfield. His consolation was the fact that he was in some very restrictive terrain with a major highway running through the mountains and thus his TOWs wouldn't be as effective due to the short distances. His Dragons and AT-4 would have to be his armor punch.

Frank was making the rounds visiting with his soldiers when his RTO came up to him.

"Sir, Bastogne Six is on the horn for you."

Taking the hand mike, he transmitted, "Bastogne Six, Bulldog Six, over."

"Bulldog Six, you have vehicles approaching your position. Identity is unknown. Over."

"Roger, Bastogne Six. We'll be on the lookout for them, over."

"Keep me posted. Bastogne Six out."

Handing the brigade command radio hand mike back to the RTO, Frank reached for the battalion command net hand mike.

"All Bulldog elements, Bulldog Six, over." Each of the three remaining companies responded in order. "This is Bulldog Six. We have vehicles approaching from the south. Be advised the identity is unknown. They could be bad guys or friendlies. Make positive identification before engaging. How copy?" Each company came back that they understood. Now it was just a matter of waiting.

The sector 1st Battalion occupied was easily defended. It was the southern end of Mogayra, with two major roads entering from the one major road that the 7th and 37th Iraqi Divisions had used in approaching for their initial attack. The sides of the road were littered with broken and destroyed Iraqi vehicles and equipment. Frank had inspected the positions earlier but was concerned that night was approaching and identification of friend or foe was going to be difficult. All day, Iraqi elements had been attempting to get through his sector. Previously Frank had been instructed to allow individuals to continue north without vehicles or weapons. The corps couldn't take more prisoners at this point. Vehicles were another matter—stop or destroy. The Dragon and AT-4 weapons had done just that throughout the day. The fight at the airfield had quieted down and the 1st Battalion Delta Company, the antitank company, was back in his sector and moving to positions.

"Bulldog Six, Bulldog Pup, over," the scout platoon leader, Lieutenant Bradshaw, called using his unauthorized call sign.

"Bulldog Pup, Six, go ahead."

"Six, we have vehicle traffic approaching." The platoon leader gave the coordinates.

"Roger, I copy. Can you identify? Over," Bulldog Six asked.

"Negative, over."

"Roger, continue to observe. If you make positive ID, let me know immediately. Bulldog Six out."

****

The 29th Infantry Division had launched their attack as the elements of the 101st were flying out to seize the airfield. The road trip was eight or nine miles of stop-and-go traffic for the frontline unit, the 1st Battalion, 115th Infantry Brigade. The stop-and-go was caused by a combination of getting damaged Iraqi vehicles out of the road and contact with retreating Iraqi units.

"Hey, Lieutenant... Lieutenant," Sergeant Peterson whispered softly.

"Whatcha got?" Lieutenant Pile asked. They had dismounted from their vehicles and were on foot two hundred yards ahead of the vehicles, which were in overwatch positions.

"Sir, about two hundred yards up ahead, maybe more, I thought I saw someone light a cigarette. It stuck out like a sore thumb in my NODs," Sergeant Peterson pointed out. As dark as the night was, the flame from a lighter would be like a beacon.

"Okay, let's move up for a closer look," Pile instructed and notified his platoon to move up.

"Charger Six, Pony One, over," Pile called, wanting to inform the battalion commander, Lieutenant Colonel Gooderjohn.

"Pony One, Charger Six, over," Gooderjohn replied. He really hated the new call signs that the powers that be had assigned to his battalion.

"Charger Six, we have possible positions," Pile told him and passed on the coordinates.

"Roger, I have artillery on call. First round illum. Be prepared to adjust," Gooderjohn instructed.

****

"Bulldog Pup, LP One."

Lieutenant Bradshaw had placed a two-man listening post out three hundred meters forward of his position, which was three hundred meters forward of the first rifle company. "Go, LP One," he responded.

"Bulldog Pup, we have movement. Appears to be mechanized vehicles five hundred meters south of our position, over."

"LP One, can you identify? Over," Bradshaw asked.

"Negative. Will continue to observe. Standing by to adjust artillery." The LP provided the grid coordinates where he wanted the artillery to land when called for.

****

"Did you hear that, Lieutenant?" Sergeant Peterson asked, stopping in his tracks and taking a knee.

"Yeah, sounded like a squelch on an FM radio. Damn Iraqis could be setting us up for an artillery strike. I'm not seeing anything in these NODs. Let me call the BC and light this place up." Turning to his RTO, Lieutenant Pile took the hand mike and made the call for artillery support.

****

"Bulldog Six, Bulldog Pup, over."

"Bulldog Pup, go."

"Bulldog Six requests artillery now at TRP 310. One round illum. Over."

"Roger." As Frank approved the shot, his FSCOORD called the battalion mortar platoon and requested illumination on the coordinates provided.

****

"Pony One, shot over," the fire support officer called as the battalion mortar platoon dropped an illum round down the tube and it fired.

****

"Bulldog Pup, shot out," the fire support officer called as the battalion mortar platoon dropped an illum round down the tube and it fired.

Simultaneously, the two illumination rounds flew in opposite directions to the same location and ignited at fifteen hundred feet. The entire area was bathed in a white light with shadows eerily moving

171

around as the two one-million-candlepower flares, suspended under their parachutes, drifted to the ground, twisting in the night air.

Both platoon leaders suddenly realized who the other was and called, "Check fire" before any high-explosive rounds could be fired. The linkup had been made. Everyone breathed a bit easier.

Chapter 31
Not Good

24 April 1991
2nd Republican Guard HQ
Medina, Saudi Arabia

"General al-Hamdani, the last of our units is ready to depart. They will serve as a rear guard as we move to Buraydah," his aide told him. General al-Hamdani was wrestling with the thought of having to retreat from his positions as he looked over a map of the western region. *I cannot believe that the pencil pushers could not have sent one or two more divisions to me. With those additional divisions we would have broken through. With the American divisions going north, with one more division, I could break through to the coast. But no, Qusay, our military genius leader, says retreat. He thinks the Americans moving north will put them behind us and cut our supply lines—and they would, but I could also get behind them into their supply lines before they could cut mine. How stupid of Qusay.*

"Very well. Be sure to instruct all commanders that I do not want any needless destruction of property or harm to civilians. We came as liberators and we will leave as such. I will not be accused of wanton destruction, understood?"

"Yes, sir, I will repeat the order to them to make sure they understand. Your helicopter is on the pad to get you and fly you to Buraydah, where the IV Corps commander will meet you," the aide indicated. General al-Hamdani picked up his hat, looked around the office one last time, thinking about what could have been instead of what was, and walked out the door.
****

The powerful and exalted Republican Guard could not dislodge two American divisions of paratroopers. They should hang their heads in shame. Now maybe Baghdad will not treat us like the bastard children at a family reunion, Lieutenant General Galib Ghanem thought as he waited for General al-Hamdani to land. *They are coming back through my lines with their tails between their legs like some whipped dog. Maybe if they get out of my way, then I can destroy the Americans.*

General Ghanem saw al-Hamdani's aircraft landing but was not about to get out of the car until the dust had settled from the turning rotor blades. Finally, he exited his civilian-requisitioned Mercedes 400SL.

"General al-Hamdani, so good to see that you are well," Ghanem said as he approached and exchanged salutes, followed by a handshake.

"Cut the crap, Ghanem. You are only glad to see me humiliated and out of your way. Are you ready to receive my forces through your lines and provide the resupply that we requested? I have no desire to be here any longer than it takes to move my units through," al-Hamdani said. His tone reflected his sour mood.

"That is what I always admired about you. Even in the face of defeat, you come right to the point. Nice to see you too. Yes, we have everything in place to receive what is left of your force and push it on its way," Ghanem said, enjoying the not-so-subtle digs. "The sooner I get your people out of here, the sooner I can complete my defenses. I have a car and driver standing by to take you to a residence for you. If you need anything, they know how to contact me. Good day, sir." Ghanem saluted and returned to his car. *The arrogant bastard. He loses practically his entire corps and still he thinks his shit does not stink. We will see who is smiling when I crush the Americans.*

"Driver, back to headquarters," Ghanem directed.

Arriving back at the headquarters he had established at the Aramax logistic center, he went straight into the operations section. Spotting his operations officer, he motioned him to follow the brigadier to his office.

"You wished to speak to me, General?" Brigadier General al-Bu Muhair asked.

"I just spoke with General al-Hamdani. He says the Americans are heading north after the 2nd Corps and not coming this way. There may be some Saudi forces following the remnants of his corps, but nothing that one or two divisions could not handle. I am concerned, however, about the 1st Republican Guard Corps pulling back and giving us all their area. The Americans destroyed the IX Corps in the UAE. I will not have them do that to us. We need to shift forces to the east and quickly. The 21st Infantry Division is at Al Hawlyan, south of Al Hofuf, so we will leave them in place. The 6th Armour Division is at Al Kharj, which could position them well to attack the flank of an American push out of Kuwait. However, since we do not expect to see any significant force following the 2nd Republican Guard Corps, we need to thin the center of our sector and shift east," General Ghanem said, almost as if he was thinking out loud.

"Sir, we could leave the 16th in Buraydah and the 20th in Unaysah while bringing the 1st Mech east as well as the 30th Infantry. We have two divisions in Riyadh where one would be sufficient. That would give us three more divisions to move east to meet the American attack," Brigadier General al-Bu Muhair offered.

Ghanem heard him and began looking at a map on the wall in his office. Without looking away from the map, he said, "Issue the order to get them moving. I will know in an hour where I want them positioned. Notify the 6th Armour to be prepared to counterattack to the east."
****

High above the Indian Ocean, a Magnum geosynchronous satellite had been in position since November of 1990, replacing another satellite that had been up for four years but was running low on fuel for repositioning. With its huge one-hundred-meter circular antenna, it soaked up electronic communications over the airwaves like a sponge. The information it gathered was quickly downloaded to the NSA and, from there, forwarded to the Department of Defense and CENTCOM, almost in real time. Within hours of Ghanem giving the order to move his divisions, General Schwarzkopf was reading the order at the same time as Ghanem's division commanders read it.

"How sure are we that this information is accurate?" Schwarzkopf asked O'Donnell.

"Sir, it appears to be very accurate as Keyhole and Lacrosse/Onyx are providing the same information. He's shifting his forces to the east. The 1st Mech Division has the furthest to travel, about two hundred miles, and his reconnaissance elements pulled out about an hour ago. At best, maintaining forty miles an hour, they'll be down in the new locations in five hours. The 6th Armour Division is sitting pat at Al Kharj and the 21st is in Al Hawlyan. We'll see either the 34th or the 36th heading for Al Hofuf shortly. He's going to try to blunt the offensive and counterattack with the 6th Armour Division, I suspect," O'Donnell speculated.

"Alright, let's get this info to all the division commanders. We'll let III Corps take Al Hofuf; the Marines can take the 21st, and VII can head for Al Kharj and the 6th Armour Division. I suspect that the 1st Mech Division will come right into the middle between Al Hofuf and Al Kharj in an attempt to put all his mobile forces together for a counterattack. He'll put the two infantry divisions somewhere between Al Hofuf and Al Kharj, but on line with the 21st Infantry Division."

"What are we looking at as far as obstacles and minefields are concerned?" Schwarzkopf asked.

"Keyhole shows us an extensive obstacle belt between Al Hofuf and Al Kharj. He has time to put in one good tank ditch, wire and artillery registrations," O'Donnell said.

"First priority for the Air Force is to start bombing the crap out of them. I'll speak with Horner about this. I want him to get on it tonight," Schwarzkopf said, heading for the door and General Horner's office.

Chapter 32
Command Brief

25 April 1991
CENTCOM HQ
Abu Dhabi, United Arab Emirates

Almost as soon as Abu Dhabi was liberated, the CENTCOM headquarters moved to the new location. General Schwarzkopf was greeted openly and warmly by the Emir, who had returned as soon as US forces had rolled into the city. He ordered the best accommodations for General Schwarzkopf and found suitable quarters and space for the headquarters. Now was the time to put phase two into action.

"Keep your seats," Schwarzkopf said as he walked into the room. All of the division commanders were present from MARCENT, III Corps and VII Corps. General Luck represented XVIII Airborne Corps as they were continuing their operation in the west and their plans would not change at this time.

"Good morning, sir," General Schless said. "First slide. Sir, significant events in the last twenty-four hours are the completion of all resupply of the units in the UAE; the completion of two new POW camps and the turnover of POWs to Oman and the UAE; and the linkup between the 29th Infantry Division and the 101st at Mogayra."

Turning in his chair to see General Luck, Schwarzkopf asked, "How did it go, the linkup?"

"Went well, sir. The 29th is consolidating at this time and will push off in the morning as 2nd Brigade launches his attack in support of the 28th. The 3rd Brigade of the 101st will flow into Mogayra today and be ready to launch tomorrow night in support of the 29th's next objective."

"And the 82nd?" Stormin' Norman asked.

"Jump went well. The port is secured and the ground movement will be completed today. I wish we had the full division, but we had to leave the one brigade as strategic reserve back at Bragg," Luck said.

"So, no changes in your plan."

"No, sir. We're on track."

Turning back to General Schless, Schwarzkopf said, "Sorry, Jim, go ahead and continue."

"Sir, if there are no questions about significant recent events, I will be followed by the G-2," Schless indicated and stepped to the side.

General O'Donnell stepped up to the podium. Internally, Schwarzkopf chuckled to himself as O'Donnell reminded him of a leprechaun because of his red hair, freckled face and small stature. He also brought a pot of gold with his very accurate intelligence estimates.

"Morning, sir. Indications are that the Iraqi IX Corps does not offer any threat to our operations at this time. We believe that Lieutenant General Juwad Assad Rasol Shitnah was killed, along with most of the IX Corps staff, in an air strike. What elements of the Corps that have survived are attempting to move back and join forces located in Saudi Arabia and specifically the IV Corps.

"In the past two days, we have seen a shift in Iraqi forces with the 1st Republican Guard Corps pulling out of their positions and being replaced by elements of the IV Iraqi Corps. The IV Corps had eight divisions spread out now on a line from Al Hofuf to Buraydah. He hasn't received the attention from the Air Force that the 1st Republican Guard Corps has received, and so he's at eighty percent strength and consists of six infantry divisions, one mechanized division and one armored division. The mechanized division is equipped with the BMP, and the armored division has T-62 and some T-72 tanks." O'Donnell paused to let his comments sink in.

"In the west, the 2nd Republican Guard Corps is also withdrawing back towards Buraydah. They're at fifty percent strength at this time and we expect that they may withdraw all the way to King Khalid Military City, where there's a considerable stockpile of equipment, both Soviet and American vehicles that they captured," O'Donnell noted.

"Schless, make a note," Schwarzkopf said. "Let's get the air guys to start hitting those vehicles at KKMC, but not the buildings or infrastructure, understood?"

"Yes, sir. Will get them on it right away," Schless replied, jotting down a note to himself.

"Pardon me, O'Donnell, please continue," Schwarzkopf directed.

"Sir, in the area of Tabuk, the II Iraqi Corps headquarters is there now as well as the 2nd Iraqi Division. Remnants of the 7th, 51st and 37th Infantry Divisions are attempting to link up with the 2nd in Tabuk. The 14th, or what's left of the 14th, is also attempting to consolidate in

178

Tabuk. The XVIII Airborne is putting a lot of pressure on the 7th, 51st and 37th, making it difficult for them to rearm or refuel. Reports indicated many vehicles are abandoned on the side of the road due to lack of gas," O'Donnell stated, which brought a smile to Schwarzkopf's face.

"We've witnessed a decrease in his air defensive systems, which we believe is due to the attrition that has happened to his search radars as well as the weapons and early-warning systems. This past week, he launched a total of twenty sorties against our ground forces, down from three hundred at the start of the war. His SAM systems and defenses around and inside Iraq have not been damaged and are intact at this time," O'Donnell concluded.

"And his naval forces, where do we stand on those?" Schwarzkopf asked, not looking up from the notes he'd been writing.

"Sir, his naval forces attempted to interdict the mine-clearing operations in the Strait. Two F-18 aircraft sank two of his corvettes off Sirri Island, and the *Princeton* sank another with a Harpoon missile. Other vessels have withdrawn and are now standing off the coast of Kuwait and the Saudi cities of Dammam and Al Jubail. We have confirmed that a submarine believed to have been given to the Iraqis by China through Iran has been sunk. We retrieved debris in the debris field that confirmed this information. We suspect there may be another sub operating in the area of the Gulf of Oman or Arabia, and the Navy is keeping an active search program for them," O'Donnell stated. "Sir, if you have no more questions, General Schless will continue."

"Good rundown, O'Donnell. Tell your people they're doing a great job," Schwarzkopf said. O'Donnell nodded with a broad smile. as he walked away as Schless stepped up.

"Sir, for phase two, we recommend no change in the task organization—"

"Is everyone okay with that?" No one objected. "Okay, then, but we need to discuss a possible change that affects you, Ivan," he said, looking at the III Corps commander.

"And that is…?" Ivan said.

"Baker called me and it seems that the King wants an Arab commander controlling the Arab forces, an Arab corps commander. We may be replacing you and your staff with an Arab corps headquarters.

"Sir, we do recommend that we bring everyone up on line with III Corps on the right, allowing the bulk of host nation units to enter the cities, our two Marine divisions along with the 1st British Armoured Division in the center, and VII Corps on the left flank. This places our heaviest corps opposing the bulk of the IV Iraqi Corps and the 2nd Republican Guard Corps should they attempt to swing into the flank of VII Corps, which we feel they won't attempt," Schless stated. As he spoke, he pointed to a large wall map showing the direction of advance for the respective corps and their sectors.

"Fred," Schwarzkopf said, gaining General Franks's attention, "how do you feel about this?"

"Sir, from what I've seen so far, this doesn't concern me as long as I retain my attack helicopters to give me ample warning and deep battle interdiction capability. Our Air Force brothers have been pounding the IV for the past three days, so I don't see a problem if they've been as accurate as we've experienced thus far," General Franks concluded, to Schwarzkopf's satisfaction.

"So, everyone is good with this plan of maneuver, I'm hearing. Good, Let's get it done. We commence phase two at 0800 tomorrow morning."

Chapter 33
Phase 2 Commences

25 April 1991
Team Delta, 3rd Battalion, 69th Armor
Al Sila, United Arab Emirates

Captain Poggi watched the evening before as the 2nd Armored Cavalry Regiment passed through them, heading west. He knew that they would be following them shortly, and in the middle of the night, Lieutenant Colonel Altamire, the battalion commander, called a commanders' meeting and issued the orders commencing at 0800 hours the next day. Poggi had to give up one tank platoon to their sister infantry battalion and received one platoon from the infantry, equipped with Bradley fighting vehicles. Lieutenant Kincade was back, much to Lieutenant Bagel's satisfaction. Bagel felt that he and Kincade had worked well on Medina Ridge and was glad to be able to work with him again.

Assembling his platoon leaders, tank commanders and first sergeant, Poggi gave the company order for the day's operation. He spread his map out on the ground and squatted down next to it. He used a new pencil as a pointer. "Okay, the battalion moves out at 0800. Order of march is us on the left flank, Team Bravo on the right flank and Team Alpha following in the center. We'll spread out on the left flank. No need to eat someone else's dust. From left to right, 1st Platoon, 2nd Platoon, Infantry and 3rd Platoon. I'll be between 2nd and Infantry. First sergeant will bring up the headquarters section at five hundred yards behind us. There's no paved road but hard-packed sand from what intel's telling us. We depart from our current location and take a heading of two hundred and forty degrees for one hundred and seventy-eight miles to Yabrin. Anticipate hitting an Iraqi infantry division after we pass through there. The Cav will feel them out before we get there, and I'm sure we'll receive more instructions as we approach. Maintain speed of thirty miles per hour. Any questions?" Poggi asked, looking at the platoon leaders' faces.

"Sir," Lieutenant Bagel said, "where is the rest of the division?"

"The division is the left flank for the corps and we're the left flank for the division. There's a possibility that the Iraqi 6th Armour Division will attempt to counterattack, and if so, he'll be coming right at us. He's located west of Haradh in Al Kharj. The Cav should be able to give us a heads-up if the 6th decides to move against us," Poggi said.

"Sir, what about resupply of fuel? One hundred and sixty miles is going to stretch us pretty thin," Bagel asked.

"The Cav has secured a refuel point for us at eighty miles out. That heading will take us right to it, but just in case, these are the coordinates." Poggi read them. "Plug that into your sluggers so you don't get lost. Kincade, how are you for fuel?" Poggi asked.

"We're topped off, sir, and good for about two hundred and fifty miles at thirty miles per hour," Kincade replied.

Poggi nodded. "Alright, be sure you're topped off with fuel and ammo and plenty of bottled water. Let's keep the radio chatter to a minimum. Mount up. Give me an up when you're ready. That's all," Poggi said and stood up as he retrieved his map and folded it.

Lieutenant Bagel was deep in thought as he walked back to his tank. *We're going into another fight, it looks like, after driving for five-plus hours, plus a refuel stop, so it'll be later in the afternoon before we get into it and we'll have the setting sun in our eyes. Maybe we'll get lucky and the attack will be delayed until dark. Much rather do this after dark. Our night sights are so much better than theirs. Night would be so much better.* Once he was seated in the commander's hatch, Bagel made a net call on the platoon radio.

"Panther One-One elements, give me an up when you're ready," Bagel transmitted, within sight of his three other tanks. Looking about, he got a thumbs-up from each of the tank commanders.

"Panther Six, Panther One-One, all elements up and ready. Over," Bagel announced on the company command net.

"Roger," was all the response he received from Poggi. Moments later, Poggi issued the order, "All Panther elements move out."

Bagel's tank lurched forward and Bagel was convinced that this was caused by his driver enjoying bouncing him off the commander's hatch. Watching his four tanks move on parallel azimuths, Bagel looked back. The huge dust cloud could mean only one thing—VII Corps was on the move and heading west.

****

The 36th Infantry Division had its orders. Move from the really nice south side of Riyadh to Haradh, a really shitty place nowhere in the desert. *Haradh has the only paved road from the coast to Riyadh, and the Americans are going to need it for the MSR. We must stop them at Haradh,* MG Maheer al-Amili, commander of the 36th, thought as he moved down the one paved road to Haradh. His lead brigade was almost there now, and the other two would arrive shortly after him. His defense would be two brigades forward and one brigade back. All three brigades would be in strongpoint positions that others had placed along the road. The way they were situated, all three could fire on a unit that attempted to move between the two forward strongpoints. He had few armored vehicles in the division, being an infantry division, and few tanks, T-63s, which were older Soviet tanks. He knew that on a fluid battlefield, these tanks wouldn't stand a chance, but dug down in a defensive position they should be okay. Keeping the American close-air support aircraft off the tanks' backs would be the problem.

Arriving at the first strongpoint, al-Amili saw the first problem. The brigade commander met him as he pulled up.

"General al-Amili, very good to see you," the brigade commander said as he saluted.

Al-Amili's salute was fast almost as fast as his tongue. "Colonel, don't you think you should have camouflage over your tanks in their hull defilade positions?"

"Yes, General, we were going to get to that right after the men had a chance to rest," the brigade commander said.

"Rest? They will have a very long rest if the American attack aircraft show up. Get them on it right away, *now!*" al-Amili practically shouted. Even the soldiers at the nearest tank could hear the conversation and without further orders began getting their netting in place.

"Come with me," al-Amili said, pointing at his vehicle. The driver already knew where they were going. It didn't take him long to pull up in front of the division artillery commander's tent. "Get out," al-Amili said to the infantry brigade commander. The division artillery commander recognized the voice and exited his tent.

"Ah, good afternoon, General al-Amili. I was—"

"What is so good about it? Why is your artillery not camouflaged? Have you and this commander worked out your target reference points? Have you registered your guns as yet? I have not heard a shot fired yet. Are you waiting for the Americans to show up before doing it? What have you two been waiting for? Get it done and get it done now or you will be on the first helicopter to Baghdad. Am I clear?" al-Amili said, not too subtly. Both officers were sweating profusely and not from the heat.

"Yes, sir," they both responded in unison and saluted. Al-Amili responded with a growl as he headed to his vehicle.

He had visited the 21st Infantry Division on previous occasions as they were and had always been in Al Hawlyan. He was satisfied with their field discipline and craft. Their positions were well camouflaged, but they had lost some artillery and tanks to the American close-air support that seemed to come down from on high and attack well-camouflaged positions. They had a good obstacle belt across their entire sector. He felt confident that this unit was ready.

He had initially planned on putting the 30th Infantry in Al Hofuf but decided that it would be quicker to move the 34th Infantry Division from Riyadh to Al Hofuf and move the 30th to Riyadh in their place. The 34th should be in Al Hofuf now and he could check on them in the morning.

"Driver, back to Riyadh," al-Amili ordered.
****

The HEMTTs with their five-thousand-gallon holding tanks of diesel fuel were standing by in Yabrin when 3rd Battalion, 69th Armor rolled into the refuel point. The refuel point had followed the 2nd Armored Cavalry Regiment and set up the refuel point at Yabrin. This was just one of six spread across the front of the VII Corps to take care of the vehicles. Each point was operated by a National Guard unit trained just for this sort of mission—a tactical military truck stop. A tank would pull up and immediately start being refueled. When topped off, it would move to the next station and all fluid levels would be checked and topped off if necessary. Once the vehicle was serviced, the tank crew was served a hot meal, cold water and coffee. They would then wait for the rest of the unit to be serviced before proceeding on. At some point short of the designated line of departure for the attack, units would wait for the entire division to be ready. This was not a rapid process, considering the entire division was being serviced. It was 2100 hours when the word came down to resume the movement to contact in the direction of At Tawdihiyah located on Highway 10 between Al Kharj and Haradh.

Lieutenant Bagel was satisfied now that he didn't have the sun in his eyes and they would be advancing under the cover of darkness. Their night vision sights on the tank, to include thermal imaging sights, were very effective. The slightest heat difference clearly showed up and the heat generated by a tank or vehicle was much greater than the surrounding sand of the desert. Bagel was hunting this night—hunting for Iraqi tanks.

"Ramos, take it slow coming up on this crest. I want to see what's over there before we charge across. Got it?" Bagel said to his new driver. In fact, Bagel was running with an entire new crew that hadn't worked together before. His previous crew had all gotten promoted out of his vehicle for other vehicles. His master gunner had moved up to become a tank commander for one of his other tanks. His driver had moved up to be a loader on another vehicle, and his loader had become the gunner on another vehicle. Movement of crews wasn't unheard of in combat, but everyone attempted to avoid it.

"Anderson, be ready with a sabot round when we fire," Staff Sergeant Adams, the new master gunner, directed.

Ramos had his night vision goggles on and could clearly see on this moonless night. The tank's night sights provided excellent visibility of the terrain for Sergeant Adams, and he was switching between the night sight and the thermal sights. As the tank reached the crest of the ridge, Lieutenant Bagel whispered, "Holy shit."

Laid out before him and his platoon at two thousand meters was the defense of one of the Iraqi divisions. Bagel could see both vehicles and fighting positions. Light discipline was almost nonexistent with vehicle headlights on and soldiers smoking. A cigarette stood out very well when viewed through the night observation devices.

A sabot round was already loaded, so Bagel gave the commands for the first engagement.

"Gunner, tank."

"Identified," Adams responded.

"Up," yelled Specialist Anderson.

"Fire!" Bagel ordered, and immediately the tank rocked from the sabot round leaving the muzzle of the tank. Almost instantaneously, the turret of a T-62 tank two thousand meters away exploded. Bagel immediately looked for another target. On his right and left, the other tanks of the platoon were engaging Iraqi vehicles and bunkers. Although he couldn't see what the other platoons were doing, he knew they were engaging as well.

"All Panther elements, move up," Captain Poggi ordered.

"Ramos, move out," Bagel ordered, and Ramos gave the tank some gas. He had already picked the next position he would sprint the tank to—a position that would offer some defilade of the hull and yet allow the gunner to engage targets. As they rolled forward, Bagel spotted a bunker that was engaging with a heavy machine gun.

"Gunner, HEAT, bunker."

"Identified."

"HEAT up."

"Fire!" And again the tank rocked with the HEAT round leaving the muzzle. The Bunker disappeared in a cloud of sand and flame. Bagel was concerned about his other three tanks, but a quick glance showed they were holding in formation, each covering the other. As he continued to scan for other targets, he saw a group of Iraqi soldiers emerge from the ground. They were carrying what appeared to be RPG antitank guns.

"Bunker from my position." Bagel let a long stream of .50-caliber rounds enter into the middle of the group. When he stopped, no one was moving. As they closed on the infantry positions, Bagel came to rely more on his .50-cal, as did the others. Finally, the shooting died down due to an absence of Iraqi vehicles and soldiers. To the northeast they could see flashes of artillery being employed and some tracers from .50-cal machine guns and small arms. When Bagel got the call to halt, his platoon was well past the first line of Iraqi positions. Bagel contacted each of his tanks and got a status report on damage, fuel and ammo. They all reported no damage and sixty percent on ammo. Most of what had been used was the .50-cal ammunition, as there were few tanks.

****

At 0400, Brigadier General al-Bu Muhair knocked on the door to General al-Amili's bedroom. It took a couple of hard raps on the door before he received a response to come in.

"General, this best be good to wake me," al Amili said, still half-asleep.

"Sir, we are getting reports from the 21st and 36th Divisions of heavy contact. The 36th does not know if he can hold much longer. He estimates that three divisions are coming at him. He is sure he has two divisions attacking at this time," al-Bu Muhair said. Even before he finished, al-Amili was out of bed and getting dressed.

"What is the status of the 1st Mech Division and the 6th Armoured?"

"Sir, the 1st Mech Division has arrived in its assembly area and is refueling at this time. General Alavi says he can be ready to launch a counterattack in one hour. According to General Faizan, the 6th Armour Division is ready whenever you issue the order," General al-Bu Muhair said. He wanted to be sure that al-Amili knew that this was General Faizan's estimate and not his own.

"Good. Tell General Faizan to counterattack along Highway 10 to Haradh. Tell General Alavi to counterattack also towards Haradh as soon as he is ready. They will link up together there, and then we will have them drive towards As Salwa, thus cutting right through the rear of this attacking corps."

****

"Panther Six, Cheetah Six, over," Lieutenant Colonel Piscal transmitted.

"Cheetah Six, Panther Six, over," Poggi replied to his battalion commander.

"Panther Six, when you reach Highway 10, I want you to set up a blocking position on the south side of the road. Cougar elements will take a position astride the road with Tiger elements north of the road. Be prepared for a possible counterattack by the Iraqi armored division located in Al Kharj. Give me a heads-up when you have them in sight. How copy?"

"Cheetah Six, Panther Six, I have good copy. Will be moving into position in one-five mikes, over."

187

"Roger, give me an up when you're in position. Cheetah Six out."

On Captain Poggi's orders, the company turned and faced to the west, taking up positions overlooking very broken terrain with numerous washes and wadis. Bagel conducted a visual reconnaissance of the terrain and determined quickly that this was not conducive to tank operations.

"Panther Six, Panther One-One, over."

"Go ahead, One-One."

"Six, this terrain is crap for tanks. I doubt if we'll see anyone coming this way in this stuff. It's deep wadis and washes, over."

"One-One, that should make your job easy, then. Be prepared to pull out and attack north if they get through on Highway 10. How copy?"

"Six, I have a good copy."

Chapter 34
FOB Falcon

26 April 1991
2nd Brigade, 101st Airborne
FOB Copperhead

Activities at FOB Copperhead had quieted down. The half-hearted ground attack against the 3rd Battalion and the 1st Battalion had been destroyed with a couple of hundred prisoners taken. 2nd Battalion, along with the attack helicopters, had cut the attack on the airfield to ribbons. There were few prisoners. The lift battalions got a chance to get some crew rest and during the night had flown to FOB Copperhead for the anticipated lift of the 2nd Brigade to FOB Falcon. Once established at Falcon, CH-47s would fly in with five-hundred-gallon fuel blivets of JP-4 aviation fuel for the lift ships and attack helicopters. The 28th Infantry Division would conduct a linkup and move in with their HEMTTs to refuel their track vehicles. Establishment of the FOB was critical to the ongoing operations.

Colonel Dean Anderson sat in his vehicle, which would be in the ground convoy. Fuel was too important to waste flight time hauling unnecessary vehicles into the FOB. His operations officer's vehicle had the same radios and would be flown in on the lift. Dean was a bit nervous about this operation.

"Hey, Keith," Anderson called to his operations officer, Major Keith Hurbert.

"Sir," Hurbert replied, looking up from his map, which he had spread out on the hood of Anderson's Humvee.

"What's the status of the lift?" Anderson asked.

"Sir, it's a go. Weather is good with no fog now that we're away from the coast. No wind today, so no need to worry about a dust storm. Only adverse factor is the temperature. It'll get back into the low nineties today. Aircraft are all up and ready. Troops should start loading in another ten minutes, with liftoff at 0430 hours."

"And flight time to the objective?"

"Sir, it's seventy-five miles to the objective, which is eight miles north of Al Buriekah. It's astride the main highway to Tabuk, which is another eighty-five miles beyond that. The 28th Infantry is currently eighty miles south of Al Buriekah. Once we land, we should be operational for the attack helicopters in two hours. You seem a bit antsy about this operation, sir. What's bothering you about it?"

"No, nothing really, just 'what-ifing' in my head. CH-47s are bringing a battery of artillery on the first lift, correct?"

"Yes, sir, and two more batteries on the second lift with a third lift for the artillery. Sir, we have it all covered. Let's load up. That's your aircraft over there. We'll be following the first lift," Major Hurbert said, folding his map and pointing to the UH-60 Black Hawk one hundred feet away.

****

Night flying could be some of the most pleasant flying, especially in a large formation of Black Hawk helicopters. Generally there was little turbulence, which made for a pleasant ride. With fifteen soldiers in each aircraft plus the door gunner and crew chief, it was necessary to close the doors until just prior to touchdown to prevent anyone from falling out.

Captain Simms commanded Bravo Company, 1st Battalion, 502nd Infantry, 1st Brigade of the 101st. An officer candidate graduate, he had been a young sergeant when he'd attended, so he'd been around the block as an enlisted soldier. He knew all the tricks, schemes and excuses that soldiers would use when they screwed up. His soldiers were proud of the fact he had come up through the ranks but frustrated that they had a difficult time pulling the wool over his eyes. Simms was flying with his two RTOs and a rifle squad of eleven men and a medic. They were in the chalk three position on the sixty-ship lift of Black Hawks. The night was a dark as the bottom of a dry well with no moon and no lights on the ground. He estimated their altitude to be no more than two hundred feet. A glance into the cockpit showed that the pilots both had their NODs on and the green instrument lighting turned down very low, so he couldn't really see the altimeter.

Looking around at the faces of those with him, Simms noticed that the kids he had brought to Saudi Arabia eight months before were all gone. Now they were battle-tested men. Same faces, but instead of anxious looks, all he saw were determined professional glances. There was no bravado as before. A few that had originally come over were not present, having been sent home with wounds—some repairable, some permanent, some life-ending. He would remember the faces of those kids. Simms was proud of his boys, who weren't much younger than him, and the squad leader was the same age as him.

Simms's concentration was lost when the crew chief yelled, "Two minutes."

Unlike the days of Vietnam when, at the two-minute mark, the Cobra gunships would roll hot and shoot up the landing zone, the attack aircraft raced ahead and flew low over the landing zone, looking for targets. None engaged unless they had a target, and no targets were engaged. At the one-minute mark, the aircraft went into a noticeable deceleration and that was the signal to open the doors. As the doors slid back, the dust from the landing aircraft swirled into the main cabin, but the soldiers ignored it. As the wheels touched, the first soldiers were out the door with the rucksacks they had been sitting on following them to the ground, where each soldier immediately took a prone position, searching for a target or waiting to be engaged. In less than four seconds, the aircraft was lifting off, empty except for the crew. Simms and company waited for the dust to settle before they moved out. In those few minutes, Simms checked his map, took a compass head to his objective and made a company net call to his platoon leaders.

"All Banshee elements, Banshee Six. Give me an up," he said on the company radio net. When he received the last up from the newest platoon leader, he gave the order to move out.

Bravo Company had landed on the west side of a rocky ridgeline that was to the west and parallel with the main road north to Tabuk. His battalion was the eastern side of FOB Falcon and the priority unit, as they had what was expected to be the most dangerous avenue of approach into the FOB. On the south end of the ridge was an open wadi right into the FOB. This had to be closed to prevent an Iraqi force from entering. To do that, the battalion commander had assigned his antitank company to the south of Bravo and had placed one platoon of his antitank vehicles in Simms's sector. The rest of the antitank company, Delta Company, was south of the opening or deep within the opening to take advantage of its long-range fire.

As Simms reached the top of the ridgeline they would defend from, he looked down on the highway. There was no movement on the road, but wreckage lay everywhere. Iraqi trucks, tanks, and BTR-60s were all scattered along and across the road. The smell of burnt rubber and human bodies was strong. Through his NODs, he could make out the details of the carnage before him. He quickly turned, as he had things to do before daylight to get his company ready for what might come.
****

Colonel Maloof, commander of the 3rd Regiment of the 51st Iraqi Division, or what was left of it, decided that movement in the day was a kiss of death. After the disaster that had taken General Zogby and the other regimental commanders, he had regrouped the remnants of the other two regiments and his own and was conducting a delaying action against this new mechanized threat that had come before his elements. Expecting the light infantry of the airmobile division, he was now being pressured by a mechanized force. They weren't as aggressive as the paratroopers with the chicken patches on their shoulders, but this force had the heavy weapons that the paratroopers lacked. *If I could just keep the attack helicopters and the close-air support off, then we would have a chance of getting to Tabuk*, he thought.

In the cool night air, he was pleased at the discipline he was seeing in his elements as they slowly moved up the one paved road to Tabuk. His map was spread out on the front of his vehicle. He had a poncho over his head and covering the map so he could use a flashlight to read the map and not give away his position. *Before daylight, we have to get off this road. We are twenty kilometers south of Al Buriekah. We should be there in an hour at 0500, so that gives us another hour before the sun comes up*, he calculated. *This large wadi twenty kilometers north of Al Buriekah should do nicely for us to hide in today. Then two more days to get to Tabuk. Hopefully, this nightmare will be over for me.* Colonel Maloof folded his map and began giving instructions to his operations officer.
****

"First Strike Six, Anvil Six, over," the Alpha Company commander radioed.

"Anvil Six, go ahead," Lieutenant Colonel Donald replied.

"First Strike Six, we have company approaching from the south and it doesn't sound like friendlies, over." The other company commanders heard this net call and right away alerted their subordinate platoons to be prepared.

"Anvil Six, confirm who those people are before you engage. I've had no word on the location of friendlies."

"Roger, First Strike Six. Anvil Six out."

Donald quickly grabbed his brigade net radio and called Colonel Anderson. "Strike Six, First Strike Six, over."

"First Strike Six, Strike Three, over," Hurbert replied as Strike Six was overlooking his map and nodded for Hurbert to take the call.

"Strike Three, we have company approaching from the south. Do you have any contact with the friendlies moving north for the linkup? Over."

"First Strike, that's a negative. We've had no contact, over."

"Roger. Is the artillery in yet. Over."

"We have one battery on the ground and ready to receive missions. Over."

"Roger, what about the attack aircraft? Are they on station?"

"Negative. They returned to refuel after escorting the first lift. They should be back in one hour, over."

"Strike Three, you best be getting some tac air up, then, because we're about to get into it. First Strike Out." Donald was not a happy camper. Minimal artillery support from a battery of 105mm howitzers with no attack helicopters was not his idea of a fun morning. Donald wanted to see for himself who this was before he allowed his people to commence an engagement. Grabbing his two RTOs and his S-3 and fire support coordinator, he set out, moving to Anvil's positions on the south side of the wadi.

****

The 3rd Regiment, 51st Infantry lead elements moved at twenty kilometers per hour, constantly scanning into the night sky for the American attack helicopters, which they had learned to fear more than anything. They hadn't experienced any American tanks but knew that some American mechanized force was trailing them north. They had engaged some infantry fighting vehicles and some scout vehicles, but no tanks. The tail end of the regiment was all those from the other two regiments who had somehow survived the onslaught that had happened days before. Everyone now just wanted to get to the safety of Tabuk with the 2nd and 37th Divisions under their air-defense umbrella.

Colonel Maloof had moved his vehicle forward and was following behind his lead element, the 1st Battalion of the brigade. If something was going to happen, he wanted to know about it immediately and be able to react, not waiting for a radio call. His options were limited as he had lost all artillery and there were no attack helicopters. The divisional artillery had come north first, but he had received a report that they had been hit by an airstrike along this road the day before. The road was already covered with destroyed vehicles from both his division moving north and corps supply vehicles that had been moving south weeks before. Most bodies lay where they had fallen as there were few inhabitants around to bury the dead in accordance with Muslim tradition.

They have to pick up the pace. The sun will be up in an hour and we need to get the entire regiment hidden in that wadi before then, Maloof thought when the first sound of trouble reached his ears. Small-arms fire was crackling at the front, and the distinct sound said it was not only AK-47s but also American M-16s. Then the sound of an American M-60 machine gun entered the orchestra. *Damn, let this be just a small patrol*, he thought as his vehicle dodged wrecked vehicles, attempting to move toward the sound of the guns. When he heard the first explosion and saw a vehicle to his front become a burning cauldron, he knew this was no skirmish.

****

"First Strike Six, Anvil Six, we have BTR-60s. Am engaging."

"Anvil Six, what's their strength?" Donald asked but got no response. Then he heard the first explosion but didn't think it was a TOW round.

"Dawg Six, have you engaged? Over," Donald asked his Delta Company commander.

"First Strike Six, that's a negative," the commander responded in a near-whisper. "We're letting them get into the kill zone before we engage. I believe that was an Alpha Tango Four from Anvil elements, over."

Two more explosions went off, briefly lighting up the night sky. *Damn, I wish the sun would come up. Another hour, I suspect*, Donald thought.

"Sir, Anvil is calling in artillery at this time. He has asked for illum first, followed by HE VT," the FSCOORD said.

"Good, we'll get a better look at what we got," Donald replied. From where he sat, he could clearly see the exchange of small arms but not who or what was doing the shooting. He was concerned, as he only had half of this battalion on the ground—the second half wouldn't be arriving for another thirty minutes. Only ten of his twenty antitank vehicles were on the ground. When the first of five artillery flares illuminated the night sky, his heart sank. This was an organized battalion of BTR-60s with infantry. He grabbed the hand mike for the brigade command net.

"Strike Six, First Strike Six, over."

"Go ahead, First Strike Six," Anderson came back.

"Strike Six, contact. Appears to be a BTR-60 battalion with follow-on forces, over."

"Roger, what is your situation?"

"Anvil is engaging, but I have only the ten TOW vehicles that came on the first lift. I don't think we can hold them with just ten. Over."

"Roger, I'll have Second Strike send his to assist. Break, Second Strike, Strike Six, over."

A moment later, the voice of the 2nd Battalion commander came over the net. "Strike Six, I monitored and am sending them to assist. They'll contact First Strike Six when they approach. Over."

"First Strike Six, did you copy?" Strike Six asked.

"Strike Six, I copied and am standing by, over."

Donald began to breathe a bit easier, knowing that ten more TOW vehicles would be joining the fight on his side.
****

In the time that Donald had been talking to Strike Six on the radio, VT fuze artillery began to hit the Iraqi column, stripping anything that was on the outside of the vehicles away, to include antennas. Although

Colonel Maloof couldn't transmit, it was a gift from God, as American antitank gunners were trained to shoot command vehicles first and the antennas on the vehicles were a dead giveaway. Maloof began to realize that where he planned to turn the column off the road for the day was exactly where the Americans were defending. He had to move them out of this kill zone, and that meant accelerating up the road. With his antenna shot away, he had to issue verbal orders. He quickly found the commander of the first battalion and told him to move north out of the kill zone and find a place to hide for the day. Quickly, that commander was moving his entire force north up the road, racing through the gauntlet of enemy fire. Some vehicles made it, others did not.

Once Maloof had coordinated with the 1st Battalion, he raced his vehicle back south to find the next commander. The 2nd Battalion commander hadn't had his antennas stripped, so Maloof climbed aboard his vehicle so he could use the radio while his crew was replacing his own antenna. His message to the subordinate commanders was clear: race through the engagement area going north and find a place to spend the day in hiding, or stay here and die for sure. Returning to his vehicle, he ordered his driver to move north with all possible speed.
****

As Donald had been watching the battle unfold, he was surprised that the Iraqis didn't attack but drove as fast as they could through the engagement area. They weren't stopping to fight but merely attempting to escape.

"Strike Six, First Strike Six over."

"Go ahead, First Strike Six," Anderson replied.

"Strike Six, these guys aren't attacking but merely attempting to escape north. They're putting up minimum resistance in the engagement area but accelerating into and through it. We're being selective on the engagements, taking out BTR-60s first and anything else second. Have not seen any tanks, over."

"Roger, understand you can hold your positions at this time, over."

"Strike Six, that's affirmative, over."

"Roger, First Strike Six. Keep us informed. Out."

As Donald sat with Anvil Six, watching the Iraqi vehicles attempting to race through the engagement area, he noticed one vehicle that had raced through the engagement area twice, and now it was entering a third time. Tapping Anvil Six on the shoulder, Donald pointed at it and asked, "You see that vehicle?"

"Yes, sir, the one turning around?"

"Kill it. That's got to be a leader," Donald stated. Anvil Six was on the radio immediately. Moments later, two AT-4 antitank rockets hit the vehicle. The vehicle instantly stopped and smoke poured out of the engine compartment. Then the flames began to escape through the side portholes and the top hatch. One figure cleared the top, with the flames licking at his boots as he rolled off the top and dropped to the ground. Donald noted his fall and lack of movement once he hit.
****

Colonel Maloof had already driven through the engagement area twice, guiding and encouraging his forces to get through the danger zone. *One more trip should do it*, he thought when the first round hit the forward right-side wheel, followed by a second round, which hit the rear engine compartments. The first round caused the vehicle to lurch to the right as the wheel disintegrated. The second round set off fuel and killed the engine. Lying on the floor in the front of the vehicle, Maloof looked back and quickly realized that the burning fuel was coming for him. He attempted to jump up but could barely move as his back had slammed into something with the first explosion. Slowly, too slowly, it seemed, he dragged himself up to the top hatch and pulled himself up on top of the vehicle. As he rolled away from the flames coming out of the open hatch and licking at his boots, he misjudged the distance he had before he rolled off the top. The night suddenly got much darker and then peaceful.
****

Colonel Maloof slowly opened his eyes. He had trouble getting them to focus at first, and when they did, nothing made sense. He was lying on a stretcher with an IV bottle stuck in his arm. He closed his eyes, knowing that his soldiers had retrieved him and brought him to safety. That illusion was quickly broken when he heard a voice that wasn't speaking Arabic.

197

"Yes, sir, we'll have him on the next chopper going back. He has a bad back injury but should recover in a couple of months. They may want to do surgery and then physical therapy for a month or so," one voice said.

"How much morphine is he on?" another asked.

"As much as I dare give him," the other voice answered.

"Can I talk to him?"

"You can try. Don't know if he'll comprehend anything," the doctor answered.

"Colonel Maloof, can you hear me, sir?" Donald asked, squatting down beside the man on the stretcher.

Maloof attempted to focus his eyes. "I hear."

"Colonel, you have a bad back injury. We're flying you out to a hospital in Yanbu for treatment. You're heavily drugged with morphine," Donald told him.

"And my regiment—what—" Maloof's eyes became very wide with pain.

"Just lie there and don't try to move, Colonel. Some of your brigade got out of our engagement zone. Some didn't, and the tail is now caught between us and the 28th Infantry Division moving up from the south. If they surrender, they'll be taken prisoner and treated well. We aren't here to kill anyone. Only to move you out of Saudi Arabia and Kuwait," Donald said.

Maloof tried again to say something, but the pain prevented it.

"Colonel, just lay there and rest. The chopper is on short final and you'll be out of here soon. You take care, sir," Donald said as he stood and watched two medics pick the colonel up.

If I get captured, I hope they treat me this well, Donald thought, knowing that he would not be captured. The 2nd Brigade as well as the 1st Brigade commanders had discussed this and all agreed, they would not be captured.

Chapter 35
Rethink This

26 April 1991
Republican Palace
Baghdad, Iraq

Lieutenant General Igor Petrov had seen the satellite photos before he'd left the Russian embassy that morning. He had already seen them before he'd left Moscow but wanted to be sure nothing had changed on the latest pass by the Zenit reconnaissance satellite. The photos were clear and clearly indicated what Petrov had feared. Almost more frightening, though, was having to bring this news to Saddam Hussein— but the powers that be had insisted that a high-ranking general officer present the evidence. *At least he cannot have me shot, I don't think*, Petrov thought as he walked into the Republican Palace.

The Republican Palace had been built in the 1950s, commissioned by King Faisal II for his wedding, which hadn't occurred because he'd been assassinated before it could take place. Saddam had found it to be to his liking and met dignitaries there for important meetings. As Petrov walked through the entrance, he appreciated the architecture but thought the Ikea furniture was out of place in such a place of such beauty. He was ushered into an office where Saddam rose from an overstuffed chair to greet him.

Extending both arms, Saddam grasped Petrov by the shoulder and kissed him on both cheeks. "Please, General, sit down," Saddam said, pointing to a chair next to the one he had been seated in. Between the chairs sat an interpreter. Saddam didn't speak Russian and Petrov didn't speak Arabic. Petrov could speak English, but Saddam always said his English skills were very bad.

Once the two were comfortably seated and all the minions had been excused from the room, Saddam looked to the general. "So, what is so important that Moscow has sent you to talk to me?" he asked.

"Mr. President, Moscow has great concern for your victory in this conflict. We want to see you win a great victory over the puppets of America. We want you to become the leader of the Arab world," Petrov said.

"I am that already, General. My army has rolled over Saudi Arabia and the UAE. My navy controls the Strait to the Arabian Gulf, and my air force controls the sky above," Saddam boasted.

Is this guy for real or what? Petrov thought as he studied the man's face. *He's not joking—he believes this fairy tale.* "Yes, sir, and we want to see you to continue this way. That is why I have been asked to show you these latest satellite photos we received on the last pass this morning," Petrov said, handing the photos to Saddam. He did not take them.

"And what would these photos show me that I do not already know?" Saddam questioned.

Petrov was a professional, but his temperature was rising at the thought of this arrogant despot. "Sir, these photos will show you that the American XVIII Airborne Corps is very close to seizing Tabuk. That the III Corps in the east is moving on Al Hofuf with both Arab forces and an American division. The Marines are moving to the west of Al Hofuf with three divisions, and the VII Corps, their heavy corps, is about to cross Highway 10 and cut Riyadh off. In addition, they have a sufficient supply line to sustain them for another six months of combat. Their airfields are full of aircraft; their fleet is unchallenged. In San Diego, California, another National Guard division is loading onto ships, having completed its rotation at the National Training Center. They will be here in a month," Petrov concluded.

"General, I know most of this information without looking at photographs. We are slowly drawing the Americans away from their supply bases in Oman, thus extending their supply lines. Soon they will be stretched so thin that when the 1st Republican Guard Corps attacks, the Americans will be exhausted," Saddam said, rather pleased with himself.

"Sir, that is fine, but at the rate the Americans are advancing, they will take Dammam, and when that happens, their resupply operations will shift from Oman to Dammam and be very short again. As these photos show, they have supply ships loaded and just waiting to come in to offload in Dammam," Petrov indicated.

"General, the 1st Republican Guard Corps has moved back into Kuwait as we speak and joined the VII Iraqi Corps, which has three divisions outside of Kuwait as a screening force. It was never my intent to hold Saudi Arabia but merely to cripple it. Destroy its oil fields, which we have successfully done. This will raise the price of oil to an acceptable level for me," Saddam said. Petrov could not believe what he was hearing.

"Now Kuwait is a different matter. They are the nineteenth province of Iraq, the Basra province, and as such will be retained by us. The meddling British cut them loose almost one hundred years ago and we are now taking them back." Suddenly, Saddam's tone changed. "And no one, American, British, Iranian or Russian, is going to tell us different," he said with anger etched across his face.

I wonder if he is going to have me shot now, Petrov considered.

"Sir, we are not telling you to surrender Kuwait. Merely advising you as to what forces are arrayed before you and offer what help we can without being directly involved in the conflict. As you know, we are having our own internal struggles right now and can do little militarily to assist you," Petrov stated. That is the party line.

"General Petrov, I am glad we had this meeting. I would like to give these photos to my minister of defense if you do not mind," Saddam said as he stood, signaling that the meeting was over.

"Those are for you, Mr. President, in the hope that they will assist you in your victory," Petrov said. *Fat chance*, he thought, however.

Chapter 36
Counterattack

26 April 1991
6th Armoured Division
Ain Wasia, Saudi Arabia

The 6th Armoured Division had established their forward command post in the industrial area of Ain Wasia with forward elements on the west side of At Tawdihiyah. In the early-morning hours, they had monitored the actions of the Americans against the 21st and 36th Infantry Divisions as well as the movement of the 1st Mechanized Division. All subordinate units had been placed on alert for future actions. Vehicles had been topped off with fuel and ammo. One regiment was in defensive positions forward of At Tawdihiyah along Highway 10 to prevent any movement by the Americans towards Riyadh.

"General Faizan," Colonel Ghafor, his operations officer, said, gaining the general's attention. General Faizan had been awake for almost twenty hours and was studying the map and the intelligence reports for the hundredth time. "Sir, the lead elements of the Americans are crossing Highway 10 at this time."

Looking up from the maps, Faizan smiled for the first time in many hours. "Now is the time to hit them. Order the 1st and 2nd Regiments to attack as we planned. Notify the 1st Mech that we are attacking and request they do likewise on our left flank."

"Yes, sir, I will issue the order," Colonel Ghafor said.
****

Captain Bouzizi sat in his T-62 tank, waiting for an order to move. The plan for the counterattack had been gone over several times with the battalion commander. Every company commander understood their objective and every crew member understood their job. Bouzizi felt blessed, as he had maintained the same crew since the war had started. They had been bombed and strafed by the American Air Force. They had eaten the dust of dozens of tanks moving ahead of them. They had been through discomfort together, and that had molded them into a strong crew. Each relied on the other and, as brothers, they would not fail one another.

As Bouzizi sat in the position, his mind wandered back to Basra, where he had been born, and the home his parents had raised him in. He thought of the school he'd attended as a boy and the soccer team he'd played on, scoring several goals over the years. The trip to Baghdad to attend the university had been marked by fear as Iranian jets had attacked the road he was traveling on. That one event had told him to become a soldier. He didn't like carrying the load of an infantry soldier and had scored high enough on examinations to be selected to attend the armor course. On graduation, his first assignment had been as a platoon leader in a tank company, and he had seen action along the Iranian border in the closing days of the war. His actions had been noted by the battalion commander and he'd quickly been promoted and given this company to command. His sixteen tanks were fairly new and all in good working order.

"Sir, when are we going to move? My butt cheeks are getting sore from sitting in this driver's seat for so long," Private Allaf complained.

"Hey, Allaf, maybe you want that pretty thing you were with this weekend to massage your ass, yes?" Corporal Atwan, the loader, chimed in.

"Oh, shut up, Atwan. You know nothing," Allaf retorted.

"I heard you were with your sister this weekend, Allaf. Are you really close to her?" Sergeant al-Jabiri asked, half-joking, from his gunner position.

"Alright, you guys, knock it off," Bouzizi said. "Try and get some sleep before we move out. It's going to be a long day, I suspect."

"Captain, do you really think we'll mix it up with the Americans? I have heard that their tanks are very good," Sergeant al-Jabiri inquired.

"Their tanks are no better than ours, and we are attacking to reach Haradh. Whoever gets in our way, we engage. It is that simple," Bouzizi said. Just then, the radio crackled and the voice of the battalion commander came on.

"Move out," was the only command. Bouzizi didn't need anything more.
****

The 1st Battalion, 18th Armor, a tank battalion of the 24th Infantry Division, had crossed Highway 10 and was encountering resistance from Iraqi infantry. The level of resistance was almost nonexistent, however, as the infantry had only RPGs and 9M14 Malyutka antitank guided missiles. The missiles had an effective range of three thousand meters, but also a major flaw. The missile was wire-guided to the target but had to be flown with the use of a joystick. The fastest way to defeat the missile was to simply shoot in the direction of the launch site, which would cause the shooter to flinch and fly the missile off target. The Cheetahs, as 1-18 Armor was called, had one infantry company moving with them, and they had been busy clearing bunkers while the tanks remained in overwatch and fire support.

"Cheetah Six, Lion King Six, over," Colonel Jose, the brigade commander, transmitted. Colonel Jose was a Cajun from Louisiana. His annual crawfish boil for the brigade officers was an event everyone looked forward to.

"Lion King Six, Cheetah Six, over," Lieutenant Colonel Piscal responded.

"Cheetah Six, hold your current location. Be prepared for a counterattack on your left front. We have intel that an armor force is approaching from the west and a mech force from the northwest. How copy?" Lion King Six asked.

"Lion King, I have good copy and will hold in place," Piscal responded.

"Roger, out." Lion King signed off.

Piscal thought about the current and future situation for a minute, then switched from intercom to FM 1 radio. "All Cheetah elements, this is Cheetah Six, over," Piscal transmitted. Each company-size element responded, letting him know they were listening. He explained the situation and directed each of the companies to assume a defensive posture with the threat to the west and northwest. All responded and immediately moved to the best terrain for their defense, much to the relief of the fleeing Iraqi soldiers that had been attempting to defend against the 3-69 Armor. Suddenly the raised Iraqi bunkers were useful places to hide behind, providing a hull defilade position for the M1 tanks and Bradley fighting vehicles.
****

Captain Bouzizi's company was eating dust, having been designated the reserve company for the battalion. He hated being in that position, as did everyone. Each vehicle turned up enough dust to choke the crews, but following another company made it worse. The one consolation was the fact that the dust cloud helped mask your vehicles from the enemy. Slowly, Bouzizi could hear artillery begin to impact to his front. When this occurred, you were generally within a thousand meters of the impacting rounds as the tank was so loud when buttoned up you couldn't hear much outside it. Bouzizi just hoped the impacting artillery was friendly and not American artillery.

"All units. The American forces are withdrawing east. Continue to press the attack to Haradh," came over the radio.

"Captain, did I hear right? The Americans are falling back?" Sergeant al-Jabiri asked.

"That's what I heard, Sergeant," Bouzizi replied, looking through the pillow blocks to see targets. He hadn't found any as yet.

"Captain, that doesn't make sense," Sergeant al-Jabiri said.

"Oh? And why is that, Sergeant?"

"Captain, why would the Americans be withdrawing? I haven't seen one American vehicle either engaging, retreating or burning. All I'm seeing is destroyed Iraqi equipment and dead Iraqi soldiers," Sergeant al-Jabiri said, pressing his point. Captain Bouzizi hadn't thought about this but now began to confirm Sergeant al-Jabiri's observations.

"Maybe, Sergeant, we have not reached the place where the Americans were. We will see their destroyed vehicles soon," Bouzizi said to reassure his crew and himself as they pressed the attack forward.
****

In accordance with the brigade plan, Lieutenant Colonel Piscal had ordered his Cheetah elements to begin an eastward withdrawal when the Iraqi artillery began to fall. He covered his withdrawal with his own artillery support, which further masked his movement. He was going to drop back two klicks, two thousand meters, which would expose the flank for the attacker to 3-69 Armor.

"All Power elements, Power Six. Execute plan Bravo," Lieutenant Colonel Altamire ordered. The battalion staff and company commanders had developed and gone over a plan for just this sort of situation on several occasions. They had executed it at the National Training Center in Fort Irwin, California, and it had worked very well. Now it was time to test it with live rounds and live targets, targets that were going to shoot back with live rounds. The plan was for one defending battalion to withdraw two thousand meters, sucking the attacker forward while the second battalion attacked the flank behind the lead elements, destroying the follow-on force while the first defending element engaged the lead elements.

As soon as Captain Poggi received the command, he ordered the Dawg elements to execute. Lieutenant Bagel immediately pulled back his platoon, which was the southernmost platoon, and moved into the trail position, center with 2nd Platoon and 1st Platoon abreast, all heading in a northerly direction to cross Highway 10. The terrain was low sand dunes, five to ten feet high and perpendicular to the route of march but ideal for taking a quick hull defilade position.

"Dawg One-One, Dawg Six, over."

"Dawg Six, Dawg One-One, over," Lieutenant Bagel responded.

"One-One, watch our left flank. Would not be good to be surprised by these guys while we surprise them, over."

"Roger, One-One has you covered." With that, Lieutenant Bagel led his platoon to the left flank but maintained five hundred meters behind the 2nd Platoon.

****

"Allaf, maintain your distance on the north side of Highway 10. Keep it in sight but run parallel with it," Captain Bouzizi said over his intercom system.

"Roger, sir."

Bouzizi was getting reports of enemy contact from the more northern companies, but as yet he had not had any contact with the Americans. *Everyone else will be bragging about how they drove the Americans back and we have nothing to show for it*, Bouzizi thought as the tank on his right side exploded.

"Tank, three o'clock," Sergeant al-Jabiri yelled, turning the turret to face the new threat.

"All elements, engage, three o'clock," Bouzizi ordered his company, and both turrets and tanks turned to face the threat. Before they could fire their first shots, two more of Bouzizi's tanks were destroyed. He watched in horror as his vehicles were being systematically destroyed from the left and right inward.

"Allaf, put us behind a dune and halt," Bouzizi yelled, wanting to be in a hull defilade position, which would offer some protection.

"Sergeant, do you see them?" Bouzizi asked.

"No, sir. I just know where the fire came from, but—" His words were cut short when something ripped the left side of the turret off, and the side of Sergeant al-Jabiri's head with it.

****

"Gunner, sabot, tank," Lieutenant Bagel ordered.

"Identified," Sergeant Adams replied.

"Up," Anderson yelled.

"Fire," Bagel commanded. In the time it took to give the commands, the T-62 tank with the antennas and flag had dropped behind a sand dune that partially covered the turret. Bagel's shot, although it covered the distance in less than one second, had to punch through the top of the dune, which slowed the round to some extent. When it hit the turret, some of the kinetic energy in the round had been dissipated.

"Check your work," Bagel directed and sought out their next target, which he quickly found. He didn't see that Captain Bouzizi had somehow crawled out of the tank and was lying on the ground. There was too much to do to notice.

****

"Power Six, Avenging Angel Six, over."

"Avenging Angel Six, Power Six, go ahead," Lieutenant Colonel Altamire said, wondering who this was on his net.

"Power Six, Avenging Angel Six is a flight of six Alpha Hotel Six-Four. Understand you have targets for me, over."

"Affirmative, Avenging Angel. Regiment of T-62 tanks." Altamire read off the coordinates of the lead vehicles opposing his battalion.

"Roger. We will commence our attack in five mikes. Over."

"Good copy and good hunting. Power Six standing by," Altamire said and began to look around for the Avenging Angel aircraft. He didn't see them but could see the dust that was being generated by the rotor wash from a hovering helicopter. From out of the swirling dust clouds, four flashes could be seen, immediately followed by four more. The flashes made a beeline for the lead tanks, which simultaneously exploded. Between the fifty-two tanks of the 3-69 Armor, the fifty-two from 1-18 Armored and the six Apache helicopters, the first regiment of the 6th Armoured Division was stopped and being systematically destroyed.

Chapter 37
Boundary Shift

27 April 1991
III Corps HQ
As Salwa, Saudi Arabia

The III Corps operations order had the 1st Cavalry Division on the right flank and the 50th Armor on the left flank. The move to As Salwa had been relatively unopposed although littered with broken toys that the Iraqis had left behind. The 3rd Armored Cav Regiment was screening the left flank, maintaining contact with the 1st Marine Division, who was going into Al Hofuf. Although the movement north for the 1st Cav and the 50th Armored was going smoothly, the Egyptians were struggling to maintain their equipment and keep up. TF Abu Bakr and TF Tariq were not having maintenance problems but were stopping frequently to rifle through equipment and supplies left behind by the retreating Iraqi units. III Corps Tactical Operations Center was in As Salwa.

"Ivan, Yeosock here," the voice on the other end of the satellite phone said.

"And a good day to you, sir. To what do I owe the pleasure of this call, may I ask?" Lieutenant General Ivan Smith loved screwing with his old friend.

"Yes, you may. Slight mission change for you. VII Corps got hit yesterday afternoon with a counterattack by the 6th Armoured Division and the 1st Mech Division and was in a fight with the 36th Infantry Division. We're going to turn him slightly and let him liberate Riyadh— that's causing us to shift the two Marine divisions and the Brits to take on the 21st Infantry Division located in Al Hawlyan. Can you take Al Hofuf?" Yeosock asked.

"Sure can. That'll give Rich Schneider something useful to do," Smith said.

"Good. How soon can you start that engagement?"

"In about three hours. I'd like to have the Al Fatah Brigade from Kuwait along with the 2-5 Kuwait Mech Battalion accompany him to reassure the locals that we're friendly. Once we get up to Buqayq, I'm going to have the 3rd and 4th Egyptian Divisions take the lead along with

TF Abu Bakr and TF Tariq as we move to Dammam. Put an Arab face on this exploitation. I'll put the 1st Cav in reserve to back up 50th Armor if necessary," Smith explained.

"Sounds good to me. Just keep me in the loop," Yeosock directed. "One more thing I need to discuss with you. The King is making noise about wanting a host nation commander leading the host nation forces. He thinks that would lend credibility to the Arab forces liberating Kuwait." Yeosock explained.

"I don't care for the sound of this," General Smith said with a sigh.

"Well, this is just a heads-up. Norm is blocking that right now. Just continue to march and let him sort it out."
****

Major General Rich Schneider, commander of the 50th Armored Division, sat outside his TOC and watched the lone UH-1H aircraft circle. *Who the hell is this now?* he wondered as the aircraft made a final turn to an approach. *Like we don't have enough damn dust around here already—now we have to add a bit more from a helicopter.* He continued to watch as three individuals hopped out and the helicopter began a shutdown procedure. As the group approached, he recognized Lieutenant General Ivan Smith, the III Corps commander. They had only met a few times, but he liked the man from what he had seen.

Standing, Schneider rendered a proper salute, which Smith returned with a smile.

"Rich, how goes the war?" Smith asked, extending his hand.

"My little piece of it is boringly quiet, sir. Can't speak for everyone else," Schneider said.

"Well, I think I might just be able to make it more interesting for you," Smith replied and guided Schneider to a map mounted on an easel.

"The Marines are shifting to the west, and we're moving the boundary between them and us. This shift put Al Hofuf right in our expanded sector. The city has well over five hundred thousand residents. We expect that most of the Iraqi forces have pulled out but cannot say if they left stay-behinds or sympathizers. You and 1st Cav are going to clear it out. The 1st Cav will clear the eastern side and you the western side. While you're doing that, Task Force Abu Bakr and Task Force Tariq will conduct a passage of lines while 1st Cav will clear these residential areas and date orchards on the eastern side. You get the city proper. My ops people will send over some graphics with boundaries later today. It's paramount that you and the Cav are talking so we don't have a fratricide incident. This will set up our approach into Dammam with Arab forces. Once you and the Cav have cleaned out these residential areas, then we can push north and isolate Dammam for the Arab forces. Any questions?" General Smith asked.

"I understand the order for minimal collateral damage still applies, so no use of my artillery in the city?" Schneider asked.

"Order still stands," Smith indicated.

****

Sergeant First Class McCoy was in the commander's position on his Bradley Fighting Vehicle with a squad of soldiers spread out in front of the vehicle, cautiously moving down the street on both sides. Their platoon had been told to participate in clearing out King Faisal University. When they entered the main gate, their battalion, 1-114 Infantry, along with the rest of 2nd Brigade, went to the east side. Each battalion of the brigade was formed into task forces with two tank companies from the two armor battalions, flipping with two companies from each of the infantry battalions. The area they were slowly moving through was partially wide open and partially very urban. Parking lots were the very open areas, measuring the length of two or three football fields. As they progressed north, however, it became more urban with dormitories and multistory classroom buildings.

"Big Dog Three-One, Big Dog Three," Sergeant McCoy's platoon leader transmitted.

"Big Dog Three, Three-One, go ahead," McCoy responded.

"I just came across a track vehicle next to this dormitory that was squashed like a bug with one of those concrete bombs. We need to check this dormitory out. You come in the back way and secure the downstairs. I'll bring Second and Third Squads in the front and start clearing floors. How copy?"

"Big Dog Three, I have good copy. Let me secure the ground floor and then you come in over."

"Roger, standing by for your call."

McCoy stopped his vehicle and gathered the squad around him. "Okay, this is what we got. We're going to secure the ground floor of this dormitory and the rest of the platoon is going to clear the upper floors. It's only three stories high, so it should go fairly fast. You two stay with the vehicle. The rest on me. Move out."

The squad approached the back door and loading dock at the back of the building. From the smell, McCoy figured that the loading dock must be at the back of a kitchen. They lined up on both sides of the passageway door, and McCoy nodded to the point man, who grabbed the handle and pulled the door open. The second man entered quickly at a low crouch with his weapon raised, ready for an engagement. Nothing happened. The rest of the squad filed in on opposite sides of the hallway. As they passed each door, the room or closet behind it was cleared and the squad moved on. Two squad members peeled off to clear the kitchen. No one was present and it didn't appear that anyone had cleaned the place in days, as spoiled food was on the counters. Dirty dishes were piled up in the sink and, from the appearance, the food hadn't been professionally prepared. However, there was a pot of water boiling on the stove.

As two members scoped out the kitchen, the remainder of the squad looked into the dining area. It was equally a mess, with dirty dishes everywhere. McCoy touched one plate with the back of his hand. *Still warm. Someone has just been here…*

McCoy gave the appropriate hand signal to indicate they had company in the building.

"Big Dog Three, Three-One, over."

"Go ahead, Three-One," the lieutenant said.

"Be advised, we have company in the building."

"Have you seen anyone?"

"No, Big Dog, but we interrupted their dinner, it appears."

"Roger, let me know when you're ready for us to come in, over."

"Roger wilco."

McCoy signaled for the squad to move on, since this area was clear. McCoy looked around the corner of the doorway leading out of the dining hall. It emptied into a large open area with couches, tables and reading stands with magazines, newspapers and books. The magazines and newspapers were all six months old. On the far wall were windows

212

overlooking the parking lot. To the right were a staircase and elevators. McCoy motioned for everyone to spread out and begin sweeping the room towards the elevators. As they approached, an elevator bell rang. Everyone froze, weapons trained on the elevator doors with Private Hanna standing next to the door, back to the wall. As the door opened, a young man cautiously stepped out. He took three steps before the barrel of a weapon was in his face. Then he heard the voice.

"Take another step and I'll blow your fucking head off." The young man spoke enough English that he fully understood and did not move.

"Hog-tie this bastard. Check him for weapons," McCoy ordered, and the young man was tossed to the floor, zip ties placed on his wrists.

Leaning over, McCoy quietly asked, "Do you speak English, Mohammed?"

"You bet your sweet ass I do, and my name is Frank, not Mohammed," the young man answered with a slight Boston accent.

"What the—are you bullshitting me?" McCoy asked as he pulled the young man to his feet.

"I kid you not, Sergeant, my name is Frank, and I'm from the south side of Boston. I was born in Iraq and moved to Boston with my parents in the late seventies," Frank explained.

"So what the hell are you doing here?" McCoy asked, suspicious of the young man.

"Well, I was enrolled in the university studying engineering when the Iraqis attacked. I couldn't get out of the country, so I figured I would just hunker down and stay here until it was safe to leave or until you came and got me," Frank said. "Now can you untie me?"

"No, not until your story checks out. You got a passport?" McCoy asked.

"Yeah, it's hidden in my room with my Massachusetts driver's license. But you don't want to go up there," Frank replied.

"And why is that?" McCoy asked with renewed interest.

"Because there are about twenty Iraqi soldiers up there on the second and third floors, scared as shit. They were told to stay here and defend the campus with a bunch more, but everyone else already left. These guys didn't have a vehicle and so they were left behind," Frank informed him.

"And they just let you ride down here?" McCoy interrogated with suspicion now.

"No, actually they asked me to come down and negotiate a surrender. They offer two options. Option one is you can surrender to them and they'll take your vehicle and leave you here. Option two is they'll surrender to you if you promise not to shoot them and give them a vehicle. Those are the two choices that their lieutenant would consider. What do you want me to tell them?"

McCoy was dumbfounded when he heard this.

"Big Dog Three, Three-One."

"Go ahead, Three-One."

"Big Dog, you need to come in here and hear this."

"Roger, be right there."

Entering the building, the lieutenant was surprised to see the squad actually relaxing but covering the stairs and the other elevator door. McCoy let Frank offer the lieutenant the options for surrender.

"Gee, Frank, I'm going to have to consider these terms of surrender," Big Dog said. "*Hmm*... let me think about this for a minute." He walked towards the front door. Frank couldn't believe that the lieutenant was considering both options.

"Okay, Frank, we'll do option two but they are not getting a vehicle. You go back upstairs and tell them I want every weapon, grenade, pistol, rifle, and toothpick placed in an elevator and sent down. Then I want everyone to walk down the stairs, five steps between them, with their hands above their heads, not behind their heads but above their heads with palms open. If I see someone that isn't that way, we shoot them. Understood?"

"Hey, Lieutenant, I speak Bostonian English, so no need to spell it out for me. I'll take the elevator back up and start sending them down," Frank said as he motioned for them to untie his hands.

"Untie him," McCoy said to a squad member. "Oh, Frank—when you come down those stairs, the same applies to you, and you best have that passport in your back pocket along with that driver's license, or you'll be with your friends a long time. You read me, bro?" McCoy asked in his best New York accent.

Ten minutes later, the elevator bell rang again. When the door opened, a collection of weapons, to include rifles, automatic weapons, RPG rockets, grenades and knives, was on the floor.

A voice called out from the stairwell. "Okay, guys, we're coming down." It was Frank.

"Just be sure they understand the procedure, Frank," McCoy yelled.

"They do. I rehearsed it with them."

The first Iraqi soldier appeared around the corner. His steps were very measured as he showed all his teeth in a wide smile. "Allo, American GI. Allo. I go Boston with Frank."

"Just come on down nice and slow," McCoy said, not sure if anyone understood him.

As each Iraqi soldier approached, they all said the same thing. McCoy and the lieutenant, as well as the entire platoon, were wondering about this. Finally, Frank showed up.

"Hey, Frank, what's this shit about them all going to Boston with you?" Big Dog asked.

"Well, I had to offer them something in return for them not getting a vehicle to leave in, so I told them I would take them to Boston with me. They believed me, I guess. Can you get us all on a flight together?" Frank asked with a broad smile.

"I'll see what I can do," Big Dog replied as he shook his head and began to chuckle.

****

On the other side of the campus, 2-113 Infantry, part of 1st Brigade, was not having a fun time. A company-size unit was trapped in the administration building, and some had taken refuge in the university mosque.

"Guardian Six, Patriot Six, over," the Alpha Company commander, Captain Dietz, radioed.

"Patriot Six, Guardian Six, go ahead," Lieutenant Colonel Jimmy Heinz replied.

"Guardian Six, I need some Arab forces over here. We have a platoon-size element holding up in the mosque and engaging, over."

"Roger, I'll try to get someone over there. Right now I don't think we have anyone following, over."

"Understood, we're standing by but cannot get these areas cleared until we get these guys out. Patriot Six out."

Turning to his Ops officer, Major Duvall, Heinz instructed, "Get Brigade on the horn and see if we have any Arab forces following us that we can get to come over and talk these guys out."

An hour later, Major Duvall came to Heinz's position and indicated, "Sir, Brigade says it'll be three hours before they can get an Arab force over there to get these people out. But... 2nd Brigade says they may have a solution to our problem here in ten minutes. Seems one of their units captured a guy that claims he's an American from Boston. He talked a platoon into surrendering an hour ago. Speaks fluent Arabic."

"Shit, get the guy over here and let's see what he can do," Lieutenant Colonel Heinz directed.

"I figured you'd want him, and he's on his way now. Should be here in a few minutes," Major Duvall said with a grin.

"Well, send him right down to Dietz so he can put the guy to work. Tell Dietz to put him in a helmet and flak jacket. Last thing I need is some civilian being shot because we didn't offer him the proper equipment."
****

Climbing out of the Bradley fighting vehicle, Frank was amazed at the inner workings of the beast. The pinging sounds off the side of the vehicle told him he wasn't in Kansas—maybe the south side of Boston, but not Kansas. He was met by Captain Dietz, who was standing behind the vehicle when it stopped. In his hand was a white flag.

"I'm Captain Dietz. Who are you?"

"Sir, I'm a civilian. Name's Frank."

"Well, Frank, you're now a civilian contractor for me. Put this helmet and chest protector on. Won't stop a bullet, but it'll help with shrapnel," Dietz said as a soldier handed the items to Frank. "Okay, here's the situation. We have about a platoon-size force in that mosque. We can't go in and they don't appear to want to come out. I need you to talk them into surrendering and come out. Can you do that?" Dietz asked.

"I can try, sir. Worked with the last group, but I had been with them for almost a month," Frank replied.

"Well, work your magic and carry this flag. Hope they recognize it. Good luck," Dietz added.

Luck? I'm going to need a lot more than that in the next few minutes. I'm going to need a fucking miracle, Frank thought as he raised the flag from behind the Bradley and slowly emerged. The shooting stopped. *Well, that's the first good sign.* Frank slowly walked across the parking lot to the front door of the mosque.

Dietz and the company watched as Frank walked up the front steps and started speaking, but they couldn't hear what was being said. Dietz got a bit worried when the front door opened and Frank went inside. *I didn't want that to happen. Now they have a hostage if they want one.* Dietz kept checking his watch. Frank was in there for thirty minutes. *What's taking so damn—*

Dietz didn't get to finish his thought before the sound of a gunshot emanated from the mosque. *Oh, shit, they shot Frank* ran through Dietz's mental database. Everyone was still in their battle positions and the Bradley's 25mm Bushmaster chain guns were trained on the mosque. After a minute, the front door opened, and the white flag came out. Frank was holding it and waving. Slowly he walked forward, leading a line of thirty Iraqi soldiers with their hands held high, palms out and open. The soldiers of Alpha Company slowly moved in to surround them.

Dietz approached Frank. "What the hell was the gunshot? I thought you were a goner."

Frank placed the white flag against the Bradley. "It seems that there was a vigorous discussion after I made them the offer to surrender. Seems the officer was against it, wanting to hold out for reinforcements. A vote was taken—he lost and protested. He lost the protest as well. His body is in the mosque."

Chapter 38
Major Decisions

29 April 1991
Iraqi Army HQ
Kuwait City, Kuwait

All the key players in Saddam's inner circle were present. Sultan Hashim Ahmed al-Tai, the Defense Minister, was chairing the meeting, but Tariq Aziz, the Deputy Prime Minister, was sitting in to hear the discussion. Ibrahim Ahmed abd al-Sattan al-Tikrit, the Armed Forces Chief of Staff, was present, as well as Sayf al-Din Fulayyih Hasan Taha al-Rawi, the commander of the Republican Guard. Hamid Raja Shalah al-Tikriti was present to address Air Force issues. Corps commanders were not present.

"Why isn't Admiral Hassan present for this meeting?" al-Tai asked.

A naval officer on the sidelines answered the question. "Sir, he was aboard ship when it was hit by a missile on the first day. A rescue operation failed to find any survivors."

"Alright, let's get started. The purpose of this meeting is to look at the current situation and decide what to do from here. First let's hear from the air force. General al-Tikriti," al-Tai indicated.

"The air force has sustained great losses in the past month. The Americans now have five aircraft carriers operating within strike distance of most of Saudi Arabia, and with inflight refueling, they can loiter over the target area for over an hour. The American and British air forces are flying out of Oman and Egypt and also are capable of striking almost anywhere in day or night conditions. Their heavy bombers are coming from Diego Garcia and Great Britain. What fighter-capable aircraft we have left are attempting to protect our ground forces. Our close-air support aircraft are being mauled by the American fighters whenever they lift off. The air-defense forces have been inefficient in curtailing the American attacks. The—"

General Muzahim Sa'b Hassan al-Tikriti slammed his hand down on the conference table. "How dare you blame the air-defense forces for your inability to maintain air superiority? If you count the number of downed American aircraft, the air-defense forces have brought down more than double what the air force has shot down. And our losses have been equally high. We turn on a radar and there is a good chance that their Wild Weasel missile will engage the system," he protested with a raised voice.

"Enough!" Sultan al-Tai yelled. "We are here to examine the current situation and decide the future. We are not here to point fingers and make accusations. General al-Tikriti, please finish your assessment of the air force without making accusations."

"Yes, Mr. Minister. The air force has as of this morning about three hundred aircraft left, to include ground attack and interceptors, compared with probably three thousand aircraft, most being close-air support and fighters, that the Americans have. If we are having a good day, we can put up sixty sorties a day. If the Americans are having a bad day, they can put up about fifteen hundred aircraft a day for thirty days. They are currently averaging about two thousand sorties a day. At this point, I am recommending that we hold what aircraft we have in reserve for the defense of Kuwait and our own homeland," General al-Tikriti concluded.

"General al-Tikriti, is there anything else you would like to add about our air-defense forces?" al-Tai asked.

"Sir, we have sufficient air-defense assets at the division and corps levels and we are in good supply of more missiles. Kuwait and northern Saudi Arabia are under the umbrella provided by the SA-2 and SA-3 systems as well as the SA-6 systems. These systems overlap with those that we have over Baghdad and major cities in Iraq. There is also a good supply of air-defense guns guarding our key installations under these missile umbrellas. If our ground forces pull back closer to Kuwait, they will come under these umbrellas," General al-Tikriti announced. Unbeknownst to the others, he and General Ibrahim al-Tikrit as well as al-Rawi had already discussed the air-defense situation, noting the lack of air force support.

"General Ibrahim al-Tikrit, your assessment of the ground campaign," al-Tai asked.

"General al-Rawi and I have discussed the ground situation and are in agreement. The Americans have an uninterrupted supply line from Oman and now they have a port on the Red Sea as well as from which they are supplying the XVIII Airborne Corps. They have crushed the IX Corps and reduced the II Corps to two divisions and remnants of three

219

others as best we can tell. The 2nd Republican Guard Corps is at fifty percent strength and withdrawing through Hafar al Batin so it can be reconstituted. The IV Corps is engaged right now with the American VII Corps, the American III Corps and two Marine divisions, all of which are enjoying air superiority. General Ghanem doubts he can stop them from destroying his entire force as they are mostly armor and mechanized forces and he is mostly infantry. The 1st Republican Guard Corps has already pulled back to Kuwait and taking up defensive positions there. The VII Corps has a screen line south of Kuwait with only one armored division and seven infantry divisions. We doubt that they can stop the American mechanized and armor forces. Our recommendation is to pull everyone back to Kuwait and prepare a rigorous defense to stop the Americans. This would put our forces under a strong air-defense umbrella, shorten our supply lines and allow our infantry units to fight from prepared positions en masse instead of spread out over the vast desert," General Ibrahim al-Tikrit concluded.

Al-Tai looked around the room and the faces confirmed his thoughts. They had gone too far and needed to pull back before the entire army was lost. He turned to two members of the Ministry of Defense, General abd al-Jabbar Shanshal and General abd al-Jabbar al-Asadi. "Gentlemen, your assessment, please?" al-Tai asked. He did not want to be on this sinking ship alone.

The two members looked at each other before al-Asadi spoke. "We are of the opinion that the recommendations made are valid and should be implemented as soon as possible," General al-Asadi answered.

"Mr. Aziz, you have heard our recommendations. These recommendations should be instituted quickly," al-Tai said.

"I will convey your recommendations this afternoon to Mr. Hussein, and you will have your answer very soon," the Deputy Prime Minister said. Everyone hoped the answer wouldn't be a bullet in the back of the head.

Chapter 39
Joint Air Assault Operations

30 April 1991
3rd Brigade, 82nd Airborne Division
Jeddah, Saudi Arabia

"Sir, you can go right in. General Ford is waiting for you," the general's aide said as Colonel Jim Irons walked into the outer office.

"Morning, sir," Irons said, pausing in the door to render a salute.

Returning his salute, Ford motioned to an overstuffed chair in the office with a coffee table in front and two cups of coffee already poured. Picking up a cup and sitting down next to Irons, Ford took a sip. "Good things come to those who wait, Jim," Ford said.

"I've heard that, sir," Irons replied, not sure where this was going.

"Well, you've waited long enough. Is your brigade ready for a drop?" Ford asked. Irons nearly spat his coffee out.

"You're damn right we're ready. When and where, sir?"

"The where is the airport at Tabuk. The when is in question. The 101st is leapfrogging FOBs north towards the airfield and the garrison compound that's adjacent to the airfield. The 28th and 29th Infantry Divisions are conducting a ground move to link up at each FOB, but we want those facilities intact when the infantry divisions get there. Powers above us are afraid that the Iraqis will blow everything and make it unusable to us. I'll keep you posted on when, but it'll be short notice. We'll have the C-130 aircraft to support your full brigade, infantry, artillery, and TOW vehicles. Wish we kept a couple of Sheridans here to send in with you, but hindsight..." Ford left his sentence hanging.

"Sir, this is great. The boys will really be excited to get a combat jump in and a star on their wings," Irons said as he finished his coffee. His mind was racing with what had to be done.

"Yeah, looking forward to that myself," Ford replied with a big smile.

"Sir, you're... sir, you shouldn't... sir, you can't...," Irons stammered.

"And why not, Colonel? You don't think I'm going to keep the division staff here in the perfume palace waiting. Shit, I have one plane

just of the Division staff and one for vehicles in the follow-on. I want to be standing on the runway and greeting Peters."
****

Several hundred miles away in Tabuk, General al-Douri had just placed the phone back in the cradle. The call from General Ibrahim Ahmed Abd al-Sattan al-Tikrit had sobered his mood.

He looked up at his aide. "Please have General Arif Jahid come see me immediately."

Twenty minutes later, General Jahid entered the corps commander's office.

"You wished to see me, sir?" Jahid commented.

"Yes, sit down," al-Douri said, motioning to a stiff-backed chair while he remained behind his desk. "Hear me and hear me good. There will be no discussion. We have been ordered to move from Tabuk in the next twenty-four hours and head back to Iraq. As your division is the only division left mostly intact, I want you to leave as quickly as you can. Take all the supplies you can carry, and fuel. Speed is of the essence, so you will take Highway 15 to Highway 80 to Sakakah. You may spread your division out where the terrain permits, but where it doesn't, use the highways. Attempt to cover as much distance as you can under the cover of darkness in blackout drive. The air-defense forces are going to position along the highway and travel with you to protect you from the American aircraft, but there are no guarantees at this point. Just get back into Iraq as quickly as possible and continue to move east to the Kuwait border. When you cross back into Iraq, head for the airfield at Al Salman. Supply points along your route are planned and will be coordinated with you. Any questions.?"

"Where will you be?" Jahid asked.

"The corps headquarters are flying out of here tomorrow from the airport to Al Salman. Once there, we will move a jump TOC west to stay in contact with you and coordinate the resupply points. As we speak, supply convoys are heading west to link up with you," al-Douri explained.

"What about the other units? When are they coming out?" Jahid asked, worried not about their safety but about the congestion on the highway in front of him.

"What other units, Jahid? The 51st and General Zogby do not exist. We have heard nothing from them, and the last transmission was from Colonel Maloof, who was caught in an ambush. The 14th has been attempting to refit but only has one regiment capable of doing anything and is south of Tabuk. He and what's left of the 37th Division will attempt to slow the American advance to give you time to get out of here. What was left of the 7th Division has joined the 37th Division. As it stands now, I have managed to lose most of the corps. I can only imagine what will be waiting for me in Baghdad when and if I return."

****

Lieutenant Skroggans had been in a good position to receive transmissions from both Mallory's and Mays's positions as well as transmit back to XVIII Airborne Corps. Staff Sergeant Mays and Sergeant Smith were covering the garrison complex and had discovered the SA-6 air-defense missile site. As they watched, activity at the complex picked up to the point of almost being frantic.

"Hey, Smitty, look at this shit," Mays said, poking Smith awake.

"Yeah, what we got?" Smith asked, raising himself up from his sleeping position to look through the bushes that were offering concealment to the pair. "Oh shit... they're fixing to bug out. Look at the way they're loading supplies on those vehicles. No order to it, just get it on a vehicle," Smith pointed out.

"Makes you wonder where they're going in such a hurry, doesn't it?" Mays said.

"We best report this. The LT is in a position to observe if they roll south. Mallory and Peppers should be able to see if they roll east," Smith said.

Mays picked up his radio mike. "Shit, we changed frequency and call signs last night. Do you have the new codes?" he asked with some frustration.

"Yeah, let me dig it out... I put the new code in last night but forgot the call signs. Wait one," Smith responded, a bit embarrassed that he'd forgotten the new call signs already. "Here it is. Our new call signs are Starlight Two for the lieutenant, Starlight Two-One for us."

Mays pressed the mike switch. "Starlight Two, Starlight Two-One, over."

"Starlight Two-One, go ahead." Mays immediately recognized the lieutenant's voice over the radio.

"Starlight Two, sitrep. Complex is alive with activity in the last hour. They appear to be loading up to move out. Not sure of direction of movement, but they're definitely loading to bug out," Mays reported.

"Roger, Two-One. Break, Starlight Two-Two, over."

"Starlight Two, this is Two-Two, over."

"Two-Two, did you monitor Two-One? Over."

"Roger. We aren't seeing any above-normal activity. Will watch to see if anyone comes by our location. Over."

"Starlight Two-One, is that Sierra Alpha Six still in position, over?"

"Roger, has not moved," Mays responded.

"Roger. Starlight Two out." As soon as he could, Lieutenant Skroggans changed radios and passed this new intelligence activity to XVIII Corps.

****

"Bob, is your brigade all here now?" General Peters asked the 3rd Brigade commander. Colonel Bob Clark had been with the division as a battalion commander and now as a brigade commander, and he couldn't be happier. From his early days as a platoon leader in Vietnam, with a follow-on assignment as company commander at Fort Lewis in the early 1970s and ultimately as aide to the Chief of Staff of the Army, he'd had a great career. His soldiers loved the man. He was the epitome of a soldier statesman and a warrior. 3rd Brigade had been under the command of another officer, but a change of command had occurred just before the invasion of Kuwait.

"Yes, sir. We closed on Falcon last night. My ground convoy is pulling in now between elements of the 29th Division," Colonel Clark responded.

"Yeah, the 28th is going to push off to the east of Tabuk and the 29th following up right behind us. Your upcoming mission is to conduct an insertion into the military complex on the west side of Tabuk. Intel is telling us that the Iraqis are bugging out. We've got to give the aviators some downtime as we've been pushing them hard for the past ten days, so you have twenty-four hours to get organized and come up with your plan. Aviation commanders will be over later today to discuss aircraft availability. I'm going to give you another infantry battalion. Any one in particular you want?" Peters asked.

"Sir, how about my old battalion, 3rd of the 327th? I know Dan Cory—we served in Vietnam together, me as a rifle platoon leader and him as a pilot. That battalion did really good at JRTC and did a number back on the defense. I'd like to take him," Clark requested.

"Okay, I'll put a priority on getting him moved up here. He'll be here by tomorrow morning. May not have all his stuff, but it can convoy up soon enough," Peters said, pausing for a moment. "Oh, one more thing. Your air assault will be in conjunction with a brigade drop from the 82nd going in on the airport just to the east of your objective. Sure would be nice to be standing in that compound when Ford finally gets there," he added with a grin.

****

"Cory, Hall here. Get your battalion ready to move. Aircraft will be arriving in two hours. Two turns of twenty Black Hawks with ten CH-47 for vehicles. Everything else goes by road. Have your XO put a convoy together and head for FOB Falcon. When you get there, you're attached to the 3rd Brigade. Colonel Clark wants to see you as soon as you arrive. Don't get comfortable—you're not going to be there long. Any questions?" Colonel Hall asked.

"No, sir, that's pretty clear. I'll move the battalion to PZ posture in thirty minutes. Anything else, sir?" Cory asked.

"No. Good luck." That was the last thing Cory heard before the line went dead.

****

Cory dismounted from the first of the Black Hawk helicopters, delivering his battalion to Falcon. He was met by Colonel Clark, who was sitting in his vehicle.

"Cory, toss your ruck in the back and let's take a ride," Clark indicated with a thumb pointing to the back.

"Yes, sir. How you doing?" Cory replied happily, removing his hundred-pound rucksack from his back and placing it in the back of the Humvee.

"Doing good. Your boys ready for some contact?" Clark inquired.

225

"They're ready to go home, and if this is the road home, then they're ready." As they drove to the TOC that 3rd Brigade had set up at Falcon, Clark briefly went over the upcoming mission with Cory. "When we get in the TOC, the Ops guys will brief the plan to you and the other battalion commanders," Clark said as the vehicle came to a halt in front of a GP Medium tent.

Going inside, Cory saw another battalion commander that he recognized but knew little of the other commanders as they'd only really met at social functions and had seldom worked together, but everything was done by well-defined SOP, so that shouldn't be a problem.

"Gentlemen, if you'll take a seat, we'll get started," the Operations officer said, approaching the front of the tent and the map board, on which there was a 1:50,000 map and a blown-up photo of the military complex. The seats were absent, so most just stood and took notes on their maps.

"As of yesterday, elements of the 2nd Iraqi Division were occupying this military complex and the headquarters of the II Iraqi Corps. Yesterday afternoon a signals intercept indicated that the II Corps is leaving and the 2nd Iraqi Division has been pulling out since last night. Remnants of the other divisions are attempting to move quickly through the area, with no organized command and control from what's being observed," the ops officer explained.

"Our mission is to secure landing zones on the perimeter of the compound for follow-on insertion by the 2nd Brigade from Falcon and hold the area until the arrival of ground linkup forces. Simultaneously, the 82nd's going to conduct an airborne insertion into the airport with their 3rd Brigade. Once 2nd Brigade arrives, we'll push out and clear the complex. Any questions?"

"Fire support?" asked Andy Berdy, the 2nd of the 187th commander.

"Fire support will be our attack helicopters and tac air. Major Bledsoe will be on the first lift going in with the brigade commander and myself."

"Who's the linkup force?" Hank Kinnison, who commanded the 1st of the 187th, asked.

"Hank, that's a good question. The 29th and 28th Divisions are coming up from the south on two different axes. The 29th is closest to

Falcon right now, but the 28th is closest to Tabuk and approaching it from the southeast. We'll just have to wait and see who comes knocking first. As long as it's not Iraqi, I couldn't care less. Oh, and as long as it's not the Marines coming to rescue us like we rescued them at Khe Sanh in Nam," Clark concluded, with everyone snickering.

"Okay, here are your assigned landing zones. Battleforce, you'll be in the north in this open area. Your LZ is a klick long and plenty big enough to get all the aircraft in. You're to secure these buildings along the south side and north of this major thoroughfare. Prevent any direct fire from these buildings on the northwest side. Questions, sir?" the Ops officer asked.

"No, I got it," Cory said. The Ops officer then addressed the locations for the other three battalion commanders and the flight order. Cory would be the first of twenty Black Hawk helicopters, with a load of fifteen soldiers per aircraft. That would get half of the battalion's infantry soldiers into the landing zone on the first lift, with the second lift an hour plus later bringing in the remaining half. The battalion also got five CH-47s in two turns to bring in vehicles. Cory decided that the first five loads would be the battalion ops officer's vehicle along with the TACP vehicle, and eight TOW vehicles as the CH-47 could carry two vehicles at a time. The second lift of CH-47s would bring in four more TOW vehicles, four cargo Humvees loaded with ammo, C-rations, and batteries, one ambulance, and his vehicle. He noted that both northwest and south of his objective were hospitals if he needed to get soldiers there. If so, then one would be seized early on.

"Gentlemen, if there are no more questions, we load at 0345 and launch at 0400 with an anticipated landing time of 0440. See you all on the objective," Bob Clark said.
****

The 3rd Brigade, 82nd, was consolidated at the airport in Jeddah. All day, C-130 aircraft had been arriving and lining up in the taxi area. Soldiers were in the haji tents waiting for orders to begin chuting up. Squad leaders had gone over the unit packing lists earlier in the day to ensure the soldiers had just what they needed and nothing more. Soldiers will always attempt to pack creature comfort items that only weigh them down and exhaust them in the heat. The day before, Colonel Jim Irons

227

had received the mission and had worked his plan for the brigade takedown of the airfield. He appreciated the fact that the 101st was going to be air assaulting the military complex to the west and tying up any potential reinforcements at about the time he was scheduled to drop. What really warmed his heart was knowing that the 101st would also be bringing Apache helicopters and medivac aircraft if needed. His orders were to hold the airfield until relieved by ground forces. It would be either the 28th Infantry Division or the 29th—no one could give him a satisfactory answer as to which.

As Colonel Irons sat under a haji tent drinking a warm soda, an Air Force colonel approached. "You the commander of this bunch?" he asked with a smile and an extended hand.

"Sure enough am and proud of the fact. Who might you be?" Irons said, standing and accepting the outstretched hand.

"Billy Butane, colonel, USAF, and I command these aircraft that you're crazy enough to want to jump out of over an enemy-held airfield."

"Well, Billy, we figure that's a lot safer than being on them when you attempt to land them. Take-off optional, but landing is mandatory, I understand. Jim Irons," Irons joked.

"Got me there. Thought I'd go over the flight route and time with you," Butane said as he pulled out his map and spread it out on a table. "We'll take off from here"—he pointed at Jeddah—"and turn out over the Red Sea. No need to worry about air-defense missiles out there. We'll then proceed north in a trail formation. The Navy is providing us with a CAP in case an Iraqi fighter shows up unexpectedly. At this point"—he paused to point at a specific point on the map—" we make a ninety-degree right turn to a zero-nine-zero heading and drop to six hundred feet AGL, above ground level, before heading straight to the airfield at Tabuk. One pass and everyone out. How does that sound to you?"

"Sounds good. How's the weather?" Irons asked.

"Should be a fairly smooth flight. No wind to speak of and a moonless night on top of that. GPS has the airfield dialed in, so we should hit the drop zone with no problem," Butane indicated.

"Please hit the drop zone. Too soon and we wind up right in the middle of a major enemy concentration. Too late and we're going to be running to get back to our objective," Irons said in all seriousness.

"Don't worry, I promise to hit the green light the minute we're over the drop zone. What drop altitude do you want?" Butane asked.

"We train at twelve hundred feet, but I'll take six hundred and be happy. Don't want the boys sitting up in the sky too long. Six hundred gives us time to deploy our reserve if there's a problem. At Corregidor in World War II, the drop altitude was three hundred and fifty feet and no reserves were worn. Everyone made it okay... a few strains and broken legs, but that was crappy PLF and not the drop altitude," Irons explained.

"PLF?" Butane quizzed.

"Parachute Landing Fall," Irons answered. He noticed that Butane had no jump wings on his flight suit. "Any idea what the air-defense situation around the drop zone is?"

"There are some guns and they've been pinpointed. We've been told they'll be taken out before we arrive. There's also an SA-300 along the flight path near the military complex, but it's scheduled to be taken care of as well," Butane explained.

"God, I hope you're right. Any idea who's going to take them out?" Irons quizzed.

"Nope, and I have to just put my trust in God on those items," Butane said, pausing to look around at the young soldiers surrounding them. "Where do we find men that are willing to do this? Their average age is what, twenty-two?" Butane asked.

"Actually, the average age of my brigade is twenty. I'm the old man at forty-three. We find these guys passing footballs on the high school playing field, or working on their cars in the driveways, or attempting to impress the girls at the mall. Hell, if you look closely, we have some women that'll be making this drop as well. It's not just a man's game. I have women that operate our Stinger missiles, our ground surveillance radar, our medics. They all do this looking for a challenge, trying to prove something to someone, or to themselves. No one steps out of a perfectly good airplane without some sense of fear. Overcoming that fear is the challenge, and I've yet to have a jump refusal in the brigade. I don't expect any tonight. What aircraft are you flying? You are flying tonight, are you not?" Irons asked.

"Jim, I lead my formations. I'll be in the chalk one position," Butane said, looking Irons right in the eyes.

"Good, I'll be on your plane, then. I'll be in the door position. Let's pray it all goes well," Irons said, extending his hand.

"Drop time is 0430. I'll try to be on time," Butane said, accepting the handshake.

****

"Starlight Two, Home Plate, over," XVIII Corps called.

That's unusual, Lieutenant Skroggans thought as he picked up the hand mike. "Home Plate, Starlight Two, over."

"Starlight Two, you will have company at 0430 hours. We need you to clearly mark that Sierra Alpha Six by 0400 hours. How copy?"

Skroggans had to think about this one for a moment. "Roger, how about India Romeo chem sticks? Over."

"Starlight, that'll work, but we need a sufficient number to mark the target," Home Plate stated.

"Home Plate, that's about the best I can do. We don't carry heavy weapons to create an explosion, over."

"Roger, then that will have to do, but have it marked by 0400 hours. Out."

Skroggans looked at his watch. It was 0200. It would waste too much time for him to run down to Mays and Smith's position for him to do the job himself.

"Starlight Two-One, Starlight Two, over."

"Starlight Two, Two-One, go ahead."

"Two-One, how many IR chem sticks do you have?" Skroggans held his breath, afraid that Mays hadn't taken any with him.

"Wait one, Two," was the response. He knew Mays was tearing through his rucksack looking to see how many he had. Then he would shake down Smith to see what he had. "Two, this is Two-One. We have six IR chem sticks, over."

"Roger, they'll have to do. I need you to take them and lay them out around that Sierra Alpha 300 in your sector, over."

"Two, are you nuts? Over."

"No, we're going to have friendly company soon and that site needs to be marked plainly by 0400. Do you copy?"

"Two, we copy, but we want you to know that our mothers are not going to be happy about our taking this action," Mays stated and dropped the hand mike.

****

No Mercy Six was leading a flight of four AH-64 Apache helicopters. Each was armed with eight AGM-114 Hellfire air-to-ground missiles and two pods of Hydra 70 rockets for a total of thirty-eight rockets, in addition to the 30mm M230 chain gun in the nose of the aircraft with twelve hundred rounds. Sitting in the armored cockpit, No Mercy Six was fairly confident that tonight's mission would come off very well. He had to be on station by 0400 and it was coming up on 0345 as he glanced at the clock mounted on the console of the aircraft. The four Apache helicopters were flying nap of the earth, very low and very slow, using their night vision systems to avoid running into anything and scanning with their target acquisition system for the intended target. They had the coordinates of the target, but things tended to look a bit different when navigating at night.

"Sir, do you think these guys never heard about light discipline?" asked Warrant Officer Conners, sitting in the copilot/gunner's position of No Mercy Six's aircraft. In front of them, at a range of six kilometers, was the southern end of a military complex that they were told had the target, an SA-6 system. It was well marked as most of the lights were on. A trickle of vehicles could be seen moving out of the complex to the west.

"Okay, let's move up and see if we can locate the IR chem lights that are supposed to be marking the target. They should be around a clump of trees just south of the complex," No Mercy Six said to his copilot. The other three aircraft just followed his lead. They had decided in the mission brief to maintain radio silence until after the shooting started. They hoped that they were below the capabilities of the acquisition radar on the SA-6. No Mercy Six scanned the terrain for the next hill mass that they could fly to and hide behind as he pushed the nose over the gained some speed for the move. Two klicks closer to the complex was the next hide position, where they came to a hover.

"Okay, coming up," No Mercy Six said.

"Roger. I'm looking," Warrant Officer Conners said over the aircraft intercom. They crested the hill, and Conners said, "Got it!" Using his TADS, or Target Acquisition Designation System, he focused on the target. No Mercy Six glanced at the other three aircraft and noticed they all turned to a heading parallel to his.

"What are you seeing?" No Mercy Six asked.

"I've got three of the chem sticks, but the launcher is generating a lot more of a signature. He's running his engine. Appears that the commo nets are down. I think he's getting ready to move," Conners speculated.

"Fire when ready," No Mercy Six ordered. The words had hardly cleared his mouth when the first Hellfire missile left the aircraft. Almost immediately, the other three aircraft launched missiles. The four missiles converged on the SA-6 launchers. The combination of four Hellfire missiles and the three missiles on the launcher all exploding at the same time left no doubt in anyone's mind that the launcher was destroyed.

"There's another," Conners almost yelled as the fireball silhouetted another SA-6 launcher.

"Engage," No Mercy Six ordered. He then broke radio silence. "No Mercy elements, engage targets of opportunity. It appears we've hit a battery." Flashes in his peripheral vision told him the other aircraft had heard the order and were engaging as another launcher was destroyed in a spectacular display of fireworks.

"No Mercy Six, No Mercy Four-One. Scratch another launcher."

"Roger, there should be two more somewhere and the command radar vehicle."

"No Mercy Six, I have the radar in sight. Engaging." No Mercy Six recognized the voice of No Mercy Four-Two as another Hellfire missile was launched. Moments later, there was another explosion—not as spectacular are the others, but a kill nonetheless.

"No Mercy Six, I have a launcher attempting to move north. Engaging," reported the voice of No Mercy Four-Three. In the distance, another spectacular explosion. *Three launchers destroyed but one is still alive*, thought No Mercy Six. *Got to get that last launcher.* He knew that, besides the centralized radar for guidance, the SA-6 also had a visual sight system to engage aircraft. He had to kill this last launcher.

"No Mercy elements, there's one more launcher alive. We've got to get it. He can visually acquire and engage us. Be careful, but we have to find him. Over."

"Six, this is Four-One. I'll swing to the east. He should be in that treed area where the others were located."

"Roger. Break, Four-Three, how about you wing more to the west? Break, Four-Two, you and I will approach from here. Stay low."

"Roger, my wheels are rolling on the ground I'm so low," Four-Two reported.

As the four aircraft converged on the stand of trees, the heat signatures of the burning vehicles dominated their night vision systems, making it difficult to locate a vehicle that wasn't generating any heat. Approximately one thousand meters from the grove of trees, No Mercy Six made a decision.

"All No Mercy elements, close to one thousand meters and engage the area with rockets. Let's see if we can flush him out." He received a positive response from each aircraft. Coming to a hover, Mr. Conner moved his sight onto the southern portion of the grove and launched four rockets, then moved the aircraft slightly and fired four more. The other aircraft were employing the same tactic. The grove of trees was experiencing the same effect as if they were being hit with 105mm artillery rounds. Flushed like a flock of quail, six vehicles raced out of the grove. The launcher was clearly identified. No Mercy Four-One scored the kill. The other aircraft engaged the ammunition carriers and command vehicles. At 0410, the area was clearly marked with burning vehicles.

****

"Six minutes," the jumpmaster sounded off as the flight of C-130 aircraft approached the Tabuk airport from the west. Billy Butane had received the reassuring call that the SA-6 battery had been destroyed, which he passed on to Jim Irons, who was standing in the number one stick position next to the door. For the next six minutes, everyone mentally prepared themselves for what was about to happen. Almost everyone on the plane had conducted at least one jump since jump school, but not this low and not in combat. Anxiety was running high and certainly got the adrenaline flowing.

"Stand in the door," the jumpmaster directed Irons, who moved immediately to take his position. The red light was still illuminated, and he waited in anticipation for the green light. As the green light came on, Irons was out the door before the jumpmaster could say "go," and a stream of paratroopers followed him. Irons looked up to check his canopy first and it was good. Then he glanced to see if he could see the other aircraft. He could not, as they were all blacked out.

Dropping his rucksack on the end of its thirty-foot tether, he looked down and realized the ground was coming up, quickly. *Damn, six hundred feet doesn't give you much time.* His PLF was a good one in the soft sand. He was thankful he didn't land on the concrete runway. Quickly removing his parachute harness and gathering his rucksack, he remained kneeling and oriented himself as to where he was and the layout of the airport. He found himself on the west side of the 31/13 runway and next to the OMNI beacon. *Perfect drop, Billy,* he thought. The rest of the brigade was being dropped along the 24/06 runway south of the main terminal. He heard soldiers landing all around him as well as the occasional piece of equipment that someone had lost in the jump; he just hoped none landed on him. That was the most dangerous sound he was hearing, as no shots had been fired. *Could we have totally surprised them?* Irons wondered.

Looking down the 24/06 runway, he saw chem light markers illuminating rally points for the different units. Soon, the last plane passed overhead and disgorged its jumpers. They had thirty minutes to clear the 24/06 runway before more C-130 aircraft would be coming in with heavy drop and LAPES loads. No one could be on the runway for those drops. Troops liked to watch the low-altitude parachute-extraction systems, but it was too dangerous to be anywhere near the runway, as some loads were known to crash into the ground after sliding out of the back of the aircraft. Aircraft were also known to belly onto the ground when dropping the load, resulting in a total crash.

Slowly, the chem light patterns spread out across the airport to seize their respective objectives. A few shots were heard and then the rhythm of automatic weapons fire was accented by the green and red tracers crisscrossing the airfield. Irons grabbed his rucksack and the squad of soldiers around him and moved out for his objective, the control tower eight hundred yards to the northeast. *Damn, I just had to have the door*

234

position. If I'd been fourth or fifth in the stick, I'd only have about two hundred yards to hump. Lesson learned, he mumbled to himself as he jogged with the young soldiers around him.

****

Cory was in chalk ten of the twenty-aircraft lift. He wanted to be positioned in the middle of the objective on landing. The first five aircraft contained Alpha Company soldiers, and they were to cover the area to the northwest of the landing zone. Captain Mulford only needed to suppress and direct fire weapons that could range the landing zone as the nearest building was about one hundred and seventy-five yards to the edge of the landing zone. A dirt berm offered some good concealment for those soldiers. Bravo Company had the southwest side of the landing zone with Charlie Company taking the southeastern side. Until the second lift came in, the battalion could only clear the immediate buildings on the landing zone and secure only a few of those. The area appeared to be some sort of racetrack with a high tower on the south side. Cory immediately gathered his commander team and climbed to the top of the tower, which offered good visibility and good radio reception. After ten minutes, reports started to come in.

"Battleforce Six, Gladiator Six, over," Mulford called, not used to the new call signs that the battalion had been issued. *Who was the dumbass that had us change call signs and frequencies right in the middle of this operation? Let's add more to the fog of war,* Mulford was thinking.

"Gladiator Six, go ahead," Major Wells, the battalion operations officer, responded.

"Battleforce Three, Gladiator Six. We have secured the north perimeter. All is quiet. Over."

"Roger. Break, Spartan Six, over."

"Battleforce Three, we have secured two buildings and are clearing others. Negative contact with anyone. Place is deserted. Over," Captain Grubich reported.

"Battleforce Three, Centurion Six, over," Captain Agather radioed.

"Centurion Six, go ahead."

"Roger, we've secured three buildings and are clearing the others. We've detained two people who are telling us that everyone bugged out of here early last night, heading east. Over."

"Roger. After the next lift comes in, let's get those two up here so we can send them back to higher. In fact, have them on the LZ and load them onto a bird. Tell the pilots to deliver them to higher. How copy?"

"Battleforce Three, I have good copy and will have them standing by."

As Major Wells was communicating with the company commanders, Lieutenant Colonel Cory watched the CH-47 aircraft approaching with his vehicles. He couldn't relax until he had an antitank capability on the ground with the battalion minus now. The four battalions of the brigade had landed in a circle around the military complex but a mile apart from each other with an urban terrain between them. Cory prayed that a large force wasn't in there as this would not be an easy fight for one brigade, even a reinforced brigade.

Chapter 40
Clear the Road

1 May 1991
1st Brigade, 82nd Airborne TOC
Almazari, Saudi Arabia

The 1st Brigade had made a successful parachute assault on the port area. Only scattered enemy contact had been made, and so the brigade had pushed out reconnaissance elements to scout the road to Tabuk. The locals were assisting the soldiers in any way that they could, which made the chain of command a bit worried that the soldiers might get too relaxed. Just after landing, and using local transportation, Colonel Kinser had met with the mayor of Almazari, sixteen miles south of the port at the intersection of the highway to Tabuk and Jeddah.

"Hey, sir, Checkpoint One just reported meeting up with a couple of Sheridans accompanying the 2nd Brigade," Command Sergeant Major Hill reported.

"About time they rolled in here. Tell the S-3 to notify the 1st of the 325th that they can return to 2nd Brigade's control...and see if he can get Colonel Allen over here to meet with me, or I'll go there... wherever he sets the meeting up," Colonel Kinser directed.

Two hours later, Kinser and Allen were sitting in overstuffed chairs, sipping tea in the Marsa Diba Hotel, where the Emir of Dubai had secured rooms for them. In fact, he'd secured the entire hotel for the US commanders.

"How was the trip from Jeddah?" Kinser asked.

"Long and slow," Allen replied. "The highway was fine. It was all the engineer equipment we brought that was slowing us up. I have an entire reinforced road construction battalion at the end of the column that we're moving up front right behind a screen force so we can get the road to Tabuk opened," Allen replied.

"I took the liberty of pushing some reconnaissance folks in civilian vehicles that the locals gave us. They went about forty miles up the road before they hit a major landslide in a very narrow pass," Kinser said.

"Yeah, that's what we've got to clear to get the supply convoys through. I also have a Quartermaster battalion coming up that will continue on to the port to start offloading ships," Allen said, taking another sip.

"Already started. The first ship came in yesterday and left this morning. They have a great area for offloading and a yard for storage."

"Great. Then as soon as we get the road open, we can get supplies moving to Tabuk. That'll make Peters happy," Allen indicated.

"Yeah, then maybe we can get out of here and join Irons," Kinser commented.

****

"Colonel, this battalion makes roads. We do not move mountains. Half of that mountain is in that pass and it would take more explosives than we're carrying to move it. At that, it'll be two weeks before I could put a path through that mess," Lieutenant Colonel Bullock explained in frustration. Colonel Allen wasn't buying it.

"We don't have two weeks to get these supplies through. We're wasting time when you could be working on that rock pile," Allen argued.

"Look, sir, give me twenty-four hours to find a way around this pass and make a road for you," Bullock said.

"Don't you think the Iraqi 14th Division thought of that and didn't do it?" Allen responded with.

"Sir, the 14th was getting its ass kicked with air strikes when they attempted to come through there. I bet we'll find a junk pile of destroyed vehicles when we get around there and none will be engineer equipment. Give me twenty-four hours, sir," Bullock almost pleaded.

"Alright, you got twelve to tell me you found a way and another twelve to have it passable to vehicles. Doesn't have to be pretty, just functional," Allen agreed in frustration.

****

Sergeant First Class Haggenback loved his work. He was a surveyor, and surveying roads was his job. It was a job that kept him and his team away from the flagpole with no one looking over his shoulder. He also liked the fact that he would retire from the Army at age thirty-seven with a fifty percent retirement check and still be young enough and experienced enough to get a good job with a civilian road construction company. *Sweet*, he thought.

"Alright, guys, let's get off this road and try going up this wadi to see if we can get around the roadblock," Haggenback said to his eight-man team riding in two Humvee vehicles. He folded his map and everyone began to move back to their respective vehicles. It didn't take that many to survey a route, but to survey a route in Indian country with hostiles about, Haggenback wanted security. While Haggenback navigated off his map, his driver, Private Ford, attempted to avoid the deep ruts and larger rocks in the wadi. Even with careful driving, the ride was anything but smooth.

"Sarge, this is, what, the fourth wadi we've been up that we've had to turn around because it went nowhere?" Ford commented.

"Now, see, that's where you're wrong, Private Ford," Haggenback said. He always prefaced a soldier's name with the soldier's rank.

"How so, Sergeant?" Ford asked as the left front wheel dropped into another hole.

"You see, Private Ford, every wadi we've been in leads to someplace. However, none of them lead to where we want to go. All these wadis go someplace. It's just a matter of us finding the right wadi. Be patient and have a little faith," Haggenback said, looking over at Ford.

"Oh, I have faith, Sarge. Faith that we're going to get so far and turn around to look up another wadi," Ford said as he attempted to miss a large rock. Haggenback buried his head in his map, looking to see if there was a branch off this wadi that might prove successful. He was lost in thought when his concentration was broken by Ford.

"Holy shit," Ford mumbled, causing Haggenback to look up.

"Damn, I don't believe it," Haggenback said, looking out the front window of the vehicle. Before him was a junkyard of burnt, broken and destroyed vehicles rounding out the entire inventory of Iraqi combat vehicles. There was also the stench of burnt and decaying bodies. Off to the left was a paved road disappearing into a pass.

Ford stopped the vehicle and Haggenback got out and stood next to it. The other vehicle pulled up behind him. Everyone got out, just mesmerized by the scene in front of them. Finally, Haggenback snapped out of it and got things organized.

"Alright, there's no need to break out the survey equipment. The road is going to follow this wadi. Specialist Anderson, I want you to drop a flag at every turn in the wadi as we head back. You should have enough. Specialist Moore, when he drops a flag, you shoot a compass heading back to the previous flag. Call it out and, Sergeant Jamison, you plot it. Any questions?" Haggenback asked.

"What are you going to do, Sarge?" Anderson asked.

"Specialist Anderson, I am going to do what a sergeant first class in the Army is supposed to do," Haggenback answered.

"Which is?" Sergeant Moore asked.

"Supervise your work, scrutinize the work to make sure it's done properly, criticize if it's not done properly, and ostracize you when the project is done. Now let's move."
****

"Colonel, the engineer road builder is here to see you," Command Sergeant Major Colburn said, disturbing Colonel Allen's sleep.

Sitting up from his prone position on the ground, Allen saw the lieutenant colonel approaching with a nonchalant look. *Hell, it's only been eight hours. He better not be throwing his hands up already*, Allen thought.

"Sorry to disturb you, Colonel," Lieutenant Colonel Bullock apologized.

"Well, what is it now?" Allen said, ready for an argument.

"Well, sir, I was wondering when you wanted to get this convoy rolling again," Bullock said.

"What the hell are you talking about?" Allen retorted, confused.

"Sir, we have a road mapped out that goes around this mess and puts us back on the highway. I have some EOD folks out right now clearing the last of some unexploded ordinance at the end, but with headlights on and chem sticks, the road around is clearly marked. I thought you would want to know. So how soon do you want to be rolling?" Bullock asked, truly enjoying himself as Allen rose in a fluster. Fifteen minutes later, the convoy was rolling slowly through the wadi and heading to Tabuk.

Chapter 41
Eye in the Sky

1 May 1991
Pentagon, Basement Level
Arlington, Virginia

The satellite had just made a second pass and confirmed to those watching that the Iraqi forces were pulling back to Kuwait. It appeared that two divisions were moving back towards King Khalid Military City following a trail of broken toys of the 7th Medina Division and the 5th Baghdad Division. One division was still in Riyadh and remnants of four divisions were moving north across the open desert, bypassing Al Hofuf. Their paths across the desert were marked with black smoke clouds of burning vehicles and trails of dust marking their progress. Three and possibly four divisions could be seen in defensive positions south of the Kuwait border.

"So, Paige, what's your assessment of this?" Cliff Jeffery asked.

"I think it's pretty clear that he's withdrawing back to Kuwait," she said.

"Yeah, but why? What does he gain by pulling back into Kuwait? What's the one big advantage that this gives him?" Bob Daley asked out loud.

"Well, it shortens his supply lines for one," Paige answered.

"It puts him closer to his air support," Cliff said, studying the computer screen.

"There has to be something more to get him to withdraw this far back. I don't think we've hurt him bad enough yet to cause a total withdrawal. He's leaving this one division in Riyadh, it appears. Is he going to make the city a rubble pile with street fighting?" Daley asked.

"Wait one…what's the status of his air-defense weapons? Have we found any SA-300s as of yet? And how much of Kuwait is covered by the SA-2 and 3 batteries? He could be attempting to get his people under an air-defense umbrella. His air force has lost so many aircraft they're almost ineffective at keeping our guys off the ground forces' backs," Paige commented. "Let's look at what he has for air-defense weapons." She grabbed a three-ring binder off an adjacent desk. Flipping through pages, she found what she was looking for. "Okay, he has SA-2, SA-3, SA-6, SA-8, SA-9 and SA-10. The SA-2 were Vietnam vintage and have an altitude of eighty-two thousand feet and a range of forty-five kilometers. These are generally easy to spot because they'll have the six launchers in a circular pattern with the radar in the center. However, in the open desert, with camouflage applied, they may not be as easy to spot as they were in Vietnam. They're considered a strategic weapon, so we should find these around major cities such as Baghdad," Paige said.

"What about around oil fields?" Bob asked.

"I doubt it—they know we won't strike an oil field," Cliff stated.

"Not unless he was protecting the launchers by placing them in an oil field, knowing we would be worried about hitting the oil wells," Bob interjected.

"I hadn't thought of that. We best be looking in the Ramadi oil fields to see if there are any there," Cliff directed. "Okay, Paige, what's next?"

"The SA-3, which we saw in Vietnam as well, is mobile or fixed-based. Has a range of twenty-two miles and an altitude of fifty-nine thousand feet," Paige read off the information page.

"Being mobile, they could be about anywhere, but again, I think we'll find these around more important targets such as the naval bases, supply depots, and fuel storage areas. Again, if they are around the refineries, I think it's more to protect them than to guard the refinery," Cliff concluded.

"All the rest are mobile and generally are found at the corps and division levels oriented in low-flying aircraft," Paige continued. "In fact, the SA-10 is primarily an antihelicopter air-defense weapon and highly mobile."

"What about the SA-5?" Bob asked.

"Nope, Iraq isn't known to have those," Paige indicated, going down the list. "And we suspect that the SA-300 will be in Iraq around Baghdad."

"Okay, folks," Cliff said, looking up from the list that Paige had just scanned, "we need to make locating air defense a high priority on the next passes. If we can identify his systems' locations and plot out fans of coverage, it may give us a better picture of where he's pulling his forces back to and why. You can almost bet that where his SAM coverage is located, he won't be flying his own aircraft there. Might give our people a better idea of where they can expect any air attack to approach from."

Chapter 42
24th Gets the Prize

3 May 1991
3rd of the 69th Armor
Riyadh, Saudi Arabia

The engagement with the 6th Iraqi Armoured Division was violent and long. The 24th committed all three brigades of tanks and Bradley fighting vehicles as well as attack helicopters. The 6th Iraqi Armoured Division didn't hold back and committed all their T-72 tanks, BMPs and Mi-24 Hind helicopters. In the end, the superior capabilities of the American equipment won out over the Iraqi numbers. After twenty-four hours of fighting, even through the night with the Americans' advantage in night optics and thermal sights, the battlefield was a graveyard of burning and broken vehicles as well as bodies. Comparatively, the 24th had few casualties, but regrettably, several soldiers had been killed in a fratricide engagement—a case of miscommunications and direction.

When the 3-69 Armor moved westward, they approached Prince Sultan Military Airfield cautiously two days ago. Lieutenant Colonel Altamire was told that this had been the central control facility for the Iraqi Air Force once they'd invaded Saudi Arabia but that it had been heavily bombed when the offensive to take back Saudi Arabia had begun. As the battalion rolled up on the perimeter fence, it became obvious that it had in fact been extensively bombed. The runways had several large craters and most of the hangars were destroyed, with Iraqi Frogfooter aircraft still inside. Most of the billets were also destroyed. Three HAWK air-defense launchers were piles of junk scattered around the outer perimeter. Altamire knew that this airfield wasn't going to be operational anytime soon, but it wasn't his problem.

Passing through Prince Sultan Military Airfield, the battalion rolled through Naajan on their march to Riyadh. They hadn't encountered any combat Iraqi forces but were being slowed down by the number of rear-echelon Iraqi soldiers they were policing up. Each group would have to be collected, searched, and held until another force could take responsibility for the prisoners. Generally, it was a military police unit that had several cattle trucks and was just loading prisoners in them. Thankfully, the prisoners didn't offer any resistance or cause any trouble.

Local Saudi residents demonstrated mixed emotions. Some waved; children darted between the vehicles as soldiers tossed candy to them. Old men just stood on the side of the road with their arms behind their backs and just stared at the Americans. Women in their all-black attire scurried along, not acknowledging the Americans. As far as the soldiers were concerned that was good, as the women in black gave the soldiers an uneasy feeling. The one group Altamire was not seeing was young men. It made him wonder.

****

The small group had been moving west ever since the first night of the battle. Their regiment had been chewed to pieces before the battle was even an hour old. They watched their company commander, Captain Bouzizi, crawl out of his vehicle and roll to the ground, but they couldn't get to him due to the intense automatic weapons fire. They didn't see anyone else exit the burning vehicle. Their own vehicles had also been killed, but Allah had allowed these five to survive. They didn't know how or why but were thankful to him for allowing it to happen. Lieutenant Arif al-Jaziri had been a platoon leader. Now he led four other men, hopefully to safety. They had seen others walking towards the Americans with their hands held high, waving white flags, but they weren't convinced that this would be better than getting back to their division headquarters. Entering Al-Kharj, they found a smoldering ruin that had once been a command post. MG Parshan Faizan was present, but not alive. Colonel Ghafor was also present and in a state of shock as far as Lieutenant al-Jaziri could tell. It appeared that they had been abandoned by the rest of the division headquarters staff.

"Colonel Ghafor, what happened?" Lieutenant al-Jaziri asked, squatting down in front of the man, who was sitting on the floor with his back to a wall. Noticing the colonel's cracked lips, al-Jaziri offered him a drink of water. The colonel drank as if he was addicted to water.

"We got a report that the Americans were withdrawing, and the general wanted to press the attack. I cautioned him, but he ordered a full attack. It was then that the American artillery and rockets began hitting our position. I think they may have been listening to your radio transmissions and found us that way. We thought we were safe, that they would not dare fire artillery on a Saudi town," Colonel Ghafor lamented.

Sergeant Ibrahim Kadar entered the room with two other soldiers. "Sir," he addressed the lieutenant, "we have found a vehicle that Private Sadar has running. We should be going and quickly."

"Alright, help me with the colonel and let's head to Riyadh," the lieutenant said, standing and assisting the colonel in doing the same. Walking as if intoxicated, the colonel was assisted to the Toyota pickup truck and placed in the back, while Lieutenant al-Jaziri took the passenger seat.

"Private Najm, head to Riyadh and disregard the speed limits," al-Jaziri said, pointing towards the front of the vehicle.
****

"Power Elements, Power Six," Colonel Altamire called over the command radio net.

Each company commander responded in order to acknowledge that they were listening.

"Power Elements, it appears that the Iraqi division that was in Riyadh is bugging out. They're moving to the north, it appears. Command doesn't want a firefight in the city, so we're going to hold at Al Haeer. Alpha is to move to the northeast and secure the prison. When you get there, give me an update on the condition and number of prisoners there. Check to see if any American or Allied prisoners are being held there. Bravo, take up a position between the prison complex and the town. Charlie, you take the northern part of the town and Delta the southern part. See if all the Iraqi forces have pulled out. We'll stay on this highway and peel off to enter the town from the east and move through it to the west. I want you to take up positions along the river. Any questions?" Altamire concluded. There were none.

Delta Dawgs were tail-end Charlie in the column of armored vehicles, and Lieutenant Bagel's platoon was the last of the column. Some days that could be good, and some days not so good.

"Dawg One-One, Dawg One-Four." It was the last vehicle in the column and Bagel's fourth tank.

"Dawg One-Four, what's up?"

"Dawg One-One, I got a white Toyota pickup coming up fast behind me. Permission to traverse my turret one-eighty? Over," the tank commander asked. Normally tanks would travel with every other tank having their main gun pointed to the opposite side of the road from the vehicle in front, but not a complete reverse turret with the gun pointed over the engine compartment.

"Roger, permission granted. Stop him if you can. It may be a panicked civilian trying to get his favorite loving sheep to the vet," Bagel joked. Off-color jokes about the Arab men and their sheep were very common among the Allied troops.

As the last tank turned his turret one hundred and eighty degrees from the line of march, the Toyota continued to close the distance at high speed but was still over a mile behind the tank. The dust from the tanks made it difficult to see the Toyota clearly and for the Toyota to see the tanks clearly.

****

"Lieutenant," Private Najm said, shaking the doxing officer awake.

"What... are we there yet?" al-Jaziri asked, attempting to remove the sleep from his eyes.

"No, sir, but there's a column of tanks and vehicles ahead. They fade in and out in the dust they are creating," Private Najm said.

"Good, let's speed up and join them," al-Jaziri ordered, and the good private pressed the accelerator to the floor. The Toyota pickup still had a lot of life in it and increased speed significantly. So did the dust blowing across the road, masking signs and other vehicles. Occasionally, al-Jaziri would catch a glimpse of an armored vehicle through the dust as they raced to catch up to the column.

"Stop!" al-Jaziri screamed. Private Najm slammed on the brakes, throwing everyone in the back against the cab. Al-Jaziri was looking down the barrel of an American M1 Abrams tank fifty meters in front of him.

****

Sergeant Boman had been a gunner on the tank for only a year and in the last three weeks had had more gunnery practice with live targets than most senior noncoms sitting back in the States. Looking through his

247

gun sight with the thermal imaging capability, he had been watching this pickup truck barreling towards him. *Could this guy be a suicide bomber?* he considered.

"Hey, Sergeant Rollins, this guy is coming fast. I doubt if he can really see us in our dust, but he's coming fast," Boman said.

"Spivey, stop the vehicle," Rollins ordered the driver as he turned in the commander's hatch and looked over the back of the tank. He couldn't see anything initially in the dust trail that they had left. As the dust cleared, he caught a glimpse of the white Toyota.

"Boman, don't get trigger-happy. This might be some guy with a wife and kids," Rollins said as they sat and watched the dust clear.

"I think he just hit his brakes," Boman said as Najm came to an abrupt halt.

"Well, hello, Mohammed," Rollins said softly, recognizing the Iraqi army uniforms the passengers were. "Guys, I think we just captured a few prisoners," Rollins said over the intercom as he waved the pickup truck forward, the main gun still pointed at the truck.
****

"Private, drive very slowly. I think the war is over for us," al-Jaziri said with resignation.

Chapter 43
Move to Riyadh

6 May 1991
CENTCOM HQ
Riyadh, Saudi Arabia

General Schwarzkopf was anxious to get CENTCOM displaced from Oman to Saudi Arabia. ARCENT and MARCENT had displaced earlier to Abu Dhabi and Dubai, but not CENTCOM. Schwarzkopf wanted to lead from the front, and sitting back in Oman was not his cup of tea. The Iraqi forces had barely left Riyadh when the first headquarters elements began arriving. Even the King would be returning shortly, which Schwarzkopf recommended against as the Iraqi Air Force was still operating—ineffectively, but they could get lucky.

"Bob, get General Powell on the phone for me, please," Schwarzkopf asked his aide. A few minutes later, the aide indicated that General Powell would be on the phone shortly.

"Morning, General," Schwarzkopf said when Powell answered.

"Afternoon, Norm—or is it evening there? I can't keep it straight. How are things there?"

"Well, I can tell you Riyadh is a mess. What wasn't nailed down, the Iraqis stole. The royal palace has been trashed, and I recommend that the King stay in Spain until they get that place squared away. That'll also keep him out of my hair for a bit longer," Norm said.

"I'll talk to Baker about it and see if he can convince the King to hold off for a bit. What's the tactical situation?"

"Right now, XVIII Airborne has taken Tabuk and is mopping up remnants of the II Iraqi Corps. The 2nd Iraqi Infantry Division hauled out before they got there and is heading back towards Iraq along with the II Corps headquarters. The road from the seaport to Tabuk is open, so our supplies are flowing from the seaport to Tabuk, and the airport at Tabuk is now operational. We aren't moving any Air Force assets there yet—just cargo is flowing into there," Schwarzkopf said.

"How did the two National Guard divisions do... the 28th and 29th?" Powell inquired.

"They did good. Chased the remnants of the 7th and 37th Iraqi Divisions back to Tabuk and right into the 101st, which was leapfrogging FOBs and engagement areas. I tell you, those Apache helicopters are eating these guys for breakfast, but they require a lot more maintenance support than what we had with the old Cobra gunships. There are some lessons learned here as far as maintenance requirements in this environment. The sand is eating rotor blades on all the aircraft."

"The logisticians have raised the flag already back here. I told them to send whatever you need and we'd sort it out after this is over."

"Good."

"So how's the rest of the operation going?" Powell asked.

"VII Corps has taken Riyadh, which you knew, and is moving northwest, clearing out the area between Riyadh and Buraydah. They're finding only scattered elements of the IV Iraqi Corps left behind. That's becoming a problem with the number of prisoners we've taken in. We're turning them over to the Saudis for safekeeping. The Saudis have built a huge POW compound south of Haradh. No fencing, but there's no place to take off to either. No water holes except at the compound. They're just dropping them in the middle of the desert, giving them a haji tent and that's it. They're feeding them and have set up a field hospital and latrines. We have a medical unit there to treat the people—otherwise I think we'd have the Red Cross or Red Crescent breathing down my neck. The Saudis signed on to the Geneva Convention, and as best as my people can tell they're following it," General Schwarzkopf explained.

"That's good. We certainly don't need any bad press on that subject."

"You're right. But the Iraqis aren't a signatory to Protocol 1 or 2 and they're considering this an internal conflict, Arab to Arab. That removes some protection to the people of Saudi Arabia and Kuwait, by their interpretation."

"Have you seen some evidence of violations?"

"Some units are reporting that young men are missing from towns that we're liberating. Locals tell them that the Iraqis rounded them up and took them when they pulled out. Might be attempting to conscript them into the Iraqi Army. We'll just have to wait and see about this."

"Okay, how goes it with the other forces?" Powell asked.

"The Marines have secured a line along Highway 522 between Riyadh and Al Hofuf. The III Corps has secured Al Hofuf and has pushed his host task forces as far north as Buqayq. They're going to clear out Dammam. Trying to keep our guys out of the cities and let the host nation forces clear them out. Didn't have a choice when it came to Riyadh, but things went well and the guys are respectful of the situation."

"So where are you going from here?" Powell asked.

"My weather guys tell me that tomorrow and for the next forty-eight hours, we're going to have one of the damn dust storms rolling through on the east side here. That will shut down everything for forty-eight hours. If you've never been in one of these things, believe me, you're missing nothing. That's going to cover the Iraqis pretty good, and I suspect they'll continue to push getting back to Kuwait. We'll hold in place for that time. Let everyone get some rest, if it's possible in those conditions, then we'll push on. Looking at having the XVIII Airborne swing into Iraq on the west side of Kuwait. Have VII Corps do likewise, linking up with airborne elements and driving into the northern part of Kuwait. Have III Corps and the Marines come in on the south side with III Corps host nation forces taking Kuwait City. That's the plan right now. My question for you is what's my final objective? I've been asking that question since the start of this thing and I'm still waiting for an answer. I'd like to have it before we get to Kuwait. Otherwise, I'm planning on Baghdad as my final objective."

"Now wait one, Norm. You can't just go charging into Iraq," Powell said.

"Well, then, give me my final objective."

"Okay, I'll get with Cheney and the President and get you an answer. Anything else?" Powell asked.

"No, that's about it. Keep the supplies coming. I'll give you a call in a couple of days, but get me an answer to the million-dollar question," Schwarzkopf said and hung up the phone.

Chapter 44
Blinded

7 May 1991
1st of the 3rd Aviation Regiment
Udhailiyah, Saudi Arabia

The attack battalion had been covering the 1st Cavalry Division since it had arrived in the Middle East, deploying out of Fort Hood right along with the 1st Cavalry Division. The division was on the west side of Al Hofuf between the city and the Marine division on the left flank. The 1-3 Aviation Regiment was a battalion of attack helicopters sitting on the abandoned airfield at Udhailiyah. Unfortunately, there were no hangars for the aircraft, but there was one building for the crews. A short distance to the east was a complex that the support personnel had taken over for shelter. The unit had been racking up the hours flying, and the toll on the aircraft was showing. The AH-64A attack helicopter had been in the Army inventory for three years but had never been pushed this hard until combat operations had started. Nor had the pilots been pushed this hard. Flying the helicopter in training exercises and flying the aircraft in combat presented significantly different stress levels. Levels not experienced by this younger generation of helicopter pilots. Some of the old Vietnam-era pilots had experienced this level of stress, but they were few and far between as those that had stayed in the Army after Vietnam were eligible for retirement and many had already retired from the Army. Those that were still on active duty were most likely not qualified in this new attack helicopter.

"Okay, listen up," Lieutenant Colonel Bodine said, looking over his group of pilots and crews. "Tomorrow is a down day." Smiles and small cheers could be heard. "Don't get your hopes up. We have a down day because we have one of those desert dust storms we've heard about and seen in the old movies." Looks of wonder were exchanged between the pilots.

"Sir, what old movies?" one of the younger pilots asked.

"You know the Jimmy Stewart movie, *Flight of the Phoenix*, where he's a pilot and crashes in the desert? It was a hit in 1965 and had this scene where a sandstorm blows in and covers them."

"Sir, I wasn't born until 1968. Wasn't there a sandstorm in *Star Wars*?"

"What movie had sandstorms isn't the point. The point is that it's going to get very nasty around here and you all need to be sure you have a mask over your nose and mouth. Wear goggles if you have them and find a place to just hunker down and sleep if you can. If you get up to go piss, don't go far as you'll probably have difficulty finding your way back," Bodine said.

"How bad can it get that we would get lost going to take a piss?" a senior NCO asked.

"Sergeant, you'll be lucky if you can see five feet in front of you, I'm told. I can't imagine that, but we'll see. Make sure you all have two liters of water with you before it hits us. Any questions?" Bodine asked.

"Sir, how long will we be down?" another pilot asked.

"I'm told the storm will last eighteen to twenty-four hours. We'll need time after to check over each aircraft and clean out the sand. So you might get two days. Make the best of it. Any other questions?" He paused. "Okay, then, get some rest."
****

The morning sun came up as pretty as ever. The temperature was even pleasant, and in fact it had been a bit cool the night before, requiring everyone to wrap up in their poncho and poncho liner if they didn't have a sleeping bag. Pilots were creatures of comfort—not to the extent of their Air Force counterparts, but well above the level of the infantry soldier. Unfortunately, the AH-64A attack helicopter didn't have a lot of room for pilot comfort items. Those went into any cubbyhole the pilots could find. Attack pilots traveled light as a result.

Several of the pilots had moved outside to enjoy the morning sun and pleasant temperature while they sipped their coffee made on a can filled with sand and some JP-4 aviation gas. Made a pretty good little stove. Breakfast was a cold MRE, whatever one drew. With luck, a pilot would draw scrambled eggs and bacon and somehow be able to heat it. Luckless pilots drew lima beans and ham. Hot or cold, that tasted like crap. Some were reading well-worn letters from home and others were writing letters home.

"Damn, it would be nice if we could talk to our wives and let them know how we're doing. Sally says the TV is covering a lot of stuff but not specifically about our unit or where anyone is except to say in the desert," Phil complained.

"You can damn well bet the REMFs are talking to their wives. I know for a fact that the battalion chaplain was talking to his wife almost daily back in Oman. 'Official business,' he would say," Pete said, holding his hands up and imitating quotation marks.

As the pilots sat making small talk, the morning sun continued its path but the temperature didn't rise noticeably. A few of the pilots had a card game going when a puff of breeze scattered the cards.

Grabbing for the loose cards, Phil looked up. "Holy shit," he said, his face in awe of what was coming. "Guys, I think we best get inside, *now*." They all turned to see what he was looking at. A wall of sand was approaching rapidly. It appeared to be a couple of thousand feet high, but they couldn't tell for sure as the leading edge at the top was closer than the main body. They did know it was a solid wall of sand, however. The realization of what was about to happen hit them all at the same time, and the pilots sprinted to the shelter of the building. Entering, they closed all the doors and windows.

"That should keep it out," Pete said as he closed the last window. No one said anything. There was no doubt in anyone's mind when the wall of sand hit. The doors and windows shook with the wind, which built very quickly to over thirty miles an hour. Almost immediately, sand began swirling around inside the room. Jet streams of sand entered through every nook, crack, and cranny around the doors and windows. Soon everyone was wearing a mask and covered their heads under their poncho and liner. Minutes ticked into hours with no relief. No one wanted to get up to go piss. If they did, they used a trash can that the commander had placed in the room just for the purpose. Even then it was painful to get up and go to it—no one was about to open the door and go outside. Once it got dark, no one bothered to light a light as no one had a need for one and no one wanted to come out from under their poncho. The fortunate ones went to sleep, and eventually everyone slept.

At first light, the storm had not abated. By this time, everyone was covered in a fine layer of sand and some even had piles on their ponchos. Nasal passages were clogged with sand that had clung to nasal hair.

Water from water bottles had a muddy taste to it. Some used their bottled water to wash out the sand that had settled in their lower eyelids during the night. Their eyes were red from the irritation.

Lieutenant Colonel Bodine lay under his poncho liner with his mask covering his nose and mouth. *How much longer is this shit going to keep up?* he wondered. *How much of this fucking sand is the dust covers on the engines going to keep out? We're going to have to flush the engines and inspect rotor blades after this. The maintenance guys will be working for twenty hours. Pilots are going to have to get out there and give them a hand cleaning this crap. And all the while, the Iraqis will have clear sky before us and be running north before we can even think about getting off the ground. Damn it.*

Chapter 45
Continue the Attack

9 May 1991
CENTCOM HQ
Riyadh, Saudi Arabia

As soon as Riyadh was liberated by the 24th Mechanized Division, CENTCOM moved from Muscat. They arrived just ahead of the sandstorm that was bearing down on the eastern side of the country, playing havoc with everything. Even in the city, dust managed to find its way through the slightest of openings. A fine coating of sand layered furniture, food and drinks. As frustrating as it was, the CENTCOM staff knew it must be miserable for the soldiers, Marines and airmen that were enduring it outside. They also knew not to openly complain about it in front of General Schwarzkopf unless they wanted to see him rise to his nickname of Stormin' Norman.

The staff had determined that some adjustments had to be made in the attack plan. This storm and the fact that the enemy has a vote in any plan developed called for some modifications. They were ready to run it by the general and get his approval to issue the orders for the changes.

"Good morning, sir," General O'Donnell, the G-2 intelligence officer, said.

"What's so damn good about it? Is that your weather report for today?" Schwarzkopf asked.

"Afraid not, sir. As for the weather, this will continue to blow until late this evening and then be done. Around midnight, we should see a clearing sky. Tomorrow, temperatures will be back to normal for this time of year—high nineties to one hundred degrees."

"Wonderful," was Schwarzkopf's only sarcastic comment.

"Sir, the enemy has used this sandstorm as cover for his retreat. Satellite imagery shows that he's pulling back to Kuwait and continuing to build his defenses there. Not previously found before is the fact that, despite his naval losses, he's placed sea mines all along the coast of Kuwait. The minefield is rather extensive, being about one hundred and fifty miles long and fifty miles wide. It's laid in three belts, about ten miles between belts," O'Donnell explained.

"Why the hell did we not find this sooner?" Schwarzkopf asked.

"Sir, previously, use of the satellite time to look for sea mines had very low priority and the folks in D.C. weren't looking for them."

Schwarzkopf jotted down a note.

"Okay," was all he said.

"Sir, satellite imagery shows a large number of air-defense missile sites in both Kuwait and Iraqi. We suspect that he's pulling back to get his forces under this umbrella as his air force hasn't been able to maintain or gain air superiority or even parity. Our air campaign is mauling him badly, and we believe he's thinking that by moving under this umbrella, he might feel some relief. The umbrella contains SA-2, SA-3, SA-6, SA-8, SA-10 and SA-300 missiles as well as the usual SA-9 that's found at the regimental level. The five-sided palace is working up detail locations and overlays of the air-defense threat, to include radar locations, and will get that to us in the coming days. They've put a priority on that," O'Donnell explained.

"What they call a priority, I sometimes call a delay. If you need me to energize them in getting that information, you let me know," Schwarzkopf directed.

The old man is definitely in a foul mood this morning, O'Donnell thought as he prepared to provide the next bit of news.

"Iraqi ground forces continue to move north, taking advantage of us being under this sandstorm while they're almost out of it. The II Iraqi Corps is moving back into the western desert. The IV Iraqi Corps has moved back to KKMC, and it appears they're continuing to move to Wadi Al Batin and along the Iraq-Kuwait border region. The 2nd Republican Guard Corps is being refitted and is moving into western Kuwait, and the 1st Republican Guard Corps has been in southeastern Kuwait for some time now. The VII Iraqi Corps has a screen line south of Kuwait and we believe that once all Iraqi forces have passed through him, we'll see him withdraw back into Kuwait as well. We might see him take the 1st Republican Guard Corps position, with the 1st Republican Guard Corps assuming the role of a reserve force," O'Donnell explained.

"What about his air force? How bad have we hurt them?"

"Sir, they've moved all their aircraft back into Iraq. They're staging out of several bases. He has six major military airfields, another twenty-five backup airfields and sixteen other lesser airfields. His air-defense around each is formidable, and he has over two hundred hardened shelters for this fighter aircraft," O'Donnell explained.

"Where are they?" Schwarzkopf asked. In anticipation of the question, a map was projected on the screen.

"Sir, the main bases are Basra, Kirkuk, Mosul, Rashid, Tikrit, Ash Shuaybah, and Al Iskandariyah," O'Donnell indicated, pointing to each on the map.

"Of particular interest, sir, is this airfield in Tallil. This is a major airfield with hardened bunkers for aircraft and personnel. More important, however, is the fact that Saddam's major chemical biological laboratory is located in Salman Pak, but there's a lab adjacent to this airfield in Tallil. He doesn't store his chemical weapons there—they're stored north of there in a five-by-six-kilometer ammunition dump here, south of An Nasaria." O'Donnell pointed on the map. "His chemical weapons production facility is in Samarra, sixty miles north of Ramadi."

"Have we seen any indicators that he's planning on using his chemical weapons?" General Schwarzkopf asked.

"No, sir. We had a report that some chemical weapon—mustard gas, I believe the report said—was used earlier, in the Battle of Medina Ridge, but we suspect now that may have been a false report. We've found that a large concentration of sheep shit will trigger the chemical detectors and think that might be what happened there," O'Donnell explained, to the chuckles of the audience.

General Schwarzkopf wrote another note before he asked, "Anything else, General?"

"No, sir, that concludes my portion. I will be followed by General Schless," O'Donnell said, picking up some notes and moving aside for General Schless. General Schless took the podium and called for the first slide.

"Morning, sir. Our task organization remains the same. In the past twenty-four hours, offensive operations have halted due to the current weather conditions. XVIII Airborne is consolidating in Tabuk. VII Corps is occupying from Riyadh to Buraydah. The Marines along with 1st British have covered down on the line from Al Kharj to Al Hawlyan, and the III Corps from Al Hawlyan to the coast with the host nation forces on the coast. When the weather clears and on order, all units know to continue to move north. We—"

"Gentlemen," Schwarzkopf interrupted, "I've spoken with the King, and we're going to make a few changes in the task organization." As he invoked the name of the King, they all suspected some political pressure had come into play. "We're standing up another corps headquarters under the command of the Saudis, and it'll consist of the Saudi Mechanized Brigade, the Northern Omani Brigade, the UAE Mechanized Battalion, and Task Forces Othman, Abu Bakr and Tariq. This will be known as Joint Forces Command East. They will remain along the coast and drive to take Kuwait City. On their left flank, I want the two Marine divisions, hence known as Marine Central Command. 1st British will shift and come under VII Corps along with 1st Cavalry Division. III Corps will retain the 50th Armored Division along with the 3rd and 4th Egyptian Divisions and the Saudi-Kuwait Joint Task Force Sa'al and Muthanna and will be known as Joint Forces Command North. It will be on the left flank of the Marine Central Command and the right flank for the VII Corps. The VII Corps will give up the 24th Mech to XVIII Airborne Corps. VII Corps and XVIII Airborne Corps will be under Army Central Command," Schwarzkopf stated. Horseholders were frantically writing notes as Schwarzkopf stood and walked over to the map. He picked up a pointer.

"I want Joint Forces Command East to cover from the coast to vicinity of Al Wafra. Marine Central Command will cover from Al Wafra to the elbow in the Kuwait border here," the general said, pointing to the almost ninety-degree turn in the Kuwait border. "Joint Forces Command North from the elbow to the border of Kuwait and Iraq. Army Central Command from the Kuwait-Iraq border west. This array gives us several options depending on what I'm told is our final objective. Alright, you have the laydown, now get back to me with the options for the plan," he said, placing the pointer down and heading for the door. Over his shoulder, he told the aide to have Lieutenant General Boomer come to his office.
****

"Excuse me, General, but you wanted to see me?" General Boomer said, entering the office.

"Yeah, Walt, I want to bounce something off you. Please sit down," Schwarzkopf said, indicating a chair. "You know about this minefield off the coast of Kuwait that the boys found?"

"Sure do, big damn thing. Why?"

"Well, we sure as hell can't run an amphib op through it, but I wonder if the Iraqis know that?" Schwarzkopf said with a smile.

"I suppose if we ran some minesweepers up there and started operations, that may just scare the crap out of them, making them think that's what we're going to do. What you got in mind?" Boomer asked.

"I'm thinking of doing just that. Run some minesweepers up there and move the Gator Navy up as well. Let them be seen and get it into the Iraqis' heads that we're going to do an amphibious assault in the vicinity of Kuwait City. How many divisions do you think they would position along the coast to oppose such a landing?" Norm asked.

"Well, considering that they learned that one division in the UAE wasn't enough, I'll bet he'll hold three divisions along the coast just to oppose a landing," Boomer said.

"I was thinking the same thing. Might even place an armored division centrally for a reserve," Norm added.

"Let me get with the Gator Navy boys and work up something. We could really get into his head with this," Boomer said as he stood to leave. "I'll have something for you next week if that's okay?"

"That'll be great. Until then, General," Norm said with a smile. He loved screwing with the enemy's head.

Chapter 46
Resume the Offense

2 May 1991
B Troop, 1ˢᵗ Squadron, 15th Cav
Al Qalibah, Saudi Arabia

The sandstorm that racked the eastern portion of the county hadn't descended on the western side, much to everyone's joy. The XVIII Airborne Corps was able to consolidate the forces in and around Tabuk. The aircraft and crews were dragging from a lack of sleep and overworked machines; thus, the decision had been made to give them a down day for maintenance and crew rest. For the ground forces of the 28th and 29th Divisions, it was business as usual. Rearm, refuel and get ready to move out. The 82nd Airborne Division was consolidating at the airport, their forces from the coast having come by truck overland to join those that had conducted the airborne assault of the airport.

"Okay, let's load up," Lieutenant Pile yelled to his platoon with their four M3 cavalry fighting vehicles. "We're point, so let's move up," he told his driver, who engaged the vehicle and proceeded to move to the head of the four-vehicle column. The rest of B Troop, 1-15 Cav, would be following about three hundred meters behind them.

"What's the route, Lieutenant?" Specialist Thompson asked. Lieutenant Pile was new, having been transferred over from another unit. Thompson liked what he had seen so far, but this was his first experience going into Injun territory with the new platoon leader.

"We're going to follow Highway 15 and clear it, reporting roadblocks and mines. We're not coming back to Tabuk, it appears."

As they cleared the cultivated farmland, they spread out, with two vehicles on each side of the road. Pile was pleased to see a Cobra helicopter and scout aircraft ahead of them flying an S pattern over the two-lane asphalt road. Occasionally they would come across a burned-out vehicle or a vehicle that had run out of gas. They didn't encounter any Iraqi soldiers, nor any that wished to be taken prisoner. Sheep still grazed on stubble grasses as their forefathers had for a few thousand years. Little changed with time in this part of the world.

"Silver Sabre Two-One, Crossbow Three-Two, over." Pile recognized the call sign as that of the Cobra pilot.

"Crossbow Three-Two, Silver Sabre Two-One, over," Pile replied.

"Sabre, I'm going to have to break for fuel. My replacement, Crossbow Three-Four, is about thirty minutes away and will join you. Good luck. Out."

Thanks a lot for the heads-up, Pile thought, switching his microphone to intercom. "Okay, heads up. The Cobra and scout had to break station, so there are no eyes forward of us." He received an acknowledgment from each of his crew. He then notified each of his track commanders. They'd been moving down Highway 15 for a little over two hours and were ten miles from Al Qalibah, a wide spot in the road and the intersection of Highway 15 and Highway 80, which continued on to Sakakah, right where they were going. Six miles from Al Qalibah, the highway went through a small pass between two escarpments. The southern escarpment could easily be bypassed to the south. Pile determined that this looked like an ideal location for an ambush and so approached cautiously.

"Sabre Two-Two, Two-One," he called his platoon sergeant, who was on the north side of the road with the other cav vehicle.

"Go, Two-One," came over the headphones.

"Two-Two, let's check out these two escarpments and make sure Abdul isn't setting an ambush, over," Pile instructed.

"Roger, we're going to dismount and move out," the platoon sergeant transmitted.

"Roger, Two-Two, we'll do the same. Stay in contract," Pile said.

"Roger, Two-Two out." Pile switched to intercom. "Okay, guys, let's dismount and check this area out," he ordered his soldiers.

The backs of the two Cav fighting vehicles opened and six scout soldiers exited each vehicle. The gunner and driver, as well as the track commander, remained in the vehicles to provide overwatching fire if it became necessary. As Pile dismounted as well, Sergeant Blair, the gunner, took over as the track commander. Blair had been promoted once the unit had been activated as he had more experience than others and it was recent experience as he'd only been out of the Army a couple of months when they were called up. Fortunately, only a few guys had been injured and no one had been killed. As almost everyone in his guard unit was from the same town, they were a pretty tight-knit group. They still referred to the company commander as Sheriff.

Pile was leading the twelve scouts who had fanned out, placing about ten meters between each man. No point in having one hand grenade or machine-gun burst take out more than one man. Suddenly, a scout on the left flank dropped to his knee and raised his hand with a closed fist. Everyone dropped to a knee and became very alert. Pile remained in a low crouch and made his way over to the soldier.

"Whatcha got?" Pile asked in a whisper.

"Listen, sir," the young scout said and pointed towards the edge of the escarpment overlooking the road. Waiting, Pile dropped to all four and began a slow crawl to the edge when he heard the sound of a rifle bolt slamming a round into a chamber. A chill ran down his back. Then he heard the voices. He had no idea what was being said, but it wasn't in English, and that meant caution was required. Pile looked over his shoulder and saw that everyone was watching him. *Good, they're paying attention.* He raised his arm and spun it in a circular motion. Everyone began coming to him in a crouched walk and took a knee when they arrived. No one said anything. They didn't need to as they all could hear the Iraqi soldiers just over the edge.

Using hand signals, Pile communicated what he wanted done and everyone separated into groups of two along the escarpment. On Pile's signal, each man withdrew a hand grenade and pulled the pin. Again, on Pile's signal, the grenades were dropped over the edge. For the first two seconds, nothing was heard from the Iraqis, then the shouting started as realization set in. Three seconds later, a series of explosions went off. Pile and his men stood and began spraying the Iraqi position with automatic weapons. As each man emptied their magazine, they stopped shooting and replaced the magazine but didn't shoot. Few could have lived through that onslaught, and if they did, they would be in no condition to fight.

"Okay, stay on your toes, but let's move down and see what we hit. Johnson and Travis, go first and we'll cover," Pile directed. The two soldiers moved cautiously over the edge of the escarpment while others trained their weapons on the lifeless Iraqi soldiers. Pile's radio came to life.

"Two-One, Two-Two, over."

"Two-Two, Two-One, go ahead."

"I heard some music over there. Everyone okay?" the platoon sergeant asked.

"We all good. Have one unfriendly position taken out. Squad-size with automatic weapons and suitcase antitank rockets. How's the hunting over there?"

"Two-One, we have indications they were here but have left maybe three hours ago."

"Roger, let's load up and head to the checkpoint."

"Roger, will join you on the road. Two-Two out." *Another five miles and we can wait for everyone else while someone else takes point*, Pile thought. Al Qalibah might have been a wide spot in the road, but it was a welcome relief point at least for Troop B.

****

This was a long ride in the UH-60. For almost an hour, half the soldiers of 3-327th Infantry Battalion along with half of the 1st Brigade, 101st Airborne Division, had been in the aircraft. Their destination was FOB Bastogne, which they were to establish one hundred and twenty miles northeast of Tabuk at an oasis known as Al Hawi. All indications were that there had been some mining or oil drilling in the area. Accompanying the UH-60 troop lift aircraft, there were CH-47s with sling loads of vehicles, fuel blivets, and 105mm howitzers. This would be the first of two lifts coming. Once the first lift touched down, they would be on their own for three hours before the next lift arrived. As the Iraqis were retreating, the powers that be felt that this wasn't a long period of time for the force. The purpose of the FOB, as it had been explained to the soldiers by Lieutenant Colonel Cory, was to provide a refueling point for the AH-64 attack helicopters in support of the ground forces coming up Highway 80 and to repel any Iraqi forces attempting to move against FOB Bastogne.

"Two minutes," the crew chief yelled above the pounding of the rotor blades and the scream of the turbine engines. A soldier on each side pulled the cargo doors back quickly as the aircraft flared for its landing on the paved road. As the front wheels touched, Lieutenant Colonel Cory and the other fourteen soldiers bailed out and assumed a prone position next to the aircraft, weapons pointing out from behind their rucksacks.

"Battleforce Six, Gladiator Six moving out," the Alpha Company commander, Captain Mulford, reported. Mulford had crossed swords with the colonel over one major point. Mulford's RTO was the worst in the battalion and was seldom by his radio to answer when the colonel called. Cory had gone so far as to relieve Mulford's RTO and made Mulford carry the radio himself. After a few weeks of that, Mulford had found a reliable RTO and things had improved significantly in their relationship.

"Roger. Break, all Battleforce elements, move out. Notify me when you've secured your objectives. Battleforce Six out." Turning to his two RTOs, Specialist Mahnken and Specialist King, Cory asked, "Are you two ready to move yet?"

"Sir, we're just waiting on you," Mahnken said. Mahnken was a very good RTO, as was King, but both liked to push it to the edge with the colonel. The colonel would dish it out just as well in return, especially if it did go over the line. If both hadn't been as good as they were, the colonel would have changed them out long ago. Truth was, he liked the banter with them. They were both nineteen and Cory was forty-four. He had to work at keeping up with them physically, and seldom did he falter, they noted. "The Old Man is in pretty damn good shape for his age," was stated on more than one occasion when they were with their fellow soldiers.

"Okay, let's move out and hook up with the S-3. He should be heading for that cluster of buildings to the north," Cory said, and they began to walk that way when the first shot could be heard. They stopped and dropped to a knee.

"Did you hear that shot?" Cory asked.

"Yes, sir, but that didn't sound like an AK or a PKM," King said, looking around.

"Sir, Gladiator Six is calling for you," Mahnken said, handing the hand mike to Cory.

"Gladiator Six, Battleforce Six."

"Battleforce Six, Gladiator Six, we have a sniper. One man down. Need medivac. Over."

"Roger, how bad?"

265

"Bad. Chest wound. Haven't identified the sniper's location, but he's east of my location. Over." Without being told, King was on the brigade command frequency requesting a medivac aircraft.

"Roger, Medivac has been notified. Break, Scout One, Battleforce Six, over."

"Battleforce Six, I monitored and am looking," the scout platoon leader reported. The scout platoon had two snipers of their own who were very good at what they did.

****

The scout platoon had been inserted the night before, six kilometers away, along with the scout platoons from the other battalions, each in the respective battalion sector. Lieutenant Stahl had pushed the platoon out in two locations to form a perimeter to the east and south of the battalion sector. He'd established a central position for himself from which he could communicate with his teams and the battalion commander. As soon as the shot was heard, Stahl knew what was going down.

"Team One, any sign?" Stahl asked the first team.

"Negative, not in my sector."

"Team Two, any sign?"

"Wait one—he's in our sector, and we're looking now."

Stahl waited.

Five minutes later, the team leader reported, "Scout One, Team Two, we have his location. He's moving around and kicking up some dust about three hundred yards from my location."

"Roger, take him out as soon as you can," Stahl ordered. That wasn't necessary as he knew they would.

Specialist Daniels and his spotter, Specialist Alexander, had been working together for two years now. They were a good team and either could be the shooter or the spotter. In fact, they were so confident in each other's ability that they frequently swapped positions for a day or so.

"There's a rise at three hundred yards with two rocks sticking up like a pair of tits," Alexander said, lying prone behind his spotting scope. "Have you got that?" he asked Daniels, who looked through his rifle scope. Daniels's weapon was the newly issued M24 rifle, manufactured by Remington Arms. It chambered a 7.62mm round, but these rounds weren't pulled off a machine-gun belt but specific match ammunition,

266

M118LR long-range 175-grain bullets. The scope was a Leupold Ultra M3A 10x42 fixed-power scope. On the range, Daniels could place five rounds in the center of the target at eight hundred yards and four out of five rounds at one thousand yards.

"Yeah, I see it," Daniels replied.

"Okay, come right fifty meters and you'll see a dip in the ridge. Ten feet below that dip is a bush. He's at the base of the bush. See him?" Alexander asked.

"Oh, yeah. Hello, Abdullah. Today you meet forty virgins in paradise," Daniels said as he studied the target and noted the wind, which was negligible and not a factor today.

"Okay, here goes," Daniels said. He took a deep breath and then released half of it, his trigger finger slowly applying pressure to the trigger. At some point, the trigger tripped the firing pin inside the bolt, and the round exploded out the barrel at a speed of two thousand five hundred and eighty feet per second. As Alexander watched, he couldn't see the bullet but he could see the air move as the bullet passed through heat waves on the desert floor. The spray of red at the end of the bullet's flight told him that Daniels had racked up another kill. Once the remainder of the battalion was in the FOB, they would walk out and examine the kill.

Chapter 47
Duraki

15 May 1991
Iraqi 3rd Squadron
Shaibah Air Base, Basrah, Iraq

Major Vitaly Popkov sat across the table from his friend, Major Konstantin "Kostya" Ayushiyev. The two men were locked in a test of will and wit. Popkov studied his friend's eyes, wondering how he would attack. After what felt like hours, Kostya slapped a queen of spades on the table. Popkov defended with the king of spades. Kostya came back with the king of hearts. Again Popkov was able to edge out his friend, this time with the ace of hearts. With the ace in play, Kostya made his next attack with the ace of spades. Popkov defended with a trump card, the seven of diamonds. Kostya halted his attack, and play moved across the table.

Popkov lashed out with the ace of clubs, hoping to draw out any of Kostya's trump cards. The move worked as Kostya defended with the eight of diamonds. Popkov looked at his cards. With two trump cards left, he felt confident that he had the game in hand. Each player was down to their final two cards. Popkov looked around the room at his squadmates.

"I don't know about you, Kostya, but I really like my cards," said Popkov. Everyone in the room knew what would happen next: Popkov was about to make a wager.

"Just play your next card, idiot. You're wasting time."

"No, no. Hear me out. These two cards"—he waved the cards in his hand— "are unbeatable."

Kostya rolled his eyes.

"Okay, I'll bite. What do you want?" asked the pilot.

"It's not about what I want—it's about what I don't want," replied Popkov.

"You're impossible, Vitaly, get to the point!" said one of the onlooking pilots.

"I don't want to submit my after-action report for our next mission. If I win this hand, Kostya will write it up for me." He shifted his gaze to

Kostya. "If you somehow defeat my unbeatable cards, I'll cover you for the rest of the week."

Kostya turned it over in his mind. He looked at his cards. He had one more trump, the queen of diamonds. Next to that, he had a relatively weak ten of spades. It wasn't great, but it could be worse. In the end, he decided, it wasn't about the cards, it was about the challenge. He would rather lose the bet than have Popkov calling him a coward, even in jest.

"Fine, if it'll speed up your play, I'll take your bet."

Popkov played the nine of diamonds, which forced Kostya to burn the queen. Popkov then hesitated before dropping his final card, the ten of diamonds.

"Shit," said Kostya, knowing that he couldn't beat that card. The room burst out with laughter and cries of "*Durak!*" the Russian word for *fool* for which the game was named.

"Kostya, let's go for a walk," said Popkov once the room quieted. "We can go over the format I like to use in these reports." As soon as the two had left the barracks, Popkov apologized to his friend. "I know that wasn't particularly fair in there, but the men needed a diversion and I thought I'd lighten the mood."

"Oh, I don't mind. I'm always up for some theater, as long as it's for a good cause."

"With our new accommodations here, I think improving morale definitely qualifies as a good cause."

The Iraqi Air Force had moved the squadron to Shaibah Air Base in Iraq just north of the Kuwaiti-Iraqi border. It wasn't too primitive by combat pilot standards, but the men had gotten a bit too accustomed to the facilities in Saudi Arabia and the UAE.

"Yes, our new home isn't exactly up to the standard of our old base, is it?"

"And it's not just the facilities, Kostya. It's the rationale behind the move." Popkov looked around to ensure they were alone. "No matter what our Iraqi minders say, there's no hiding it from the men—we're losing this war."

"It would seem so," replied Kostya. "We can no longer guarantee air superiority outside of our SAM coverage. That much is obvious. The question is, what comes next? How do they turn this around, and more importantly, how long will we be a part of that turnaround?"

"You think that Moscow will pull us out of here?" asked Popkov.

"I don't think they'll have a choice. Right now we're an incredibly valuable asset. We're experienced combat pilots. If they leave us here in a losing effort, how many of us will remain to return and pass on our knowledge to the rest of the VVS?"

As if on cue, the two men heard the distant wail of air-raid sirens.

"Shit, let's go!" said Popkov as he raced to get to one of the air base's fortified bomb shelters. In the distance, he could see the ready fighters screaming down the runway, and he wished that he were flying instead of running.

The two pilots made it into an underground shelter just as the first of the bombs fell. They sat out the attack in the shelter, impotent, unable to do anything except exist. After ten minutes that stretched on into what felt like hours, the all clear sounded, letting them know it was safe to return to the surface.

"My God," said Kostya as they emerged. The entire airfield was glowing with the fires from the POL facility off to the northeast. Popkov looked to the revetments where the squadron's MiG-29 fighters were parked. His heart sank as he saw smoke and fire rising from the storage pens. Unfortunately, unlike some of their other airfields, Shaibah didn't have any hardened shelters. From the wide swath of destruction, Popkov concluded that they must have been hit by a massive amount of cluster munitions. The thousands of tiny bomblets would tear through the unprotected planes. He had no idea what had ignited the POL facility, but at this point, what did it matter?

"I think this answers our question, my friend. I do believe that we are going home," said Popkov just as Kostya was reaching the same conclusion.

Chapter 48
Seeking Help

15 May 1991
The Kremlin
Moscow, USSR

Tariq Aziz was shown into Gorbachev's office and received a warm welcome.

"Mr. Prime Minister, thank you for seeing me on such short notice," Aziz said, extending his hand as he approached the Soviet leader.

"It is good to see you, Mr. Aziz, but I wish it was under different circumstances. This exercise has not gone as we anticipated, even with the more modern equipment that we have provided," Gorbachev said, motioning for them to sit in the overstuffed chairs.

"I welcome you to Moscow," he continued. "We see the goal of this conversation as finding out whether any new considerations have emerged from the Iraqi leadership that would facilitate the search for a political solution to the dangerous crisis in the Persian Gulf."[4]

"We are very much appreciative of anything that you could do—" Aziz began, but Gorbachev cut him off midsentence.

"With regard to Iraq, we have cooperated with you in the past and would like to preserve this cooperation. Our interest in this is clearly manifested in the fact of today's meeting. In addition, it is quite clear that if Iraq participates constructively in political efforts to untie the tight knot of problems that have emerged in the Persian Gulf region, then there will be one outcome. If there is no such participation, then everything, in my opinion, will end badly. Taking into account our relations in the past and present, I would like to say quite frankly that this conflict carries

---

[4] Extracted comments from National Security Archives, Gorbachev MemCon with Iraq Foreign Minister Tariq Aziz, September 5, 1990. www.nsarchive.gwu.edu. Mikhail Gorbachev, Sobranie Sochinenii (Moscow: Ves Mir, 2012), v. 22, pp. 30–34.

great danger. You can say that, supposedly, this assessment stems from the insufficiently courageous position of the Soviet Union. We don't think so. Our position is strong enough. But I cannot say that about the position of Iraq."

The Soviet leader paused for a second before continuing, "The last thing we want would be to lose everything that has been created in our bilateral relations over years of cooperation. That is why, even in such an acute situation, we are in favor of dialogue, for Iraq to participate in the search for a settlement. In a recent speech, I noted that the course of action of President Hussein is unacceptable to us. But for us, a massive, prolonged presence of US troops in this area is also unacceptable. We are advocating a return to the original situation with the provision of the necessary security guarantees to all parties involved in the conflict. Of course, it would be preferable for us if the process of finding political solutions took place with the active participation of the Arabs. However, it has become increasingly clear that the Arab states are unable to agree among themselves. What are you going to tell me? As your friend, I advise you to move as quickly as possible to the search for political ways out of the crisis, because in the international arena, voices are ringing out more and more loudly, urging that 'harsh measures' be applied to Iraq. It is clear what is meant by this. Are you comfortable with this? I cannot believe that the Iraqi leadership would be willing to abandon its people to the mercy of such a cruel fate." Gorbachev paused, taking a sip of the tea that had been served. The pause gave him an opportunity to see Aziz's reactions. Satisfied he was reading the Foreign Minister correctly, he continued.

"Now three possible scenarios have moved to the foreground. The first is the current situation, the military path. In our opinion, the one who makes the choice in favor of it is dangerously mistaken. It does not matter who we are talking about—President Bush and Prime Minister Thatcher, who have made many statements on this topic, or President Hussein. The second option is associated with the preservation, and most likely also the tightening, of the blockade of Iraq, which, of course, will place the heaviest burden on the Iraqi people. Ultimately, it is inhumane, and indeed simply cruel towards the Iraqis, to whom it offers bitter suffering. Even if the sympathies of the Arabs will trend more and more in favor of Iraq, even if the Arab countries view the victims of the Iraqi people with sympathy, this path is extremely difficult, and most importantly, it does not contain structural elements and does not lead to a way out of the crisis.

"In short, it is realistically only possible to speak of the third option, which involves a serious search for a political solution. This alone, in our opinion, meets the interests of Iraq and will curtail the current situation. We will persistently argue against a military option and convince Bush of its danger and futility. However, frankly speaking, this requires constructive, realistic steps on your part. It was about these that we had expected to hear when we approached President Hussein with the question of whether there were new developments in the Iraqi position. Do you have any new proposals? The Americans do not want us to take on a mediating role yet. We told them that the process of finding solutions does not exclude the use of mediation missions, although we did not specify whose missions we were referring to. We appreciate that our dialogue with Iraq continues, despite the severity of the situation. We do not wish ill upon Iraq. However, there is the logic of history, the logic of development, with which both you and we must agree. You should take such a factor as public opinion into consideration. Our public opinion is very alarmed by the events in the Persian Gulf. And we must admit that there are grounds for concern. In the future, it will be much more difficult for us to placate this anxiety. What do you say? What did you come here with?" Gorbachev asked.

Aziz took a deep breath. *I need to make our case now*, he thought. "We in Iraq were fully confident of our strength and did not fear a confrontation with the Americans. At the same time, we recognized that such confrontation could lead to an extensive conflict along all the lines, consequences of which would affect not only our Arab region, but the entire world. However, such a prospect did not scare us. The Americans deceived themselves when they talked about a possibility of conducting a so-called 'surgical operation' against Iraq. Deciding to undertake something like this, then, is giving them a long and a very bitter conflict, which could turn everything upside down in this region of the globe. We, on our part, as revolutionaries, naturally, are not afraid of such an outcome and are prepared to make sacrifices for months, even years if that is what it takes. Peace for us is a sacred goal. We are talking about peace in which our security would be guaranteed," Aziz said as he

273

paused to sip his tea. A game of statesmanship was being played. Who would blink first?

Aziz continued, "Life itself put the entire complex of problems on our agenda and we should resolve them together. I have in mind the Palestinian problem and the Israeli occupation of the Arab lands, suffocating economic conditions in which many Arab states found themselves, a scandalous gap between the rich and the poor in the Arab world, the tragic situation in Lebanon and a mass of other problems. The entire Arab world, from Iraq in the East to Morocco in the West, is seething. Arabs are no longer able to wait," Aziz concluded forcefully.

Gorbachev smiled. *Aziz has lost his cleverness as they say.* "We have been persistently looking for many years for a key to solving the most important problems of the Middle East, particularly the Palestinian problem and the Arab-Israeli conflict in general, and the complicated entanglement of the Lebanese crisis. However, a way out has still not been found. Now, after the actions committed by Iraq, the task has become a great deal more complex. Finding a solution to the region's problems has become even more difficult."

"In essence, you gave very strong arguments to the Americans for building up their military presence in the Middle East and the Persian Gulf. American troops won't just leave the area. We see that Japan and Saudi Arabia are already joining in their funding. So, the United States has achieved its goal... The fact that Kuwait was occupied, and then ultimately declared the nineteenth province of Iraq, gives an additional reason for the strengthening of the American military presence in the land of the Arabs, for the entanglement of the Western partners of the US in this ... The United States is also using the fact that Iraq promised President Mubarak not to commit military action against Kuwait, but broke this promise and deceived the Egyptians. The Americans told the world that Iraq could not be trusted and Iraq has proven their point," Gorbachev said and could see from Aziz's facial expression that he had scored.

Aziz began to protest but did not get the first word out when Gorbachev continued. "Frankly speaking, you do not leave us any other choice. We really would not like to see Iraq in total isolation, and we are taking this into consideration in our practical steps. It is possible that you receive instructions from the Supreme Being, but I would like to give

274

you some advice, and it is up to you to decide to use it or not. We believe that we must not give up the search for a political solution on a realistic, constructive basis. So far, I feel, you are not ready for this. But it would be wise to consider that in the future the situation will only get worse. There is a limit beyond which the people will no longer be able to bear sacrifices, suffer adversity and hardship. Then it might present a bill to its leadership. I think that this is not the result you aspire to. There is a play by Shatrov— 'The Brest Peace'—that is playing now in the Soviet Union. In that play, the director used the following scene: Lenin, trying to persuade the head of our delegation at the negotiations in Brest— Trotsky—to conclude the peace treaty with the Germans, says that he was ready to practically plead on his knees. It was a critical moment in our history, when they had to save our revolution. Later, they had to conclude the peace treaty anyway, but with much harsher conditions. Lenin even called that peace treaty 'bawdy.' We had a lively exchange of opinions. I cannot say that I am satisfied with what I heard. It would be preferable if the Iraqi side came up with new approaches. You only presented the known positions. That is why we have different assessments of this meeting. But we are not rejecting the contacts. Give President Hussein my greetings."

Gorbachev shook his head in frustration as he ended his meeting with the Iraqi representative. They had given the Iraqi's every possible chance to achieve a victory, but they chose to not pursue from a position of strength. Now they are on the cusp of defeat and want us to intervene to save them.

I need to speak to our generals and have the last of our advisors pulled out of Iraq. We have all gambled and we have lost. It is time to cut our losses and pull our people back before this escalates any further, the Soviet leader thought, *and get that damn Kilo sub we sold to Iran back in port someplace.*

Chapter 49
Decisions

15 May 1991
Oval Office, White House
Washington, D.C.

The President had been maintaining a hands-off approach to telling General Schwarzkopf what to do and what not to do. He really didn't want to know the minor details. Now, however, the SecDef and SecState were asking for a decision on what the endgame was going to be and he needed to give them an answer.

"Send them in," the President said, speaking into his intercom. The door opened and the SecDef and SecState entered, with General Powell behind them.

Cheney entered as well. "Mr. President, I have asked General Powell to join us."

"That's fine. Have a seat, gentlemen." The President motioned, coming from behind the Resolute desk and taking his usual single chair just as the side door opened and a steward entered with a tray and four cups along with the pot of coffee. He placed them on the coffee table and departed. Powell took the pot and poured four cups, passing them to each man. All drank theirs black with no sugar.

Mr. Chaney began the meeting by bringing them up to speed on where things sat in the Gulf. "Mr. President, the actions in the Gulf are moving rapidly, with Saddam's force pulling back into Kuwait and Iraqi. That two-day sandstorm gave him an opportunity to run without us on his backside. He has pulled most of his forces back into defensive positions along the Kuwait-Saudi border and some forces along the Iraq-Saudi border. His navy has been swept from the Gulf or is tied up in ports in Kuwait and the one port in Iraq and not venturing into the Gulf. His air force is hunkering down in airfields scattered around Iraq but is still a formidable force if they surge. His army has been mauled pretty good but is still a fighting force."

"So what you're telling me, Dick, is that he isn't defeated yet and could come back in the near future once we run him out of Kuwait," the President summarized.

"Mr. President, if he decides that the pressure is too great and does pull out of Kuwait back into Iraq, yes, he will be left with a sizeable force capable of rolling right back into Kuwait after we leave the area. We will be doing Gulf War Two."

"Do you think he's going to pull out of Kuwait?" the President asked.

"Sir, we have no indication to support that opinion," Cheney responded, "but..." He looked to Jim Baker.

"Mr. President, I have it on good authority that Tariq Aziz is flying to Moscow today to meet with Mr. Gorbachev. We believe the purpose of the meeting is to have the Russians propose a cease-fire with the Iraqis retaining Kuwait or at least an annual payment from Kuwait for their intrusion into the Rumaila oil field with their slant well drilling," Mr. Baker said, placing his coffee down on the table between them.

"How do we know he's going to Moscow?" the President inquired, sipping his coffee.

"We got word from the Swiss as they didn't want us to shoot his plane down. They'll let us know when he's flying back," Baker responded.

"Mr. President, we need to tell General Schwarzkopf what his final object is and soon. He's been pushing the Iraqis out of Saudi Arabia and closing in on Kuwait, but he needs to have a final objective to plan the continuation of his campaign," Colin Powell interjected.

Bush paused in thought for a moment before answering. *Colin is right, but I need to see what the results of Tariq's meeting with Gorbachev are. It may result in a complete withdrawal and end the fighting. I've just got to wait and see.*

"Gentlemen, I understand that we need to give a final objective to General Schwarzkopf, but let's wait to see what the Russians propose. I don't want to cut Gorbachev off at the knees when he may offer a viable alternative. A few more days won't make a difference to General Schwarzkopf. Dick, get the general on the phone and I'll talk to him. Anything else?" the President asked as he stood, signaling that the meeting was over.

****

"General Schwarzkopf, let me congratulate you on your success in this campaign," the President said. General Schwarzkopf waited for the other shoe to fall.

"Thank you, sir, but we still have a ways to go," he replied, cautiously.

"That's what I wanted to talk to you about. I want you to pause the attack for a few days. Aziz is in Moscow meeting with Gorbachev, and I want us to see what comes out of that meeting. Gorbachev may come up with a viable alternative to ending this fight and get the Iraqis out of Kuwait. A few-day pause won't hurt your ground plan, will it? You can still run the air campaign, but I want you to hold off on charging into Kuwait or Iraq. Conduct reconnaissance operations, but not a full-blown attack. Is that a problem?"

"Sir," Stormin' Norman said, attempting to keep his voice under control as his blood pressure rose, "a pause of a few days will allow the Iraqis to rearm, refuel and reinforce their forces. If Gorbachev does offer a plan that leaves the Iraqi Army intact, we could very well be looking at coming back here in a couple of years when he tries this again, having learned the lessons already. I'll follow your orders, sir, but I believe a pause like this may be costly to us in terms of lives."

"I understand, General, and you make a good point. We'll get back to you just as soon as we evaluate the situation. Have a good day," the President said as he hung up the phone. *I don't care if you don't like it—I'm the President and I give the orders.*
****

"Son of a bitch," could be heard down the hall coming from General Schwarzkopf's office. No one wanted to venture into that cave for fear of being shot on the spot. Finally, Major General Schless built up the nerve to do so.

"Sir, I take it your conversation with the President wasn't what you wanted to hear," Schless said.

"No, damnit, it was not. Get Pegasus in here. I need to talk to both of you," Schwarzkopf directed. Twenty minutes later, both general officers reluctantly entered Schwarzkopf's office.

"Here's the thing. The President wants us to hold off on rolling into Iraq and Kuwait. Seems the Iraqis are having a meeting with Gorbachev,

278

and he wants to see what comes out of that meeting before we cross over. Damn politics. It'll screw up a great military campaign every damn time," Schwarzkopf fumed.

"Sir, I'll get an order out right way having all forces hold in place. We can still move to our tactical assembly areas, right?" Schless asked.

"Yeah, and they can continue to conduct reconnaissance of the Iraqi defenses, but no major engagements. The air campaign continues," Schwarzkopf indicated. There was a moment of silence before General Pegasus spoke up.

"Sir, this may not be a bad thing."

"How do you figure?" Schwarzkopf asked.

"Sir, we've rolled across Saudi and the UAE in record time. We have the logistics to support the operation, but we're at the end of a very long logistical tail. Our supply trucks have done yeoman work but are starting to show the effects of long hours and long hauls. With this pause, we can get the port of Dammam opened and begin supplying from there instead of having to bring everything up from Oman. This will give us an opportunity to push forward supplies to the units in a more timely manner, especially fuel and ammo. I was going to come to you and tell you that we were going to have to pause when we got to the Euphrates River, but now we can resupply here and be prepared to go all the way to Baghdad without a pause. There's a silver lining here," General Pegasus explained as he tried to lighten his mood.

Schwarzkopf thought about it for a moment. "Alright, let's use this time for resupply and maintenance. Tell the commanders they have two days as of right now to refuel and rearm before we order the attack to continue. How soon can the port of Dammam be opened?"

"Sir, the first ship arrived there this morning and is being unloaded. The refinery at Al Jubail is pumping diesel fuel to our tanker trucks as we speak," Pegasus said. Schwarzkopf just smiled and dismissed them with a hand wave.
****

The VII Corps had great combat power—five armor/mechanized divisions and a cavalry regiment. Supporting them were also corps artillery units, to include multiple rocket launcher batteries and attack helicopters.

"General, we always knew that the logistical tail was going to be the weak point, but not this bad. The attack is going so successfully and so quickly that unless we change our tactics a bit, we're going to have to pause to get things caught up," Colonel Cherry said.

"So what do our logistic requirements look like right now?" General Franks asked. "What did we eat up yesterday?"

Cherry looked over at Brigadier General Holt, the corps G-4, responsible for logistic planning.

"Sir, we've fielded one hundred and forty-two thousand soldiers, which means a minimum of one hundred and forty-two thousand MREs if everyone only gets one a day. We have forty-eight thousand vehicles and aircraft with one thousand five hundred and eighty-seven tanks, one thousand five hundred Bradley and Cav fighting vehicles, six hundred artillery tubes, and two hundred and twenty-three attack helicopters. Yesterday we used five point six million gallons of fuel, consumed three point three million gallons of water, and fired six thousand rounds of tank, artillery, and large caliber ammunition. Right now, trucks and CH-47 aircraft are moving all that again today," General Holt explained.

"How close are we to what we planned?" Frank pressed, sensing a problem developing.

"Sir, if we go by the schoolhouse textbook for combat consumption, we would have far exceeded the numbers, but watching what we were using back in Oman for training and what we've used on a daily basis since we crossed into the UAE, we're pretty much on track," Holt said.

"So what's the problem?" Franks questioned.

"The problem is turnaround for delivery back to depots to reload and get back to the front. Units are running out of supplies before the transportation can drop off, get back to the depot, reload and get back to the unit, and the further we get from Oman, the more acute the problem is going to be," Holt pointed out.

"So what's the solution? Surely you brought me a solution along with this problem," Franks commented.

"Yes, sir, but you may not like it," Holt said hesitantly.

"Try me," was Franks's only response.

"Sir, if we could cut back on the artillery shooting, then we can solve part of this problem," Cherry said. Franks gave him the *Okay, explain this one, Colonel* look.

"Sir, we've been pounding the hell out of everything with artillery. If an attack helicopter finds a target and fires on it, they then adjust artillery on the same target that they just killed. If a Bradley platoon takes out a bunker complex, they pound it with artillery before they continue. We're wasting a lot of artillery ammo, sir. Instead of every battery firing on the same target, we only need one battery to fire on each target. The artillery guys are treating this as a massive live-fire exercise back at Fort Bliss or Hood if you ask me and we're chewing through ammo like this is World War II."

"Sir," General Holt said, jumping into the conversation, "the other thing we could do, sir, is have half of the artillery displacing forward while half remain in firing positions and refuel and rearm at the same time. That way the logistic tail won't be chasing after the people on the move. The artillery batteries can leapfrog past each other as they are resupplied."

"Well, you two have succinctly laid out the problem and the solution. I don't like either but understand the need. Okay, implement your plan. But get back to me tomorrow and let me know how it's going. Remember, fighters win battles, but logistics wins wars. I'll talk to General Yeosock about this and see what's being done to push the logistics."
****

The next afternoon, the gang of three were again knocking on the President's door. The President didn't rise to meet them and didn't offer them a chair. *If they sit down, they'll never get out of here and a ten-minute meeting will become an hour*, the President thought privately. Barbara had told him in no uncertain terms that he was not to be late for the state dinner that night.

Baker was the first to speak up. "Mr. President, we have a good idea of what Aziz was told by Gorbachev. It appears the Russians are not happy with how the whole thing was handled despite them providing equipment and advisors at the outset. We now believe the Russians felt he was going only into Kuwait and not Saudi Arabia or the UAE.

Gorbachev told him to basically sue for peace on our terms, that they would get no more assistance from the Soviet Union."

"Well, that's good news. Now are we seeing anything out of Saddam to show that he's listening?" the President asked, steepling his fingers on his desk.

"No, sir. In fact, he's moving supplies into Kuwait and shoring up his defenses," Powell answered.

"Sir, we really need to give General Schwarzkopf some guidance on the final objective, so he knows how and what to plan on doing next," Cheney almost pleaded.

Baker interjected, "Sir, we may have another problem," as all eyes turned to him.

"And what might that be, Jim?"

"Sir, I'm getting some rumblings out of the Turks about their feelings on the invasion of Iraq. Seems they feel if Saddam is removed, it'll have a destabilizing impact on the Middle East," Baker said.

"Translation?" the President pressed, a frown starting to appear on his face.

"Translation is they believe if we topple Saddam, then they alone are going to have to deal with the Kurds. They like the idea that he keeps his thumb on some of them and they don't have to deal with the whole Kurdish issue alone."

"What do you think they'll do if we do take him down?" Cheney asked.

"They could kick us out of our air bases in Turkey. They could drop out of NATO—"

"I would call their bluff on those two options," Cheney interrupted. "The air bases bring in some very nice revenue to the Turks, and as long as Greece stays in NATO, the Turks will stay if for no other reason than to make life miserable for anything the Greeks want to accomplish. The two hate each other beyond words."

"Alright, tell Schwarzkopf that his final objective is Baghdad and the seizure of Saddam. Enough of this screwing around. If we don't take him, and his army down, we're going to be right back here in five to ten years. If by some miracle Saddam comes to his senses and sues for peace, we can always curtail operations. Oh, as far as bombing inside Iraq goes, all military and government targets are on the table. Let's be careful with hitting the civilian population, but military and government targets are fair game. Anything else?" the President asked indicating they shouldn't say anything further. "Alright, get out of here or I'm going to be negotiating with Barbara, and I always lose those negotiations."

Chapter 50
The Ball is Rolling

20 May 1991
3-327th Infantry
Tactical Assembly Area Campbell, Saudi Arabia

Lieutenant Colonel Ray Fitzgerald deplaned from the C-130 while its engines were still running. The flight was a short one, from Tabuk to Rafha. His battalion was one of the first to arrive and was being assembled on the north side of the runway, where a column of trucks were waiting. Asking soldiers of the 82nd to load trucks in anticipation of combat wasn't something a commander wanted to do. Especially as the rear elements of the 1st Brigade, 101st Airborne Division, were co-located at the airport. The "grunts" had already flown to the tactical assembly areas they were occupying just south of the Iraqi border. The jeering between the Screaming Eagles of the 101st and the Sky Soldiers of the 82nd was common, but someone from another organization best not jeer either, as both would turn on them like a snake on a mouse.

"Ray! Ray Fitzgerald," a voice called out. Ray turned to see where the voice was coming from and saw an approaching soldier waving his arm and looking at him. As the soldier got closer, Ray recognized him.

"Cory, is that you? Damn, what are you doing here?" Ray said, extending his hand. Ray and Cory had lived in the same fourplex at Fort Benning in the mid-1970s. Their kids had played with each other and gone to school together. Ray had even purchased Cory's skydiving gear when Cory had moved up to a new rig that had nearly gotten him killed and put him in the hospital for two weeks.

"I command a battalion in the 101st, we flew in here yesterday. I'm just back here getting some commo gear in my vehicle checked out. You?" Cory asked.

"Same, commanding a battalion in the 82nd. I guess we're moving into an assembly area as well. Hopefully we'll be making a drop in Iraq. Have you heard anything?" Ray inquired of his friend.

Cory shrugged his shoulders, "I know my first objective. Planning for two other contingency missions though I've been given a final objective. Can't say where, but I think we'll both be arriving there by air at about the same time."

"Well, you know a hell of a lot more than me. We were told to get here, and we'd be told later. Hey, I have to go. Good seeing you. Take care, and hope to see you on the other side," Ray said, holding out his hand, which Cory took.

****

TAA Campbell was the jump-off point for the 101st into Iraq. It was also nine kilometers from the Iraqi border. A Saudi border guard post was one klick from the Iraqi border with a similar border guard outpost on the Iraqi side. From a distance, both looked like the French Foreign Legion forts of the 1930s movies. Cory was the first to go up to the Saudi border post and was quickly greeted and accepted by the commander there. The Saudis that had returned to man the post were very happy to have the American units around them. So happy they invited Cory to leave a team there with a radio for joint communications.

When Cory arrived in the AO, it was after dark, and it wasn't until the next day that he had an opportunity to get the lay of the land. On the battalion's right flank was 2-187th Infantry and on the left flank was 2-327th. The battalions of the 2nd Brigade, 502nd Regiment, were located behind the two forward brigades. Colonel Hall had a morning commander's call and an evening commander's call. His three infantry battalion commanders were always present, along with Lieutenant Colonel Lynn Hartsell, the artillery battalion commander.

"Okay, here's the deal. We're going to depart here and fly about one hundred and ten miles into Iraq and establish an FOB—FOB Cobra. Basically, we're going to be a gas station for the attack helicopters and a waypoint for the 3rd Brigade to pass through as they leapfrog north to the area around As Samawah. Cory, you have a be-prepared mission to go with them. You need to get with Colonel Clark and see what he might have for you," Hall said. Cory just jotted notes and shook his head.

"When we get to Cobra, Cory, you have from twelve to three on the perimeter. Jim, you will have from three to six, Thomas six to nine, and Frank from nine to twelve. Any questions?" Hall asked. No one had as they had been individually consulted by the brigade S-3.

"Okay, then, I'll see you guys in the morning," Hall said, standing up.

"One question, sir. When are we launching into Iraq?" Thomas asked.

"Good question, and I don't know. The Air Force is softening up the area with air strikes, hitting his units, his infrastructure, and airfields. When Schwarzkopf feels confident that the Air Force has pounded them sufficiently, then we go over," Hall said.

"Sir, do we know our final objective yet?" Cory asked. This was the question they all wanted answered. Hall looked first at the ground, lost in thought. When he looked up, he saw four sets of eyeballs staring at him, seeking an answer.

"Keep this to yourselves, but As Samawah is only one hundred and forty-seven miles southeast of the Baghdad International Airport," Hall explained. Everyone responded with wide grins.

Chapter 51
Khafji

22 May 1991
TF Shepherd
Khafji, Saudi Arabia

TF Shepherd had been tasked by Division with providing a general outpost screen along the Saudi-Kuwait border in the division sector. Each of the four companies had a section of LAV-ATs with their thermal night sights, TOW missiles and 25mm cannons.

"Captain Pollard, I want you to move your company to a position four kilometers northwest of this police station. The reconnaissance platoon leader is there to coordinate with you," Lieutenant Colonel Myers directed. Captain Pollard commanded Delta Company, part of 7th MEB, and had only recently joined TF Shepherd, Lieutenant Colonel Myers's command.

When Pollard arrived at the police station, he made the coordination with the recon platoon leader and moved his company into position. The position was four thousand meters long, and he covered that with his thirteen LAV-25s, seven LAV-ATs and his command vehicle, an LAV-C2. Once everyone was in position and had been checked by Captain Pollard, they all settled in for a quiet night.

"Charger Six, Knight Two, over," the recon platoon leader called Pollard.

"Knight Two, Charger Six, over," Pollard responded.

"Charger Six, we have a column of thirty, I say again thirty, armored vehicles moving towards the police station. Over," the platoon leader indicated in a surprisingly calm voice.

Pollard immediately switched radios and notified Lieutenant Colonel Myers, who passed the information up the chain of command. Soon Myers was back on the radio, wanting more information.

"Knight Two, Charger Six, over."

"Charger Six, Knight Two."

"I was just about to call you. We now have five, I say again, five, Tango Six-Two and several Bravo Mike Papa with infantry moving on the police station with the recon platoon. Recon is engaging. Request tac air, over." As the platoon leader watched, his recon platoon engaged the Iraqi vehicles with what little antiarmor capability they had which wasn't much. LAW rockets, AT-4 and M203 rounds weren't much of a match against BMPs and tanks.

"Charger Six, Knight Two. We need to vacate this property. Am pulling back," Knight Two reported.

"Roger, we will cover. Break. Charger elements, engage."

On that command, the right side of Delta Company that was within range of the Iraqi force opened fire with their TOW weapons systems while Colonel Myers was adjusting artillery on the approaching column. As Pollard watched, reports of more Iraqi vehicles were received from his own platoons, which he passed on to Myers.

"Shepherd Six, Charger Six, over."

"Charger Six, Shepherd Six, go," Myers said, tension thick in his voice.

"Shepherd Six, we have a large force at the police station, and it appears that they're attempting to move back into Saudi. Over."

"Charger Six, understood. Requesting air support now. Stand by," Myers instructed.

Stand by my ass, Pollard thought. *I've got to move some vehicles to within range of these guys.* Immediately he was on the company command net.

"Pawn Two, Charger six, over."

"Charger Six, Pawn Two," Lieutenant Williams, the 1st Platoon leader, answered.

"Pawn Two, I want you to reorient to engage those people at the police station. Break, Bishop Two, Charger Six."

"Charger Six, Bishop Two, over."

"Bishop Two, occupy a position to the right of Pawn Two. Engage when they're within range. How copy?"

"Charger Six, good copy. Moving now."

Captain Pollard watched as the platoons reoriented their positions and the LAV-AT vehicles did likewise. However, he didn't see the recon platoon moving from the police station. In fact, the firefight within the police station compound was still intense.

"Knight Two, Charger Six, are you out of there yet? Over."

"Negative, we haven't been able to break contact. We're almost out of ammo, over."

"Roger, wait one. Break, all Charger elements, engage." On that command, all the vehicles in Delta opened fire on the Iraqi force. A tank blew up almost immediately and burned, providing an excellent reference point for future air strikes. However, three more T-55 tanks emerged from the darkness and began engaging the recon platoon.

Shit, I've got to get those guys out of there.

"Bishop Two, Charger Two."

"Bishop Two, go ahead."

"Bishop Two, form up on me. Break, Pawn Two, remain in position and provide cover fire."

"Pawn Two, roger." Pollard gave his driver the go-ahead and they moved out to lead the 2nd Platoon towards the police station. As they moved forward, Pollard observed the actions at the police station compound and had to make snap decisions.

"Bishop Two, hold position and engage," Pollard ordered. Immediately TOW missiles and 25mm fire raked into the Iraqi forces. An Iraqi tank exploded, but so did one of his LAV-AT[5] vehicles. Then a second T-55 was hit and destroyed, which halted the Iraqi attack for a moment. This provided time for the recon platoon leader to break contact and vacate the police station compound. As the night fighting continued with the Iraqis occupying the compound, which offered some cover and concealment, it became more difficult to identify their positions. Muzzle flashes provided the location of the enemy forces, but that was all.

This is a damn dog fight with them in cover and concealed positions. Got to make some adjustments and work some options, Pollard thought as he inflicted some casualties on the Iraqi forces but also took some of his own. Assessing the situation, Pollard began giving commands.

"Pawn Two, Charger Six, over."

"Charger Six, Pawn Two, over," Lieutenant Williams responded.

---

[5] In the real Battle for Khafji, this LAV was lost in a friendly-fire incident. A LAV in a support role accidentally engaged this LAV destroying it.

"Pawn Two, I want you to come up on the right flank of Bishop. Break, Bishop Two, Charger Six, over."

"Charger Six, Bishop Two, over."

"Bishop Two, hold your position. Pawn Two is coming up on your right flank, over."

"Roger, Charger Six."

"Charger Six, Pawn Two is on the move." Looking through his NODs, Captain Pollard could see the 1st Platoon moving into position on the right flank of the 2nd Platoon. As the platoons were now three thousand meters from the police station compound and all vehicles were online, to include the LAV-ATs, which were scattered throughout the company, Pollard was able to engage the Iraqi forces with all of his 25mm cannons and TOWs without fear of a fratricide situation. The firefight continued.

"Captain, we have tac air on station," Pollard's forward air controller told him.

"Good. Send him after any tanks he can see around that burning tank," Pollard instructed the young man. Pollard watched for the plane. The night sky was too dark to see the aircraft, but he could see the damage it was inflicting with guided bombs. He could tell right away it wasn't an Air Force A-10, which was the preferred close-air support aircraft, but it would do for right now.

Pollard was aware that his 25mm cannons couldn't penetrate the T-55s' armor, but they would separate the BMPs from the tanks. In addition, the ricocheting bullets were marking the targets for additional air strikes that were arriving on station.

"Captain, I have another flight of aircraft on station. A-10s this time," the FAC said. "They want us to mark targets, as they say our tracers are insufficient for them to identify them. They can drop a flare and adjust off that," the FAC indicated.

"Fine, have them drop it and we'll adjust," Pollard ordered. Within minutes, the distinctive sound of the A-10 could be heard as it made a low pass and dropped its flare. Instead of landing forward of position, however, it landed in his position.

"Banshee Four-Five," the FAC called to indicate the enemy's positions in relation to the flare. Before he received a response, an LAV-25 in close proximity to the flare exploded.

"Son of a bitch," Pollard yelled. "Pawn Two, did you just lose a vehicle?" Pollard screamed into the radio.

"Roger, Charger Six, the A-10 hit us."

Turning to the FAC, Pollard said, "Call those bastards off. They're hitting us damnit!"

While Pollard was sorting out the loss of another LAV-25 and, more importantly, the crews and Marines, the Iraqi forces began to back off. Pollard was able to disengage his company, moving one thousand meters further away and linked up with Company A, which allowed him to rearm, refuel his company and care for the casualties. The battle for Khafji would continue for another day before Iraqi forces retreated.

Chapter 52
It Is Time

24 May 1991
CENTCOM HQ
Riyadh, Saudi Arabia

The meeting had been called the night before. Phone lines between Riyadh and Washington had been busy all night. Suspected but not confirmed, a phone call had also been made to the Kremlin in the late hours of the night. Decisions had been made.

"Mr. President, I feel that the time has come that we end this affair. My forces are in place and are rearmed and refueled. Indications are that our air campaign has sufficiently degraded the Iraqi forces. I'd like to launch the ground offensive the day after tomorrow and end this war," General Schwarzkopf said.

"OK, how do you visualize this going down, General?" the President asked.

"Sir, I've moved our amphibious fleet off the coast of Kuwait as part of a deception plan. That'll hold two, maybe three of his divisions in place on the coast. The Joint Forces Command East will attack north along the coast. The Marine Central Command will attack north and east alongside Command East. Joint Forces Command North will attack north and swing east above Marine Central Command. Army Central Command has VII Corps, and XVIII Airborne Corps. VII Corps will drive north, then turn east, attacking into northern Kuwait and southern Iraq. The XVIII Airborne Corps attacks north to the Euphrates River, blocks reinforcements seizing the bridges over the Euphrates River and prevents the withdrawal of Iraqi forces. Once this is completed, we'll move on to the next phase and be well positioned to continue the attack," Schwarzkopf summarized.

"Has General Bilal taken command of host nation forces under Joint Forces Command North?" the President inquired.

"He has, sir, but I can tell you General Smith is not happy about it," Schwarzkopf indicated.

"I can understand that he might not be, but politics trumps personal and professional feelings on this," the President replied.

A voice in the background could be heard. "Mr. President, we want to be very careful about continuing the attack," Powell said. "We have indicated that our objective was to remove Iraqi forces from Kuwait and Saudi Arabia. If we push it further, we're subject to global criticism."

Ever the damn politician, John Sununu thought as he sat and listened to Powell.

"Mr. President, let me point out that Saddam still has a large stockpile of chemical weapons and isn't afraid to employ them on his own people. If we continue the attack further, he may see no reason not to employ them on our forces as well," Powell continued.

"General Powell," Sununu said, cutting Powell off, "have we seen any indications that he's moving his chemical weapons from their storage facilities? No, and we've been watching those sites very closely. I say we continue with the plans until such time as we get an indication that he might be doing that."

The President turned to Jim Baker. "Jim, what do you think?"

"Sir, the world community finds Saddam to be a pain in the ass but a good puppet to some, such as the Soviets. Most nations want this conflict to end and end quickly, but they don't want to see Saddam in a position of power when it's over. The Saudis feel that if he's left in power, then he can come back and do this again. The Israelis definitely want him out before his Scud missiles start coming over with chemical weapons on board. The Middle East would be a quieter place without him," Baker explained.

"Who do you think would take his place? If we remove him, are we replacing him with something worse?" the President asked.

"Sir, that's the million-dollar question. We just don't know unless we occupy the country, and do we really want to do that?" Cheney asked.

Hearing this background conversation was driving Schwarzkopf insane. *All I want is a freaking go-ahead to launch the ground offensive into Iraq. This crap should have been asked and answered months ago.* "Excuse me, gentlemen, right now I need an answer on the immediate question. Can I launch the ground offensive into Iraq the day after tomorrow? When that phase is completed, then these other questions can be decided," Schwarzkopf said, attempting to cover his rising anger at the lack of decisions.

"Mr. President, may I suggest that we send a communiqué to Saddam through the Swiss and ask one more time for him to withdraw his forces from Kuwait?" Powell asked.

Before the President could respond, Schwarzkopf had heard enough. "Mr. President, the longer we delay, the more damage he's going to do to Kuwait. The oil fields are already a towering inferno, and each day, he destroys another fifty or so wellheads. He's already released oil into the Gulf, which we were able to shut off with a missile strike. He has mined the Kuwaiti coast for miles and robbed the city of anything that wasn't nailed down. How much more damage are we going to allow? Sir, the time to launch is now," Schwarzkopf said, allowing his tone to demonstrate his displeasure with those in Washington. There was silence from the Washington side, and Schwarzkopf thought for a minute that they had been disconnected. Finally, the President spoke up.

"General, you may proceed. Launch the attack the day after tomorrow, and may God be with you."

Chapter 53
Air Assault

26 May 1991
Day 1, G-Day
Saudi Arabia

The sixty UH-60 Black Hawk helicopters, along with CH-47 Chinooks and AH-64 attack helicopters, had been made ready the night before. Soldiers of the 1st Brigade, 101st Airborne Division, rehearsed exiting the aircraft with fifteen infantry soldiers per aircraft for the most part and then slept next to the aircraft. For replacements or newbies, this was their first combat air assault. The assault was scheduled for an 0400 takeoff. Everyone wanted to be on this assault, even the cooks for the 3-327th Battalion. They had volunteered to be stretcher-bearers, and at first Cory had turned them down, but when he'd seen the confidence in the infantry soldiers move up a notch, knowing that stretcher-bearers were going, he'd decided to let them participate. The 0400 launch time had come and gone and still they sat on the ground. Fog in the objective area was the reason. Pathfinders had been inserted the night before and were reporting the weather conditions in the area. Finally, at 0530 the pilots began to crank the aircraft.

The flight to the objective was quick, being only 110 miles inside Iraq. The flight altitude was fifty feet, and at the speed they were flying, they passed over isolated pockets of Iraqi troops before they even knew the aircraft were coming. No one shot at the aircraft, nor did the aircraft shoot at anyone. The aircraft put the battalion right on the spot for the three landing zones the battalion was using. Almost immediately afterwards, five CH-47 aircraft came in hauling eight TOW equipped Humvees and two command-and-control vehicles, one being the S-3's vehicle and the other the TACP vehicle. Within the hour, Battleforce had captured ten Iraqi soldiers in two positions. Now it was time to wait for linkup with the Brigade's ground convoy and elements of the 24th Mechanized Division, which was scheduled to cross the border that night.

****

The dust from the CH-47 as it lifted off made it impossible to see. It had deposited Command Sergeant Major Bob Nichols and eight soldiers, along with eight motorcycles and one Humvee. They were alone, unable to see anyone or anything in the open desert.

"Alright, let's set up a defensive position. Motorcycles in the center," Nichols directed. The soldiers immediately went to work digging foxholes and camouflaging their position. If things went according to plan, the ground convoy would arrive in four or five hours. When it did, motorcycle riders would lead each element to where the respective ground unit was located.

"Sergeant Major," a soldier said, gaining the command sergeant major's attention. "Just how big is this Objective Cobra? I see helicopters landing off in the distance, but just how big from one side to the other?"

"Collins, do you think we would have motorcycles if we could just have you walk to where each unit is located?" Nichols asked.

"No, Sergeant Major," the young soldier answered with a sheepish look.

"Alright, everyone, gather around and get your maps out," Nichols ordered, spreading his map out on the hood of his Humvee. Once everyone had their maps out, Nichols began to point out the necessary features. "We're located right here. Mark that on your maps." When all had done so, he said, "At this point"—he pointed and read off the coordinates— "is the artillery location. Mark it." He continued indicating the location of the perimeter infantry units, the brigade element location, the aircraft refueling point and other lesser unit locations within Objective Cobra.

"Okay, now that you have everyone plotted, how far across is the objective?" Nichols asked, looking at Collins.

"Damn, that's twenty miles across," Collins exclaimed.

"Okay—now, as each unit comes here, if they need a guide, you'll take them to where they need to go. Some will have a leader with a GPS tracker so they can find their way without a guide, but some won't and it'll be up to us to get them to the right location. Any questions?" Nichols asked. As he was talking, the sounds of gunfire could be heard to the northeast.

"Sounds like someone has made contact, Sergeant Major," Specialist McFarland observed.

"That's in Battleforce's area. He's over there. Bastogne Bulldogs are on his left and First Strike is on the right flank. No Slack is to the left of Bastogne. Wonder what Battleforce got into?" Nichols mumbled.
****

"Battleforce Six, Gladiator Six," Captain Mulford called on the battalion command net.

"Go, Gladiator Six."

"Battleforce Six, we have a bunker and are engaging. Over."

"How many people do you have in the bunker? Give me types of weapons too." Lieutenant Colonel Cory could hear the distinct sound of AK-47 fire but also the rapid fire of a PKM machine gun. He also knew that Mulford was busy and wouldn't be talking on the radio until the action was over. Cory would just have to wait. Reaching for the brigade command net radio hand mic, he called Colonel Hall.

"Bastogne Six, Battleforce Six."

"Battleforce Six, go ahead." Due to the distances, each infantry battalion could hear Bastogne talking back to a call but could only receive one side of the conversation. The distances were just too great for a battalion to communicate with another battalion.

"Bastogne Six, we have contact in Alpha sector. Small force in a bunker. Will send an after-action when complete. Over."

"Battleforce Six, you are the first to report contact. Keep us posted, out."

"He didn't seem too concerned, sir," Major Wells, the operations officer, said.

"He probably isn't just for a bunker. Now if we see that Iraqi brigade that's two hours northeast of us coming down that road, then he'll get concerned, and so will I," Cory said without a smile. *I'll sure feel better when the rest of our TOWs and the convoy arrives*, he thought.
****

Major David, executive officer of Battleforce, had been drafted by Colonel Hall to develop the plan for the convoy to travel from the Iraq-Saudi border to Objective Cobra. Although the brigade had a full staff, it seemed they didn't have the expertise to make such a plan. David was an excellent officer and his intelligence intimidated Colonel Hall to some extent. David would lead the convoy the 110 miles across the desert, and therefore he placed Battleforce elements in the lead. Ten TOW vehicles performed as security on the flanks of the convoy's lead elements along with several cargo Humvees equipped with SAWs and M60 machine guns on top of the cabs. The convoy consisted of not only the brigade's vehicles but also the five-thousand-gallon HEMTT tankers for the aircraft refuel point and ammunition for every weapons system in Objective Cobra, to include small arms, artillery and rockets and Hellfire rockets for the AH-64 helicopters. A total of seven hundred vehicles would eventually follow this trail across the desert.

"Sir, how long do you figure before we reach the objective?" Leonard, David's driver, asked.

"Leonard, I figured we could make the trip in just over four hours. However, I didn't calculate us stopping so damn many times to change tires," David grumbled. "We've been driving what, six hours now? We should be coming up on the checkpoint soon." David checked his GPS tracker and looked down at his map for the hundredth time.

"Sir, we didn't expect to be driving through these areas of flint. The flint rock is cutting tires to ribbons. We've been driving an hour and have had to stop six times already to change tires. At this rate, we'll run out of tires," Leonard pointed out.

"I'm not worried about the tires on the Hummers as they're run-flat tires. The deuce-and-a-half's, however, are another story, and so are those fuel and water tankers. We run out of tires for them, this whole thing could become an exercise in futility," David stated.

"Those big rigs have some pretty thick tires, sir. They may get cut, but cut to the point of leaking air, I don't think you need to worry," Leonard said.

"Leonard, I get paid the big bucks to worry, about everything."

"Well, sir, you can stop worrying. I think that's Command Sergeant Major Nichols's vehicle on that crest. We're there, sir," Leonard said, looking over at David, who had just looked up from his map. A smile finally appeared.

Chapter 54
Ground Attack

26 May 1991
G-Day

"McCafferty, how soon could you launch your attack?" General Luck asked at 1300 hours, eight hours after the 101st had taken FOB Cobra.

"Sir, I'm not scheduled to roll until later tonight, but if you give me the word, my brigades can launch in thirty minutes. Why, what's happened?" McCafferty, the commander of the 24th Mechanized Division, asked.

"Nothing's happened. The 101st and everyone else to your left is unopposed except for some minor crap. The 1st of the 327th came upon an Iraqi infantry battalion from the 48th Iraqi Division and captured the entire battalion. The counterattack we were expecting against the 101st hasn't materialized and doesn't appear that it will, so I want you to launch your attack now. If they won't come to us, we'll go to them. Let me know when you're on your way," General Luck directed.

"Yes, sir," McCafferty said enthusiastically. Turning to his Operations officer, he instructed him, "Give the order to attack in thirty minutes."

"Sir, we're getting reports from the 3rd Armored Cav Regiment giving us positions of the 48th and 26th Divisions. The Cav says they're running through them like shit through a goose and meeting almost no resistance. They're telling the prisoners to just sit on the ground, and someone will be along to police them up. It's a repeat of the UAE operation," the operations officer said.

"Good, let's see if we can beat the 101st to the Euphrates River," McCafferty said as he headed for the command track.
****

1st of the 4th Cav Squadron, the Quarter Cav as they were known, had a long heritage of combat actions stretching from the Civil War to the present day and including every conflict along the way. Organized with two troops consisting of Abrams tanks and cavalry fighting vehicles, it also had two ground troops along with lift helicopters and attack aircraft. Their mission was to breach the Iraqi initial positions forward of the 1st Infantry Division, the Big Red One.

Lying on the ground, four soldiers had crawled within twenty meters of the berm the Iraqis had placed in front of their positions. The Saudi berm lay five klicks to their rear. In front of the berm was a tank ditch where the spoil for the berm came from, and in front of the ditch was the concertina wire that had to be removed. Each soldier had a Bangalore torpedo.

In a whisper, Staff Sergeant Billings said, "Clements, you move to the left. Carter, you're next to him. I'll be next to you and, Dobbins, you're on the right. Five meters between us and don't ignite until you get the word—then get the hell out of here. Got it?" Everyone acknowledged as they had gone over this several times in the past two days. "Okay, move out."

Each member crawled to his respective position and waited for the signal, which would be easy to identify. It was every combat vehicle in the squadron opening fire on the Iraqi positions. Once in position, each soldier shoved his torpedo under the wire, ensuring that it was squarely in position. When the shooting started, each ignited his torpedo and scurried back a safe distance before the horrific explosions occurred.

"Holy shit! Look at that hole we made," Clements said in amazement. He had practiced with the Bangalore torpedoes but had never actually fired one.

"Get out of the way. Here come the dozers," Billings said as the dust settled and an Abrams tank with a plow blade appeared, followed by several others, each with round steel culverts that were pushed into the tank ditch, all under the withering fire from the squadron. Once the last culvert was dropped, a bulldozer came forward, crossed over the culverts and began pushing down the berm while infantry soldiers scampered up the berm on both sides of the dozer and engaged Iraqi positions. When the dozer broke through, the tanks and CAV vehicles of the squadron followed through.

"Sarge, the combat dozers are still pushing dirt. We're through, so why don't they stop?" Clements asked, dropping an empty magazine out of his M16.

"Those are Iraqi bunkers that they're dozing. I just hope the Iraqis aren't still in those bunkers," Billing commented. Within hours, the squadron was leading the 1st Infantry Division ten miles into Iraq. There was no stopping them now.

****

1st British Armored Division, positioned behind the 1st US Infantry Division and the 1st Cavalry Division, initially crushed through the 27th Iraqi Division with no difficulty. The 1st Cav breached the initial defensive line and the 1st British poured through. As had been noted previously, the Iraqi command couldn't coordinate his artillery with his maneuver forces, and there was an absence of initiative to maneuver on the part of the Iraqi command. On their own, the 1st British came upon the 12th Armoured Division in a defensive posture and, using artillery and airpower along with maneuver, had pretty much decimated that division by the end of the day—a day that had gone much better than anyone could have imagined. Lieutenant Colonel Moore, commander of the Queen's Royal Irish Hussars, was a bit surprised at the day's actions.

"Sergeant Major," Colonel Moore said as the sergeant major approached with two canteen cups of tea.

"Sir, I thought you might like a cup," the sergeant major said, handing him one.

"Thank you, Sergeant Major. How are the lads doing?" Moore asked, blowing over the top of the cup.

"Sir, the lads are fine. Full of piss and vinegar as they say. I didn't have the heart to tell them that those T-55 tanks were no match for our Chieftains. No point in deflating the men at this point. They've been beating up on these poor Iraqi chaps so bad it's almost a shame," the sergeant major said.

"Well, we move out in a few hours and it appears that we're going to be running into the first of the 1st Republican Guard Corps divisions, the 3rd Tawakalna Mechanized Division. They have T-72s and BMPs, so this will be a bit more of a challenge," Moore indicated.

"Word has it, sir, that the flyboys have been pounding the daylights out of that division for the past two weeks," the sergeant major observed.

"That's what we're being told, but I won't believe it until I see it. Pilots have a habit of exaggerating their accomplishments. When we get home, I'm sure they'll tell the world that they did it all by themselves, winning the bloody war. I want the lads to think that this is still a tough fight that we cannot let up on. This isn't over yet. Let's not get overconfident until we're on our way home. There's still a fight ahead."

Chapter 55
2nd Marine Division

26 May 1991
Assembly Area Red 1
Saudi Arabia

The night sky was illuminated by the burning oil wells in the Umm Gudair North oil field. The air was heavy with the odor of hydrogen sulfide fumes coming off the wellheads. Everyone had been briefed earlier in the day by Lieutenant Colonel Howard Shores, a division staff officer, on the operation to mark and open eighteen cuts in "the Berm," as it was called. The Berm was as a three-to-six-meter-high berm along the Saudi-Kuwait border about one to five miles from the actual border on the Saudi side. It had been built several years prior by a Japanese company. Nine cuts were to be made in front of the Tiger Brigade, which had been attached to the 2nd Marine once it arrived in-country. The Tiger Brigade was the northwestern flank of the division with the remaining cuts in front of the 6th Marine. As soon as the first cut was made in front of the Tiger Brigade, the 2nd Light Armored Infantry Battalion moved through and commenced to operate forward of the Berm in this area as part of a deception plan.

"Okay, here's what we got for this evening," Captain Wolf, commander of B Company, 2nd LAI Battalion, said, facing his platoon leaders. "We're going to mark six lanes through the Iraqi minefields. I'll go with 1st Platoon and provide overwatch while 2nd and 3rd Platoons mark the lanes. You all have used the mine detectors, so this is nothing new. Any questions?" he concluded.

"Sir, how many lanes do we need to mark?" the 2nd Platoon leader asked.

"I want each of you to mark three lanes. Once you've completed those, I'll come forward and mark the last two lanes myself. Any others?" Wolf said, looking at each platoon leader. "Okay, we move out at 1800 hours."

****

Lance Corporal Jamison didn't mind walking with the mine detector and listening for the telltale sound indicating something metallic was in the ground. He did mind that the Iraqi infantry was only eight hundred meters away while he was doing it. Fortunately, they were silhouetted in front of the burning oil wells. He was not.

"Hold," Jamison said in almost a whisper. Walking beside him was Private Louis from San Antonio, Texas, new to the Marines, Saudi Arabia, and combat. He was a replacement that had only arrived in-country two weeks before. His job on this night was to push a flag into the ground next to any mines they found. Their flags were marking the right side of the lane. They had walked about three hundred meters when Jamison took a knee.

"I think we're through the minefield. I'm not getting any other readings," he said to Louis.

"What are you stopping for?" a whisper came from behind them. They recognized the voice.

"Sir, I'm not getting any more readings. I think we're through the field," Corporal Jamison stated to the platoon leader.

"Okay, then, let's sweep back to the Berm and get the hell out of here," the platoon leader ordered, adding, "And be careful."
****

"Sir, one of the problems we're going to have is the fact that our artillery batteries are too far back to range the Iraqi artillery batteries. When we launch the attack, they're going to be able to pound us, but we won't be able to hit their artillery with counterbattery fires," Colonel Palm, commander of the 10th Marines, explained. His brigade was an artillery brigade.

"Sir, the Iraqis have about five hundred guns that are within range of the breach points. Some of these are those South African guns that outrange our M198 155mm howitzers even if we use RAP rounds."

"So what do you propose?" asked Brigadier General Sutton, the assistant division commander.

"Sir, I think we should move the artillery forward of the Berm and forward of the assault elements before the assault forces cross the Berm. This will place the guns within range of the Iraqi guns and allow us to better support the attack. I know this violates all the schoolhouse doctrine, but tactically, I think it makes sense in this situation. The 2nd LAI Battalion is out there and can provide some security for us," Palm pointed out.

General Sutton said nothing for a minute, just staring at the map.

Finally, he said, "Do it. Coordinate with the Tiger Brigade and do it."

****

The desert night sky had been clear except for the smoke from the burning oil well heads, which masked the setting sun to some extent. Iraqi positions along the first defense belt were backlit by the fires but were about seven klicks from the Berm. As the night progressed, the Milky Way that everyone was used to watching disappeared behind the black smoke and clouds that moved into the area. By the early hours of the morning, a light rain began.

"I don't want to hear any sniveling about the weather. If it ain't raining, then we ain't training," Gunny Sergeant Allen said, looking over his platoon of Devil Dog Marines of Alpha Company, 1st Battalion, 6th Marine Regiment. The most miserable of the young Marines were the replacements that had just arrived and who were subjected to the usual treatment of being a "newbie or Cherries."

Most Marines were quiet, lost in their personal thoughts about what was ahead of them. Old Marines thought about what *needed* to be done, newbies thought about what was *going* to be done. Gunny Allen had been around the block enough to know of the concern in some and the lack of camaraderie that the newbies were feeling. He thought for a moment and stood. As he did so, most of the eyes of the platoon followed him—after all, he was their father figure of sorts.

"Gentlemen," he said, gaining the total attention of the platoon now in the darkness and drizzle.

"This day is call'd the feast of Crispian:
He that outlives this day, and comes safe home,
Will stand a' tiptoe when this day is named,
And rouse him at the name of Crispian.
He that shall see this day, and live old age,
Will yearly on the vigil feast his neighbors,
And say, 'To-morrow is Saint Crispian.'

305

Then will he strip his sleeve and show his scars,
And say, 'These wounds I had on Crispin's day.'
Old men forget; yet all shall be forgot,
But he'll remember with advantages
What feats he did that day. Then shall our names,
Familiar in his mouth as household words,
Harry the king, Bedford and Exeter,
Warwick and Talbot, Salisbury and Gloucester,
Be in their flowing cups freshly rememb'red.
This story shall the good man teach his son;
And Crispin Crispian shall ne'er go by,
From this day to the ending of the world,
But we in it shall be remembered—
We few, we happy few, we band of brothers;
For he to-day that sheds his blood with me
Shall be my brother; be he ne'er so vile,
This day shall gentle his condition;
And gentlemen in England, now a-bed,
Shall think themselves accurs'd they were not here;
And hold their manhoods cheap whiles any speaks
That fought with us upon Saint Crispin's day."[6]

There was silence in the platoon, but he could see the facial expressions changed. Old Marines now turned to the newbies and extended handshakes and exchanged names. A new bond was created in the platoon as the new guys were suddenly welcomed with open arms by the veterans.

"Alright, let's saddle up. We have a job to do," Gunny Allen said, picking up his rucksack. The platoon followed suit as they headed for the line of departure and crossed at 0530 hours. For the last hour, the sound of artillery booming was heard, and the sky was alive with multiple rockets from the M270 Multiple Launch Rocket System commonly referred to as MLRS, all pounding on the Iraqi artillery positions. Each

---

[6] William Shakespeare, *Henry V*, *The Riverside Shakespeare*, ed. G. Blakemore Evans et al. (Boston: Houghton Mifflin, 1997), 4.3.40-67.

launcher fired the M-26 rocket, which contained 644 antipersonnel/antimateriel grenades that were dispersed over the target and detonated upon impact. Each launcher could fire twelve M-26 rockets, and each battery could fire 108 rockets in a matter of minutes.

As the platoon reached the colored tape marking the lane for them to follow, Corporal Hallie asked in a low whisper, "Gunny, do you hear music or am I imagining things?"

"Hallie, if we were back stateside, I would ask if you were smoking dope again, but as we're here at this time and place, I know you're not doing that. What you're hearing, young man, if you listen closely, is our song, the US Marine Corps Hymn. It's being played on loudspeakers by the psychological units. Scare the crap out of the Iraqis. They know we're coming," Gunny said.

As they approached the North and South Umm Gudair oil fields, Gunny halted the platoon. "Okay, remember—stay out of any low spots. There is H_2S gas in the low spots due to the burning oil rigs and your MOPP suits won't protect you from that, so stay out of them and any bunkers. Got it?"

A resounding "Yes, Gunny" could be heard.

"Alright, here we go." Gunny proceeded to lead the platoon forward. As he did, they came under direct and indirect fire from an Iraqi position that was between the minefields. The platoon engaged—at least until they heard the sound of diesel engines and rolling tracks. Out of the morning rain, an armored vehicle appeared. It was the lead element for Task Force Breach Alpha.

Task Force Breach Alpha was a special combat engineer unit consisting of eighteen amphibious assault vehicles (AAVs) with the M154 mine-clearing line charges, M60A1 dozer tanks, M60A1 track-width mine plows, M60A1 tanks with mine rakes, and twenty AAVs with engineer squads and an assortment of other vehicles to clear the way through the minefields. First up were the vehicles with the M154 mine-clearing line charges.

"Gunny, what the hell is that?" one of the newbies asked.

"Watch and learn," was Gunny's response. As the first vehicle moved up, they noticed off the rear top of the AAV was some sort of launcher. The twin machine guns were hosing the Iraqi position, forcing the Iraqi soldiers to keep down. Suddenly a rocket launched off the back

307

of the AAV, trailing what appeared to be a rope behind it. It flew out about one hundred meters.

"Well, that's pretty damn worthless," the young newbie said. "The damn thing never exploded. What good is it?" he asked as he started to rise up. Just then, a huge explosion went off in front of the AAV and the concussion wave shoved the youngster to the ground.

"What the fuck!" the young Marine yelled.

"That, my friend, is called a mine-clearing line charge or MICLIC to you. It just cleared a one-hundred-by-eight-meter path through that minefield and now he's going to fire two more charges to make it a bit wider, I suspect. He'll be followed by those M60 tanks with rollers and plows to clear out any mines that didn't go off. Watch and learn," Gunny instructed. The platoon held their position as Task Force Breach Alpha performed its assignment. At 0740, the platoon and 1st Battalion, 6th Marines, were through the minefield.

Chapter 56
Omens

26 May 1991
Pentagon
Washington, D.C.

Satellite imagery had been flowing into the basement office all night. Paige Harrison had to be told to go home and get some sleep and come back in the morning to relieve Bob Daley, who would work the all-night shift. She would get the day shift, and Bob would bring her and Cliff up to speed at the shift change brief.

"Last night was something else. As you scroll through the photos, you can see just how fast this thing is moving. Over here on the west, the two divisions have set up a screen line from Saudi to the Euphrates River. The 101st put in one FOB and has pushed to the Euphrates with another FOB blocking the highway. Their attack helicopters are destroying anything that moves on that road. The 24th linked up with the 101st and has turned east now," Bob pointed out as photos streamed across the computer screen.

"How much resistance are they meeting?" Paige asked.

"Out here in the west, it doesn't appear to be much. Got to the Euphrates with very little resistance to be truthful. Now in the VII Corps sector, they did meet some resistance, as you can see in this photo. This is the 1st Infantry Division, and you can see he blew through two Iraqi divisions with some fighting along this berm and tank ditch that the Iraqis have been building since the start of hostilities last year. Over on the right flank of the 1st Infantry is the 1st Cav, and they shot through a gap in the Iraqi defense with the 1st British right behind them. It appears that the 1st Cav widened the gap and let the 1st British punch through and nail this tank division that's sitting here. Took the Brits all day, but it appears that they've pretty well destroyed that division. The Brits are turning to the east now," Daley summarized.

"Okay, what about the Arab forces on our side?" Cliff asked.

"Joint Forces Command North has the two Egyptian divisions and the Saudi task force. They, I understand, are under the command of the Egyptian Corps, which is under Joint Forces Command North. They've hardly moved. In fact, they're still sitting on the border and have barely moved across. Something is amiss here, I think," Daley indicted, pointing at the computer screen.

Paige quickly added, "You know, if the 1st British and the Egyptians drive eastward, they're liable to cut off all these units that are south of Kuwait City. Their eastward movement is going to place them on top of Mitla Ridge and block everything attempting to get back to Iraq."

"You're probably right, and I think the Iraqis see that too. Look here," Bob said, pointing at another picture. "These units in front of the Marines and the Arab forces along the coast are already starting to fall back. This road going up to Mitla Ridge is already packed with vehicles moving north, all kinds of vehicles. I don't think they're reorienting to oppose the threat from the west—I believe they're attempting to withdraw completely," Bob said, zooming the picture in for a close-up. The clarity surprised everyone.

"Well, let's write up our analysis and get it upstairs to the Deputy SecDef. He may want to get it to Schwarzkopf and the President. What are we seeing with the Iraqi Air Force?" Cliff asked.

"Ha, we're seeing several of their frontline jets sitting on runways in Iran," Bob said with a chuckle.

"What! You're shit 'in me, aren't you?" Cliff blurted out.

"I shit you not," Bob announced as he scrolled through more photos. Finally, he found what he was looking for. "See, those aircraft at the Tehran Airport have Iraqi markings, and they're some of the fighters in their inventory. Here's another of one of the transport planes unloading what looks like families. I think the pilots have had enough of the US Air Force and are bugging out. I tell you, Cliff, I think the whole Iraqi military force is falling apart and quickly," Bob observed.

"Paige, I want you to look this stuff over and confirm what Bob has said. No offense, Bob."

"None taken. I understand we want to be doubly sure before we start raising flags," Bob acknowledged. "Paige, if you need anything, please just call me and I'll come back in."

"I hope I don't have to do that. I suggest that we do the same on shift change tonight and have you review my write-up. Okay?" Paige offered.

"Sure thing," Bob said as he stood to head home for some sleep. Turning back, he added, "You know, we could be looking at the beginning of the end. Peace in the Middle East. Boy, that would be nice for once."

Chapter 57
Joint Force Command North

27 May 1991
Day 2
VII Corps HQ, Saudi Arabia

"Sir, we have a problem," Colonel Cherry said. Cherry was the assistant operations officer, G-3, for VII Corps, and like General Franks, he had lost a lower leg in Vietnam, but it didn't slow him or General Franks down one bit.

"So, what's the problem?" Franks asked.

"The forces under Joint Forces Command North haven't crossed the border. Our right flank is exposed," Cherry explained.

"What! You are joking, right? That's a bad joke," Franks said.

"Sir, I wish I was. I spoke with both the 1st Cav and 1st British, and they've confirmed it. Seems that the Egyptian division commanders, are reluctant to move Arab forces against Arab forces," Cherry replied. "I spoke with the G-3 of Joint Forces Command North, and he said General Smith is hopping mad."

"Call ARCENT and see if they've talked to Marine Central Command and are getting the same info. Get back to me when you've spoken to them," Franks directed. Cherry left and came back an hour later.

"Sir, I spoke to the Ops people at Marine Central. They're getting the same report from the 2nd Marine Division. The Arabs from Joint Forces Command North have not moved into Kuwait," Cherry said, hoping that Franks wouldn't shoot the messenger.

"We have to get this resolved and fast. Our flank is wide open for a counterattack in this case. Have 1st Cav secure our flank until we get this resolved. Let me get General Yeosock and General Smith on the phone and talk to them about getting those forces to move."
****

"Joe, what's the deal with the Arab forces? They're not moving. My right flank is exposed to a counterattack," Franks said, as calm as ever. He seldom got excited. It just wasn't in his personality. Some generals were screamers, but not him.

"Frank, I'm aware of the situation. Boomer and Smith have been talking to me and I've talked to the Egyptian commanders personally. Seems those divisions had no problem fighting up to the Kuwait border because the Iraqis were surrendering rather than fight, but now he feels that they will fight and they are reluctant to move their forces against their Arab brothers," Yeosock explained, frustration evident in his voice at the situation.

"Well, what are we going to do about it? He has, what, four divisions sitting in front of him plus a mech division? And right now there is no pressure on any of them," Franks pointed out.

"For right now you're going to have to protect your flank as best you can," Yeosock said. "Ivan has the 50th Armored moving but he can't get the Egyptians off their asses to fight right now."

There was a sigh before Franks responded. "I get it. I'm doing what I can to protect that flank, but these so-called Arab allies are leaving my ass to flap in the wind. The 1st Cav opened the first defense belt and the Brits passed through and are beating up the Iraqi 12th Armoured Division. It appears they have only T-55 tanks. They're no match for the Chieftains. He'll turn east then, with the 1st Cav covering the flank and together they'll hit the Tawakalna Division, but we need to get the Egyptians off their asses."

"I agree. Let me talk to Norm and see what he can do. I'll get back to you," Yeosock said and hung up, turning to an aide. "Get General Schwarzkopf on the line."
****

"I know, I know. My guys have been watching the satellite feed and have told me. Bilal doesn't want to move or can't get his people to move because he feels that it's not right for Arabs to be fighting Arabs in Kuwait. I asked him what the hell the difference was in the UAE and Saudi, but not Kuwait. His answer: 'Kuwait is a province of Iraq,'" Schwarzkopf explained.

"Isn't there something we can do to get him moving? This could be a major problem for both Marine Central and VII Corps," Yeosock pointed out.

"Don't you think I know that?" Norm said and then continued, "Sorry. But this just really pisses me off. They should have raised this flag before we ever got this far. I have a call into Baker at State to talk to Mubarak and quick. I'll get back to you after I hear from him."

"Okay, but I hope this doesn't take long. Thanks," Yeosock said and placed the phone back in the cradle.

****

"Mr. Secretary, is Mubarak going to get them moving?" Schwarzkopf asked when Baker came on the phone.

Mr. Baker sighed as he tried to explain to the general in charge of all allied forces. "I spoke with him, General, and he's reluctant to order General Bilal, who is their overall commander, to move aggressively. Seems that even though he was in support of our actions and of ejecting the Iraqis out of the UAE and Saudi, he's reluctant to go into Iraq proper. Seems you've been too successful in his eyes, and he fears you'll overrun Kuwait so fast that the door will be open to go into Iraq and topple Saddam."

"Sir, at this point my mission is to eject Iraqi forces out of Kuwait and sufficiently destroy the Iraqi Army so it doesn't pose a threat in the future. I have US forces moving in Iraq, and the Egyptians won't cross into Iraq. Tell him that and maybe he can get them back on the move," Norm said.

"You can assure me that the Egyptian forces won't venture into Iraq once Kuwait is liberated?" Baker questioned.

"Yes, sir. I promise the Egyptians will not put one tank track in Iraq. They'll be fortunate if their equipment doesn't fall apart just trying to get to Kuwait City."

"Alright, General, I'll go back to him and give him assurances to that fact. Please don't make me go back with my hat in my hand, rendering an apology," Baker said—he was half-joking, but Schwarzkopf got the message.

Chapter 58
Continue the Attack

28 May 1991
Day 3
Iraq/Kuwait

"Alright, listen up," Lieutenant Colonel Altamire said to his company commanders, who had gathered around his tank. Iron Mike, as he was called behind his back, had spread out his map. "Here's what we got today." As he spoke, he pointed to the map. "We're here, according to the GPS. We're going to move on the left flank of the brigade and take this airfield at Tallil. On the north side of the airfield is where the garrison is located along with the flight crews and hangars. To the north of the airfield, in this area, is a bioweapons lab. The lead scientist is a woman. Tell the troops to detain all women but not to remove any veils. We have female MPs that will do that. We suspect that in this grove of trees there are some Iraqi aircraft hidden under camouflage netting. Our job is to secure these hangars on the northwest side and this garrison area on the north side of this major street. Piscal and 1-18 Armor will take that area, so we want to be careful with firing into that area. We'll attack from the south to the north abreast, which should minimize the chances of us potentially shooting at each other. Poggi, your company will be on the right flank and maintain contact with Piscal's left company. We're moving about sixty miles northeast to get to Tallil. Any questions?"

"No, sir. Do we know which company that will be?" Poggi asked.

"The three will get that info for you before we move out," Altamire replied. "Sever, I want you and Alpha Company to secure these hangars on the left. Billings, you and Bravo Company take these buildings between Poggi and Sever. Gill, you and Charlie Company are reserve and follow Billings. If there are no questions, let's mount up and get ready to move out."

"One question, sir," Poggi asked. "What are the other brigades doing? Are they going to be on the airfield as well?"

"No, while we're taking out this airfield at Tallil, they're going to bypass and head for this airfield at Jalibah. Division doesn't expect much here at Tallil, but the 49th Iraqi Division has positioned itself at Jalibah and been reconstituted with personnel and equipment. This will position the 24th as the northernmost of the forces and put the Euphrates River on our left flank. Any other questions?"

"Any idea what VII Corps is doing? I'd hate to run into those guys in the dark and start shooting each other," Poggi said.

"They're well east of us, and the 2nd ACR is in the lead, screening their front. We shouldn't have to worry about them. Now let's get rolling."

****

"Jesus, get me through this night," Specialist Ramos, the driver in Lieutenant Bagel's tank, prayed as another round left the main gun. Each time he heard a ping off the side of the tank, he flinched. He had been the driver since the start of hostilities, but nothing was as intense as this. The Iraqi 47th and 49th Divisions were dug in on favorable terrain and putting up a fight. Fortunately, the T-55 tanks they were employing didn't have the range or accuracy or thermal sights of the M1 Abrams tanks.

"Lieutenant, we've gone through half our sabot rounds," Specialist Anderson said over the intercom system. The chattering from the .50-cal machine gun almost drowned his voice out.

"We're just going to have to make every round count… tank, two o'clock," Bagel called out.

"Identified," responded Staff Sergeant Adams, slaving the main gun onto the target.

"Up," replied Anderson.

"Fire," commanded Bagel, and the explosion for the fired round rocked the tank rearward as the sabot round exited the main gun. In less than a second, the turret of an Iraqi tank could be seen tumbling in the air.

"Lieutenant, I'm seeing white flags. I think maybe these guys have had enough. It's been, what, four hours since this dance started?" Staff Sergeant Adams asked.

"Yeah, and I've had enough. Thank God we didn't lose a single vehicle in the platoon, or anyone killed. I cannot understand how lopsided this war has been. Are we that good or are they that bad that we're rolling over them?"

"Sir, I think it's a combination of both," Adams replied in a weary voice. He was tired as they all were, and thirsty.
****

"Fire!" The battery of five 155mm self-propelled howitzers roared, sending five HE rounds across the battlefield to an awaiting Iraqi artillery battery of the 26th Infantry Division. The 1st Infantry Division had been engaging the 26th all morning and was closing in on their final units. The AN/TPQ-37 Firefinder Weapon Locating System was picking up incoming rounds from Iraqi artillery, plotting the location of origin and feeding that information to the battery fire direction centers, where the information would be plotted and the firing data sent to the batteries' guns.

"Sir, we're getting indications that the Iraqi batteries are withdrawing and moving out of range for our guns," Captain Dade said.

"Alright, I'll get DIVARTY on the horn and see about displacing to a new firing location. We need to be moving closer to the maneuver forces to keep the Iraqis off their back. While we displace, DIVARTY can have the MLRS boys hit these targets. Hell, they have the range. We should be concentrating on supporting the maneuver forces and not this deep battle shit. We're direct support to 1st Brigade. Any other missions come down that aren't 1st Brigade, send them back. Priority of fire is 1st Brigade, understood? Not deep battle and general support for Division. Anyone gives you shit about that, you tell them to call me," Lieutenant Colonel Dan Morgan said, chewing on his cigar, which he still hadn't lit yet.
****

"According to GPS, we're due to turn east at this point," Captain Triplett said, sweat dripping onto his map from under his Kevlar helmet. Triplett had been with the 2nd Armored Cavalry Regiment for a year, commanding E Troop, 2nd Squadron, consisting of one hundred soldiers and twelve M3 Cav fighting vehicles. Nine M1 Abrams tanks from the troop followed behind the M3 Cav fighting vehicles. He was dog-ass tired, having been on the move all night identifying and engaging Iraqi positions. His path was marked with burning vehicles, Iraqi bodies, and destroyed bunkers.

"Where do we head from here, Captain?" First Sergeant Burns asked, pulling his map out to compare notes.

"From here, we're heading southeast towards this highway coming over this ridge, Mitla Ridge. Our limit of advance for tonight is this 73 north-south grid line named Phase Line 73 Easting. We're to clear away the Iraqi security forces, conduct a passage of lines with the 1st ID and not become decisively engaged. I do like that term, 'not decisively engaged,'" Triplett pointed out with a smile. "How are the troops holding up?"

"They're doing good, sir. A few guys took some light wounds, but nothing to send them back to the rear. None want to go back to the rear either. We patched them up and they're good to go. I got ammo redistributed, and chow, so they're happy. Fuel status is good for another couple hundred miles. We did pick up a few prisoners," First Sergeant Burns indicated.

"How many?" Triplett asked.

"About two hundred."

"Shit, what the—" Triplett asked.

"No worry, Cap'n. We already turned them over to the EPW collection point and they're out of our hair. Hell, there must be a couple thousand located at that place. Even got a corps commander from the VII Iraqi Corps. He was strutting like a frickin' peacock until a lieutenant informed him that he was a prisoner just like the rest of them ragheads," Burns said.

"Don't bet on it. His ass will be shipped off to ARCENT before the sun reaches its apex today," Triplett said and paused for a minute. "Okay, let's mount up and get moving. We have a ways to go before we sleep."
****

The 18th Iraqi Armoured Brigade had been expecting an attack by the Americans from the south and east. Their positions reflected this line of thought and were well dug in preparation for destroying the American attack. Sector of fires had been marked. Artillery target reference points had been passed to the supporting artillery along with minefields laid to channel the Americans into kill zones. As Colonel al-Jaziri studied his map in his command bunker, he began to hear the sound of incoming artillery. *That sounds like it's to the west of our positions.* "Captain

318

Darwish, see who is shooting to the west of us," al-Jaziri told a young captain, a staff officer who was on a radio.

"Sir," the captain responded with some level of excitement in his voice. "Division is on the radio. The Americans are attacking from the west and not the south or east. Division wants us to reorient our defense. The 50th Brigade is establishing a screen line along the 60th north-south grid line to give us time to reposition."

"What!" al-Jaziri almost screamed. "Get the battalions on the radio. We need to reposition everyone and right now," he ordered. Turning to another staff officer, he said, "Get the artillery commander and tell him to get over here immediately so we can readjust our target reference points." To Captain Darwish, he said, "Have the 1st Battalion pull out of his current position and move to the west five kilometers and orient his defense around these buildings on the 69 Easting north-south line. Have 2nd Battalion move to this location at 73 Easting and take up positions facing west. Have 3rd Battalion follow 2nd Battalion."
****

"Are you seeing this in the thermal sight?" Lieutenant Bowling asked his gunner in their M1 Abrams tank. Sand was blowing, obscuring their normal vision. Lieutenant Bowling was the platoon leader for a tank platoon in E Troop.

"Eagle One-One, Eagle Six," Captain Triplett called.

"Eagle Six, Eagle One-One," Lieutenant Bowling responded.

"Eagle One-One, I want you to move up on line. We're picking up numerous targets. I suspect we're going to be decisively engaged. How copy?"

"Eagle Six, roger, On the move now," Lieutenant Bowling stated and gave the order to move out to his driver as well as the rest of his platoon. It was 1530 hours, he noted on his watch and jotted down in a small diary he was keeping.

"Sir, I ain't ever seen this many targets in my life and all coming at us," Staff Sergeant Crandell indicated.

"What's the range estimate?" Bowling asked.

"Sir, they're at three thousand meters. Some are masked in buildings and alongside the buildings," Crandell indicated.

Bowling switched his intercom to the troop net frequency. "Eagle Six, Eagle One-One, tanks and vehicles at twenty-five hundred meters."

"Eagle One-One, roger. All Eagle elements, engage enemy positions in the cluster of buildings. Eagle Two-One, take the right flank. Eagle Three-One, maneuver left flank."

Both platoon leaders acknowledged and commenced maneuvering against the Iraqi position in the small cluster of buildings. As his vehicle lurched forward, Crandell depressed his trigger and the first round streaked across the night sky in less than a second, resulting in an Iraqi tank exploding. Now the battle of 73 Easting was on.
****

"Colonel, 2nd Battalion reports that the Americans are engaging, but they are beyond the effective range of his guns. The 2nd Battalion reports he can barely see the Americans through the dust," Captain Darwish exclaimed.

"Tell them to remain hidden until the Americans are within two thousand meters. Then engage," Colonel al-Jaziri ordered.

"Sir, the Americans are seeing them at twenty-five hundred meters and hitting them. They report they have lost twenty tanks and fifteen BMPs. He is asking to withdraw before his battalion is destroyed," Darwish almost pleaded.

"Where is his artillery support?" the colonel shouted, turning to Captain Farouq, the artillery fire support officer.

"Sir, the batteries are under attack from rocket artillery and are attempting to pull back. They have not been able to carry out any fire missions in support of the brigade," Farouq reported, almost ashamed of the artillery.
****

"All Eagle elements, let's move out," Captain Triplett ordered, leaving the cluster of smoldering buildings behind along with a small group of prisoners that were stripped of their weapons and told to just sit and wait. As the troop moved eastward, it came on a low rise. The troop was traveling M3s abreast with the M1 platoons following.

As they crested the low rise, the master gunner screamed, "Shit, sir! Tank front, five hundred meters. Engaging." He engaged with a TOW missile and his Bushmaster chain gun.

Triplett didn't have time to give an order when every M3 opened fire on the surprised Iraq tank company. Immediately, Iraqi tanks began to explode as TOW missiles slammed into exposed turrets. Eight Iraqi tanks were burning when the M1 Abrams tanks crested the hill and destroyed the remaining tanks. Not wanting to be a target for Iraqi artillery, Triplett gave the order to move out and continued his advance past the 73 Easting phase line.

"Eagle One-One, Eagle Six."

"Eagle Six, One-One."

"One-One, move north and regain contact with Golf Troop."

"Roger, moving north. One-One out." Triplett continued to move the remainder of the troop east, probing for the main defense of the Iraqi forces. Then all hell broke loose.

"Eagle Six, One-One. Thirteen, I say again, thirteen Tango Seven-Two. Engaging now." One-One passed the coordinates. *Crap*, Triplett thought, knowing full well that two cav vehicles were no match for thirteen T-72 tanks. The TOW was a good weapon but took time to load. The scouts were outgunned.

"Eagle Six, Iron Six," another troop commander was calling.

"Go, Iron Six," Triplett transmitted.

"Eagle Six, I have Eagle One-One in sight and his target. We're moving to engage," Iron Six said, only to be interrupted by another troop's commander.

"Iron Six, I'm coming up on your east side and will engage as well," Killer Six said without his call sign, but everyone recognized the voice.

"Killer Six, Ghost Six. I'll cover your flank overlooking this north-south wadi. How copy?"

"Ghost Six, I have good copy. When we take care of this, I'll join you. Killer Six out."

****

"Colonel al-Jaziri, the Americans have reached the 73 north-south phase line with their reconnaissance elements," Captain Darwish said as he plotted the position on the map.

"Contact 3rd Battalion and have him attack. His T-72s will smash this attack. Contact the brigade from the 12th Armoured Division on our flank and ask him to commit one of his battalions as well. We will coordinate the attack. He only has T-55, but it will help relieve pressure on our tanks."

****

"Holy crap," Sergeant First Class Harrison said as he saw the first of what appeared to be twenty T-72 tanks drop down into the wadi his tank was overlooking.

"Eagle Three-One elements, engage," Harrison heard over the radio. He didn't need to be told and immediately gave the command to fire. The gunner identified a target, the loader indicated the round was ready and the gun roared. This would keep up for the next six hours, and the Battle of Easting would become one of the largest tank battles since World War II.

Chapter 59
The End Is Near

29 May 1991
Day 4
Mitla Ridge

"Three, two, one…" And the director shot a finger at Arthur Kent.

"I am standing with elements of the 1st Infantry Division overlooking the main highway from Kuwait City to Basra, Iraq. The highway is a two-lane paved road and the only paved road in this region. Right now, it is a highway of death. Iraqi vehicles of every kind, tanks and armored personnel carriers, are attempting to move up this road to escape the American advance. They are under constant artillery bombardment and attacks from American jets and attack helicopters. It appears that the entire Iraqi Army is attempting to flee before the American forces that have launched this attack into Kuwait only ninety-six hours ago. The speed of the American advance has destroyed many Iraqi divisions and overwhelmed the Iraqi military leadership. Some civilian cars and buses may be seen, but they are occupied by Iraqi soldiers. The attack helicopters are avoiding striking them, but the artillery and jets cannot make that distinction. This is Arthur Kent reporting from Kuwait." As Arthur Kent reported, the camera scanned the devastation along the road from its vantage point, showing burned-out vehicles scattered all over the road and to the side. The bodies of those trapped in the vehicles were clearly visible as well. It was obvious that no one was escaping this trap that the Americans had closed.
******

In the Oval Office, the President watched the pictures being broadcast across the nightly news.

"Mr. President, Mr. Baker, Mr. Cheney, Mr. Sununu and General Powell are here to see you," the intercom announced.

"Send them in," the President said. *Now what shitstorm is this going to bring?* he thought when the four walked in.

"Mr. President, have you seen—" Cheney started, referring to the events playing out on the television.

"Yes, I have and so has the whole world. So what have you got?" the President asked.

"Sir, we're getting a lot of calls from world leaders about this Highway of Death. Many are expressing the feeling that we have decisively defeated the Iraqi Army and driven them out of Kuwait and the fighting should stop. Saddam has made overtures to the UN that he will leave Kuwait and not return," Baker said.

"Not good enough. I want his head on a platter. He's an international environmental terrorist, for God's sake. He's butchered his own people with chemical weapons. He invaded three countries and started a war with Iran and did it all in ten years. The man has to go," the President insisted.

"Mr. President, the Turks have come up very loud on this matter. If we invade and remove Saddam, they will close our bases and they intend to come to his aid or at least partially occupy northern Iraq. They feel strongly that his removal will have a destabilizing impact on the region and especially for them with the Kurds. The Iranians have let it be known they feel the same as the Turks, as they have a Kurdish problem as well," Baker went on to say. The President glanced at Cheney and Baker, both with daggers.

"Well, Colin, what's your opinion on this?" the President asked.

"Mr. President," Powell began, "at a minimum, a cease-fire should be imposed to allow the Iraqis to flee out of Kuwait and for CENTCOM to sort itself out. We have almost ten divisions all packed into an area the size of Rhode Island and mixed together. To continue an attack, it will take some time to unscramble the forces and reposition them. Add in resupplying the units and getting the oil fires under control, and it's all going to take time. Time that could be used to bring Saddam to the peace table and an honorable surrender for the Iraqi Army."

"John, what do you think?"

Sununu leaned forward in his chair as he responded, "Mr. President, I believe that what General Powell just offered is the best course of action. Declare a cease-fire and put the ball in Saddam's court. The world will see that we're offering an olive branch and he can take it or have us come knocking on his door."

The President sat staring at the four advisors standing before his desk. *I have to make the final decision on this. Collectively, they've never*

324

given me bad advice. I know in my heart if I let Saddam off the hook now, we're just going to have to go back there in five or ten years and do this all over again. I can see that, but the world cannot, and that's who we have to appease at this point. Damnit, I don't like this one bit...

"Alright. Issue a cease-fire order for 0800 tomorrow morning Kuwait time and make it public, so the whole damn world knows we've issued it. But also let it be known that if one damn artillery shell, one damn tank round, one anti-aircraft missile is fired, we're marching right into Baghdad. Jim, get a list of demands for Schwarzkopf to present to the Iraqi delegation. Schwarzkopf will handle all the negotiations. I'm not going to lower the prestige of the United States by formally meeting with Saddam. This is a surrender, not a peace treaty."
****

Sergeant Nidy, Specialist Holmes, and Specialist Rhodes all sat in their respective foxholes as the sun rose. They had air-assaulted into another flat spot in the desert to establish another refuel/rearm point for the attack helicopters of the 101st. Their company, Company A, 3rd Battalion, 327th Infantry, had seen some action when taking Objective Cobra, but things had been quiet on this insertion. In fact, they questioned why they had even come here as it appeared from the abandoned US vehicles that a heavy force had already gone through this area the night before.

"Okay, what now?" Nidy said, sipping his morning coffee.

"It looks like we sit on our ass until we move again. Maybe Sergeant Seabrook knows something," Holmes said as he noticed the platoon sergeant approaching. Sergeant First Class Seabrook had the respect of these guys. A large, not fat, black man, he was soft-spoken and only seemed to speak when necessary.

"Hey, Sergeant Seabrook, what we doin' now and how long are we going to be here?" Rhodes asked.

"Why? You got someplace to be and something else to do, Rhodes?" Seabrook asked. He didn't look happy.

"Just curious is all," Rhodes responded, picking up on the negative vibes that Seabrook was sending out.

"Hey, what's the matter, Sergeant?" Nidy asked.

"I'll tell you what the matter is. Effective at 0800 hours today, a cease-fire goes into effect. We can't shoot at them, and they can't shoot at us. Now the politicians and generals get involved and we wait," Seabrook said with some disgust.

"You're shitting us, right?" Specialist Mauzy said, walking up to the group.

"I shit you not. On top of that, the colonel says we're pulling out of here later today and flying back to Cobra, and there we'll wait for however long it takes for the brass to get a formal cease-fire signed and the Iraqis out of Kuwait. The colonel is pissed," Seabrook added.

"Damn, he should be," Nidy said. "The old man knows that we're going to be coming right back here in five, ten years and have to do this all over again. Shit, we have the Army in place to do the job and finish it right now," Nidy concluded in disgust. For a few moments, no one said anything.

Standing, Nidy threw the last of his coffee into the desert and began to walk away. Over his shoulder, he said, "Like in Korea, Vietnam, and now here, the damn politicians have sold us out again. We will never win another war because of them."

References

The following publications were researched in the writing of this series. Almost all are available online.

Association of the United States Army, *The U.S. Army in Operation Desert Storm: An Overview.* Arlington, VA: Association of the United States Army, 1991. https://www.ausa.org/sites/default/files/SR-1991-The-US-Army-in-Operation-Desert-Storm.pdf

Brown, Ronald J., LTC, USMCR. *US Marines in the Persian Gulf, 1990–1991, With Marine Forces Afloat in Desert Shield and Desert Storm.* Washington, D.C.: History and Museums Division, Headquarters, U.S. Marine Corps, 1998. https://www.usmcu.edu/Portals/218/U_S_%20Marines%20in%20the%20Persian%20Gulf%2090-91%20MARINE%20FORCES%20AFLOAT%20IN%20DESERT%20SHIELD%20AND%20DESERT%20STORM%20%20PCN%2019000314500.pdf

Carpenter, Mason P., Major, USAF. *Joint Operations in the Gulf War: An Allison Analysis.* Maxwell Air Force Base, Alabama: Air University, 1995. https://apps.dtic.mil/sti/pdfs/ADA291616.pdf

Cureton, Charles H., LTC, USMCR, *US Marines in the Persian Gulf, 1990–1991, With the 1st Marine Division in Desert Shield and Desert Storm.* Washington, D.C.: History and Museums Division, Headquarters, U.S. Marine Corps, 1993. https://www.usmcu.edu/Portals/218/With%20the%201st%20Marine%20Division%20in%20Desert%20Shield%20and%20Desert%20Storm.pdf

GAO Report to the Chairman, Subcommittee on Oversight of Government Management, Committee on Governmental Affairs, U.S. Senate, Operation Desert Storm, Transportation and Distribution of Equipment and Supplies in Southwest Asia, GAO/NSIAD-92-20. Washington, D.C., 1991. https://www.gao.gov/assets/nsiad-92-20.pdf

Joint Publication 3-09.3, *Close Air Support*, Washington, D.C.: Joint Staff, November 25, 2014. https://irp.fas.org/doddir/dod/jp3_09_3.pdf

Joint Publication 3-15, *Barriers, Obstacles, and Mine Warfare for Joint Operations.*, Washington, D.C.: Joint Staff, September 6, 2016 https://www.jcs.mil/Portals/36/Documents/Doctrine/pubs/jp3_15.pdf

Matthews, James K and Cora J. Holt. *So Many, So Much, So Far, So Fast, United States Transportation Command and Strategic Deployment for Operations Desert Shield/Desert Storm.* Washington, D.C.: Joint History Office, Office of the Chairman of the Joint Chiefs of Staff and Research Center, United States Transportation Command, 1995. https://www.jcs.mil/Portals/36/Documents/History/Monographs/Transcom.pdf

Melnyk, Les', CPT, USANG. *Mobilizing for the Storm: The Army National Guard in Operations Desert Shield and Desert Storm.* Arlington, VA: National Guard Bureau, Office of Public Affairs, Historical Services Division, 2001. https://permanent.fdlp.gov/lps28302/desertstorm.pdf

Michael, Steven B., CPT, USAF. *The Persian Gulf War, An Air Staff Chronology of Desert Shield/Desert Storm.* Washington, D.C.: Center for Air Force History, 1992.

Mroczkowski, Dennis P., LTC, USMCR. *US Marines in the Persian Gulf, 1990–1991, With the 2D Marine Division in Desert Shield and Desert Storm.* Washington, D.C.: History and Museums Division, Headquarters, U.S. Marine Corps, 1993. https://www.usmcu.edu/Portals/218/With%20the%202d%20Marine%20Division%20in%20Desert%20Shield%20and%20Desert%20Storm.pdf

Nelson, Robert A, Major, USA. "The Battle of the Bridges: Kuwait's 35th Brigade on the 2d of August 1990." *Armor*, September–October 1995. https://www.benning.army.mil/armor/eARMOR/content/issues/1995/SEP_OCT/ArmorSeptemberOctober1995web.pdf